MW01234251

i

The First Sheet

Lula Rivera

1/5/15

Melissa,
 I hope you enjoy Lil's story.
(Patience through the three
longer chapters -- the story is there.)
I hope it's worthy of your time.
 Love,
 Lu

The First Sheet
A Novel.

ISBN-13
978-0-9905250-0-4

Printed in the United States
Printing Number
10 9 8 7 6 5 4 3 2 1

Do	Don't
1.	
2.	
3.	

To our daughters

and to our sons.

Value one another.

Speak loudly for one another.

And take care of the water.

The First Sheet

Act III
Rewrite

vii

Prologue

Lil Swann can't get her act together. Act III that is, the third act of the script of her life, the script she's been writing in her mind since middle school drama camp. The third act is by far the most important of the five-act script. Sure, Lil knows Hollywood has its affinity for the condensed movie in only three parts, but her high school English teacher's adoration for Shakespeare had been contagious, and Lil was still a believer in the antiquated plan to take her time and use all five. Besides, now she has to cram twenty-five years into the first two acts-- the dumping grounds for all the necessary information her fictitious audience needs. The third act though, the third act contains the climax, the whole reason for buying the ticket to begin with. It's what everything from the first two sections is leading up to, the one to which the fourth part is merely the "falling action" with perhaps a minor unresolved issue or two. The fifth act? Simply the "dénouement," the tying up of loose ends from all the previous acts. Everything up until this point has gone pretty much according to plan, but without a breathtaking Act III, it's just plain . . . just plain . . . well, just plain.

Lil knows her story won't be the stuff legends are made of—she actually prefers a simple life--but she wants her time on earth to matter, and she wants it to contain a love story. If her children are the only ones to read things she might jot down one day, she just wants it to be worthy of their time. But that's not looking likely. Children aren't even looking likely.

Nothing is coming together--the casting, the setting, the timing, the music, the meet cute, the sequence of events--the gobsmacking she and her imaginary audience expect in a good story. And they expect it immediately. None of it's panning out. How can she ask her audience to have patience—the one "p" even Jane Austen's audience had to supply themselves—when Lil has lost her own? She's done everything she can to make it work.

It's time. Time for the dreaded rewrite, a major one. A pivotal plot change. She knows what she has to do. The hardest part is admitting her friends were right. No, actually, the hardest part is giving up the dream, the fantasy, the way she had scripted it, beautifully, all the way back in high school. Or that knowing this new twisting of events can't be untwisted. But all that's neither here nor there anymore. It's decision time, and for Lil, that always involves a list.

1

The List

"Let's do this thing," Lil mumbled to herself as she pushed a fresh pencil into the old-fashioned sharpener she kept on her desk and cranked the handle until the motion became smooth and the fragrance of shaven wood met her nose.

She removed the pencil, blew away all the powdered remnants, and examined the sharpened graphite point. She retrieved a package of college-ruled notebook paper from her work satchel, the first pack she'd purchased since she'd graduated from the University of Alabama four years ago. She closed her laptop and slid it aside. Some things are too precious to type on a computer that could tell your secrets to the World Wide Web. Some things are just sacred enough that you take a simple sheet of notebook paper, and you use a number two pencil.

She tore the plastic wrapping off of the package of paper, removed the advertisement slick, and placed them in the trashcan under her desk. She leaned close and breathed in the nostalgic smell of new paper. She missed paper. She lined up all the edges in the stack, and ran her hand across the top to smooth the first sheet. She liked writing on the top of the whole inch of paper, feeling the sharpened pencil press in, leaving an indention below, a hint to that second sheet of what might follow this one. She made two headings, "Do" at the top left, "Don't" to the right. She lined her ruler precisely up the center of the sheet vertically and drew the dividing line, that tempting strip of caution tape, that threshold you dared or dared not to cross, the speed breaker between Do and Don't. The juxtaposition of that solitary segment across all the horizontal blue lines on the paper that were waiting on her entries, set her in list-writing mode. She was familiar with the process, though she never followed her own advice at the end of it.

Lil had constructed many lists over the years, the Do/Don't list for going out with Blaze Hardaway in high school, her first. That decision caused the loudest, yelling argument ever in her house, pitting her mom, who argued they should trust Lil, against her father, who just had a "bad feeling about that Hardaway boy." The Do column filled up quickly. "He's the cutest boy in school," "He's a senior," "Every girl wants to date him," "Wide receiver," "Point guard," "Shortstop," "Cleft chin." The only thing in the Don't column: "My dad says there's just something about him." She went on the date. Her father had been right.

The Do/Don't list for whether to go to Auburn University had had the same imbalance, twenty-five to one. Auburn was the clear winner. The only thing in her "Don't" column:

"Hinton, Mac, and Sims are going to Alabama." The list for studying journalism versus the dos and don'ts for choosing business. Ironically, on paper, business clearly made the most sense. She chose journalism. Her first two lists for college degrees had been a comparison between journalism and drama. Drama had won, but her father wouldn't pay for a drama degree. It was killing him already to make his checks out to the University of Alabama. He was an Auburn alumnus.

"Just make that acting thing a hobby," he'd argued. "No girl from Alabama has any business in Hollywood or New York City when Birmingham, Alabama, is chock-full of theatres."

She had taken his advice on that one. She might as well have; he wasn't going to pay for it anyway. She learned from that one-sided discussion, not to mention her double-major plan. She'd fallen in love with Spanish in high school, and going beyond a minor to a major in Spanish wouldn't cost her dad a penny more if she took heavy loads for a few semesters. That decision didn't even require putting pencil to paper. She was doing it.

Today's list didn't take long. She had been walking around with it in her head forever. She didn't have to revise it even once. The first sheet said it all. The imbalance in the columns was the same, kazillion to one. The weight of the pros clearly trumped the only con.

Lil gently ran her index finger across the one Don't, feeling the engraved depression her pencil had made, saying goodbye to that solitary reason not to. Her eyes moved to the left, across the line, to the number of reasons in her Do column, and she inhaled a theatrical acceptance of her new life plan. This time she would listen to the list. This time, she would change her stars.

"Just do it," she told herself.

Like a true journalist, Lil flipped past two pages in her calendar, looked at her deadline that was circled in pencil, scooped up her pen, and circled it in ink. She put the pencil and pen in her drawer. She put the pack of paper in her bag, straightened her desk, put on her jacket, hung her bag across her shoulder, and picked up her list. She passed coworkers meeting late-afternoon deadlines.

"Got a show tonight, Lil?" Craig Jenkins asked as she passed him.

"Nope, going to meet the firing squad for coffee."

2

The Firing Squad at Hot's Café

Lil saw them through Hot's Café window, all four of
them, in their same chairs, at their regular
Wednesday table. She had known these girls since
before grammar school. No one had bailed at the last minute
today, texting that a child was sick or that a meeting had run
long. Lil had gotten a temporary reprieve from the previous
Wednesday's coffee, which had been cancelled since it was the
day before Thanksgiving. She only could hope they had
forgotten their marching orders from the Wednesday before that
one. That day they had ordered her to come to the next coffee
with the list in hand, an intervention of sorts. Lil made a point
to be the last one at coffee today. She was braced for one
unified attack. She didn't want to have today's conversation
four times, backing up and starting over as each one arrived,
giving the first ones there time to reload.

She took a breath, stiffened her back, opened the café door, and walked over to the table. She didn't even get a "hello" today. Hinton saw her first and merely said, "Hand it here." Lil put her list in Hinton's outstretched hand, glanced over at the big café clock, and watched the second hand as she took off her jacket and sat down. She'd give it thirty seconds to turn raunchy.

Hinton ran her finger quickly down the "Do" column, not giving herself time to read the individual entries.

"Hint, what are you doing?" June asked as she fanned her face, pink from pregnancy hormones that heated her up until her skin clashed with her strawberry hair.

Hinton lifted her bangled arm and held her hand up, motioning for the others to wait until she'd finished her perusal of the list. She smacked the list down on the table, and looked at Lil.

"Darlin," Hinton drawled, "you don't even know how to make this list," she said, clearly disappointed in Lil's effort. "I feel like bang'n my head on this table," Hinton added, looking at the others.

"What?" Mac asked, picking up the list.

"There's not a word in that 'Do' column that starts with the letter 'O,' " Hinton complained.

"And there it is," Lil said, as the second hand hit its thirtieth second.

"There what is?" Sims asked, taking the list from Mac.

"Crude," Lil said. "I told y'all if you made this conversation crude, I wasn't going to have it."

8

"Darlin, we'll talk about oil in a minute," Hinton assured her, "but a list of why to do it with a man cannot exist without the word 'orgasm.' "

"What?!" June gasped. "Lil! That should be number one!" she said, grabbing the list from Sims and looking for the word.

"That's not *why* you do it," Lil defended her list. "That's a wonderful thing that happens because you *chose* to do it."

They all got quiet, stared at Lil, then burst out in simultaneous laughter. Everyone in the café glanced over at them, but they frequently had an audience. June noticed even the group of senior ladies eavesdropping at the next table laughed, the gray-streaked, redheaded one choking a little on her coffee at Lil's reasoning.

Lil had known these girls since their "Bach, Brahms, and Babies" mother's-day-out program the year before they started 4K. Even back then, Hinton was a toddling little fashion icon. Today, as always, she was the epitome of professional elegance, wearing a formfitting, ivory wool suit and ivory patent leather, stiletto pumps, suggesting some executive at work had retired. The only other blonde in the group besides Lil, Hinton paid Humbert DuBleaux $30 every four weeks for each golden strand. Everything about her jingled, from her bracelets to the chain handle on her Chanel purse. Always dressed for an office that didn't recognize business-casual, Hinton didn't work. She didn't have to—Denton L. Vandercleave, IV, Esq., made a fine living, and he had put a mighty big ring on it. But Hinton loved looking like she worked, hustling around the city next to people who did and sitting next to her working friends at coffee. With the girls, Hinton dropped the "E" from Denton's "Esquire," and referred to Denton as "the squire," as if she were some kept chambermaid wearing the anachronous French maid uniform. Plus, she was proud of Denton, and she liked reminding everyone of his title. Hinton dressed to make men's heads turn, and they did. She especially liked that Denton was aware of the attention she got. Hinton said, "It keeps the squire on his toes, especially when he's horizontal."

Mac sat beside Hinton. She had the shortest name of them all. And not the Mac part. Baptized MacKenzie Shorter Salter-Sparks Buchanan Lee, she had shortened it all to Mac in first grade. Except for June, these girls' mothers, in the Southern tradition, had sewn yards of surnames together from generations of kin, governors and bootleggers long forgotten. Enough surnames, should the money ever run out, to remind people that at least they used to have it. Enough names to make the Spanish monarch, Felipe Juan Pablo Alfonso de la Santísima Trinidad y de Todos los Santos de Borbón y de Grecia, look like he'd been cheated with only a nickname. Eventually they'd whittle it down to one name. Mac had gone a step further, impatient with stretching "MacKenzie" across the primary paper with the fat primary pencil. She shaved it down to Mac, much to her mother's horror.

"That 7-year-old girl is savvy," her father, Big Daddy, as everyone called him, expounded. " 'Mac' on a business card is gonna open doors for that girl quicker than 'Tuliplee Magnolianna Rosepetal would!"

Mac didn't know about all that. She didn't even know what savvy meant, though she liked the way Big Daddy smiled at her when he said it. She was just pleased that "Mac" on the teachers' class rosters accidentally got her invited to "boys only" parties all the way through the seventh grade.

Mac, like Hinton, looked every bit as though she, too, had stepped off the cover of *Executive Models Magazine*. Mac didn't have to work either, but she did, for her daddy. Her Jack sold enough furniture to take care of two families, but Mac's daddy would have taken care of her even if Jack came back from one of his trips to market carrying the winning Powerball ticket. In truth, Big Daddy didn't have to take care of Mac. With her profit numbers, she was setting him up for an early retirement.

A brunette bombshell, Mac had been a fixture at Big Daddy's Imports since she was the little girl in Big Daddy's commercials. She was something of a Birmingham celebrity because of the ads, too. She was as renown in the tri-county area for her slogan of "Let me take ya for a ride," as Paris Hilton was for "That's Hot." The older women in the office at Big Daddy's loved Mac. They didn't even care that Mac peeled off the car lot four hours after showing up, announcing she had a one-on-one with her trainer, a teeth whitening, or a microdermabrasion. At 27, she was vocal about her facelift fund. But the older women saw Mac's untouchable sales numbers, and they knew she wasn't needed on the lot. She was drumming up business for Big Daddy's Imports wherever she was. They knew most daughters in the same Jimmy Choo's wouldn't have shown up to work at all.

11

Sims sat next to Mac. No one would guess that Sims had a dime, always showing up to coffee still wearing the T-shirt she had slept in along with the running pants she woke and added. No makeup, the perennial ponytail, the P.E. whistle still around her neck, Sims had walked right out of a 70s "I'd Like to Teach the World to Sing" Coke commercial. Her mother's timber family had married into her father's construction dynasty. Two countries joining their royal heirs couldn't have formed a better union. All they needed now was a good realtor, but Sims couldn't have cared less about the money. Living paycheck to paycheck would have made her just as happy.

Sims' parents divorced when she was in tenth grade. Both remarried. Her mother and two brothers moved a couple of miles into Mountain Brook, but Sims stayed with her father so she could graduate with her friends. She was the strongest female athlete in their school. Sims had every intention of going to the University on a volleyball scholarship to study physical education to teach P.E., but she got pregnant at the end of eleventh grade, and gave birth to Tanner during the twelfth. Her family was so well off that the out-of-wedlock child didn't push Sims even one rung down the social ladder. Her family grew the trees and built the ladder; everyone else was busy just trying to be them. Lil's mom was the solitary whisperer in Sims' situation. What Mrs. Swann didn't know was that she and her idol, Amy Vanderbilt, were partly to blame for Sims' condition.

Mrs. Swann taught a highly sought-after etiquette class for seventh graders, the hefty fee for which only could be called tuition. Mothers would clamber to enroll their future little

CEOs, sports attorneys, and ambassadors, a year in advance in Swann Academy. Mrs. Swann would struggle to keep the 12-year-olds' attention, teaching the kids the fine art of using a grapefruit spoon, the difference between a water goblet and an iced tea glass, where to put their napkins when they had to go pee, how to tie a tie and dance the tango, and whom to introduce first when a third party approaches. The graduation gift was the 841-page, hardback edition of *The Amy Vanderbilt Complete Book of Etiquette*.

Hinton had used her book everyday in high school, on top of her head, to practice walking in her mother's high heels that she would sneak to school in her backpack. Mac couldn't have functioned without the book. It raised her makeup mirror perfectly to eye level. And Sims' edition kept her bedroom window propped open for Malcolm Lefoy to climb through after he properly walked Sims to the front door and shook hands with her father. But Mrs. Swann didn't need to worry about "poor knocked-up Sims and her Mama, bless her heart." Sims was fine.

When she discovered she was having a boy, Sims swore she'd never make him cut his hair or wear shoes or a shirt, and she held true to her word until the 4K teacher required all three things. They celebrated Tanner's birth with an enormous baby shower, the biggest event in country club history until Hinton's wedding reception following her marriage to Denton whose father owned law offices across the state. That baby shower celebration was the one time Sims said with a smile, "I don't care how much it costs." Sims remained the rebel, always showing up to coffee in running attire with the P.E. whistle still around her neck, having finished her education at the University of Alabama at Birmingham.

June was Lil's college roommate. She was crimson to the core, all but her Auburn hair. The only one not from Birmingham, June grew up in Montgomery. She moved to Birmingham after college to stay near her friends, and she found a good job in insurance. She roomed with Lil until she met Auggie at the shooting range he owned with his brothers when she went to watch Lil practice. June and Auggie made a decent living together. She couldn't afford to quit work to stay home with their first baby that was due in about six weeks, plus she loved her job. Her Homewood fixer-upper was in shambles at the moment, so she had lined up a daycare and had interviewed babysitters for when she would have weekend work events.

June had fit right in with the others as early as Lil's first conversation with her in their freshman dorm. With Sims deciding not to go to the University, their foursome became a threesome. Lil lost at Rock-Paper-Scissors, and was the odd man out, having to request an unknown roommate. She got June.

"Were you born in June?" Lil asked June while they were putting sheets on their Tutwiler dorm beds the first day of rush.

She needed to break the silence of "I'm fixing to have to spend an entire year living with this girl I've never laid eyes on before."

"No," June answered, "but if you count backwards nine months from my birthday, it's June," she said, having a full body chill. "It gets worse. My full name is Savannah June, and

14

yes, they did the 'nasty' on their honeymoon in Savannah nine months before my head crowned," she said before she acted like she was spitting to get the grossness of those words out of her mouth. That started the constant laughter.

Lil and June were in a dorm room next to Hinton and Mac's room. Both Lil and June worked part time during their college years to pay for textbooks and sorority expenses, and it helped one to look across the dorm room to see the other cramming in her studies while the other girls were tanning on rooftops. Lil doubled her hours at work at the beginning of her senior year when her father lost his job. She didn't tell her parents when she was diagnosed at the infirmary with mono three months into the school year. She was determined to power through. She had no choice though, but to cut back on her sorority activities, but she knew she had her sisters. Hinton, Mac, and June were good nurses to Lil.

Years before the others ever met June, they'd concocted a whimsical plan to solve the maid of honor conundrum they knew they'd face one day. They had stood in a circle and dropped a coin in the middle. Heads meant left; tails, right. The quarter landed on heads, and the girls looked to the left, and smiled at their maids of honor. The plan also stipulated that the brides would name a child after their maids of honor one day. The whole ritual was Lil's idea. The others couldn't imagine ever being married, but they humored Lil anyway.

When June entered the picture and weddings started happening before Lil even had a suitor in sight, she convinced the others to let her step out of the circle and let June step into her place. The others wanted to add June without letting Lil step out, but Lil knew her standing there could ruin it all, could break the continuous cycle.

"Besides, Mac," Lil smiled, "you've always wanted to name a girl 'Savvy,' and June's 'Savannah' sets you up for that beautifully. I'll figure it out when . . . if my time ever comes."

" 'Savvy Jackson, reporting live from the White House,' " Mac pretended to be her successful daughter, named after her new maid of honor, June.

Sims road-tripped to Tuscaloosa a lot. Malcolm Lefoy's parents had divorced and remarried like Sims' parents, so with eight young grandparents always fighting for time with Tanner, Sims would pack a bag and head to T-Town to hang out with the girls. While Sims was away, Tanner pouted about his stiff shoes and confining shirts. He squealed with delight when his energetic Mama ran back into his suntanned arms. It was a great four years.

All of them settled in Birmingham, spread around the Over-the-Mountain areas, Lil in Hoover, June in Homewood, Mac in Vestavia Hills, and Sims and Hinton both in Mountain Brook. Back in Birmingham, they met for Wednesday coffee at the Original Pancake House in Five Points South. They liked their coffee in a restaurant-grade, white porcelain cup with a waitress topping it off every few minutes. The Original was located conveniently to Lil's news blog office, Big Daddy's lot, and Denton's downtown law office, which Hinton would drop by before coffee to speak to Denton and make sure he noticed all the partners giving her a once-over. June's insurance office had been situated just beneath the iron Vulcan's naked butt in Homewood, right up the mountain from Five Points. Recently, her office had been relocated farther away, so she and Sims would meet at the end of Highway 280, park one car in a gravel lot next to DeVinci's Pizza, and ride together.

When Hinton and Mac reached the third trimester of their first pregnancies, both expecting boys, they needed easier parking on Wednesday, so they all inched their way up the mountain, into Homewood, just past the Vulcan, to the empty lot where Sims and June had parked, which had become home to Hot's UndertheMoon Café. The white cups and saucers were brand new, and the waitresses topping them off wore black aprons that said, "Hot."

"Okay, somebody give me a pen," Mac said, taking Lil's list and turning the paper over.

June handed her the pen the waitress had left on the receipt clipboard from the previous customers.

"Number one," Mac said, as she created a proper list on the back side of the sheet of paper.

"ORGASM--all in caps," she said, looking at Lil. "Have we taught you nothing?" she added.

"All in caps," Hinton repeated Mac, "underlined, bold-faced, italicized, and in quotation marks."

"Here," Sims added, pulling a yellow highlighter out of the pocket of her running pants. "Highlight it, circle it, and follow it with an exclamation mark."

Mac made those adjustments, and they all looked at June to make sure they'd thought of everything to accentuate the importance of the orgasm.

"Really?" June said, squeezing lemon into her water while she waited for them to figure out their clear omission.

"Do I *really* have to point out the obvious?" she commented, stirring the water, giving them time to think, then setting the spoon on the table.

"Ladies," she conceded, "make it plural."

"Yes!" "Of course." "What were we thinking?" was the simultaneous consensus.

"Crude," Lil said again, defeatedly, knowing there would be no serious conversation today.

"Skip down to around number ten and write 'oil' before we forget, darlin," Hinton said to Mac, who actually wrote it.

This conversation was a decade old, but Lil still wasn't used to it. Her virginity had been the ice-breaking topic of their visits since Sims lost hers at 17. The others couldn't wait to get rid of theirs, but Lil had voiced early, her plan to wait.

"Wait for what?" Hinton had asked at their post-prom sleepover, checking herself in the mirror to see if there really were such a thing as afterglow, only to discover the only thing about her that was glowing was the TaylorMade-sized hickey she would have to conceal for two weeks.

"Wait for love," Lil answered Hinton. "Wait until I find the right guy, the right time, the right place," Lil had answered dreamily.

"Well, maybe before you wait for all that," Mac interrupted, "you'll find your right mind."

Lil guiltily wished their toddlers had come down with something today, nothing bad, just an odd 24-hour fever or a runny nose. They met at Hot's every Wednesday afternoon, and when they harped on Lil's virginity, Lil merely had to say, "Why did June say she couldn't make it today?" Then the conversation would flip to June or to whoever was missing, but they had ordered her to make this list, and today, they owned her.

"Why don't y'all take a minute and actually read the list?" Lil protested.

"She's right," Sims said. "What does she say for number one?"

Mac turned the list back over and read aloud with a romantic, wispy voice.

"'You've met the right guy.' Darlin'," Mac said, now in her regular voice, "I haven't even met the right guy, and I've been married for three years."

"Mac!" Lil started.

"Oh, Lil, you know I love Jack," Mac stopped her, "but you've looked for this nonexistent man until you've blown out candles on 25 cakes, and I smell another cake baking! Just do it! Then resume the hunt, one mattress at a time, for this man you think is walking around out there somewhere waitin' on you."

"Ooo, give me the pen!" June thought of something.

Lil looked over June's shoulder, and made a disgustedly sour face at what June wrote on their new list. The other three nodded at the new entry. When she finished writing, June took the credit card clipboard and fanned herself with it.

"Y'all were right about these pregnancy hormones, and right here at the end, I seem to have gotten a whole new batch," June

19

explained, her hair blowing in the fanned air. "Auggie can't even keep up with me, but he's lovin' the challenge."

"Don't worry," Hinton said to June. "Seeing that head crown will cure him. I think that's the real reason you have to wait six weeks after the baby comes. It takes a man at least that long to forget."

"Jack hunkered in the corner of my delivery room," Mac said, adding another entry to the list. "I could just make out his mumbling, 'The horror! The horror!' "[1]

Lil chuckled, wondering if Jack knew he was quoting Conrad's *Heart of Darkness* at that moment, or if he was having his own unique moment of discovery.

"Um," Hinton swallowed coffee, nodding at Mac's new entry on their list, "that takes a California king with no footboard."

Then she took the pen and scribbled something.

"Oh, my," June said, fanning harder, seeing what Hinton had written, Mac and Sims agreeing with it.

"Y'all are gonna have to throw that pen away," Lil said, reading their X-rated list.

"Back to Lil's list," Sims said, taking the sheet.

"Number two," she read, " 'You know he's forever.' "

They looked at Lil as if she were the dumbest person in the world.

"Lil, look around this table," Sims said. "Every one of us is married while you're the only one who's always dreamed about being hitched. And not a one of us waited. I'm surrounded on a daily basis by four grandmothers, all of whom 'waited,' and not a one in the pack is still married to her first. Give it up already! I gave it up in eleventh grade, Hint at senior prom, and Mac and June at sorority pledge formals freshman and sophomore years. Every one of us is happy," she scanned the group for their agreement.

She got a shrugging nod from June, and a couple of "Ehs" from Mac and Hinton.

"We're happy!" Sims ordered them into happiness. "And not a one of us married our first lovers," she finished her point.

"Well, Sims," Lil said, as the waitress brought her a cup of coffee, "I wouldn't exactly call a twelfth grade, zit-faced, second baseman in a tent on a field trip to Oak Mountain a lover."

"The point is, Lil," Sims said, "the first one doesn't have to be forever. Sam wasn't my first."

All the girls were married except for Lil. Lil figured Hinton would marry first, which she did within weeks of college graduation. Hinton always had been looking for a husband, well, for a man, but Mac and Sims had said they'd never marry, so Lil was surprised when both of them walked the aisle sooner than a year after Hinton.

Technically, Sims walked the sand in a blue jean ceremony on the Gulf in front of her family's Orange Beach mansion. When real estate mogul Sam kissed his bride, even Sims' dead and buried great-grandfathers smiled at the widening diameter of the money empire. The beach setting had been one of Lil's many options, minus the jeans. Sims pulled it off beautifully, and Lil removed the beach from her mental list of settings.

Lil had imagined Sims as one of those uncatchable beauties who would stay single, would age well, would compost, make pottery, always wear jeans, would eventually stop shaving under her arms and start smoking a pipe containing some herbal concoction. She figured Mac would work herself into a face-lifted pulp, growing her father's business into a car dynasty, but the next thing Lil knew, she was standing on a block of wood at Birmingham Blanca Brides, being pinned into a bridesmaid dress twice as expensive as Hinton's had been. Mac's wedding was a continuation of the unspoken competition between Mac and Hinton, cordially one-upping each other through life. Mac couldn't top the size of Hinton's wedding, so she was determined to double the price. Lil and June were just glad that Mac paid for the dresses.

Secretly, Lil thought she'd at least be second to marry if not first, only because she always wanted to be married, was vocal about it, had actually scripted the events in her mind over and again. She was perfectly capable of going through life solo, but she wanted to share time and all she would use it for with someone, no matter how corny it sounded to say that out loud. Within two summers of graduating from Alabama, Hinton had married Denton, Mac had married Jack, and Sims had married Sam. Yes, the first thing an editor would demand Lil remove from her script were she ever actually to write it--the trite rhyming, alliterative-assonant, or "All-Ass," as Lil called it, use of names. Cliché. Elementary even, but it had happened in real life, and by golly, she was leaving it in. Lil called the girls' husbands the All-Ass Review, not that they were asses. She loved Denton, Jack, and Sam.

Mac's Jack, Randolph Beauregard Jackson, didn't always go by Jack. Mac had gotten in the habit of calling him Jack while they were engaged, having overheard her soon-to-be mother-in-law say how much she hated it when people called "her Randolph" "Randy." She didn't like it any better when they called "her Randolph" "Beau." Randolph's mother wasn't thrilled that "her Randolph" was marrying the "Let me take ya for a ride," Big Daddy heiress, so what else was Mac to do? Plus, every time that woman talked about Randolph, she called him, "my Randolph." It creeped Mac out, and at some point, during the act, Mac started hearing that woman's voice in her head, as if she knew Mac was doing "her Randolph" at that very moment. This way he was Mac's Jack, and the voice went away.

Sam was practically begging to be part of Lil's All-Ass Review. His name would have worked with Sims' in two ways. He had been christened Samuel Mims. Lil thought it was funny to show up to coffee and ask, "How are 'All the Asses?' " Then June started dating Boone, Boone Wilkins. That's when Mac came to coffee and handed Lil a copy of the Birmingham white pages.

"What's this for?" Lil had asked.

"Oh, I highlighted all the Gils for you," Mac smiled. "I underlined the Wills, but I prefer the sound of 'Lil and Gil.' *Now* how funny is it?"

Considering that the last two guys Lil had gone out with were both Bills, it was becoming less funny to Lil at this point, too. And Hinton had turned the joke on her.

"From 'All of our Asses' to the iron buns in the sky," Hinton motioned toward the Vulcan, "seems everyone is getting some but you."

June, thank goodness, broke the All-Ass chain when she broke things off with Boone, fell head over heels for Auggie, and married him this past March. Lil still had a good time, though, with the fact that June had married an Augustus, Augustus Detroit, according to Auggie, another "nasty" city. Lil knew the girls all loved their husbands, no matter how they talked. She knew June especially loved Auggie. They were still in the honeymoon phase.

"I could shoot Auggie with his own gun!" June said to the others, pushing her glass of water away from her. "No matter how much lemon I squeeze in it, I can still taste it! Auggie has completely ruined water for me at a time in my life when it's all I can drink! Y'all are all sitting around sipping your coffee, sweetenin' your tea, and icing down your Cokes, and I'm stuck over here drinking what I *used* to think was *water*!"

"With this drought, you oughta be glad they even brought you a glass," Mac commented.

"You're being ridiculous, June!" Sims said, scooping up June's glass of water and gulping down half the glass to prove the clear liquid was safe for consumption. "You cannot taste pee!" Sims demanded.

On Thanksgiving Day, Auggie's mom showed June an old posterboard she'd come across, one Auggie had made in fifth grade when he was assigned an oral report on the water cycle. Ten-year-old Auggie had discovered in Sunday School that the water flowing through Birmingham's pipes, the rain that falls, and the lakes where he fished, contained the same water that flooded the earth for forty days and nights, the same water that Jesus had turned to wine, the same water that Pontius Pilate had used to wash his hands. Armed with this knowledge, little Auggie went a different route with his presentation than his teacher expected. Much to the teacher's shock, Auggie's main point was that we're all drinking the pee from everyone who ever lived on this earth. All his water graphics were colored in yellow pastel pencils, and his title was, "We're All Drinking Pee."

"He was only 10, and he was right," June continued. "You should have seen his yellow-tinged water following his arrows up from the rivers to the sky where it fell again as 'Peecipitation,' " she quoted Auggie's poster.

Lil smiled at how beautifully June's Act III was going now that she'd settled down with Auggie--such a cute story to tell their children. It was time to make her own Act III come together.

The curtain had dropped on Act I for Lil at high school graduation. Things had been mostly uneventful. Act II's curtain fell as the mortarboards hit the ground in Tuscaloosa, Lil graduating with a double major in journalism and Spanish, a minor in theatre. Four years into Act III, her writing career was going well, but the personal side of her life was fighting her efforts to craft the perfect script. She put down her invisible director's megaphone, took an intermission from her efforts, and got her master's in Spanish from UAB at night to help with the possibility of a Spanish language blog. But now that was finished, and her editing still wasn't fixing the scene where she already was supposed to have met and fallen in love with "The One." More exactly, the one and *only*. It was time to do a complete rewrite on Act III, thus the fresh pack of notebook paper.

"Number three," June took Lil's list from Sims, silently read the next few entries, looked over at Lil, shook her head in disappointment, and read aloud in a monotone voice, not taking a breath between the next four entries.

" 'We're in love,' 'We have the same faith,' 'He'd be a hard worker,' 'He'd make a good father,' " June looked up from the list. "She clearly lost sight of the original assignment. Should I even keep reading?" June asked the others.

"Make it stop!" Hinton said, air-banging her head an inch from the table. "Lil, we didn't tell you to make a list of why to *marry* a man. We told you to make a list of reasons to go ahead and *do it* with *any* man, and 'Lose the Virginity!' " Hinton said making an L then a V with her fingers.

The girls had a green shirt printed when they graduated from Alabama, and they gave it to Lil as a graduation gift. "L the V" was printed on the front.

"You're a compulsive list maker!" Sims said, frustrated. "You're the freak'n Pro/Con Queen! We figured once you saw the unbalanced scales in black and white, *you'd do it*! You're making way too much out of it. Hinton is right. This is the 'Do I marry him or not' list."

"Maybe in my head they are one-and-the-same list," Lil said.

"Then you need a new head, sweetie," Mac said, softly patting Lil's arm.

"Is this what sex has turned into for everybody?" she pointed to their list. " 'Cause if it is, this is so sad!"

"Lil," Mac admitted unapologetically, "you're right. We've gotten crude with the topic. The world we live in is crude with the topic. But you can't keep avoiding the conversation. The world is having it everywhere, in every theater, on television, in music videos, magazines, on billboards, cell phones, and the radio, not to mention 18-wheeler mud flaps. Even commercials should be rated," Mac said gesturing to the flat screen televisions mounted to the café walls.

The mostly professional café crowd was conducting business below the steamy commercial, pretending they didn't see the ad with the couple rolling around in the bed selling something, as the latest local drought restrictions and fines tickered across the bottom of the screen. Then the entertainment newscast resumed. The closed captions were referring to the music video by the latest one-hit sensation, B. Merry, who was going solo, leaving in the lurch, her band, "Tomorrow We Die." She was completely naked, only her shaven, tattooed head appearing above her only covering, her "ManSandwich," the title of her one and only hit. She was announcing her first concert tour, as well as her second release, "Back for Seconds, Thirds, and Fourths," weirdly, a love ballad.

"Perhaps the world has dragged us down with it," Mac continued, "but you still have to live in this world, Lil, and your way doesn't work in this world anymore. The sun is shining on a new day!" Mac smiled. "The game has new and improved

27

rules, thank goodness. The world is actually making this decision easier for you, Lil. It isn't such a black and white issue anymore. It has morphed into quite a nice 'Grey' area," Mac smirked before she pretended to crack a tiny whip.

"I get it, Mac. 'It's me against the world,' " Lil said.

"And at 112 pounds, you might as well just lie down," June added.

"Lil, you gave it a good shot," Sims said. "Your way is as primitive as your paper and pencil," she pointed to Lil's list. "Your guy is a fantasy. I'm sorry, Lil, but he is. Men don't wait on girls who do."

"Why should they?" Mac asked. "There are plenty of girls out there who don't make 'em. We caught up to the boys and passed them. No one cares who gives it up first--chicken, egg-- or would it be rooster, chicken?"

"Lil, you still get to wear white down the aisle," Hinton assured her, "but please don't, darlin. Wear ivory. White does no one's teeth any favors."

"You're that chick," June said, "the virgin on all those TV dating shows, the one the guy sends home first 'cause he doesn't know what to do with her. She makes all the other girls uncomfortable, and she's no good for ratings."

"Thanks, June," Lil said.

"And she's *lying!*" Mac said to June about the dating show virgin.

"Nooo!" June said, realizing that possibility for the first time.

Sims took the list back from June and read the only entry in the Don't column.

28

" 'Haven't met the one yet,' " she said, looking back up at Lil. "It's Justin, isn't it?" Sims said. "You either can't quit crushing on him, or you can't find someone who matches up to the fantasy you have of him in your dreams. And, Lil, it is a fantasy. The Justin in your mind isn't real. He couldn't live up to your expectations if he tried. No man could. You've cast him as the leading man in that imaginary play in your head where your life ends up happily ever after, with everyone holding hands and bowing across the stage."

"Ugh! You haven't given up on that plot already?" Hinton moaned.

"Speaking of that imaginary play, you should make it a book instead," June added. "This lady at work just self-published hers. You could do that with your short, sexless, boring little book."

"Oh, my gosh!" Lil exclaimed. "How many times do I have to tell y'all? Justin and I are *friends*, Sims! And books don't have music, June. Plays do. My story has to have music. And which came first, Mac? The girl giving it up came first!"

"Then be that girl, Lil," Hinton said, "before you're too old to be called a girl."

"Just do it with Justin and get it over with," Sims said, ignoring them.

"Stop saying that!" Lil protested.

"We know, we know--'all platonic.' We get it," Hinton said. "Well, we *don't* get it, any of it, but he won't mind being used just once, darlin."

"I wouldn't mind using him just once," Mac added, leaning back in her chair and crossing her arms matter-of-factly.

29

"Mac!" Lil shrieked.

"Okay, okay, I take it back," Mac said. "Once wouldn't do it!" she winked at the others.

"Have you ever run your fingers through his hair?" June said about Justin's shoulder-length, black hair. "He's right off a bodice-ripper cover."

"Enough about Justin," Lil demanded. "He's the dearest friend I have besides y'all. I'm not losing him for ten minutes in the sack. And even if I were interested in him, I'm nothing like his type."

Lil always refused to let the girls take aim at Justin.

"Admit it though. You've thought about it. He's a tad gorgeous," Hinton said.

Both statements were true. Lil *had* thought about it, and Justin *was* strikingly handsome. His face was nice, a strong jaw and chin, a perfect mouth, intense, dark eyes, thick brows. His shoulders were broad, his body, fit, and his long-again, short-again black hair made him look Latin or Greek, exotic, the way he liked his women. Much about Justin was dark and mysterious--he was good at keeping the topic off of himself-- but that mystique made him even more attractive.

The first time Lil's parents met him, her father took one look at Justin's ponytail.

"I hope you're growing that mess for Locks of Love."

Justin had replied honestly.

"Yes, sir, I am. This is the third time."

Lil had just grinned at her daddy. Justin was the first person she could leave alone with her parents and not worry.

30

Justin had spent a little time alone with her parents last week when he joined Lil at her parents' house for Thanksgiving supper, for the leftover portions. Justin's presence somehow lifted the somber mood caused by the absence of Lil's brother, Peter, who was in another part of the world with a Close Quarter Battle Receiver strapped to his shoulder. Justin's arrival also ended the harangue that always followed the Swann Academy Thanksgiving Boot Camp.

As Mrs. Swann unpacked and checked for chips in her stemware that the most recent "little Neanderthals" had used, she loudly defended the fine art of manners, still unsettled from having caught the students imitating her behind her back and sticking expensive squares of sugar up their noses. Her newest insult came in the form of the kids recording their bad behavior on their cell phones when she wasn't looking and with a push of a button, sending their antics for the world to see. Lil and her father heard this monologue three times a year, most loudly after the dreaded boot camp.

" '. . . there is no new thing under the sun,' Lily Letitia Swann!" she quoted Ecclesiastes.[2]

She had been tossing around the "no new thing under the sun" theme since Lil was a little girl. This time Lil smiled, thinking about Auggie's report that even the water under the sun is the same old water that has been here since creation.

"Good manners have been around since Adam graciously shared a rib with Eve," Mrs. Swann continued. "This world with its new rules and lack of decorum! There are *no* new morals, *no* new etiquette, and *no* new way to teach math!"

31

Lil and her dad mouthed that last part toward each other, knowing math would be part of the equation. Mrs. Swann would always throw math in, having been a product of a horrible phase called "New Math" when she was in fourth grade. Even Lil had been the subject of yet another "new math" experiment. Once math entered the filibuster, Mrs. Swann's argument would branch off into random directions.

"This world isn't going to hell in a handbasket anymore. Oh, no! It's going to hell smack dab in the middle of a 'ManSandwich'!"

Surprised at that contemporary addition to the argument, Lil and her father swapped expressions of being impressed. Lil listened for the pearl. Every so often, during one of these diatribes, there would be one rare, hard-to-unshell pearl of wisdom, a pearl that in her random ramblings, Mrs. Swann unintentionally would dislodge.

" 'ManSandwich,' my Aunt Sister's fanny! When women devalue themselves and don't value one another, then how do we ever expect men to value us? And when our own men don't value us, then we are at the mercy of the world."

There it was, the pearl, this time concise and easy to spot.

"We place value on the dumbest things—all of us—men and women alike. Yahoos, the whole lot of us. We still think diamonds and gold trump food and medicine! Neither will feed us nor cure us! Then there's the new gold--anything with a designer label," she rambled, though she had saved for a Louis Vuitton purse for three years.

She'd had more than enough money in an envelope for two years, but she couldn't pull the trigger on the purchase. She loved the bag--the timeless shape, the more than century-old name, the way the leather trim would patina. And if she took good care of it, she reasoned that she could even pass it on to Lil. It didn't hurt that it seemed to come with a sort of rite of passage. But no matter how much she still wanted that purse, she knew, every time she looked in the envelope, the total was enough to paint the wood trim on their small ranch house or, Heaven forbid, pay an unexpected medical bill. If anyone ever dusted that envelope for prints, he would have discovered ten thousand of them, all Mrs. Swann's, from every time she considered buying that purse, once even standing at the purse counter in Saks with the bag right in front of her and the envelope in her hand. She knew that day that she'd never splurge, and that knowledge occasionally hardened her opinion of those who did.

"You should have seen the clothes those 12-year-olds were wearing yesterday," Mrs. Swann continued. "Just *one* of their shirts cost more than my wedding dress! I think I could stitch 'Beelzebub' on a shirt, price it twenty times higher than the highest, get the head monkey to wear it, and out-sell all the others! And if you're wearing that shirt, then, please, behave any ole way you want, record yourself doing so, and show it to the world! The next day, a thousand copycats will have followed suit. I'm telling you, this is the 'Everybody Take My Photo! Aren't I Cute' generation! And if no one takes their photos, they just take their own. 'Selfies.' *That's* the word that'll describe this generation. If this world doesn't get back to basics . . .."

And so it went as she expounded the goodness of rules, coming full circle to, "Good manners are the beginning of 'do unto others,' she paraphrased the verse.[3] "Good manners are the mark of a person who will leave a good mark on this world. No, Lily, not one new thing under this sun."

That's when Lil's dad would point to Lil and mouth, "You are." He always told Lil to be that something new under the sun.

Justin had knocked on the door during the exposition on the necessity of rules. When no one answered, he let himself in, arriving to the dining room unnoticed, just in time to catch the summation and see Lil's father mouth to Lil, "You are." The whole scene took him back to a time in his childhood in a much different setting with his mother. Her conversation had an altogether different take on rules.

"Instead of helping us get things done, Justin, this world's rules often keep us from doing what we need to do. The good Lord took the time personally to write only ten. I figure those ten are plenty. All the other ones? Just more of this world. 'There is no new thing under the sun,' Justin," she said, kissing the top of his head, "except you and your precious, ten, unique fingerprints. I think He gave us those," she said, caressing the tips of Justin's fingers, "so He could show us one day where we left our mark on this world and also to show us where we didn't leave it when we should have. That day, your left hand should even be surprised at where your right hand left its good mark. Do good, Justin, without boasting. Be something new under the sun, Justin."

"Justin!" Mr. Swann noticed Justin standing there. "Son, welcome!" he said walking over to Justin, shaking his hand and giving him a manly pat on his shoulder.

"Justin! Honey, you must be starving!" Mrs. Swann said. "Lil, fix this sweet boy a turkey sandwich. He's been feedin' those poor winos at the Johnny Mack Mission all day."

"Mom! They're not winos!"

Lil let her eyes apologize to Justin for her mom's comment and went to make the sandwich, comfortable in the knowledge that Justin was fine, two rooms away with her parents. By the time Justin left, he got a full-on embrace from her father and a kiss on the cheek from her mother. Peter would have appreciated Justin's being there.

"His most attractive quality," Lil said when she first told the girls about Justin, "is his personality. Well, that sounded stupid," she edited herself. "Not his personality. I mean, the kind of man he is, not how he looks. Well, not that either. He's quite handsome. I say that merely as a female onlooker. He clearly is involved with someone, a stunning Latin, model type. Anywho. Why did Sims say she couldn't make it today?"

The girls had slyly cut their eyes to one another during Lil's gushing discussion of this man she'd met at the library, who was now helping her with her master's dissertation, whom, clearly, she was crushing on; she hadn't told them about any man in forever. She barely told them about the dates they arranged for her. They were smart enough to know when to put on their silencers and not comment, which would only push her back into her trench of privacy, so they let her ramble, encouraging the discussion with the mute raising of their eyebrows and nodding of their heads.

Over the next few months, Lil insisted she and Justin were just friends whenever the girls asked about him at coffee. In truth, Lil realized that Justin saw her only as that. The evidence was the trail of beautiful señoritas who were texting, calling, and leaving his side whenever she showed up for her work sessions. Secretly, Lil decided it was best to sledgehammer her crush on Justin, which she managed to do, pulverizing it into almost unrecognizable particles and forcing her feelings into friendship mode. She convinced herself that the choice had been a good one.

Two years after their first encounter, Justin was the best friend she had. He had helped Lil with her master's dissertation off and on over the first six months of their meeting, and they stayed in touch after she received her diploma. Over the last year, they had become regular companions. These girls knew things about Lil that Justin didn't know though. He didn't know she hadn't "L'd the V," as the green T-shirt said.

The girls gave Lil that shirt as a gift the day they graduated from the University, and they let her open it in front of her parents.

"What does that mean, Hon?" her mother had asked.

Lil made a mess of her answer.

"Um, well, it's a, um, a T-shirt that our sorority wears . . . when we are working with our charity."

"Lil's the charity president, four years running," Hinton said, "literally running," she added in a whisper behind Lil's ear.

Lil stepped on Hinton's toes.

"What do those letters stand for, dear?"

"Um, well, Mom, they stand for . . . 'Love the . . . um . . . Vironment.' Nobody says '*en*vironment' anymore, Mama. L the V," Lil added, making an L then a V with her fingers as her friends had done since that awkward moment.

"Of course not," her mother complained. "Anything to butcher the Queen's English. I'm telling you, y'all are the 'Aren't I Cute' generation," Mrs. Swann declared. "Mac, let me get your picture with your new Louis," Mrs. Swann said, adjusting Mac's graduation purse on her arm for the photo, studying the Damier canvas and size of the Speedy 30 to help with her own purchasing decision.

Lil's girlfriends did their best to contain their laughter that day, but they were 22- and 23-year-old girls graduating from college, two of them wearing engagement rings, big ones. Everything was funny that day. They thought their "Lose the Virginity" shirt was a classic. Lil still had hers, and that was the problem.

Like Lil's list said, she and Justin did share the same faith. Lil was raised and baptized in a Southern Baptist church, and she had been a regular attendee at a Methodist church in Tuscaloosa. The girls had promised their mothers they'd keep each other going to church while they were at the University, but when Hinton bored of the guys at Jordon River Baptist, she announced she was sleeping in on Sundays. Three Sundays later, Mac pulled Hinton out of bed. Mac's spending money depended on a selfie sent to Big Daddy, taken beside a preacher in front of a church holding a dated church bulletin, much like a ransom letter photograph taken with a current newspaper. That week's selfie was snapped with all the girls around Pastor Marks in front of the Moon Street Methodist Church where Hinton met law student Denton her senior year. When Lil asked Justin about his denomination, he said, "No denomination, just a Bible."

Justin was the smartest man Lil had ever met, if a Southern girl can think another man is smarter than her daddy. Justin could do most anything and hated not trying everything. He left one job, coaxed away from it by people who met him and were quite impressed with him. The people at the previous job would sometimes coax him back until his next venture. He hadn't stayed at any job long. Some paid well, others, not so much, but his desire to travel abroad required him to take the well-paying jobs every now and then. The University extension in Birmingham most recently coaxed him back to teach Spanish after he had been a translator at local hospitals and in courtrooms and police stations. He had stayed in this current job longer than any other.

"He's going to turn 40 one day, and all this job hopping isn't going to look like a good thing then," Lil's father would say, hoping Lil would pass the advice along to Justin whose parents were no longer alive to give him the same advice. "It's probably not looking too good on a résumé even now. Isn't he 30?" Then he would add, "But he's a good boy. Something about him . . .." Her dad would leave that thought hanging there.

Lil adored Justin's eyes. They studied her while she talked, picking up on every word she said. She compared him to guys she dated. With Justin, the restaurants seemed empty except for them. He was always a gentleman. She described him to the girls as suave, though before meeting Justin, she thought suave existed only in a Bryan Adams song. Before meeting Justin, she never believed a real person could pull off suave.

Justin was out of the country frequently as his funds allowed. If he ever did choose one girl, Lil knew it wouldn't be her. She was well aware she was not his type. She figured on one of his trips abroad, he'd fall in love with someone named Marisol at the Running of the Bulls or at a Brazilian festival, and she'd never see him again. She hoped, at the least, the lucky chica would live on the U.S. mainland and allow her to play Aunt Lil to their children, or Hot Lil, as Sims' Tanner would say.

Sims often would bring Tanner to coffee, and Sam would swing by after work and pick him up so the girls could visit. Tanner used to call the girls his "Coffee Aunts," since he had only uncles and no real aunts. Hinton quietly hated the term as it conjured for her a vision of yellow-toothed, hacky-voiced old broads. She volunteered to babysit for Sims one Saturday, as she needed a full day with Tanner. On the first stop of their day together, she took Tanner to Hot's for hot chocolate with marshmallows and borrowed one of the aprons from the kitchen. Hinton dropped Tanner at home just before dark with a new toy in each of his hands and a coon-skinned cap on his head. He wrapped his little arms around her neck, planted a wet kiss on her cheek, and shouted, "Bye, Hot Aunt Hint!" as he ran past his mother and into the house. Sims, standing blue-jeaned and barefooted on her silky Zoysia lawn, raised her eyebrows to Hinton questioningly.

39

"Well, idin't that precious!" Hinton assumed her innocence. "You know, we *did* go by Hot's today," she reasoned. "He's just adorable, Sims!" Hinton declared sincerely, having fallen irreparably in love with Tanner that day.

That day, Hinton looked at her swollen belly and smiled for the first time. And that day, they all became Tanner's "Hot Aunts." Tanner eventually eliminated the word "aunt" altogether. Hot Mac loved the new name, and Hot Lil pictured Justin's children calling her that. Somehow the thought helped.

"Justin kisses you on the cheek, very European," June said to Lil, pressing her glass of iced water against her face.

"Not exactly European, just one cheek," Sims said.

"Poor second cheek," Mac added in baby talk, poking out her lip.

"He kisses everybody like that," Lil explained.

"Nope, darlin, just you," Hinton said.

"Well, when I'm with y'all it's just me because he barely knows you," Lil explained.

"Just do it with him!" Sims said. "It might make you better friends!"

"At least tell him you've never done it," Hinton insisted. "That'll bust his zipper."

"He wears button flies," Mac corrected Hinton.

They all looked at Mac, not exactly surprised she'd noticed this detail during the few times they'd been around Justin.

"Whut?" Mac asked innocently, turning the one-word question into two syllables.

"Even better," Hinton said. "Buttons flying everywhere. Every man wants a virgin at least once. I've made that dream come true for more than one lucky man. Anyway, I thought you told him everything."

"No, no I've reserved that precious little tidbit about myself just for y'all," Lil said sarcastically, wishing they didn't know either.

"Seriously, Lil," June said. "We love you. We care about you. Do you really want to miss another year of sweaty, single sex? Do you want to finally do it, only to realize it's not such a big deal, but big enough that you'll regret you can't get back all the years you missed doing it?"

"Yack, yack, yack!" Sims complained about this never-ending topic. "Girl, lay down for the man and be done with it! You're a relic, the last virgin in the twenty-first century," Sims said, tired of arguing with Lil about it. "*You* are the new 'dirty, little secret.' I need some more coffee," Sims said looking for the waitress.

It seemed Lil's time on the firing wall was coming to a close.

"I'm bored, too," Hinton said, shutting down the conversation, her lips reaching for the rim of her coffee cup, with one last rhetorical comment.

"A waste of a sheet of paper. The sad, sexless saga continues and for who knows how much longer."

"Maybe tonight," Lil mumbled.

3

Topping It off at Hot's

Just short of a spit-take, Hinton choked on her coffee.

"What did she say?!" Hinton managed to blurt.

Mac stood erect, almost flipping her chair over, and shouted to the waitress.

"Top us off!"

Every head in the place turned.

They all set down their cups at the same time and scooted their chairs closer to the table. One of the older women at the table next to theirs shushed the people at the table next to them as their eavesdropping took on new interest.

"Tonight?!" June repeated.

"Any day now, at the least," Lil continued. "I've given myself a deadline, and I'm sticking with it. I've got two months left."

"Two months?! Why two months?!" June asked.

Sims quickly counted two months off on her fingers, "The rest of December into January, February. Why February?" she lifted the second finger and pondered any importance related to the timeline.

"Your birthday! You're gonna do it for your birthday!"

"You've met someone?" Mac asked.

"No," Lil answered.

"Why two months then? Why now?" June asked.

"Why not?" Lil answered. "I stared at this juvenile, fantasy list, and you were right. I didn't really come here today to defend it even though I tried. At 25, it's indefensible. I've passed this decade's midway mark, and I'm headed to thirty. I'm a freak! No man's going to wait for me until we're married, and no man's going to do it and then still marry me. It's an outdated notion, and I'm starting to forget why I was waiting in the first place," she said, knowing full well she remembered why.

Lil always had regarded making love to a man as something she would share only with her husband. It wasn't necessarily because she'd heard that explanation at church or even that her parents had taught her that order of events. She didn't judge anyone for making a different choice about sex. She had waited because she truly believed, for her, that that was the way it should happen. She had searched for the man who would treasure her choice, even celebrate it with her, though saying that out loud would just sound stupid. She longed for the man whose heart was in sync with hers, but she no longer believed he existed.

"You've all been right, all along, so start your chorus of 'I told you so,' " Lil said, "because I think I agree with you now. I tried! I really did! I just think it's time to give up. I'm tired!

43

And I'm full! If I have to eat out one more time!" she complained. "No man could possibly live up to what I fantasize it will be like now. It's like y'all have always said: I'm finally going to find someone, only to discover seven minutes later, it wasn't worth a hundred-year wait, then out for a waffle."

"Oh, sweetie," Mac said, patting Lil's arm consolingly, "they fall asleep right after. There's no waffle."

"Lil," June said, "there's no magical, monogamous, romantic man walking around out there waiting on you. That's all movie stuff. Even the moaning and groaning--all Hollywood. We're all in our beds imitating every movie we've ever seen. Ever thought about that?" she asked the others.

"Every Wednesday night, shuga," Mac winked at her, then took a sip of coffee.

"Wednesdays, huh?" Hinton asked Mac.

"Not 'only' Wednesdays, but 'every' Wednesday," Mac answered. "They don't call it Hump Day for nothin'."

"So, Lil," Sims ignored the side conversation, "on your birthday, by your birthday? What's the plan? Because I know you, and I know you have one."

"I don't know the exact day, but by the time I turn 26," Lil said, "maybe sooner. Before it's any weirder. Before *I'm* any weirder. I meet deadlines every day at work, and until I set a deadline on this thing, I'm not going to *let* it happen."

"Well, you gotta pick a guy," June said.

"What do you think I've been doing for twenty-five years, June? I've been looking, hard! Lately, I've accepted every date I've been asked on, regardless of who's asking."

44

"When did that start?" Mac said.

"Damn it!" Hinton blurted, looking at her ringing phone. "My sitter," she explained, looking at June. "That tenth grader you told me you'd found."

"*My* sitter?!" June complained.

Hinton answered the phone and put it on speaker.

"Yes, sweetie?" she spoke into the speaker to the 17-year-old babysitter.

"Miss Hinton, I really have to go. I have a date tonight."

"On a Wednesday?" Mac whispered to Sims about a teenager having a date on a school night. "That's a booty call," she said, pointing over to Lil. "She's totally doing it."

"Sweetie, I'll pay you $100 to stay another hour," Hinton said.

The conversation was too good to leave now.

"Are you kidding?!" the sitter asked, incredulously.

"I'll have cash. See you in an hour," Hinton said, hanging up before the girl could answer.

"Crap, Hint!" June complained. "I'll never be able to compete with that! Now I'll have to find another sitter!"

"Shhh!" snapped Mac. "When did you start this manic dating, Lil?"

"Three or four months ago at the midyear mark."

"How fun!" June said.

"No, it isn't!" Lil disagreed. "You should all go home and hug your husbands! You don't know what's out there. And I'm having to do double-time on the elliptical just to fit in my clothes. Dating is all about eating!"

"Listen to her complain. She's all talk. Where is that waitress?" Sims said, bored again already, getting up with her cup to go get a refill.

"I think you're really serious about this," June said, ignoring Sims. "I almost feel like it's me again! Oh, I wish it *were* me again. I'd be so much better with a do-over. I can't believe it's gonna happen!" she said, fanning harder.

"What's going to happen, ladies?" a man's voice came up behind them.

It was Justin. Their faces lit up with smiles, and their eyes cut over to Lil, who was frantically reaching for the list that set across the table from her, dirty version face up. They shifted their chairs to part a place for him to pull a chair next to Lil.

"Here, let me get that for you," Justin said, handing Lil the paper, who wadded it as her hand made contact with it, and crammed it into her bag.

Justin held his coffee to the side and leaned down to kiss her cheek. This time the outer quarter of their lips touched, and the girls raised their eyebrows at her. Lil tensed up as she saw the smile forming on Mac's lips as she was about to answer Justin's question of what was going to happen.

"Oh, just an intimate, little 'git-together' Lil's planning to have in the next couple of months," Mac said, smirking about her answer to Justin's question. "She's thinking about really rockin' in her twenty-sixth year."

"Don't worry, Justin," Hinton followed up on Mac's comment. "You'll most likely be invited."

Lil closed her eyes and waited for the jabbing to end. She didn't bother to kick any of them under the table. She knew there was no stopping them.

"Speak of the devil," Sims said, returning to the table holding a full pot of coffee.

"Oh, I might be bad, but I'm not the devil," Justin replied. "I think I've met him a time or two though. My name came up?"

"They were just asking how you were," Lil said. "What brings you here?"

"You, of course," he said to Lil. "I really needed to see you," he smiled. "Ladies, are you using this chair?" Justin asked the eavesdroppers behind him at the next table.

Though they were older than Lil's crowd's mothers, the women still batted their lashes at Justin.

"You're welcome to it, Sailor," one of the silver women winked at Justin.

He took it in stride and smiled at the women.

"Did she just call him 'sailor'?" Hinton giggled in Mac's ear. "That's hysterical. I'm gonna use that," Hinton said behind her coffee cup.

"Of course you are," Mac replied quietly, raising her own cup in front of her mouth. "She's you in thirty-five years. Just look at her. It's like she's shopping in your closet."

"I'm too busy looking at you sitting next to me," Hinton whispered about another of the older women. "She's found that hair color you've been searching for. What's that, sable? And she's been lifted to the high heavens."

"I wonder who she uses," Mac admired the woman's face.

"Be nice," Lil said quietly to Mac and Hinton who apparently were whispering about the crowd behind her.

At least they'd taken her mom's suggestion: "If you don't have anything nice to say, say it behind your coffee cup." Mrs. Swann's adult advice was less by-the-book.

"Thank you," Justin said to the women as he raised the chair and placed it in the new space next to Lil, winking at Lil about the older women as he sat down.

One of the older women mouthed to Sims behind Justin's back, "Justin?" Sims nodded in the affirmative, noticing the woman was wearing the same running attire she was wearing. The redheaded one mouthed, "Nice," while her friends nodded in agreement.

"I thought I'd just step in and say hello to your friends," Justin said to Lil. "Lil tells me your coffees are like an hour at the spa," he joked, knowing lately, to him, Lil called her close-knit group of friends the firing squad.

"Spa?" asked June, fanning the back of her neck.

"Yes," Lil said sarcastically, "and today I got the Siberian rock massage."

"Smart," Justin laughed at Lil's joke.

"Yes," Mac said, also with sarcasm, "she *seems* so smart."

"So, Justin, you speak Spanish and Greek fluently?" June asked.

"Yes," he said.

"*Are* you Spanish or Greek," June followed up.

"No," he answered.

"But speaking them--still sexy," Mac commented, crinkling her nose at Justin.

"So I'm told on occasion," he smiled.

"So why Spanish and Greek?" June continued.

"My parents were Christian medical missionaries, so I've lived most of my life in different places around the world, mostly South America," he answered.

Lil had heard Justin answer that question in that brief way numerous times. She was relieved Justin had joined them. At least momentarily, the women put down their muskets. And as was typical, when a man showed up, they would more than likely tone down the raunchy. The girls always got raunchy when talking about men, jokingly, and mostly for shock effect. Lil knew they loved their husbands. She usually got a kick out the girls, unless they turned their comments to Justin. But she couldn't be sure of what might come out of their mouths during the current interrogation.

"Where is home?" Sims asked Justin.

"Different places," he said, sipping his coffee.

"But home? Surely you can pick one place," Sims said. "Where were you born?"

"Right here," Lil thought she'd save him for a minute. "His parents were here for a couple of months raising funds for their missions, and he was born while they were here. He went to college at Duke. He played soccer there, too," she added, knowing Sims would find that interesting.

"Spanish, I get," started June, "but Greek?"

"When I was 10, the village we were living in was getting progressively more dangerous. My parents sent me to live with an aunt in Greece. I gave her a load of trouble, as would any kid who'd grown up in places where I'd grown up. She'd had enough after a year or so and sent me back to them," he answered her.

"So your home really is the world," June said.

"Feels like it," Justin answered.

"Todo el mundo," Mac said in her thick, Southern accent.

The others looked at Mac with pained expressions.

"Very good," Justin smiled at her, used to Southerners practicing their two or three drawling Spanish phrases on him.

He stood and turned to ask the passing waitress for skim milk. While he reached over for the milk, Hinton squinched her face and looked at Mac.

"Girl, you are rusty," Hinton mumbled.

Even Mac's older twin at the next table shook her head in disappointment as she sipped some coffee.

"I didn't mean to interrupt your visit," Justin said to Lil and the others. "I'm gonna step away and make a couple of phone calls. Good to see you all again," he said, leaving.

"Damn it!" Hinton said again, looking at her ringing phone. "The sitter again," she explained. "What *now,* sweetie?" she said into the phone.

"My mother said I can't take your hundred dollars, and I really have to go."

"Oh, all right, I'm coming, dear," she clicked off the phone. "I have to go."

"I do, too," Mac said, reapplying lipstick. "It's Hump Day."

"Call us, Lil," June said, gesturing to Justin who was now across the room, "--conference call during the afterglow."

"I never should have said a word," Lil said, already regretting the conversation.

50

"Get under that one and fast," Mac agreed, getting up to leave. "When you're married, he'll be your Mr. Regret."

The girls walked to the door to leave. June and Sims turned back to Lil and signaled, "L the V." Lil was already second-guessing the conversation. Two months were going to fly by before she knew it. She thought about the deadline she had blurted out and all the pressure she had just added to her situation.

"Me and my big mouth," she said to herself.

"Talking to yourself?" Justin asked, rejoining Lil as the waitress topped off her coffee.

"Yes, they drive me crazy, and I have to talk myself back down to sane when they leave."

"Never sit at a table outnumbered by married people," he instructed.

"You said you needed to see me?" she asked.

"Very much so."

"About what?"

"Why does it have to be about something? Can't a man just say he really needs to see a woman any more?"

"Nope," Lil said, "but I'll accept it. They wore me down before you got here, so I'm fresh out of witty."

Justin smiled. There they were, the eyes she loved so much. No one was in the café but them now, though the place was packed. She'd have to face it. She would be dear friends with a man she'd crush on for the rest of her life.

"This is the third time since Sunday you've met me for coffee, and it's only Wednesday," Lil said. "That's a record for us. *Or*," she added on second thought, "a *broken* record for you!" counting quickly in her mind how much more frequently the two of them had been meeting for coffee, dinner, movies, lunches.

They'd gone on a paintball outing the day before Thanksgiving, and Lil had assisted him with numerous soccer practices and games with kids Justin coached.

"Meaning?" he asked.

"You're in a dating slump."

"Ahhhh. But no. More like taking a dating sabbatical."

She studied him quizzically.

"Justin," she said, doubtfully.

"No, I really am. It has been coming on for a while. Months now. Haven't you noticed? Something like, 'There's got to be more.' Ever been there? Because I need guidance," he smiled at her.

"And you think I can offer guidance?"

Lil had been so busy with her increased dating life that she hadn't noticed the decrease in his. Lil never talked about her dates, not to Justin or the girls. None of them had any idea how many first dates she went on, almost as many second dates, and the less-frequent third dates, the one last night her latest. She'd learned years ago that friends and family start counting the guys and the time and wondering why no serious relationship, why no ring? Too many questions, too much score keeping, so she'd learned even before meeting Justin, that it was better to keep her dating life totally private. Even before her recent "manic dating," as Mac put it, Lil dated frequently, but the last three months had been crazy, and because of her theatre schedule, mostly during the week.

Lil was pretty. Birmingham was famous for its bounty of beauties. Among her crowd of friends, Hinton was always the first to get the men's attention and the random complimentary dessert from the smitten waiter, which Sims and June would eat. Hinton was the curse of shopping wives everywhere, as even the most self-restrained husbands in every age bracket, turned to get the rear view, in clear view of their insulted wives. She had her entrance into a restaurant perfected, waiting to remove her sunglasses until after the heads noticeably had turned in her direction, like the first accessory removed in a slow-motion striptease. All that was missing was the hair-blowing fan and seductive music, which Lil added for Hinton in her mind.

Mac let Hinton have the first wave, claiming even a snaggletoothed blonde would get the first one. She knew she'd get the second one, plus it took a minute for the men to recognize Mac from Big Daddy's commercials--and their dreams—as they matched her face with her "Let me take ya for a ride" fame. Without fail, a dirty martini would make its way on an uplifted tray, sent from some hopeful waver across the room. Mac would finger-wave back, wait a minute, then discreetly slide the drink over to Hinton who loved a martini. All five of them shared in the booty that was delivered to Hinton and Mac. It didn't matter that Hinton and Mac were wearing rings that weighed more than their hands. Their admission of "Married," to the brave swaggerers who eventually approached them, was often followed up with the still optimistic query of, "Happily?" Sims and June got their due amount of notice as well, but at the end of a decent-length conversation, Lil was the one they remembered.

Lil had long, dark blond hair, clear blue eyes, a 5' 3" petite frame, and nice legs. She was busty enough to get her share of double takes, and her teeth were sparklingly white. It didn't hurt that her one, quirky habit was brushing them incessantly. She loved the costumes and makeup she got to wear when she was on stage, but on a daily basis, she wore little makeup, did the quickest fixes on her hair, and didn't jingle with jewelry when she walked like Hinton did. She was low-maintenance at its best. Her smile was contagious, and most men found her suitably attractive.

Lil had formed a blogging company with six other journalists, two web gurus, and an advertising genius, all with whom she had gone to school. Their news blog was entitled, SameSun NewsMark, printed in old typewriter font. They dropped the "s" in the word NewsMark the way an old typewriter might have done, making the word look like "NewsMark" and "New Mark" at the same time. Black ink fingerprints were scattered around the articles in the blog. Lil occasionally included an opinion article headlined, "**I Can't Quit Thinkin . . ..**" She had begun to add a blurb in some of those articles subtitled, "**Whadda you think?**" encouraging her readers to get involved with solutions to situations. Six Southeastern papers had picked up the group's stories, and two other papers were in talks with them.

Denton had been a great help on the legal side of setting up Lil's business. Sam found the group its current downtown rental office for a steal. Jack donated discontinued furnishings from his warehouse, and Auggie and his brothers loaded it all on a big truck and hauled it for her. Big Daddy was their first big advertiser.

Lil had held on to her childhood dream of acting. Her father had been right about the opportunities to do so right here at home. She was a regular in Birmingham productions in the theatres scattered around town, from the Birmingham Children's Theatre at the Birmingham-Jefferson Convention Complex, to the Virginia Samford Theatre in Caldwell Park, and Red Mountain Theatre Company performances at the Cabaret and the Dorothy Jemison Day Theater, and shows in the arts district around 19th Street North. She had been cast in large productions, mostly minor roles with a few secondary parts, but at the moment she was the lead actress in the Broadway series production, *Only One Once*, showing at the historic Alabama Theatre.

The Alabama Theatre was rarely in the play production business, originally built in the 1920s as a film palace. The play times were sporadic, scheduled around the theatre's other events, and refreshingly, not always on Fridays and Saturdays, as Southern brides often booked the theatre and the theatre's adjacent Hill Event Center for weddings and receptions. Lil thought of her acting as a sideline, but her current reviews were good. She didn't take all the critiques seriously though, as the blog's feature writer and critic, Craig Jenkins, sat three desks away from hers.

Lil was a natural at conversation and really liked getting to know people, but she had stopped wasting time after the third date when she knew she wasn't interested enough to go further.

She could describe dating in her twenties only as a game. Men wanted sex, and men in their 20s and 30s wanted it immediately. They clocked in their hours, usually two, maybe three dates. After that, they did the math on what the meals were costing them and wondered what was wrong with the girl. The whole process for Lil became less about getting acquainted with the man, and more about the slight-of-hand necessary for her to get through the first several dates with her clothes still on. So much game playing was involved, that nobody was getting to know anybody, and very little was accomplished. She understood the different choice other women made, but because of the one unchecked reason in her Don't column, she couldn't cross the pencil line and push herself to the "Do" side of the sheet of paper. She didn't know Justin's approach to dating—he didn't kiss and tell--but she assumed his was far different from hers, and from the time of their first meeting, she knew she wasn't Justin's type.

They met at the UAB Sterne Library. Lil was working on her dissertation. Their hands bumped as they both reached for the same book, *El Corazon de Ecuador*, on a shelf in the Latin Studies section. After a few niceties, "Please, you take it," "No, I insist," Justin successfully bowed out since he worked at UAB and explained he could come back any time. A Venezuelan girl named Pía eventually showed up and smiled her 5' 10" self at Lil.

"Allo," Pía said her best English hello, sincerely, friendly, and not at all threatened by Lil.

Lil figured even Pía knew she was in a different league.

"Good to meet you, Pía," Lil said, mentally kicking herself for wearing the only pair of flat shoes she even owned. "And you . . . .?" Lil said to Justin as they were all leaving.

"I'm Justin Rock. Mucho gusto, Lily Swann," he said, reaching to shake her hand. "I'm an assistant professor in the foreign language department, so if you're working on your master's in Spanish, you'll see me around. Seriously," he added, nodding to the book she now held, "if you need any help on that dissertation, I lived a number of years in that country, and I can tell you things about that place that will never appear in any book."

"Thank you," Lil said, noticing how warm his hand was.

He was a young professor, 28 when they met, 30 for the next four months. Lil found his black, shoulder-length ponytail appealing, while at the same time, she found it out of character for herself that she found it appealing. She and Justin were obviously different people, and she figured Pía must have been his girlfriend or one of his classroom groupies. She imagined he had quite a few. Lil had taken him up on his offer to help with her dissertation, and their first meeting was at his house.

Justin lived downtown on one of the rougher sides, in a decent house, one of those bungalows people pass, wondering what the neighborhood had been like before the crime grew. Justin could have lived any place, but he chose the East side of Birmingham. He drove a 1978 BMW that a deceased neighbor had left him. He owned very few things because he wasn't about things.

At the first study session at Justin's house, Lil showed up an entire hour early. She tapped on the door, but he didn't answer.

She had seen the car parked out front, so she figured he was there. She cracked open the door and without crossing the threshold called, "Professor Rock?" He was coming out of the bedroom, putting a shirt on, having just showered. When his head appeared through the neck of the shirt, there she was, on his porch, her eyes fixed on a scar on the outer part of his chest near his shoulder. She would ask him about it a month later.

"A spear," he would say, smiling.

"One day you're going to have to tell me the truth," she would say, tiring of the fictitious answer.

"You're early, Lily, muy temprano, and call me Justin," he said smiling, seeing Lil standing at his doorway, as if he knew something she didn't.

"No, I'm right on time, 3 p.m. on the nose," she said, double-checking her watch.

"Lily, we set our clocks back in the early hours today, the end of Daylight Saving Time," he said.

Lil clapped her hand over her mouth, mortified.

"I'll go and come back in an hour!" she insisted.

"Not necessary," he smiled. "You should wear pink more often," he joked about her cheeks, flushed with embarrassment. "It has been a long time since I've seen a girl blush. Let's go up the street and grab something to eat while we work," he said, picking up his coat, and joining her on the porch.

Every girl Justin had dated from the time Lil met him was exotic to say the least, most of them from Spanish-speaking countries. Lil assumed at first that's why he had learned the language to begin with, to sweep some Latin beauty off her feet. She later learned about his parents' work, both doctors who had spent their lives in jungle clinics. He wasn't the son of wealthy physicians, traveling the world on their wallets. Theirs had never been full, but Justin was smart enough to create his own financial opportunities, and he lived wholly within his means. Her initial crush on him lasted six months, through two Marias, an Isabella, an Adriana, a Lupe, and a Pilar. Nope, she wasn't his type. His friendship would have to be enough, and it had been that and more. Anyway, she figured if you have a type, it's probably best to stick with it for long-term happiness, a trust-your-instincts kind of thing. She wanted to find someone who was looking for her type, for her specifically, someone who was so wildly mad for her that getting her would last their lifetimes. Stupid, she knew.

"Join me for dinner," Justin said, finishing his coffee.

"That would make three nights already this week. You really thought I could give you some guidance, didn't you?"

"I'm just hungry," Justin said.

"I have a small roast waiting for me at home in a Crockpot," Lil smiled.

"Very domestic of you."

"I'm tired of eating out," she said, knowing he had no idea how often that was. "I thought it would be relaxing to get home from work, open the door, and smell supper cooking, you know? A real supper. Like having a good wife waiting for me at home. Join me."

"Speaking of wives, I have a favor to ask," he said.

"What in the world?" Lil asked, as she gestured to the waitress that she didn't need a refill.

"Remember a few months ago, I told you Mitchell was getting married? I'm hoping you'll go with me to the wedding. Plane ticket's on me. I put two on hold this morning for twenty-four hours."

"Justin, seriously, take one of your Latin beauties. That would make three weddings, one funeral, two births, and a bar mitzvah in the last eighteen months I've been to as your faux date. At the last wedding, the women were whispering, 'Make him poop or get off the pot, girl.' They're starting to throw the bouquet at me hard. That last one hurt, and I wasn't even in the mob of women trying to catch it. I was sitting at a table eating cake."

"They love you," he said about his friends.

"I love them, too, but they think we're really an item."

"Just one more," Justin said.

"Uggg, when is it?" she groaned, backing down as usual.

"Saturday," he said, smiling. "I had forgotten about it."

"This Saturday?! Now I know why you 'really needed to see me.' I can't. The play," she said, referring to her role of Angelica.

"Is that still running?" he asked.

"Justin! I've given you the schedule twice! Have you ever been to one of my plays?"

"Yes, you left two tickets at Will Call, remember, when you played Lunchroom Lady Number Two in that one this summer. I took Ava."

"Oh, yes, you left two scenes before the one scene I was in, as I recall."

"I'm coming to this one. I really am."

"Did you really forget this wedding, or did you think it would take dinner every night this week to get me there this time?"

"I just came across the invitation last night," he said. "I'd forgotten about it because I'd told Mitchell I would be out of the country and not able to go, then my travel plans changed. And we have dinner because we love each other," he smiled suavely. "Can't your understudy fill in?"

"Not for a wedding, and not this Saturday. Rumor has it that Broadway scouts are coming to see our leading man, and the director isn't allowing any vacations. Sorry. You'll just have to tell them I gave you an ultimatum, or that I died, or, or take Ava!"

"How long is the acting going to work out with your real career?" he asked.

"As long as it works out! When it ends, it ends. It's fun. It's my first lead! And it's the Alabama Theatre! If it's my last play, it's my last play. What a way to go out!" Lil exclaimed.

"I'm really coming to this one. Just give that guy, Nick, a ticket, and I'll ask for him one night. Do you do any kissin in this one?" he asked smiling, putting a tip on the table.

"Oh, yes. There's even some pilfering and a bout of raping."

"Oh, my. I'll certainly have to see this one. Any nudity?"

"You'll have to find out for yourself. Are we on for roast?" Lil asked.

"Yes, let's go," he said, standing and pulling her chair out for her. "I'll stop by the store for some red wine, and tonight I'm pouring you a glass," Justin said.

He knew Lil had a two-drinks-a-year limit. She had a bit of an allergy to red wine and a low tolerance to the alcohol content, but she liked the taste. Her face would turn burgundy, and even her ears would burn when she drank it, but the year was running out, and this would count as her final semiannual glass for the year.

"Okay, while you're doing that, I'm going to stop by the gas station to fill up my car, but I should get there about the same time as you," she added, putting on her jacket. "I'm rolling on fumes. You know my garage combination, in case you get there first."

"Lil, it's dangerous for a woman to let her gas level get that low," he said. "Here, give me your keys, and you take my car. I'll fill it up for you," Justin said, putting his keys in her hand.

"Justin, I gas my own car up all the time, and the gas station is right there!" she pointed through the window.

"Well, tonight, you don't have to, and it doesn't matter how close that station is. It's dark already," he said, taking her keys.

"Well, here's my gas card," she said, reaching into her bag for the credit card.

"Consider it my half of the dinner," he said.

"Justin! I will not let you pay for my gas!" Lil argued.

"I will not let you not let me," he said calmly, smiling at her and opening the café door for her.

With Justin's back turned toward the older women who were still sitting at their table, Lil saw them for the first time, and all of them were giving her the L the V fingers followed by their thumbs pointing to Justin. Lil's eyes grew big, and she hurried out before Justin caught their reflections in the glass door.

Justin walked Lil to his car, opened the door for her, said, "Buckle up," closed the door and went to her car. It felt good, his taking care of her car.

"We're just friends; we're just friends; we're just friends," she repeated her new mantra to herself as she located his car key on the ring of keys he'd handed her.

Lately, she had to keep reminding herself of that fact out loud. She cranked the car, and a song met her ears. She wasn't familiar with the melody, though the artist was easily recognizable. She listened to the words as she turned up the heater and buckled the seatbelt. She leaned back against the seat and shook her head.

"You, too, Bryan? I get it. We're just friends," she said toward the car's stereo, not needing another reminder that she and Justin were just friends.

She glanced over toward Justin who was settling into her car. He backed out and motioned for her to back out in front of him.

"Those lucky Latinas," she whispered to herself.

4

The Virgin's Secret Handbook

The roast had shrunken to two-thirds of its original size, but the aroma when Lil walked in the door was just as she had hoped. The potatoes weren't too mushy, and the carrots added just the right sweetness. She brushed her teeth, changed into jeans, a T-shirt, and sweater boots, and started a fire. She boiled water, and steamed the broccoli to perfection just as Justin got there.

"Mmm, your wife did a good job," Justin said about her Crockpot when he walked through the door and smelled the aroma.

"It's the Dale's Steak Seasoning," Lil agreed. "Milo's Tea?" she asked, filling the glasses with ice.

They sat at her small island to eat. Justin noticed three business cards with Big Daddy's logo on them, all three belonging to Sales Associate Jet Leerson.

"Thinking about trading in the Mustang?" he asked Lil about the 15-year-old car she inherited from Peter when he joined the military.

"No, Jet's just a friend of Mac's."

"Fortunate name for a car salesman," Justin said.

"Mac made it up when he started working for her," Lil answered. "Mac said no one named Wilber Coons could sell a Ferrari."

Lil had discovered that fact on the first of her three dates with Wilber, a.k.a. Jet Leerson. Lil had agreed with the girls to go out on blind dates that each of them wanted to fix her up with, under their condition that she had to go out a minimum of five times with each guy. She agreed, bumping the number down to three. Jet picked her up in a different car from Big Daddy's lot on each of their three dates, put her in the driver's seat, and tried to sell the car the entire date, handing her his card after each of his three goodnight kisses. Sims fixed her up with Chet, a chiseled specimen doing his student teaching during Sims' P.E. classes. After three dates, Lil had a pulled hamstring and a lower body image. All June had to say about her guy, was, "His name is Neal, Lil." And all Lil had to show from her three dates with Neal was a $50,000 term life policy, but still no beneficiary in sight. Hinton let her off the hook after her one date with butt-squeezing Garrett who took Lil to a party Hinton hosted.

Hinton had thrown a cocktail party to celebrate her father-in-law's birthday and to show him how professionally Denton was running his family's Birmingham law office. Hinton had a good-looking lineup of young lawyers to select from since

Denton had hired only men so far. Denton had asked his sister in the Montgomery office to interview females for him. He hadn't told Hinton, but he never wanted her to wonder why he had selected any particular woman. His sister was glad to help. Hinton set Lil up with Garrett, Denton's newest attorney, for the formal affair.

Lil knew instantly Garrett wouldn't get a second date, before she even laid eyes on him. She knew it the minute he honked the horn for her. She walked to his car and got in to discover that Hinton was right about how unbelievably handsome he was, which Lil quickly assessed was part of his problem, and he already had one strike against him. They briefly introduced themselves, and before he pulled away from her house, Garrett earned his second strike. He retrieved a hand-vacuum from the back of the car, asked Lil to raise her feet, and sucked up the dirt he said she dragged into his new Porsche that still had Big Daddy's sticker on the window.

They didn't even make it inside Hinton's house before Garrett struck out. Walking to the front door, instead of placing a gentlemanly hand on Lil's back, he placed it on her sequined buttocks, an innocent mistake, Lil assumed, until he squeezed it. Before she could turn to confront him, ignoring her mother's voice in her head, which was shouting, "Slap him," Denton swung open the front door and greeted them. She avoided Garrett the rest of the night, which was easy, as he was busy kissing every ass in a suit. Unlike Justin, Garrett was now open game. In the company of her friends, Lil figured it was as good a night as any to forget her wine allergy and have her first semiannual "I just love you guys" night.

66

The five girls were in Hinton's kitchen replenishing hor d'oeuvre trays and creating Totem Pole Man where they took a section of each man at the party and created the perfect man: head, neck, shoulders, arms, hands, butt, legs, and feet. Sims called dibs on Totem Man's feet for Sam saying only, "Trust me." Garrett walked into the kitchen for another beer. He had been voted Totem Man's ass during Lil's only participation in the game.

"Because he is one," Lil had said, warm and sleepy from the one glass of wine she still nursed, as a solitary hiccup took her by surprise.

Mac squeezed Lil's butt, adding, "And he likes 'em."

As Garrett entered, Lil, Hinton, and Mac left the kitchen to take the freshly filled trays to the living room where some of the men were gathered, their wives scattered around the room chatting with one another. Lil had met the attorneys' wives at numerous luncheons Hinton hosted, luncheons that turned out to be a lot like Wednesday coffee. They entered the room with their trays just as one of Denton's partners said something only slightly off-color.

"Gentlemen," Denton said to his partners, "remember, we're in the presence of ladies."

Lil almost choked on her lemon square. She struggled to hold in her laughter, while her thoughts giggled, "In the presence of ladies? No you're not! And you're amateurs! Fledgling raunchateers, unknowingly in the presence of greatness camouflaged as gentility. Your wives could make a construction crew cry."

Hinton and Mac smiled sweetly, as did a few of the other women, excusing the comment, which also struck Lil as funny. She almost lost it when Hinton said in her straitlaced voice, "Don't worry about it, Martin. We've learned to tune out those kinds of comments." Lil literally had to hold her lips together between her thumb and index finger. She was thinking, "If half of you knew what your wives were willing to do in the bedroom, based on every lunch conversation I've ever had with them, no one would ever need anything blue in the medicine cabinet. Or would everyone need something blue?" she reconsidered, the wine fogging her reasoning.

She successfully suppressed her laughter, until she noticed over the men's heads, all the way back in the kitchen, Sims and pregnant June, air-dancing the bump with unsuspecting Garrett whose back was turned to them, refreshing his plate. Auggie walked in and caught them, shook his head, bumped June's rear with his, and kissed her on the mouth. Lil managed an unnoticed chuckle. She decided she better walk out of the room to collect herself. She didn't know that Sam had walked up and was standing behind her. Sims had sent Sam to retrieve Lil's wine, noticing earlier Lil was buzzed. Lil tripped over Sam's feet. She glanced down at them as she stumbled. He had to have been a size 14. Sam steadied her, taking her wine glass, but she could no longer hold her laughter. It was a silent, rocking laughter. Until she snorted.

"Lil? Something you'd like to share with the rest of us?" Mac drawled, her arms completely wrapped around Totem Jack's chosen bicep.

"Oh, no, I'm sorry," Lil said, still laughing, looking at her four dear friends who now stood side by side in the living room.

She cleared her throat and worked to pull it together.

"I was just thinking how boring my life would be without y'all. I really love you guys."

She walked Garrett to the door at the end of the evening, explaining that she was staying at Hinton's since they were in a 5K run the next morning, which they weren't.

"Well, let's walk out on the front porch," Garrett smiled, "and tangle up our tongues. After all, I did drive you all the way over here."

"After you," Lil said, gesturing him seductively through the door.

Of course, she was going to slam it behind him, but she changed her mind when he passed her on his way out and gave her fanny a pat.

"Garrett, would you indulge me for just a second?" she asked.

"In absolutely anything," he said stepping over the threshold and turning to face her.

"I just need to verify something," she said.

She reached through the door opening, placed her middle finger on the pulse of his neck, then placed her other middle finger on the pulse of her own neck.

"Kinky," Garrett smiled.

"Just as I suspected," Lil said. "Polar opposites. I just needed to make sure before--" and she slapped him hard across his cheek, "--before I did that," she said smiling. "Thanks for the ride," she added, well trained in etiquette, then slammed the door in his face.

Denton took her home and apologized for Garrett's behavior.

"He's probably going to sue me for battery," Lil said on the ride.

"He'll be plenty busy suing me for wrongful termination," Denton smiled at her, "which he can't win in an at-will state. I can't take the chance he would treat other women that way. I told Hinton I didn't think Garrett was someone she should fix you up with," Denton said, "but Hinton is a little naïve about the true nature of men."

Lil snorted again. She cloaked the snort with a couple of sniffs and coughs.

"I adore that woman," Denton said about Hinton.

"I know you do, Dent. She adores you, too," Lil said sincerely, wanting to tell Denton how hard Hinton had fought and won, to put his face on Totem Pole Man.

Lil slid Jet Leerson's business cards off the island countertop and into the waiting trashcan below. She and Justin almost polished off the roast. She would still have enough for a leftover dinner the next day. They cleared the dishes, and while Justin poured the wine, Lil put the leftovers in a to-go container.

"Enough about me and my sabbatical from dating. Let's talk about you," Justin said as they moved the conversation to the floor in front of the fireplace with their wine in tow.

He slipped his shoes off and put his feet to the fire.

"That's a good idea," Lil said. "Not the talking about me part," she qualified, "but the feet by the fire part."

She sat beside him, and he reached down and slipped the booties off of her feet for her. Just as she got comfortable, her cell phone started ringing across the room. She sighed and moved to stand up, and Justin stopped her.

"Hold on," he said, reaching in his back pocket, pulling out his old cell phone. "It's just me, butt dialing you again," he said, ending the call.

The two of them were the last two people in the free world still butt dialing, but neither could justify an updated cell phone until the old one gave up the ghost. They had a pact that the day one bought a new phone, the other would, too. Now each of them was trying to be the last to cave. Lil loved their old phones. She gave them all the credit for keeping her and Justin in contact after her dissertation was finished. Her mom had reared her believing a lady never called a man, and with her master's complete, she figured Justin now had no reason to call her. Justin's phone was guilty of the first three butt dials. His phone dialed hers as she jogged around Aldridge Gardens before work one morning. He was just as breathless as she was when she answered. He was across town running the trails around East Lake and the public golf course. The second call happened when he rolled over on his phone at midnight.

"Sorry I woke you," he said as he woke enough to realize the voice he was hearing was hers, coming from his phone.

"You didn't wake me. I couldn't sleep. I'm at the gym," she'd answered.

He looked at his clock and saw that it was 12:16 a.m.

"At this hour?" he asked, sitting up.

"That's why I joined this place."

"Are you finished?" he asked about her workout.

"Yep," she said, toweling her face.

"Then keep me on the phone while you walk to your car, get in, and lock it up. And please don't do this again, Lil," Justin said, now wide awake.

It was the first time he had worried about her. And the first time he realized she actually believed she could depend on the "kindness of strangers."[4]

The third time Justin's phone dialed hers was his all-time favorite.

"Hi, Mom," Lil said into her speaker.

"No, Lil, it's me, Justin. I butt-dialed you again."

"What?!" Lil exclaimed.

"Calm down. It was just an innocent butt dial."

"It's going to be fine, Mom!" Lil said. "I'll meet you at the emergency room! Tell Dad I'm sure it's just indigestion."

"Lil, who are you talking to? This is Justin, not your mom."

"Hold on one second, Mom," Lil said into the phone. "Marshall, thank you so much for all the work you put into planning this date. You must have pulled a lot of favors to get us into the rec center after hours. And as much as I would have enjoyed skinny-dipping, I'm going to have to take a rain check- -maybe on our second date. My father is having chest pains so I need to meet my mother at the emergency room. I'm sure it's nothing, but can you put your clothes back on and take me? What's that, Mom?" she said back in the speaker. "I'm on my way right now. Tell Dad I love him. And I love you."

"Should I meet you at the ER?" Justin chuckled, figuring out Lil's dilemma.

"That would be great, Mom. Thanks so much."

Justin was waiting just inside when Marshall dropped Lil off at the hospital. They still laughed about that one.

Justin muted his cell phone and tossed it to Lil's sofa.

"If you're ready for that new phone . . .," Lil teased, secretly hoping their phones would never quit working.

"No, I can hold out," Justin answered. "You're changing the subject. When was the last time you went out?" he asked her.

"Last night," she admitted, wishing they were still talking about cell phones.

"Last night?" he was surprised. She hadn't said anything about a date when they had dinner Monday.

"Before that?" he asked.

"Saturday."

She hadn't mentioned that date on Sunday when they repaired her deck railing and made a few other improvements around her townhouse.

"Justin, I go out quite a bit," she admitted. "I just don't talk about it. After a couple or three dates, if I'm not interested, I move on, and there's nothing to talk about."

"Not even to me?" he said.

She just shrugged.

"I'm not a yapper like some chicks," she smiled.

"When was the last time you were interested in someone worth talking about?" Justin asked.

"Hmmm. Probably before you and I became good friends. A long time ago. I just don't waste time when I know," she shrugged and started to move to the sofa, wanting physically to get away from the subject of her personal life. The shift wasn't lost on Justin.

"Maybe the guy's the one not wasting time on the relationship," he kidded her to keep her there and lighten the mood, "and you just think you're the one bailing."

"You see, that's the problem," Lil said, staying. "A couple of dates don't make a relationship!"

"Seriously, think about it," Justin continued to tease her. "Maybe you think you're dumping them, but they're really dumping you. We have ways of reading women and making the controlling ones think they're in control," he goaded her.

"They might eventually have dumped me had I hung around, but I'm the dumper," she insisted.

"How can you be sure?" Justin continued. "You have your games; we have ours."

"Mine are state-of-the art," Lil said. "Y'all's are transparent, predictable, poorly thought through, and weakly executed. A couple of mine literally involve smoke and mirrors, plus, they're still pushing their way into my bedroom when I dump them."

"No doubt, but let's visit the other theory, just for fun," he said. "Let's say it's you."

"Okay. 'It's me.' "

"Maybe you expect too much."

"Too much and more," she smiled.

"Or you're afraid it might lead somewhere."

"We all know where somewhere is."

"Or maybe it's something as simple as poor kissing skills," he smiled.

"Well, now you're talking crazy," she grinned, enjoying this.

"How can you be sure unless some objective someone, a good friend, who would be totally honest with you, scored you?"

"A good friend?" she pondered his suggestion. "Say Hinton or Mac?" she teased.

"You're stalling," Justin replied.

"Hmm. Maybe Craig from work," she continued.

"Well, he's not here," Justin smiled, "but I am. I'll take one for the team," he offered.

"And you're such a good kisser that you're certified to score someone else?"

"I've been told on numerous occasions," Justin answered. "Come on, Lil, you're an actress. We've been friends long enough to survive a little stage kissing, haven't we? I'm just trying to help," he continued.

"And all this just for little ole me?" Lil drawled, sarcastically.

"All research for the cause."

"You don't think I'll call your bluff, do you?" she said, seriously.

"Nope," he laughed.

"Well, I'm calling it, but you have to set the scene," she said.

"I should bring wine more often," he remarked, surprised she was considering his suggestion, though doubtful she'd really follow through. "Scene?" he asked, taking a swig of his wine.

"Yeah, set the scene," she touched her cheeks then her ears that were already burning from the red wine. "How many dates have we been on? Do I like him or not? Am I still undecided? You know, set the scene, so I'll know what kind of kiss would be appropriate."

He leaned forward, put his wine glass on the hearth, threaded his fingers through his long hair, pushing it back, and faced her.

"All right. First date," Justin started.

"Act Three, Scene One," Lil said.

"Do you even kiss on the first date?" Justin teased, knowing Lil was a true Southern girl whose mother not only had raised her on Letitia Baldrige's advice, but also had named her daughter Lily Letitia after Ms. Baldrige.

"Depends. Keep going."

"You like him--a lot," Justin emphasized. "You hope there's a second date. He's walking you to the door."

"Okay," she said, watching his lips as he talked, letting it sink in that she was about to be kissing them.

How in the world is this happening, she thought. How did we get from Wednesday coffee to kissing? If he's this smooth with me, just joking around, how smooth must he be when he's really interested in a girl, she wondered. She'd thought about this moment before but reminded herself this was just clean fun. Maybe this experiment would help her get him out of her system or give her something to remember. Either way. She took another sip of her wine and placed her glass next to his.

"Then we have to stand up," she said.

He smiled, pleasantly surprised she was still going through the motions. She stood up first. He stood and faced her.

"Okay, so I get to my door, and I turn to face him," she said, while acting her part. "I wait for him to move in. Then he pauses to get a read on my reaction to his stepping in," Lil said.

"True, he would," Justin agreed, stepping in and putting his hands on her waist.

"I pull my bottom lip in and half bite it, half moisten it, adding a hint of a smile. I breathe in and exhale once," she said, following her own instructions.

She'd scripted this scene many times.

"He dips his head down while putting one arm around my back to pull me slightly closer, lifts my chin with his other hand, and our lips meet."

"I don't need instructions. I've done this before," Justin smiled, pressing both of his lips around his tongue to moisten them.

As his face drew near to hers, she pulled back.

"Just to clarify," she asked, "is there gonna be tongue? I mean, won't that be weird for us?"

"Not for me, but I'm just the judge. It's your score," he smiled at her question.

Lil considered it.

"Okay, first kiss, lips only," she said, "then if it isn't weird, again with tongue--but not gross tongue," she added quickly.

"Who have you been kissing?" he shook his head, chuckling. "Not to worry," he winked suavely.

He moved the rest of the way in, and their lips met. He released her from the first kiss slowly and moved back in for the real kiss. It was good. It was warm. She had expected that. He was always warm. Her heart shifted in her chest. She continued with her first date kissing routine, placing her hand between them, at the top of his abdomen, gently sliding it up to his chest. The touch was nice. It made Justin feel manly, but he sensed in it the implied end to the kiss.

Their lips released. She breathed the smallest of sounds that implied, "I hate to stop kissing you, but I have to make myself stop." He didn't lean away, but kept his face close, in case she had just needed breath, hoping with his continued nearness to buy himself another kiss, to coax her for a while longer. Her eyes met his, then looked shyly down at her hand on his chest while touching her lips with her tongue, either to taste the remnants of his kiss or to give him a tad of hope that perhaps she was preparing for another one. She inhaled, then exhaled audibly, smiled at him and softly said, "Good night." Using the hand on his chest to push away, she turned toward her imaginary front door, opened it and walked inside, closing it behind her. She hated that it was over, but she was glad to have walked through her pretend door. She was convinced, had she stayed close to him much longer, he would have been able to hear her heart beating.

"Wow," Justin said, a little out of breath.

"So?" Lil asked.

"So what?"

"My score?"

"Oh, yeah, no problem there. I'm not dumping you. You're definitely getting a second date," he said.

" 'No problem?' " she repeated him. "That's my score?"

"If I told you how good it was, you'd kick me in the groin and shove me out of the real door. But scene two, second date," he continued. "You still really like him. Should he throw a toothbrush in his glove compartment?"

"No!" she said, "Of course not! Who have *you* been kissing?!" she threw his words back at him.

"But you *really* like him," Justin gruffly stressed the word "really," hoping to be bringing a toothbrush.

"No! It doesn't matter. I don't know him well enough yet. I could be crazy about him on the first two dates, and not realize what a jerk he is until the third date. If your girl is a jerk after the second date, I'm sure you're just glad you did the deed before you found that out. That's not how it works for girls," she said. "Well, not for me. Way too soon."

"Okay!" he said. "Don't get so riled up," he smiled, liking that she had. "So now it's date two. It went well, and he's bringing you home again," he said.

"Okay, this kiss has to be in the car," Lil explained. "The sex rejection doesn't go so easily on date two if he's gone to all the trouble of walking you to your door," she smiled.

Justin laughed at her explanation of the end of date two.

"You laugh, but all men think that waiting until the second date is 'waiting,' so he's expecting to pull up, turn off the car, and go in--which ain't hapn'n," Lil added in a comical tone. "So, he's driving me home, and I casually turn the radio knob to a gospel station."

"There's a gospel station?" Justin smiled. "That's a bucket of cold water. Instant mood killer."

"Huh, that wouldn't work in your car," Lil said, remembering his radio never had worked, only the CD player he had installed.

Justin winked at her. Lil continued setting the scene.

"So as we're pulling up out front, I say sweetly, 'We need to say goodnight here. My sister is visiting, and, well . . .,' " she finished. "That's usually enough said," she explained. "I don't mention the sister earlier in the date, because after that, he drives to his house instead of mine."

Justin nodded, impressed, and Lil continued.

"So we're in the car in front of my house, and thanks to modern car design, the console is butted up between us. Huh," she said again, thinking of something. "This wouldn't work in your car either, would it? Your car just has an emergency brake, no console."

"Too bad," Justin smiled. "I'm discovering a whole new appreciation for my old car."

Lil continued.

"So, he's not interested in going in to meet a sister, and he knows the night isn't leading anywhere because of the sister, but he's paid for dinner twice," Lil said sticking up two fingers, "so he thinks he at least has earned 'the good kissin,' " she put in finger quotes, smiling. "We have to go to my car for this," she said. "Come on."

"You're saying *that* wasn't the 'good kissin'? he asked about the first kiss as they headed to the garage.

He opened her car door for her and went around and got in the driver's seat, and Lil started the date two, goodnight scene.

"I need to say good night here," Lil said. "My sister is staying for a few days, and well . . .."

"You're right," Justin commented, out of character. "I'd rather not even get out of the car if she's in there," he said, smiling.

Lil smiled back, having proven her point.

"You don't have a sister you haven't told me about, do you?" Justin stopped role-playing for a moment, not remembering Lil ever speaking of a sister.

"No, but if we last a few more dates, he'll think that was adorable."

"True," Justin agreed.

Lil continued.

"I have to lean in first because, well, I'm to blame for having my sister visit, and he has to believe this is where the kissing has to be tonight."

Justin laughed.

"But only if I'm interested in a third date," Lil added.

"This is unbelievable," Justin commented. "Really good, but unbelievable."

"Okay, so I'm leaning in, and I'm gonna deliver the good kissin," she said, smiling at herself.

"You're so cute," he said as he watched her.

" . . . the kind of kissing that he thinks ought to come with some fondling," she continued, "but no man over 19 is going to reach over the console for fondling. That would be weird and a little desperate," she said as she started leaning toward him.

Their lips met, and the kissing was good. It lasted several times longer than the first date goodnight kiss. Justin slid his hands to the upper parts of her arms, gripping them firmly but gently, holding her as close to him as possible, but the damned console. A decade had passed since he'd been downgraded to car kissing, but the old excitement of it was still there. The kissing continued, just soft enough, just enticing enough, just moist enough. It only ended when Lil pulled slowly away, looked softly up at him, turned to open her door, opened it, got out, and shut the door, without a word. A master of words, Lil had discovered years earlier, that with men, words spoil the moment.

Justin sat there exhaling. This time he was the one tasting the remnants of the kisses on his lips, until she tapped on the driver window.

"Aren't you coming back inside?" she asked through the glass, finished with the scene, before she went in herself.

He didn't see it, but she was dizzy, and it wasn't necessarily from the wine.

"You've gotten this down to an art," Justin said, joining her at the fireplace where they each reached for their glasses and tapped them together. "All this time," he said, "and you've never told me any of this. I knew women planned in advance how to make things happen--trust me--but I never knew anyone thought out in detail how to make sure nothing did happen."

"It's the wine talking. Sorry," Lil laughed, touching her hot cheeks. "We probably should stop while we're still friends. I'll regret spilling it all tomorrow anyway. I should have made you sign a gag order. The girls don't even know about my dating system."

"Oh, no! This is the most interesting evening I've had in memory. I'm intrigued. Somehow a woman planning for things *not* to happen turns out to be more exciting than a woman planning to make things happen, things that, for most men, would have happened with very little effort on her part anyway. This way makes the man feel like the man. Date three," he continued. "A twist. You're still not sure about him at the beginning of the date, but halfway through it, you know you're not interested anymore. Now what?"

"Date three has to be my date," she said, finishing her glass of wine.

"Okay, I'll bite. What does that mean?"

"I have to pay. You see, two meals with no sex makes you guys unhappy," she said, making a puppy dog frown that he could only smile at, "but three meals with no sex, well, that just makes you mad," she said, poking fun at his gender. "So call me and ask me out."

"Okay," he said, stretching out on the floor on his side in front of the fire, placing his elbow against the floor, and resting his head on the palm of his hand.

She copied his posture, facing him. He didn't bother to pretend to be holding the phone, but he did slide toward her and move his face close to hers, kissing close, and did a good job of acting like the third-date bum who didn't know his time was up.

"Hey," he said in a breathy, pillow talk kind of way, smiling.

"Hey," she said, smiling back.

"Is your sister gone?"

Lil made an expression of "well played."

"She's leaving today," she answered.

"Ah," Justin said, out of character, "because something unexpected might come up that causes her to stay at the last minute if you need her to."

Lil nodded.

"So, I've been thinking about you," he continued, "a lot."

"Sweet," she replied.

They were smiling at each other. They were both having fun, and both enjoying how titillating acting all this out was.

"I have to see you," he said, running his finger up Lil's jaw to her earlobe. "Please tell me you saved a night on your calendar for me."

"On one condition."

"Anything."

"My treat. Let me take you out."

"Yeah, kind of surprising," Justin was out of character again. "I'm not even sure how to respond to that without sounding cheap."

Lil waited.

He couldn't think of anything.

"Please. You've taken me out for two wonderful dinners. I want to do this," she saved him.

"If that's what it takes to see you, I surrender my manly right to pay."

"I'll call you with the details as soon as I have them."

"Okay. Soon though."

"Very soon."

"You're not calling him back if you're not interested are you?" he predicted. "Now, he's the one waiting by the phone."

She just smiled.

"But still, you are curious. 'Is this guy worthy of the coveted third date?' you ask yourself."

"Okay, so," she said before she started laughing at herself.

"What?"

"You really don't want to know all this," she fell on her back and covered her face out of embarrassment.

"I really do," he said, smiling down at her. "I've never seen this side of you. I'm quite impressed with your little system."

"Well, there are many date three scenarios," Lil explained, sitting up. "There have to be."

"Explain."

"Let's say I've gotten to date three with a guy. We'll call him Tom. I plan the date, and, sadly, I dump Tom. Then I get to date three with another guy, Harry, someone who, unbeknown to me, is friends with Tom. If Tom and Harry realize they've been out with the same girl three times, comparing notes from the first two dates would be harmless. Sisters visit often, and dudes don't compare goodnight kisses with other dudes."

"You should teach a class," Justin said.

"But if they both had, say scenario A from the date three catalogue," Lil continued, "and compared notes, I'm exposed."

"Fascinating. So you've created many date three options for yourself. And did you figure this out from trial and error with an actual Tom and Harry who had compared notes or were you so far ahead of your own game, that this situation occurred to you first? You know," Justin changed his mind, "don't answer that. It's you, so of course you figured it out first."

"No Tom and Harry," Lil said.

But there had been a Wilson and a Simon who turned out to be cousins.

"You said scenario A," Justin continued. "How many scenarios are there?"

"Twenty-six, A-Z."

"Of course, twenty-six," he said, not able to contain his smile. "How many third dates have there been?"

"No more number questions, or I'll ask you some number questions."

"So we agree, no number questions," Justin said, and they laughed together.

He is so cute, she thought.

"But does a man ever make it through date three to date four?"

"Not often. Just a deadline system I've created. Three strikes--a system you guys understand."

"Give me an example of one date three scenario," Justin said.

"Hmmm," Lil thought. "My least favorite one comes to mind because I used it most recently."

"Okay, let's hear it."

"Scenario G: Bob and Weave," Lil started. "It's a progressive dinner. This one is really cheesy. I'm considering retiring it. It's the best one for guys I suspect are short on patience. They're the ones who bark at waitresses, honk at older drivers. You've seen the guy."

"Go on," he moved her forward, nodding.

"We meet at a preset place, and he parks his car," Lil explained scenario G. "If I pick him up at his place, that means I have to take him home to his place, and that's the last place I want to be at the end a date."

"Smart."

"Plus, no guy wants to be picked up at home."

"We don't like being picked up at all. We like having our cars. Gives us control."

"I know. So he gets in my car, and we go to--" Lil was saying when he interrupted.

"Wait. I'm in your car," he said, reminding her they were acting these out. "I think I get a pre-date peck on the lips by the third date, right?" Justin asked.

"Sure," Lil agreed.

They pecked. Justin put his hand around the back of her neck and pulled her in again, letting his hand slide up inside her hair, this time with a little tongue.

"I've missed you," he said, smiling at his performance.

Lil smiled back, impressed at how cleverly he'd gotten the extra kiss before the inevitable third date dumping commenced. She wasn't expecting that one, and her heart did something, something electrical and warm.

"What do you have in store for us tonight?" he asked.

"Um, a progressive dinner," Lil caught up with Justin. "We'll start at On Tap for drinks."

"On Tap?" Justin asked as himself. "Don't you have an actress friend who tends bar there?"

She nodded.

"So free drinks?"

"Maybe."

"Nice. Since when did you start drinking?" he asked.

In the two years he'd known Lil, aside from her two annual glasses of wine, he'd seen her have only one mixed drink, a strawberry margarita at a wedding he'd taken her to, that slammed her before she'd finished half of it. He'd secretly replaced the remaining half with a nonalcoholic margarita, warning her later how easily he had made a drink swap on her.

"Mine's a virgin. I'm driving," she assured him.

"Thank goodness," he said. "Nobody needs a repeat of Kirk's wedding."

Lil got back into character and continued playing her part.

"I have to say, I've gained quite a bit of respect for a man's role in planning a date. It isn't as easy as it looks."

"Again, very nice," Justin commented. "Gives him back a little of his manhood as he sits in the passenger seat," he smiled. "After On Tap?"

"Depends on where the guy lives. In Scenario G, I head back closer to where he parked his car. Things play out better that way. On the last date, we went to Mafiaoza's."

"At least you're eating good. Okay, at Mafiaoza's, you decide he's a dud," Justin instructs her. "Do you finish the date?"

"In scenario G, unfortunately, I have to."

"Why?"

"Because in this scenario, we run out of gas," she laughed, knowing that sounded stupid.

"Interesting," Justin smiled big and chuckled. "But doesn't running out of gas usually get the man what he wants?"

"Not when he didn't plan it. Men like control, and this turn of events is unexpected, so he shifts into 'fix it' mode without even realizing it," Lil said. "Plus, it happens in a public place. It involves pushing the car to the side of the road, waving a bit of traffic around you, horns honking, and walking to the nearest service station. The horn honking alone makes an impatient man snap."

"Lil, if you thought this guy was impatient, why did he get this date to begin with?"

"Well, there might have been some signs, but they could have been flukes. My bartender friend is glad to help with a slight bit of vodka on the pants for 'Absolut Confirmation,' which was the only reason I took him for a drink in the first place, certainly not to liquor him up."

"Didn't she spill a drink on my pants the time we went there?" Justin remembered.

"Guilty, but I was going to your house the next day for the first time so you could help me with my paper. I just needed a read on what kind of man you were. You passed with flying colors by the way. You didn't even order alcohol."

"Come on," Justin teased. "You had a crush on me."

"I don't remember a crush, but if I did, I'm cured," she smiled. "Get back to the scene," she quickly changed the subject.

Was he kidding, or did he know?

"Okay, the gas, I suppose you've clocked it all, done a little siphoning, and it all measures out?" Justin asked.

"Of course. There's a lot of walking, sweating--he's not happy. I claim to have just enough cash to buy enough fuel to get him back to his car, and he's not offering to top it off. It isn't a night that lands on a mattress or even with a decent goodnight kiss."

"But wait," Justin stopped her. "If the car is fueled to the correct low point for all this to happen, then you decide you *are* still interested, what then? You don't have any gas, and the rest of your night is about to be blown getting some."

"I have backup gas, a three-gallon jug of fuel in the trunk that I would tell him I forgot to leave by the lawnmower in the garage after I got it that day," Lil explained. "But I've never used the jug of gas," she admitted to Justin.

"Is that why you were almost out of gasoline tonight?"

She nodded that last night's date was third-date scenario G.

"Sorry," Lil said. "I forgot to fill up this morning. I actually still have the gas jug in the trunk," she remembered. "I hate plan G."

"Get that jug out of your trunk!" Justin said, though he was laughing at her previous night's date. "That's dangerous, Lil. Remind me, and I'll get it out for you before I leave. How many times have you run out of gas?"

"No number questions," she reminded him, glancing at the clock. "Oh, my gosh," Lil said looking at the late hour. "I've got an interview early in the morning, and don't you have a morning class on Thursdays?"

"How do you remember my schedule? I barely remember it myself," Justin said, reaching over to turn off the gas fire, then shutting the flue.

"I don't know. I'm a good listener?" she said, walking to the kitchen and picking up a container and coming back. "You don't want bags under your eyes. Your groupies wouldn't recognize you," she said, handing him his shoes.

"I'm on sabbatical, remember?" he said, smiling.

"You're a big talker! Funny break. You came over here and kissed on me all night!"

She picked his phone up off the sofa, and noticed he had a text from Ava. Lil reminded herself the kissing had been just a game.

"You have a message," she said handing him the phone. "And here, take the rest of the roast. It'll make a good lunch," she said, handing him the to-go container.

"You sure? Your wife made it after all."

"The gas cost more than the meal, so it's yours."

She followed him to the door.

"Let's have dinner tomorrow night," Justin said. "You can take me through one Date Three scenario at each of our next twenty-five meals."

"As fun as that sounds," Lil said, sarcastically, "I have a performance tomorrow night. Early Friday before show time?" she suggested.

"I fly out for Mitchell's wedding after work Friday, and the wedding is Saturday. My flight gets back around 3 on Sunday. So Sunday?" he asked.

"Sunday," she smiled. Her performance time was 1 to 4.

He opened the door to the garage then surprisingly turned back around. He reached around her and pulled her in close, his face centimeters from hers.

"So what happens at the end of date four should some lucky bastard clear the first three obstacle courses?"

"Wouldn't you like to know," she said playfully, shoving him out the door.

"Thanks for the 'good kissing,' " he smiled back at her from inside her garage.

He waited for the door to close to make sure he could hear her lock herself in for the night. From the other side of the door where Lil placed her cheek against the cool wood to calm herself from the wine and all the excitement of the night, she heard him shut her trunk, and she knew he was removing the gas jug for her. Ten seconds later she heard him shout.

"You don't even have a lawnmower!"

The two of them laughed where they stood. She heard the garage door closing as he left using her code on the combination.

"Those lucky Latinas," she whispered to herself.

She turned to get ready for bed. She touched her fingertips to her lips, closed her eyes, and remembered Justin's lips there. She opened her eyes, sighed, and started her mantra on the way to get ready for bed.

"We're just friends; we're just friends; we're just friends."

5

Saturday Night

il was brilliant in Saturday night's show. She didn't even care that Broadway scouts were in the crowd watching Gene Hope. Her number of performances as leading lady, especially in such a well-received Birmingham show, was running out, and she savored every one she had left. Gene, the "Manley" opposite her "Angelica," told her backstage that he couldn't get his focus because he was so conscious of the New Yorkers in the crowd. Not Lil. She knew she may never have this kind of spotlight again, plus she was on a Justin high. She pushed Gene's hands off of her waist and told him he was doing just fine. When they took their last bows, and the curtain closed, a crew member handed her a note explaining that the leading lineup was invited to Highlands Bar and Grill to dine with the two New Yorkers, a casting director and a producer. Gene must have piqued their interest.

The limo ride to Five Points South was her first. She could get used to being chauffeured around and not having to park a car in downtown Birmingham. She whispered to Matt Fowler who played the villain, Rodney.

"Walk me to my car when we get back?"

"Of course," Matt whispered.

They had become good friends during the months of working together. Matt ran interference for Lil whenever Gene was annoyingly handy. Gene, a couple of Birmingham directors, Darla, who played the female villain, and the two New Yorkers chatted on the drive. Wine was poured during the ride, but Lil declined, remembering she'd met her annual quota in front of her fireplace with Justin. The conversation was loud. That stretched-out car was transporting a load of egos. Lil's wasn't one of them. Acting for her was a serious sideline in her life, but a sideline. Not for the others. The two out-of-towners were making a far finer living selling what the others did than all the others combined would ever make.

At the restaurant, the producer ordered bottles of wine for the whole table.

"Four of this one," he said to the waiter.

Lil saw his finger on the wine menu indicating Coche Dury Grand Cru Corton-Charlemagne, 2004. Her eyes followed the dots from the left of the page to the right to where the hefty price was printed.

" . . . . $775 / bottle."

She accepted a glass just to have a sip, knowing she'd never have a chance to taste something that expensive again, but she got sidetracked with the conversation and forgot in her distraction to take that taste. The producer slid his empty wine glass aside and slammed Rye Hounds all night.

Highlands rolled out the red as they were famous for doing. Lil suspected this producer had placed a call earlier, and he wasn't concerned about the total he would be swiping his card for at the end of the night. Lil deduced that Gene could relax, and she transferred that thought to him at the other end of the table with a smile and a nod. With all this pomp, Gene was in like Flynn, which was a good analogy with all the zigging and zagging she had to do to keep Gene off her behind the scenes, but she was still happy for him. She enjoyed being along for the ride. She took detailed mental notes at Highlands so she would remember everything for Justin at dinner the next night.

Only One Once was a wardrobe director's dream. Set in the mid-eighteen hundreds, the play was dazzling with ball gowns and capes, headpieces and feathers. Everything was elaborate. Lil's "Angelica" wore gowns that weighed on average fifteen pounds apiece. Even the undergarments were detailed since many of them would be seen. It took fifteen minutes to strap Lil into the intricately crafted bustier under the rip-away gown for the rape scene.

"You know what they say about the boning supports in these corsets," Dottie, in wardrobe said on opening night as she struggled to strap Lil into the bustier. "These babies are going to be pushed up so high that the last man on the last row will have a little bone himself."

Lil couldn't respond to that remark. The bustier left no breath in her lungs to allow her.

"Angelica" is trapped in the age in which she has been born, an age during which women have no means of their own. They are only as good as the dowry they bring with them or the looks they had crowned their way into the world possessing. Angelica has no dowry, and she has to use her beauty to find a husband, a proper one. To get a man, she is expected to dazzle him with her domestic and artistic talents and to flaunt what she has with class without losing it in the process. She has to keep all the scoundrels off of her without offending them while also wooing her hero, keeping him at a full arm's length as well, until the bait that is her purity is bought and paid for with marriage.

Lil didn't understand, considering the present day turn of events, two hundred years after Elizabeth Bennet snagged Fitzwilliam Darcy, now that women can put food on their own tables, why their purity had become less valuable instead of more valuable.[5] Anyway, Angelica has no income, no hope of any, and has to hold onto her virginity to hook a husband. Then her husband can sneak off and do whatever he pleases, but she would have food on her table. The premise wasn't new, but the approach to it was.

The play dealt with the subject of Angelica's purity with humor. The laughter came from the raunchiest of scenes, which embarrassed only the most senior couples in the audience. They would deflect their eyes by pretending their walkers needed an adjustment or their eyeglasses needed cleaning. The music was brilliantly composed, and the lyrics were funnier than the spoken lines. The choreography, the most risqué material in the entire play, brought laughing tears to the eyes of many in the audience.

One number put a smile on Lil's face at every performance. It involved a lineup of male dancers, an All-Ass Review of sorts. Four dastardly dashards stand with their backs to the crowd, facing a lineup of Angelica's friends--Pamela, Camille, Tammie, and Samantha--lifelong friends since grammar school. The lyrics and choreography start with the girls playing teasing, coquettish games to keep the rogues at bay, but with each measure, the young women weaken to the men's ploys. The number moves across the stage in different directions as the couples split off into pairs, and the men's efforts increase.

At this point, Pamela distracts her partner with an intentionally protracted bent-over position, using the time to count the money in his wallet that has accidentally fallen from his pocket to the floor. She's pleased with the sum. Camille removes her suitor's coat to discover his recently deceased father's last will and testament. The wording, "my only son and heir," puts a smile on her face. Tammie is easily won over, as her impatient paramour clasps an enormous jewel around her neck, another around her wrist, and one on each ear. Finally, Samantha appears stunned as she looks questioningly into her companion's eyes. He shakes his head "no" in answer to her expression, opening his coat jacket to show her that his pistol is holstered around his shoulder.

At last, the line forms again, the men's backs to the crowd as before, each man facing one of the damsels. From left to right, one at a time, Angelica's friends succumb to the knaves. One by one, like dominoes, Pamela, Camille, Tammie, and Samantha fall back. A mattress magically rises at a diagonal from the stage floor to break Pamela's fall. A chaise lounge snaps up to pad Camille's surrender. Part of a hay-filled wagon appears to cushion Tammie's moment of weakness. And a block of grass floats forward to dirty impetuous Samantha's demise. Then in unison, as the symphony hits its final note using every percussion instrument in its arsenal, the men drop their pants around their ankles. The crowd goes into hysterics at the sight of the plastic, skin-colored asses strapped over the men's butts, and the curtain falls. The accompanying song through all of this, of course, "Wham, Bam, Thank You, Pam, Cam, Tam, and Sam."

The actors portraying Angelica's parents, a "do as I say, not as I do" couple, persuade Angelica to remain wholesome for their chosen Manley. But they, too, are caught in comically inappropriate situations themselves, and not always with each other, in scenes when Angelica is backstage or distracted. But the crowd loves Angelica, as her efforts to remain pure are far more clever than the rascals' attempts to subdue her. Though the spectators want to see a sex scene as much as Talladega fans secretly hope for a crash, they find themselves pulling for Angelica.

"OMG, Lil," Hinton said at Hot's after opening night, "even the characters you're playing now need to L the V."

"But the clothes are fabulous!" Mac added. "Do you ever get to borrow any of them?"

"Where in the world would I wear a gown from the 1800s, Mac?" Lil asked.

"Well, I'm not thinkin' so much the gowns as I am that bustier," Mac said, "and I'm not thinkin' so much 'you' as I am 'me,' say Wednesday night, and I'll have it back to you Thursday morning?"

June reached for the receipt clipboard to fan herself, then reconsidered.

"Oh, heck," she said, dunking a napkin into her ice water and dabbing it around her neck.

"Okay, everybody give me a cool-down lap," Sims demanded.

At Highlands, the food was superb, and at Lil's end of the table, the conversation was fascinating. She had the full attention of Phillip Guwen, one of the New York show's producers. The others at the opposite end of the table where Gene sat with great optimism were all focused on the casting director's tales of casting snafus of different Broadway productions.

The restaurant was just loud enough that when Mr. Guwen turned to face Lil, squaring his shoulders and turning them and the back of his head to the others, their conversation became private.

"You know our Angelica is being played by B. Merry," Mr. Guwen said, referring to the one-hit, "ManSandwich" sensation currently starring in the Broadway production of *Only One Once*.

"Yes, I did," Lil said. "I imagine your ticket sales went through the roof."

"Um," he nodded through swallowing a sip of his drink. "Yes, right where I'd like to shove her."

Lil couldn't believe he had said it.

"It would be one thing if the girl could act--or even sing, for that matter--but those of us around her should all receive Tonys for the roles we're playing each night, telling her what a great job she did."

"Mr. Guwen," Lil tried to save him from himself, "I'm sure you're kidding."

"Brava, Miss Swann," he said. "Please, call me Phillip. Surely you've seen it for yourself, and you know I'm dead serious."

"No, I haven't made it to your production. Of course, I would love to have been there. I saw it last year in Atlanta, but not in New York, and not with B. Merry."

"We aren't here for Mr. Hope," Mr. Guwen said about Gene, apparently cutting to some sort of chase.

"What?" Lil said, looking at Gene with concern as Gene listened intently to the diatribe with the director at his end of the table.

It occurred to Lil how ironic Gene's last name was at the moment.

"We're here for you, Miss Swann," Mr. Guwen continued.

Lil looked back at Mr. Guwen, even more confused.

"Your reviews are excellent, and your performance is better than the reviews say. You seem to understand Angelica in a way other actresses don't. Anyway, it isn't the offer you might be expecting--don't get too excited. It is merely the understudy to the understudy."

"But why--" she started.

"Let me make this quick," Mr. Guwen hurried. "Merry is breaking her contract with four weeks left on it. In three weeks, that bitch is catching a plane for some kind of concert tour her crowd threw together knowing she was under contract with us. Lawyers are involved," he waved his hands to throw away that part of the conversation quickly. "Her first understudy is ready, though I might add not as good as you, but she has a solid contract, and her agent is all up in our faces about it. This production has been drowning since it opened. One understudy has already walked because of that diva, and another one is threatening to do the same. We need you. You're ready. You can do this. Unfortunately, you might not get to, but we need you backstage for any other shit that might hit this show. I have contracts ready to sign for my next production, and I cannot let this show close early before I get them signed. There's too much money on the table for that one to let this one mess up things. We've passed our financial goals, but we have to stretch this run, at least for the Christmas and New Year crowds."

"But---"

"It's just four weeks," he ignored Lil. "The pay is good. I know, we are doing you the favor of a lifetime, but with so little notice, you'd be doing us one as well. The timing works out for you to finish your show's run here. Miss Swann, we realize you don't even have time to find a place to stay. Let me offer you a room. I have a four-bedroom place. It's huge. We won't even hear each other walking around. I'm at work 24-7 anyway. Take your pay and bring it back home. I've done it that way more times than you can guess. You won't get another chance to put something like this on your résumé. Just take the job."

101

Broadway, Lil thought. She started running the decision factors through her head. She would be fine at work. She had prewritten columns for days. She could even work from New York. What was there even to deliberate in her mind? What at all? Why wasn't she shouting, "Yes!"?

She knew the answer to that question. She thought something might be happening between her and Justin. She wanted their "game," for lack of a better word, to progress and see first. Leaving might change that, might give them time to reconsider jeopardizing their friendship. Justin would certainly have some gorgeous version of Pía tempting him away from his dating break while she was gone, but if four weeks was all that took, then maybe that would be a good reason to go, she balanced the thought. Who was she kidding? She and Justin were just friends. She didn't even know what the other night was. We're just friends; we're just friends; we're just friends.

"My card," Mr. Guwen palmed his card on Lil's thigh under the table, letting his hand linger there.

Lil took the card and held it. She looked at Gene with sincere sadness. The place went silent in her head as she looked at Gene and thought about the decision she would have to make. She didn't even notice how Mr. Guwen reacted when he bumped the waiter's arm as he was bringing Mr. Guwen another Rye Hound, causing the waiter to spill a drop of it on Guwen's pants.

Justin arrived at Mitchell's wedding in time for the reception. He missed the wedding due to plane delays that started the night before, but the weather eased up early Saturday morning, giving him a second window. The bad weather wasn't gone completely, but he got to the conference center just in time to see the bandleader introducing, "for the first time, Mr. and Mrs. Mitchell Hughs!"

Justin wasn't able to accept Mitchell's offer of groomsman when he had called ten months earlier because at the time, Justin was planning to be out of the country. He had delayed his travel plans just because. Well, because something was happening with his feelings for Lil. Whatever that something was, Justin wanted to figure it out without time and distance robbing him of the chance.

He walked in and scanned the room while the bride and groom walked onto the dance floor for their first dance. Two hands covered his eyes from behind him. Justin felt the ring-covered fingers and guessed.

"Lauren?"

"Darn right!" Lauren answered and hurried in front of Justin for a hug.

"Where's Lil?" Lauren looked around the ballroom for Lil.

"She's not here," Justin said.

Lauren's expression turned to mother hen.

"Justin, what have you done?" she scolded. "I knew it!" she said, popping his upper arm, hard. "You let her get away! I knew you were going to do that!" she popped him again even harder.

This time he rubbed it.

"You and your, 'My life is too complicated to add a woman to it,' " Lauren mocked him. "That girl was worth adding!"

Others were making their way to Justin with smiles on their faces, so glad to see him.

"Justíno!" Deano said. "Looking good, bro," Deano grabbed Justin and hugged him.

"Grab your girl, and get out here and shake a leg!"

Deano had clearly gotten into the champagne early.

"He didn't bring her!" Lauren told Deano with her fists on her hips.

"Of course he brought her," Deano said. "It's Lil. Who else would Justin bring?"

"She just couldn't make it," Justin said.

"Lee Ann!" Lauren said. "Get over here and talk some sense into Justin! He and Lil broke up."

They didn't believe him.

"And I tell people you're the smartest person I know?!" Lee Ann stormed over. "I'm going to have to call every one of them and correct that."

The conversations continued like this for the first twenty minutes of Justin's reunion with his friends. Lil was as big a hit with his North Carolina crowd as he was. Two hours into the night, his college buddy Cooper from Atlanta came over and sat by him, sipping champagne and watching the others dancing.

"Man, I'm really sorry about you and Lil," Cooper started. "Y'all seemed kind of perfect."

Justin just chuckled to himself about this sitcom he appeared to be starring in at the moment. He never thought he'd be that guy in that wedding scene. A minute passed.

"Lil's last name is Swann with two n's, right?" Cooper asked him.

Justin nodded at Cooper, studying him.

Another silent moment passed.

"I guess she's on Facebook, huh?" Cooper asked.

"Coop, what are you doing?" Justin asked, facing him.

"Too soon?" Cooper asked.

"We're not broken up, Coop!" Justin complained. "She just couldn't make it!"

Justin heard his own words. They weren't broken up, but not broken up from what, Justin wondered.

"It's not looking good," Justin said to Lil over the phone from the airport Sunday morning.

Justin had gone to the airport early because the rain had started to ice the roads. He thought he might get an earlier flight out, but he wasn't the only one with that plan. The airport was packed.

"Just be safe," Lil said. "We can have dinner another night this week. What about your flight? Has it been cancelled?" she asked.

"It's delayed already. I don't see it happening," Justin said.

Lil went to the market at five, straight from the play. Shopping took two stops, one at Bruno's, the other at Organic Harvest. Frantic shoppers were systematically wiping the grocery store shelves clean. A teasing drizzle barely broke the drought, and John-John Sandler had said the word "ice" during his weather report, so the bread, milk, and meat were flying out of the stores as if they were non-perishables. When she hadn't heard from Justin, Lil knew his flight was cancelled. She'd be

105

eating in tonight, and she felt like spaghetti. She started cooking at 5:45.

She chopped four garlic cloves, a green and a red pepper, two tomatoes, a carton of mushrooms, and a Spanish onion. The second sheet of notebook paper containing her fresh list of Do/Don't reasons to go or not to go to New York was in her bag along with the freshly, imprinted stack of notebook paper underneath it. The Dos had won. Only one "Don't" again, "Justin isn't in New York."

Of course she should go to New York. This offer was the definition of a no-brainer even if it was just the possibility, twice removed, of being on a Broadway stage. She added the vegetables to the browned and seasoned ground turkey, poured in a jar of Prego, and sprinkled the top with chopped black olives. Justin would be here when she got back, and he would be the first to tell her "go" if she told him about the opportunity. He practically lived on a plane. He was Mr. Adventure. And it was just four weeks! She sliced a loaf of bread in half, and put the other half away. It was Broadway, for Pete's sake. Who cared if it was only a backstage experience? Four weeks was a lifetime at this minute, but she knew she should do it. She knew she would do it. This chance would never come her way again. Yes. Decision made. She was going. This time she would listen to the list.

She turned to the half loaf of bakery bread and sliced it in half down the middle. She buttered one side, sprinkled garlic powder on it, and put shredded cheddar on the other half. This was way too much food. She needed to talk to her fellow bloggers and then figure out how many clothes a four-week

106

adventure required, but she had several weeks for all that. She tore and washed some Italian lettuce, then washed, peeled, and chopped a couple of carrots. So much food, but something about a cold, icy evening made her want to cook. Her dad would certainly get her mom on her first plane ever to see her, well, to imagine her backstage, at a Broadway production. She'd have enough of this smorgasbord left for four more meals, and that was fine. She could freeze half of it. She boiled the water to cook the angel hair pasta. Someone tapped on the front door. She opened it to find Justin.

Yes, decision made, she thought, looking at his beautiful face. Forget the list. I'm not going. Backstage is just a dusty corridor in an old theatre, and Broadway is just a word on a street sign.

"How in the world?!" Lil exclaimed.

"Rental car," he added, stepping in and kissing her smack dab on the lips. "I'm the only fool who would drive on these roads and the only person this far south who knows how to put chains on tires."

He was holding a brown grocery sack.

"Please tell me you didn't bring groceries," Lil said. "I have a huge mess of spaghetti cooking."

"I smell it," Justin said. "You've outdone your wife. No," he said, walking in, gesturing to the sack. "I come bearing gifts."

"And, here, I didn't get you anything," Lil drawled, jokingly.

"I didn't get you anything either," Justin said. "These are from your dear friends in North Carolina," he explained.

107

"What?" she asked, following him to the den where he set the sack down and reached in it.

He pulled out a jar and handed it to her.

"Paula's Aunt Foy sent this jelly to you. She said to tell you, she thought she'd told you wrong on the phone that day about how long to cook it," he said, then looked at her. "Y'all talk on the phone?" Justin asked Lil.

"Sure," Lil answered. "I met her at Lee Ann's mother's funeral when we went."

"She wanted you to know how it's supposed to taste so that when you make it, you'll know you got it right. She's going to email you the recipe this time, and apparently, she already has your email address."

"Ooo, good," Lil said, opening the jar and smelling the jelly.

Justin reached back in the bag.

"This is that book Star told you about. She said just skip chapters 8 and 9--waste of your time," he said, handing her the book.

"These are starting to smell," he commented about the canna lily bulbs wrapped in damp paper towels. "Parker said you better get them in the ground before the first freeze, but I think you missed that."

"Maybe not," Lil said, hopeful the plant would survive if she got it in the ground soon. "I'm not sure what a Canna Lily looks like versus a Calla Lily, but I'll find out in a few months."

People were always giving Lil varieties of lilies. The Calla Lily was Lil's favorite flower. She loved everything about it— from the things in literature it had been likened to, to things it symbolized. Even the name itself held a certain beauty. In high school, when Sims was deciding on a name for Tanner, Lil thought about the names she would choose one day. She considered naming her daughters after flowers like her mother had, and she thought Calla would be a beautiful name. Then in Spanish class, she learned that the different verb forms of the word meant "to silence," and that was not a name she'd want to give a daughter. Lil couldn't imagine that anyone without a voice could make much difference in this world, and she discarded the name Calla as an option.

"And this is some foot thing that Holly said will make your heels feel like silk," Justin said, pulling another item from the sack.

Lil took that one from him quickly and threw it back in the sack, a bit of pink showing in her cheeks.

"Oh," Justin remembered, reaching into his pocket. He handed her one business card then another. "Coop and Kilgro," he added. "They want to know, now that we're no longer an item, if you'd go out with them. Not at the same time," he clarified.

Lil's heart fell.

"Oh, I see you went with the 'broken up' scenario," she said, forcing a smile, walking to the kitchen in case the disappointment showed on her face. Going to New York after all, she reevaluated.

"No, actually, no matter how hard I insisted that you just couldn't make it, they continued to believe I had blown it with you. They're crazy about you Lil," he added.

Stirring the meat sauce with her back to him, she closed her eyes and exhaled.

Yep, definitely staying here, she thought.

Lil snapped the lid on the second container for Justin to take an entire meal home with him for lunch or dinner the next day and put one identical to it in the frig for herself. Justin took her hand and started walking her into the den.

"Come here and sit down with me so we can talk," he said.

He led her to the sofa and sat next to her. He looked at her intently.

"Lil, about the other night," he said.

The statement took her breath. She hoped he didn't notice. She didn't interrupt or try to finish his thought for him because she wanted to hear exactly what he was about to say. It could go so many ways. There could be a "We need to be careful that that doesn't ever happen again. Our friendship means so much more to me than that." Or "Lil, I'm on this dating break, and I took advantage of your friendship to make up for some seriously missed kissing time." Or even, "I met the most beautiful Argentinean girl in Mitchell's band." It could all end right here. Lil just waited.

"I've been running the entire night through my mind over and over," Justin said. "Date four," he continued, "when was the last time you let a man take you out on a fourth date?"

Lil thought for what seemed like a solid minute, the room silent the entire time, then she blinked, and a tear fell from each of her eyes.

"Oh, my goodness! I'm so sorry!" she clapped her hand over her mouth.

The two tears took her completely by surprise.

"I wasn't expecting those tears!" she explained, trying to laugh them off. "Really, I wasn't, Justin!" she said, truly embarrassed, wiping them away. "I have no idea where they came from!"

Justin's posture stiffened, and he moved closer to her. He wasn't expecting that either. Something about this worried him.

"What is it?" he asked. "No games now, Lil," he said seriously.

She sighed and thought about what to tell him. She sat for the quiet eternity of another sixty seconds, but he waited.

"I was a junior in high school," she started, "and Blaze Hardaway was a senior, two years older," she said.

Justin instantly prepared himself for the worst.

"He was the guy," she said with a theatrical smile, "the one all the girls hoped would call. No, not even that," she corrected. "He was the one we all knew would never call. But he called me," her tone getting serious. "I couldn't believe it. My mother was excited with me. She couldn't wait to tell her friends. Dad thought Blaze was bad news. The arguments at home started. My brother had graduated from college and was in the military and was too much older to know anything about Blaze to be helpful. Daddy said he couldn't even say why he didn't like Blaze. He just said, 'Something about him,' and left that thought hanging in the air. My mom said they had taught me well, and she convinced my dad that it was time they trusted me to make the right decisions. Daddy eventually agreed as long as we doubled with another couple, so that's what we did."

Justin noticed something about Lil jerked once as she spoke.

111

"It was fun. He walked me to the door, and he asked me out for the next weekend. The next date was nothing special, just a double date to the movies and home. Kissing at the door. On our third date, we went to a high school dance. A little more kissing in the truck outside of my house and that was it. On the fourth date, we pulled off with another couple as usual, but after a block or two, he turned into a parking lot, and the two friends in the backseat got out and got in the other guy's pickup truck. Blaze shouted, 'Back here at 10:45 and don't be late!' as the guy in the other truck pulled off with his date. Blaze drove straight to the lake. I'd never been there, not even on a sunny day with friends," she jerked.

Justin moved closer to her and rubbed her arms.

"He parked the SUV we were in and went to the back and opened the hatch and told me to come on. The seats in the back could turn around backwards. 'See,' he said, 'we can sit here and look at the lake.' I thought it was romantic. He started kissing me. Then he laid the seat back. He kept kissing and moved on top of me. I couldn't breathe. He was rough. He was pulling at my blouse. I was pushing him off, fighting to get out from under him. I finally did. My feet hit the ground. I didn't know where I was, and I hadn't seen a soul on the drive in, but it was all I could do--run. I took a few strides, and his arm wrapped around my stomach, lifted me in the air, and slammed me on my back in the truck. And he was back on top again. He was unbuckling his belt and pulling my skirt up," Lil said looking at her hands and closing her eyes while she talked.

"That's when he heard it," she said. "Just like on TV. The sound of a rifle being cocked. I never even knew my daddy owned a rifle, but he was standing over Blaze."

Justin grabbed Lil and held her tight to him. She wasn't crying. She wasn't shivering. She literally had the jerks, hard, uncontrollable jerks, and he held her until she was warm and her body calmed. She let him hold her, and she let two more tears run silently down her face.

Justin leaned back to look at her. She wiped her tears and shook her head at her silliness.

"I don't know why I'm acting this way," she forced a laugh. "It's not like he raped me," she laughed again, still wiping her face and continuing to ramble from embarrassment. "What kind of daddy follows his daughter off on a date, carrying a rifle?" she smiled, her tone rhetorical.

"A really good one," Justin said seriously.

Lil never told anyone that story when it happened. A few years later, she told June. June didn't know who Blaze was like the other girls, and June had kept her promise never to repeat it. Lil's mother somehow had persuaded her father to let it go, convincing him that doing anything about it would make things worse for Lil and horrible for him, a grown man pulling a rifle on a teenaged boy, the son of a prominent executive with the money and connections to spin things his way. No one would believe them. It wouldn't matter that the gun wasn't loaded. Lil had gotten the jerks only three times in her life: the night that happened, the night she told June about it, and tonight. Justin held her again. This time the embrace was for him. When he pulled back to look at Lil's face, he ran his thumbs

113

across her glistening cheeks, and she smiled an "I'm okay" smile, rolling her eyes at herself for crying.

"He wasn't the last fourth date I ever had," she said to Justin. "I'm sure I've had others. I didn't always count, you know," she said. "And my daddy taught me how to shoot a gun after that." Her dad had been an excellent teacher, too, as Justin had discovered on their paintball outing.

"Do you know how bad I want to kiss you right now, Lil?" Justin asked her. "But I want to do it right this time. I want to take you out, an official date. Lil, will you let me take you out?" he asked.

"Yes!" she laughed and four more tears fell.

6

The First Date

"I know all your dating secrets," Justin teased Lil on their first date.

He took her to Rojo, a restaurant downtown, nothing fancy, just casual. Lil had never been there. Most of their nights out together were spent in or around Hoover, near Lil's home where they were regulars at Ragtime Café. At Rojo, they sat near the hanging heater on the porch that was enclosed during the winter months. Everyone who worked there knew Justin. That never surprised Lil. People knew Justin everywhere they went.

"Lil, mucho gusto, good to finally meet you," a couple of men working at the grill said when she and Justin were inside placing their order.

Had Justin talked about her here to them, she wondered. Oh, yeah, his good friend, Lil, she thought.

"Justín, gracias por su recomendación para mi hermana. Ella consiguió el trabajo," another of the men said.

"De nada. Your sister has studied and worked hard. She was my best student. She was the right person for the job. Tell her I said congratulations."

Lil ordered Kate's Salad, and said it was good enough to blog about. She looked over the "This Week at Rojo" schedule she found on the table and read about the different events to come, many of them charitable ones. She excused herself when she finished eating and went to the ladies' room to brush her teeth before they left.

"Do you mind if I run a quick errand?" Justin asked as he opened the car door for Lil.

"Of course I don't."

They drove toward Railroad Station, pulling up in front of a six-story building on the block of 16th Street South and 2nd Avenue South, just across the street from the new minor league baseball stadium. Justin parallel parked and escorted Lil to a building in the center of the block that jutted upward like a lighthouse in the middle of the other dark, old two-story buildings around it. He carried a couple of brown cardboard boxes he had retrieved from his trunk, and they walked to the door. He pressed the speaker button on the outside of the building.

"Patrícia, soy yo, Justin," he said into the speaker.

A buzzer sounded, then the door lock clicked open.

"What is this?" Lil asked, not having seen any signage that indicated the business they were entering.

116

"It's sort of a mission tucked away in the center of the city," he explained. "My parents bought the building years ago with the intention of renovating it and creating a surgical site for people with nowhere else to turn. Who knew the area would grow and end up a destination site?" he said, pointing to the Barons' new baseball field before they walked inside. "With the help of many others and the life insurance policy my parents left, their dream is finally coming true."

They went up to the fifth floor. Patrícia met them there, and Justin introduced them. Patrícia was wearing scrubs. Her purse was on her shoulder, and her car keys were in her hand.

"Miss Betty just got here, so I'm headed home," Patrícia said.

"Please tell me those are the bears," Miss Betty said loudly, as she walked up and lifted the top box from Justin's hands. "I promised our new arrival he could cuddle up with one of these tonight, and I hate breaking promises to cute little boys, even little boys claiming they are too old for Teddy bears."

"Yes, ma'am, Miss Betty," Justin said, placing the other box on the nurses' walnut desk. "They're here?" he asked.

Patrícia nodded and pointed behind Justin. Justin turned to see a young mother, pushing her son down the hall in a wheelchair.

"Justin!" the boy smiled, seeing Justin.

Miss Betty had already opened the box and was holding out a bear for Justin. He took it and walked up the hall to where the boy waited.

"Goodnight, Miss Betty," Patrícia said.

" 'night, Sweetie," Miss Betty answered. "See you

tomorrow."

"Good night, Lil. So good to meet you," Patrícia said.

"You, too. Good night."

While Miss Betty tucked the boxes away, Lil glanced in the open doors along the hallway. The two rooms she could manage to see inside from where she stood looked like bedrooms, simply accommodated. The beds and chests of drawers were made of warm wood. One room even had a brick fireplace, and she noticed it also had a Christmas stocking hanging from the mantel. She felt like she was in an old, nostalgic hotel.

"Lil," Miss Betty said, and Lil turned her attention to her. "I read your article about the prepaid college tuition funds. I called my legislators like you suggested."

"Really?" Lil said, always surprised when someone mentioned they'd read her blog.

She didn't think she'd ever get used to that. Sometimes she felt like she was merely making a diary entry that only she and perhaps her parents were reading.

"Thank you, Miss Betty."

"No need to thank me. I purchased one of those contracts when my Keisha was a baby. I paid every month for years. She got her undergraduate degree with that PACT plan. My girl's working hard to be a cardiologist, and she'll make a fine one, too," Miss Betty said, proudly. "If that plan hadn't paid all of her undergraduate tuition, she wouldn't be making it, and this state would be short one good heart doctor. She's got a long road ahead of her, but that contract being honored was the first necessary part of this journey. Some of those families have three and four children depending on those contracts. Keisha and I owed it to those kids to call on their behalf. Shame if this state doesn't fully fund tuition for those children."

Lil nodded, and the women turned their attention back to Justin and Zach.

"Justin, we went upstairs to see the VIP box. It's like really sitting in the Barons' stadium," Zach said.

"There's a speaker in that room, too," Justin said. "We are connected directly to the stadium announcer's microphone. It was their gift to us. It'll be just like being at the ball park," Justin smiled.

"Too bad it isn't baseball season," Zach said.

"Well, what about this spring, when you're all better, and if your mother says it's okay, I take you up to the VIP room to watch the Barons practice?"

Zach looked up at his mother who smiled and nodded.

"What about we go across the street to watch them in person?" Zach asked.

"Well, that'll be up to your doctors."

"Okay! Don't forget!" Zach smiled at Justin.

"I won't. I promise," Justin smiled.

Justin hugged Zach and stood and gave Zach's mom his number.

"Uh, uh, uh, that man's gonna make a fine father one day," Miss Betty said.

Justin walked back to where Lil stood and took her hand.

"Let's make sure Patrícia gets to her car safely," Justin said to Lil. "I'll be back later," he said to Miss Betty. "Call me for any reason at any hour."

"Oh, I will. Don't you worry about that," Miss Betty said. "Now, y'all get on outta here and finish your date," she smiled.

The night was perfect. Lil's heart moved differently at moments, like when Justin reached across the restaurant table for her hand, twined her fingers in his, kissed them, and looked into her eyes. Her heart, right in there, in the middle of her chest, ached, but it felt good. Dolor. Ache in Spanish. Lil had always thought that word was one of the most beautiful in the Spanish language. Until this moment, she thought the soothing sound of it had been wasted on the word pain. Not anymore. Now she knew some aches were good. This dolor she had in her chest was not a figurative feeling like she'd thought it was when she'd read it in a book. This was a literal ache as though some ounce of strength had escaped from her chest, given away, and the loss of it made her want to press the palm of her hand against her breast to calm it.

When they got to her house, Justin walked her to the door in the garage.

"What you have to remember," he said to her, smiling, "is that the other night, the kissing was done the way you directed, but this is *my* first date with you, and this is the way I want to kiss you," he said.

He put his hands on each side of her face, the base of his palms along her jaw, his fingers pushed into her hair. He moistened his lips. He kissed her once. He tilted his head to the other side of her nose and pressed his warm lips on hers again, opening his mouth just enough that his opened hers. His tongue was warm, and the kissing didn't stop. Until Lil became breathless. Really breathless. If he hadn't stopped kissing her, she thought she would have done something similar to fainting. She was embarrassed. Justin felt it happening, and he quickly put one of his arms around her back, and leaned her against the door for support, pressing himself against her to keep their balance, his face close to hers. He watched her as she kept her eyes closed, then opened them momentarily as she tried to slow her breathing.

"Sorry," she said breathlessly, smiling, pink in her cheeks.

"Sorry?" he said. "It doesn't get any better than that."

Lil continued to breathe. She turned the knob behind her back, opened the door and went inside. She turned back to face Justin and smiled.

"Good night," she said quietly and closed the door.

"How does she do that?!" he said to himself, standing there wanting more.

Inside, Lil still felt lightheaded. She had come in when she did because she really thought she was going to faint, and she didn't want the long-running joke between them to be that he'd kissed her so well she fainted. She knew Justin would tease her for the next hundred years. She supported herself holding onto the wall and made it to the sofa where she fell face down and let the coolness of the leather do its work. She fell asleep for just a few minutes. At least she told herself it was sleep. When she woke, she smiled, and she touched that place on her heart and remembered the sweet dolor. She thought she would put music to that kiss in her script, the song that was stuck in her head from the ride home, Bryan Adams singing "Please Forgive Me."

The next day was Wednesday. For the first time, she'd be the one texting that she couldn't make it to coffee. It was the only way to keep all that had happened between her and Justin from bursting out of her mouth. She didn't want the girls to know, not if it wasn't going to last.

7

The Second Date

Several nights passed before their second date. They were both busy at work, and Lil had two performances that week. Justin checked her play schedule before he chose a night. She was sitting on her sofa working on her laptop when he called.

"Hey," he started the conversation.

"Hey," she said, her smile audible.

"Thank you for such a beautiful evening the other night, Lil."

"Thank you," she answered.

How sweet, she thought.

"How was your day?" Justin asked.

"Busy. How was yours?"

They talked for thirty minutes. Lil asked him about the people she'd met at the restaurant and at the surgical mission. There was so much about Justin that she didn't know, and she wanted to know everything. Patrícia and Betty were volunteering their nursing skills when they could, in addition to their regular nursing jobs. They and other nurses and doctors gave of their time to provide medical care for patients who had no means, not even the means to get themselves or their loved ones to medical care without assistance. A few months earlier, Justin had told Lil about a foundation, one raising money for equipment and surgical devices. That foundation was staffed with a few of these same medical professionals and had helped the mission acquire most of its current equipment. Businesses were also willing to help. A construction company and an engineering firm collaborated and donated their services to reconstruct the roof as a helipad. Lil was amazed at what Justin and these others had accomplished. He didn't want her to blog about it.

By the time she and Justin were getting ready to hang up, Lil realized Justin was calling for a second date.

"I was just wondering," Justin said, "if you don't have any sisters visiting, if you'd let me take you out tomorrow night. I know it's short notice, but I really need to see you again."

"No guests," she smiled. "I'd love to go out."

"I thought we'd dress up, and do something different," he suggested.

"Dress up like Batman and Wonder Woman or dress up fancy?" she joked.

"I was hoping you'd wear that black dress with the black lace sleeves that Vs down to the small of your back."

"You remember that dress?" she asked, touched at the details he'd remembered about a dress he'd seen her in only once, and only for five minutes.

He'd come by her house, and she was trying it on. It had to have been a year ago. She had said she just brought it home for fun and would never have anywhere to wear it. He convinced her to keep it.

"*Remember* it?" he said. "I've sworn to myself that the vision of you in that dress will be the last thing I think of on my deathbed just before I close my eyes."

He couldn't see her put the palm of her hand on her chest.

"May I pick you up around 6:30?" he asked.

"Six-thirty," she agreed.

He got there at 6:15. He knocked on the door holding flowers, not real flowers, a picture of flowers he'd cut out and tied with a ribbon. When he saw her in the black dress, he touched his heart. He was wearing black pants and a black sweater, and his hair was pulled back. He looked perfectly suave. He was clean-shaven and smelled kissable.

"I couldn't wait until 6:30," he said.

"What is this?" she asked about the paper flowers.

"Canna Lilies," he answered. "If that early freeze didn't damage your chances for success, these are what those stems you planted will look like in a few months."

"You're too good to be true," she said, smiling. "Come in, and I'll put them in some water."

She went to a drawer, pulled out a piece of baby blue construction paper, cut it in half lengthwise, then cut one side of the remaining half into soft waves. She got out a clear, glass vase, curved the paper around the inside bottom of the vase, and added the paper flowers.

"Genius," he said.

The night was simple. He took her to his church. It was a small but beautiful chapel with a Spanish terra cotta roof that rose into a cross above the arched, wooden doors. The ornate interior touches could have been copied from a grand cathedral. The church was near his house on the downtown side. The sanctuary was dimly lit with a hundred white and cream candles. When he had said "no denomination," Lil assumed he meant no church.

"A friend of mine is performing tonight," Justin said, opening Lil's car door. "I promised I would come."

The two of them walked through the walnut doors and in among the rows of walnut pews with red, crushed velvet cushions. The small crowd of people, mostly Hispanic, wandered from pew to pew speaking to one another. The women were dressed in silk and velvet, chiffon and satin. Lil could tell the evening was one of those rare occasions when these people pulled out vintage dresses and rarely used satin shawls. They embraced each other with warm affection. The women commented on each other's attire, saying where they had last worn their dresses.

"Sí, me pusé este vestido para la boda de mi hija," one woman said about the dress she last wore to her daughter's wedding.

126

"¡Me acuerdo de la bonita que fue esa boda!" the other woman remembered how beautiful that wedding was.

"Mira a mi marido, Rudy, el padre de la novia. Su traje ya es demasiado pequeño," the woman pointed to Rudy, her husband, the father of the bride, saying his suit was already too small for him.

The women chuckled as Rudy sat miserably waiting for the performance to be over so he could get out of the contraption.

Justin introduced Lil to as many people as he could, each person giving her details of how he or she knew "Justín," pronouncing the "J" as an "H" as Spanish does, punching the ending syllable with the Spanish accent.

"Justín," Lil repeated this new name, thinking about the new side of Justin she was discovering.

"Cuando sus padres estaban aquí, llevaron a Justín a nuestra iglesia. Tan guapo e inteligente," the women said, squeezing Justin's cheeks, telling Lil how his parents would bring the smart, handsome boy to their church whenever they were in the country.

The conversations came to a close when a robed man walked to the front and raised his hands, gesturing for the crowd to sit.

"Padre Rivera," Justin whispered to Lil.

"Amigos, thank you for coming tonight," Padre Rivera welcomed them. "I am glad the rain waited for all you ladies in your beautiful clothes though we really need it and will keep praying for it to come. Señor Sandler says it is coming, for us to be patient in our wait," Padre Rivera said about the television meteorologist. "It is good to see so many of you. We want to share a special welcome with Justín's Lily. Thank you for being here with us, Señorita Lily."

Lil wasn't expecting that personal welcome. The people in the front pews turned to smile at them. She could see the women nodding to their neighbors, saying things like, "Que linda," "Hermosa," and "Bonita." It was sweet, quaint, familiar, but at the same time, it was elegant.

Padre Rivera stepped aside and sat in the front pew.

A girl, 10 or 11 years old, stepped from the end of the same pew and stood in the front center of the church holding a violin. A moment of awkwardness followed as her mother insisted, by shooing her hands, that the girl step up to the platform behind her. She did. The girl's father then stood next to her. Watching him raise his violin to his chin, the girl followed, raising her bow to its strings, as did he, but it was not the childlike recital Lil was expecting. It was masterful. They started with "Canon in D Major," and the church pianist accompanied them. Justin placed his arm down the back of the pew around Lil's shoulders. He sneaked moments to glance at Lil as she watched the sweet child performing.

The concert wasn't long, but it was astonishing. Justin waited for the men to pat the young girl's back and the women to kiss her cheek, and then he approached her.

"Justín!" the little girl shouted.

Her tiny voice reminded Lil that this protégé was just a little girl.

"You came!" she squealed.

"Ava, I wouldn't break my promise," Justin smiled at her.

Ava, Lil thought. The mission, this church, these are the reasons why Justin lives in this part of town.

Justin said his goodbyes to Ava and her parents. As Padre Rivera locked the chapel behind Lil and Justin, he shouted to them.

"Justín! Be safe, and tell Papá Noel we all say hello!"

"Santa Claus?" Lil asked Justin about this Papá Noel, not surprised that even Santa knew Justin; everybody knew Justin.

And there it was, that really suave smile and wink.

Justin took Lil to a diner near his house, El Girasol, The Sunflower.

"They marinade the chicken in a salsa so hot, they have to wear gloves so it doesn't burn their hands. They flavor it with Adobo and grill it on a primitive grill outside. It's what brings their customers back," Justin explained about the Mexican diner.

"¡Justín! ¡Qué lindo estás!" the men in the restaurant joked about how "pretty" Justin looked that night. "Es la verdad de tí, Señorita Lily," they added, telling Lil she truly looked beautiful.

The place felt warm to Lil. The food arrived in Pyrex dishes as though it had been cooked at home. A waitress's teenage daughter came over from a table where she was doing her homework and sweetly asked Lil to stand up so she could admire her dress. She called her mother out from the kitchen, and in Spanish they discussed how they could replicate the dress, spinning Lil around as they needed. The mother argued that the V in the back would have to come up higher on her daughter as she was only fifteen. The daughter argued that the low back was what she liked the most about the dress. Another person or two squeezed in the booth to meet Lil and to ask Justin a favor and catch up.

While they waited on dessert, Justin took Lil's hands and twined his fingers in hers and kissed them.

"I don't think I've ever seen you without some scruffy whiskers," she smiled. "I like you both ways. Did you shave for Ava's concert?"

"No," he answered. "I've noticed, when I kiss you, my beard is irritating your soft skin. I don't want to hurt your pretty face, and I'm not going to quit kissing you," he said.

Too good to be true, she thought about him again.

"Ava?" she asked. "Is this Ava the same Ava you brought to my performance and left early?"

"Yes, she wanted to hear the orchestra, but her stomach started hurting, so we left early."

"How do you know Ava?" she asked.

"My parents rescued her when she was an infant. She was my sister for a few months."

"What?!"

"Because of a mix up in some paperwork, the only way for them to take Ava from the country where they rescued her, was to adopt her themselves. I met a member of their team at the airport who brought Ava to this country, and I took care of her until the papers were corrected making José and Marta here Ava's true adoptive parents. Ava doesn't remember any of it. She was just a few months old. But she knows the stories. She likes to pretend we're still brother and sister. I'm her godfather now."

"How do I not know any of this?" Lil asked.

She'd known Justin for two years. She knew what a private person he was, but she never imagined he was keeping details like these to himself. She imagined 20-year-old Justin, attending college and taking care of a baby girl all by himself. She was starting to see him as part of his parents' missions, and not just a boy who was in their way, giving them trouble while they worked.

"What else don't I know?"

"Plenty. A little at a time," he said as if he were afraid too much information at once would send her running. "But Lil, you need to understand that these kinds of things will always be part of my life, not just part of my past."

"Tell me three more things," Lil pleaded for other pieces of Justin's life story.

"Another time."

"Just a couple things more," she insisted.

He thought about her request.

"When I was a boy, I drank only P," he smiled.

"I'm serious, Justin," Lil said, not remembering having told him about Auggie's water cycle report.

"I am, too," he insisted.

"Okay, next thing."

He couldn't seem to come up with anything else he was willing to tell her. He shook his head no.

"Just *one* more thing," Lil didn't let up.

He thought about it for a minute.

"Please," Lil said.

She could tell he was considering it. He massaged his chest near his shoulder while he thought about it. It wasn't lost on Lil that beneath his hand, hidden by his shirt was the large scar. His expression became serious, and his tone changed.

"You know that story, 'Heart of Darkness'?" he asked.

Lil nodded.

"It's real," Justin said.

Lil could tell he was done talking about it for the night. Justin looked different to her. She studied his eyes, trying to see something in them. They seemed deeper, a little darker even. And if at all possible, more beautiful than ever.

"Even if we talked all night," she conceded, "I'll never fully know what kind of life you've had, will I?" she asked sorrowfully.

He shook his head no.

Lil was quiet for the rest of the time they were there as she realized the many differences in their childhoods and upbringings. He tried to bring her back to the moment.

"Soon I'll take you to the best taco place around. It's in the back of a gas station."

She smiled at him.

"I'm serious," he said, reaching for her hand. "Taqueria Tafoya, in a shared building with The Gas Boy," he smiled. "Best taco in Birmingham."

Lil returned the smile, knowing he was trying to change the mood.

Lil still seemed deep in thought on the drive home. Justin held her hand and caressed each finger. A couple of times he lifted her hand to his lips, held it there a few seconds, then kissed it. He thought he might have already told her too much. Only a few people were willing to lead the kind of lives his family had lived. They pulled up to her house. She gave him no excuses to keep him in the car, no date two car kissing requirements, no mention of a visiting sister. Turned out, he was the one with the surprise sister on the second date.

She merely said, "I'll walk myself in. Thank you so much for the beautiful night, Justin."

He wasn't expecting that ending to the date. She opened the door and stepped out of the car. He quickly got out on his side.

"Lil!" he called to her.

She stopped walking, turned, and stood facing him.

"I want to kiss you goodnight!"

She silently waited for him to come to her. He came at her hard, and took her in his arms firmly. He wrapped them completely around her and kissed her. He kissed her as if this kiss might be their last. She didn't know someone could hold her this closely. She kissed him back with longing and warmth and passion. His hands found their way up the soft skin of her back, exposed in the black V'd dress, and up into her hair. This time, he was the one who ran out of breath. When his lips released hers to breathe, she softly pulled away and quickly went inside. He walked back to the car, glancing back at her house. A few raindrops bounced off his windshield, then stopped.

Lil went in and locked the door. She walked over to her desk and retrieved the crumpled, first sheet of paper, her list from the coffee shop. She reread all the things she expected a man to be before she'd sleep with him. Justin met them all. But it never occurred to her until tonight to ask herself what might be on his list if he were to write one. Besides holding on to her virginity for an eternity, what had she ever done to deserve him? She already knew, even before she'd written the list, that he was her one, never expecting to be in his arms, but could she be his?

She took the paper, folded it down the vertical line, creased it, folded it backwards, creasing it again. She laid it on the desk and tore it in half, separating the Dos from the one Don't. She took a pencil to the Do column and wrote above number one, a new number one: "1. It's Justin." She wadded up the one Don't: "I haven't met the right man," and tossed it toward the trashcan because she knew she had met him. She missed the can. She'd pick it up another day. She was going to bed. She wouldn't have to add music to her memory of tonight's kiss. The right song was playing on the stereo in Justin's car when they pulled up to her house. She could still hear it playing as he ran to her and kissed her and held her tight. Bryan Adams again, "Can't Stop This Thing We Started."

8

The Third Date

F ive days passed. Lil and Justin spoke on the phone a few times, but work was hectic for them both. Justin had exam reviews and graduate boards. Lil had more performances than normal as schools were approaching Christmas break, and a special legislative session in Montgomery was making work crazy. On top of all that, she and the girls were planning June's baby shower at Sims' house, and Sims was not throwing a simple party. June had decorated the baby's room in a hippo theme, and Sims had them raking Birmingham and Atlanta for all things hippo.

A couple of times, Justin called to get Lil to squeeze in a coffee or a lunch, even a dinner, but she couldn't get away at a time that would work. After the other night, his mind was getting the better of him about what Lil was feeling. Another couple of days passed, and Justin was reluctant to get another, "I can't--my deadline" response, but he texted her anyway.

"Coffee?"

Thirty minutes later, she answered.

"Craving a smoothie. Berry Smooth instead?"

Justin looked at her reply and wondered if she had stared at the screen for half an hour looking for a reason not to have coffee.

She had. It was Wednesday afternoon, and Lil didn't want to face the girls at Hot's. Sims had a basketball parent meeting, and June was having Braxton-Hicks contractions, so the two of them had bailed already. Lil knew she would spill everything about Justin if she were at Hot's alone with Hinton and Mac, and they would suggest all sorts of antics for Lil to speed things along. They would behave even worse if Justin were to join them. Lil wanted to keep the news that she and Justin were dating, to herself a while longer. She'd have to bail on coffee.

"Meet you there," Justin answered.

As Lil walked across the parking lot to the smoothie shop, two teenage girls followed her, shoving each other toward Lil.

"Excuse me," one girl finally said, and Lil turned around. "Are you Angelica?" the girl asked.

"I am," Lil answered, surprised to be recognized from the play, though the cast had been on a couple of local morning television shows.

"Could we have your autograph?" the girl asked.

"Of course!" Lil said.

It was her first, on-the-street autograph request.

They went inside with her. She signed two napkins for them and recommended the coconut smoothie. The girls thanked her and left. Justin walked in in time to enjoy the moment with her. As the girls left, he kissed Lil on the lips.

"Now look who's got groupies," he said, before they ordered.

They had the place to themselves now that the high school afternoon rush was over, and energetic employees busily prepared for the wave of strollers filled with sweaty toddlers that would soon arrive from the nearby park on this warm day. She and Justin sat on the stools at the window bar, and Justin pointed to the wall where the owners had hung information about their mission of providing water filters to underdeveloped countries. He was quite familiar with the projects. They talked and caught up on each other's week. Justin reached in his pocket and pulled out two tickets to the movies, a Groupon for dinner for two, a gift card for yogurt, and a coupon for a cab ride. He fanned out the coupons on the concrete bar.

"What's this?" Lil asked.

"I'm about to ask you out on date number three, and this," Justin pointed to the gift cards and coupons, "this is my desperate attempt to pick you up and pay for it. I don't want to be the poor bum on your third date," he said looking at her. "Go out with me Friday night, Lil."

Lil laughed. He was clever, but she protested.

"Oh, no! You know that date three is *my* date. Just save your failed-attempt gift cards," she said, pushing them back toward him. "I get to plan, pay, and pick up on date three. I'll let you know when I have all the details worked out."

"Okay, but please let it be Friday," Justin said. "None of this, 'I'll get back to you with the details' stuff. I really need to

137

see you, Lil," he said, then he leaned in for a soft kiss, giving her a sample of what he meant by really needing to see her.

Her mother would have lectured her about "what kind of girl would be swapping slobber in public," but at the moment, Lil didn't care.

"Friday," she answered. "I'll let you know where I'll be picking you up."

Lil had no idea how to plan a third date that would end well for Justin. Every scenario in her catalogue was a dumper. She tried and tried to come up with a date that would wow him in a simplistic way, the way he had wowed her. She'd never been to a drive-in movie, and she'd heard about one in Harpersville and one in Argo, but they were closed until spring. The ice skating rink in Pelham was having a hockey tournament, so ice-skating wasn't an option. Tuscaloosa had built an outdoor rink, but she wanted to stay closer to town. She called the Heart of Dixie train people, but they were booked for a "Polar Express" Christmas party. Nothing. She had nothing. None of those ideas would pan out anyway if the rain they kept predicting came.

Friday rolled around and still nothing. She had checked all the entertainment tabloids, but the suggestions were just typical date stuff. Justin texted her at 3 p.m.

"I'm throwing a hitch in your third date system. The BMW won't crank. Can you pick me up at my house?"

"No problem," Lil texted back.

Picking him up wasn't the problem. What to do after she picked him up was the problem. She was a writer, for Pete's sake! She was creative. Why was she having trouble coming up with one simple idea?

"I'm trying too hard," she thought.

She tried to relax about it, thinking something would come, some stroke of genius, the moment of eureka. The only thing that came was five o'clock. One hour left and still no plan. She was dressing, but she had no idea for what. Six o'clock rolled around, and Lil was backing out of her garage, defeated. She convinced herself the stress of work, the play, the baby shower, and the confusion about her and Justin had exhausted her. She would use the drive over to collect herself. She turned on the radio, and heard an advertisement for winery tours in Calera. That would have been a good idea. She looked up out of the windshield at the heavy gray clouds mixed with lagging streaks of sun-setting red. But not tonight, she thought, as the radio personalities joked with meteorologist Marty Tubbs about what rain dance it would take to get the visible, gray stuff to fall. Tubbs answered in his distinctive voice.

"The water cycle is like a stalled Ferris Wheel right now, and all this moisture is just stuck at the top, looking down at us, wanting to come back down as much as we wish it would."

"Well, not necessarily," the radio host joked. "It depends on what girl you're stuck with, up there at the top of that Ferris Wheel, as to whether you're in any hurry to finish the rotation or not. My first kiss was with Dolly Huntsinger, stuck at the top of the Ferris Wheel at the Birmingham Fair," he said as others in the studio laughed, and their dialogue swung to a reminiscing of Ferris Wheel fiascos from their youths and the girls stuck at the top with them.

Justin saw Lil pull in his drive, and he walked to the car. He walked past the hood and squatted down. Lil figured he dropped something. Then he stood and walked past the passenger door toward the back of the car and knelt down again. He disappeared, then tapped on her driver's window. She rolled it down.

"What's going on?!" she said.

He leaned between her and the steering wheel and glanced up at the windshield. His hair smelled good. Then he trotted around and got in the passenger side and placed something in the glove compartment. He smiled at her and said seductively, "Puerto de guantes," remembering that was her absolute favorite term in Spanish: glove compartment. Justin preferred the word "guantera" for glove box, but he loved Lil's choice of puerto de guantes. Lil had told Justin she thought the real reason Spanish was considered a romance language or tongue, as she put it, had nothing to do with Vulgar Latin or the Romans. She said it was because so many of the words in Spanish use the tongue in wonderful ways. She told him two years ago that if a man wanted to make her weak in the knees, all he had to do was say, "puerto de guantes." Justin thought that was so funny at the time, saying, "Glove compartment?" Lil couldn't believe he remembered.

"What were you doing?" she asked.

"Well, it's our third date," he said. "What do you think I was doing? Clearly, I was checking the air in your tires, the gas in your tank, and the date on the last time you changed the oil. I'm going to survive this night and your twenty-six, date three scenarios if it kills me," Justin said.

Lil burst into tears.

She had been acting distant since their second date, and these tears worried Justin. In the whole time he had known her, Lil never had cried, except for when she told him about that Hardaway boy, but that had consisted of only four, silent tears. She just wasn't the crying type, and she was really crying.

"What?! Babe?" he said. "What is it?" . . . Please tell me! . . . . . . Lil, don't give up on us . . . Lil . . .?"

"I'm not giving up on us!" Lil cried. "I love us!"

"Then what is it?" Justin asked.

"No matter how I tried, I couldn't come up with a good third date," she cried.

Justin smiled.

"You are so cute," he chuckled, but she didn't hear him.

"I tried to think of something clever, Justin. I really did! The drive-in is closed through the winter! The hockey team has the ice rink booked. The train is having a Christmas party. I wanted it to be perfect, but I'm not programmed to make the third date good!" she cried.

Justin got out and walked around to her door, opened it, took her hand and guided her up and out of the car. He took her face in his hands and kissed her.

"Lil, this is the best third date I could have asked for," and he kissed her again.

"Can we be done with all the scenarios, all the games, please?" he asked her.

She answered by falling back against him and kissing him.

He opened the car door, got her bag and keys, locked the car, took her hand and led her inside. Lil had been to Justin's house only one time. No matter how old she was, she knew her mother would think there was something "tacky" about a single woman going into a man's house alone. She and Justin usually met at her townhouse or at their different destinations.

His was a sparsely furnished, bachelor's house. Sofa, chair, coffee table, TV, dinner table with four chairs, chin-up bar in the bedroom door frame, free weights against one wall, a bow on the wall as art, a guitar leaning against the chair, a bookcase with disheveled, often-touched books, and a desk covered in journals, papers, and maps.

Justin laid Lil's bag in the chair and picked up the phone. He went to the desk, got the Groupon for the dinner he had placed on the bar at Berry Smooth on Wednesday, and dialed the number.

"Yes, I'll hold," he said. "It was for dine in or delivery," he explained to Lil.

The dinner was good, still steaming hot when it got there. Moo goo gai pan and almond chicken always satisfied. They took their waters to the coffee table, and sat on the sofa and talked for a few minutes. Eventually, Justin's tone got serious.

"Lil, what happened the other night when we were at the restaurant and on the way home?" Justin asked her. "I lost you for a while. You were quiet, but it was a deep silence. What were you thinking?"

Lil wanted to be real with him. His dates had been real.

"The dates you took me on, they weren't like most dates. They were about who you are," she said. "It wasn't like you were trying to wine and dine me, you know, like other men do before they drive a girl back to her place hoping to stay the

142

night. It was like you were bringing me into your life, and I liked it."

He took her hand and caressed her fingers with his much warmer ones.

"Justin, a couple of weeks ago, the girls ordered me to make a list, sort of a list of the right man, my right man, reasons to be with him. Don't panic," she smiled at him, "but you check off those things on the list. Your life, it has good stuff, not like an expensive car or a big house or a fancy office, but like Zach and Teddy bears at the medical mission, translating in the emergency rooms and police departments, and Ava. You live the kind of things other people say would be nice to do one day. Like, 'We should go to the Johnny Mack Mission this Thanksgiving and help serve.' But you're the guy who does it, all year long. Yeah, you fly off to exotic places, but you earn those breaks."

"Lil," Justin said, but Lil continued.

"And I started wondering, what would your list look like if you wrote one? What on your list would lead you to me?"

Justin smiled. "Everything on it."

He got up and went to his desk, pulled out a drawer, and carried it to the sofa.

"My list," he said, looking into the drawer. "You."

Lil shuffled all the paperwork in the drawer and looked up at him, astonished.

The drawer had all of Lil's playbills in it, photos of the two of them at the weddings they'd been to, Lil holding his friends' babies in the hospital rooms when they were born, the two of them covered in paintball paint, soccer field mud, and printed copies of her blogs.

"You've been to all my plays?" she said, looking at the playbills.

"Of course," he answered.

"You saved my articles?" she asked, surprised.

"Yes," Justin said. "Look at this one," he pulled one out. "This is the one where you started asking readers to get involved."

"Have a heart, give a heart," Justin read the headline that was accompanied by the blog's signature fingerprint art.

" 'When I was a girl,' " he continued reading, "I wondered why, when there was a problem, why everyone in the state who wanted to didn't just send a dollar to the governor, the person who I thought at the time was the king of the state. Nothing mandatory, nothing like taxes, just knowing of a situation you would have helped with had you known about it, and a dollar in the mail. By the time all the dollars got to the governor, he could afford to fix the problem. I assume many of you had similar thoughts as children. That thought has never left my mind.

" 'Of course, as an adult I've learned how much tape costs, the sticky, red variety. I've also discovered how dirty a white collar can get, that even a preacher can steal, what taxes are, and where the money really goes. But I'd still like to try it, if you would like to join me. And I'm talking about a real problem, not just a bungled up traffic situation or a rogue slot machine. No. A child whose heart is worn out, a mother who's praying for a miracle, and a father who is strong enough to move a mountain but who can merely hold his child. What if a dollar in the mail could be their miracle? Would you send it? The little girl in me still wants to do just that.

" 'You see, I've heard about an invention called a Berlin Heart. A Birmingham-based foundation is trying to raise money for one. When a precious child's heart has a waning number of beats left, this heart, in some cases, can step in and do the work for a little while longer, while the miracle of a transplant inches closer.

" **'Whadda you think?** That would be a powerful, life-changing dollar if you sent it, most likely the best one you ever spent. Of course, you can send more than just one. And no offense, Mr. Governor, but we need to send the money to someone else.

" 'Giving is easy, just the click of a few computer keys or phone buttons will get you there. We push those keys and buttons all the time to crown new idols; certainly we can punch them one more time to save a child's life. Please, pick up the phone or use your computer now and give. Don't finish reading the blog first with the intention of doing it later. You'll forget. Life gets in the way so fast, you won't even know you forgot. I'll say thank you now, too. Thank you. So very much.' " Justin looked up at her.

"You worked with Melissa Powers at the foundation," Justin said.

He had introduced Lil and Melissa when he and Lil ran into Melissa at Urban Cookhouse at lunch one day, and they sat together to visit.

145

"You published the procedure for how to give, and the dollars poured in to Melissa."

"Well, I don't know how many dollars yet, Justin," Lil said, warning him not to be too impressed with black words on white paper. "Maybe two, mine and yours. Melissa's going to give me a count at the end of next month, and I'll print the results."

"Lil, I spoke to Melissa. She has enough donations."

"What?" Lil asked, astonished.

"She's calling you next week," he said. "Lil, Zach from the other night, his heart is worn out. He is scheduled to receive their first Berlin Heart. You did it, Lil, you and everyone who donated."

Lil was stunned. She touched her hands to her mouth.

"No, Melissa is doing it and these people who gave. I just used my voice," she said. "Justin, that device costs so much," she added in disbelief.

"I know," Justin smiled.

Lil was overwhelmed. Justin looked back to the drawer.

"And this opinion piece," he said, taking out another article.

" **'If your prints were all over something that was still broken, would you fix it, Alabama?'** " he read the headline and continued reading. " 'I can't quit thinking about how easily we go about our lives, looking away from fights in which we have no dog, that there-but-by-the-grace-of-God averting of our eyes, thankful it isn't happening to us."

" 'There's a pile of dust around one such scuffle right here at home. Some say it's settled, but it may be one of the most financially unsettling issues to hit a generation of promising Alabama children, that this state has ever seen. Our future teachers, our future doctors and nurses, our researchers, architects, engineers, and builders, our computer experts, pharmacists, veterinarians, and entrepreneurs, our future leaders, if after this they plant their roots here. Enough Alabama kids at the onset to fill over half of Auburn University's Jordan-Hare Stadium. Add the distraught parents and grandparents who are involved and more than half of the University of Alabama's Bryant-Denny is filled. Filled with our sons. Our daughters. We sold them a pact. Then we broke it and made it even more difficult for these young people to finish their education and move this state forward. They need your voice, even if you don't have a dog in this one,' " Justin continued.

" 'Prepaid Affordable College Tuition. Alabama's PACT. An education contract. Tens of thousands of Alabama children were just told that the full tuition their parents and grandparents paid thousands for when many of these young people were babies, will now be lowered to what tuition cost back in 2010, as many of these same babies now are reaching for their high school mortarboards and stepping onto college campuses. And this lower amount isn't guaranteed, as tuition continues to rise.'"

"You don't have to read it. It's long," Lil said.

"Lil, I remember the time you spent on this editorial. I remember the Tums."

"Economists say that people are our greatest resource and that education is their greatest tool," Lil said, "but this state seems to me to be banking on foreign companies over its children. We can't desert our children.

"Justin, I started researching this story because my neighbor bought those contracts for her daughters seventeen years ago. Now she has aggressive MS. She can't work again to provide the deficit. Hers is one of thousands of stories. Who fights for her girls' education now? Yes, the stock market plummeted, but these families didn't buy stock. They bought a contract.

"You have the details there," she pointed to the article. "These families are grateful for the 2010 amount, though clearly they need the full tuition. But one thing stood out to me when I talked to many of these families. Each of them could point to different things that upset them along the way—the last dozen pages of the ruling are state justices doing that themselves, one even holding his nose.[6]   But the parents I spoke with had one thing in common. They want others to understand the need for us all to look past our own yards and speak for one other. Justice is intangible, but we can feel it, even in movies and in books. These families don't feel it."

"What would you point to in this case?" Justin asked.

Lil thought about his question.

"One sentence from a 2010 law. That sentence protected these children, kept the Board from making changes that would 'violate the contractual relationship.'[7]   The first time through the courts, that sentence made the proposed actions illegal, so the state erased that sentence.[8] Pandora's Box was opened. We don't do business this way with foreign manufacturers operating within our state's borders, so why are we doing business this way with our own children?" she asked.[9][10][11]

Justin's eyes moved to the bottom of the article.

148

" 'Whadda you think?' " he read. " 'Hope still hunkers in the corner. We can fix this, one year at a time, until the last child graduates. She finishes high school in 2027. It will take voices. Even yours. Will you use it for someone else's child? Will you step into someone else's shoes and call or email the governor, your legislators? For Alabama's children. For Alabama's future. Honor the PACT,' " he finished and looked up at Lil.

"The court ruled that erasing that sentence backwards in time as if it never existed, wasn't unconstitutional,' " Lil closed the conversation.[12]

"Lil," he said, returning the article to the drawer, "until 1871, it wasn't ruled unconstitutional here for a man to beat his wife, but that didn't make beating her before then right.[13] You had what my mother called a 'Thy kingdom come' moment," Justin said.[14]

"A what?" Lil asked.

"Yes," Justin said. "Replace the word 'kingdom' with the word 'government.' We don't relate to the word kingdom anymore," he said. "Our states belong to a union governed by a Constitution that is beyond compare, but you saw government in a new light. Sometimes it takes that vision to really want the one, true government to hurry up and get here. '*Thy* kingdom come.' We're too comfortable in our own yards most of the time to feel that way. When ink keeps changing on a document that has already been signed, it often loses its value. The original document, the stone tablets so to speak, that first sheet of paper, is usually worth fighting for. When we stop defending it, we may find ourselves at the mercy of the world."

Justin smiled, then chuckled.

"What?" Lil asked.

"You won't see that conversation on a TV dating show, will you?" he smiled.

Lil smiled and shook her head in agreement.

"You've taken on a few missions, Lil," he said picking up other articles and letting them fall back in the drawer. "And you've taken the first steps—getting involved, making people aware, offering solutions, and asking for help, help from people who easily could look the other way," Justin said. "My parents spent their lives on missions for other people when they could have chosen their own comfort instead."

"Justin, you can't compare what I'm doing to what your parents spent their lives doing," she said as he looked back in the drawer and spotted another article.

"This one is my all-time favorite," Justin smiled, reaching in the drawer for a third article.

" 'Save the virgin; save a fortune!' " he read, retrieving the article.

"You give statistics on abortions, infant mortality, welfare costs, medical costs, fatherless/single-parent homes, the high rates of venereal disease. 'Whadda you think?' " Justin read, "'Want to save a fortune? Then we need to save the virgin. She's bound to be around here somewhere, this being the Bible Belt and all, so let's get out there and find her!' " Justin chuckled. "Lil, you're caring, smart, beautiful, sweet, optimistic. Should I go on?"

"You should," Lil smiled.

"You're the leading lady with a column that is published in six states, and you're only 25."

Only 25, Lil thought. Compared to things that fit in a drawer, young perhaps, to other things, not so much, she thought, looking back at her "Save the Virgin" article in Justin's hand.

"Okay, so we both look good on paper," Lil joked.

"And funny," Justin added.

"Do you still have that yogurt gift card?" Lil asked.

"I was thinking the same thing," Justin said, picking his keys up from the coffee table. "I'll drive."

"I thought your car wouldn't crank," Lil said, following him to the door, putting on her coat.

Justin opened the door for her and winked suavely at her as she walked through it.

After yogurt, Justin drove Lil back to his house. Their third date had been a really good one. She got her car keys out of her bag as she was getting out of his car. Justin came around the car and put his hand around her hand. He took her keys and slid them into the pocket of his jacket.

"Stay with me tonight, Lil," he said softly, pulling her against him.

It was date three, the one she'd always been in control of; she wasn't expecting this, not tonight, not with Justin. How foolish. How foolish to think Justin was on her timeline. And here it was. Justin. Justin wanting her to come inside. Justin. Of course. Waiting on date three was probably a record for him. Justin, holding her in front of his house. The man she'd wanted since she'd met him. The friend she never wanted to lose. Confusion fogged her thoughts.

He nuzzled her nose with his, then pushed his lips softly against hers. His mouth felt warmer than usual in contrast to the cold air around them. He was waiting for an answer. For the first time, Lil desperately wanted to be with a man, but she was also anxious, thinking this was not the time to be with him. Pieces of the puzzle she'd tried to fit together all her life were still missing. And she might lose Justin if all this fell apart later. She could lose him. In this moment, she fully understood she would lose him.

"Please, Lil." He kept kissing her.

There's a weakness that starts in a woman's chest when the man she wants is holding her, warmly kissing her, and pleading with her. An escaping of strength that emanates from around her beating heart and spreads to the rest of her body, delivering its weakening ache, its surrendering dolor. A physical, emotional, spiritual weakness. There's a reason a man is stronger, and a reason his strong arms wrap around his woman. This weak moment is that reason. This weak instant that literally leans a woman back as if lying down while still in his arms, still tasting his lips, is the only choice she has. Lil was weak. So weak she didn't feel, through the kissing, Justin guiding her toward his door. Justin. Her Justin.

"No," Lil whispered, pulling back from his lips. "Not yet, Justin." She was breathing hard. He was, too.

He laid his forehead against hers and breathed, as he accepted her "no." He slid his hands into her hair on either side of her face. He ran his tongue across his bottom lip, and nodded. He gave her one more kiss, and turned with his arm on the small of her back and walked her to her car. He opened her door for her and handed her the keys. He squatted down at the open door as she buckled herself.

"Damelo del puerto de guantes," he said, smiling at her.

She reached in her glove compartment and gave him his tire gauge.

"I'll guide you to the interstate," he said, standing and getting his keys out of his pocket.

The last time Lil tried to find her way from Justin's neighborhood to the interstate, she had gotten turned around. After driving into two dead ends, one with blue lights flashing and two men cuffed against cop cars, the other with flashing lights and entire families screaming at each other, she admitted she was lost and called Justin to come find her. She'd lived in Birmingham all her life, but she was not familiar with Justin's side of town.

"Nope," she smiled. "I know exactly where I am this time," she assured him. "First Avenue North, a quick right, and an even quicker left, and I'm on the interstate."

"Text me when you're home safely," he said. "Lock these doors," he added about her car doors, leaning under the roof of the car and kissing her goodnight.

He watched her drive off, and he patted his heart when she waved to him.

153

Lil got home, sat on the sofa, and stared into space. All the way home, she replayed the night in her mind. Only one part bothered her. His car was fine. He said no more date scenarios, please, no more games, but he'd gotten her to his house like any third date guy would do, by saying his car wouldn't crank. She had told one man her secrets, the one man she thought would never . . . no, not Justin.

"He just said it wouldn't crank to be funny, right?" she said aloud to herself.

She brushed her teeth and went to bed. She woke fifty-eight minutes later. The doorbell was ringing and ringing. She looked through the peephole and opened the door. Justin let his head fall back in relief.

"Justin?" Lil said, still waking herself, looking past him to his car that was running, the door left open in his rush, the music blaring.

"You didn't text me that you got home!" Justin exclaimed. "You weren't answering your phone! You scared me to death, Lil!"

He stepped in without an invitation and held her. She could hear his heart pounding where her ear rested against his chest. She could feel it. She smiled. He wasn't playing games. She reached her finger up to her own neck, curious to see if the pulsing of her heartbeat matched his, but he released her from his embrace. He kissed her on the forehead and left. He just needed to know she was safe. Lil closed the door, and Justin turned around and walked backwards slowly to his car, waiting to hear her lock up.

Lil opened the door quickly and jokingly shouted, "Text me when you get home safely!"

"Not funny!" he shouted back. "Lock that door!"

Justin got in his car, and sat there until he absorbed his relief. Until now, he hadn't realized how loud the music was. He turned down the volume before Lil's neighbors complained. He had left his car running when he ran to Lil's front door, not wanting to take the chance that it would choke on him like it had done earlier that afternoon. It conked out while he sat there. He turned the key in the ignition, and the whining started under the hood.

"Not again!" he urged it, pumping the gas.

Lil should have sunken back into her sheets that were still warm after Justin left and been asleep before he reached Interstate 459. Instead, she lay there knowing something about herself that she hadn't known until she heard his heart beating in her ear. She loved him. It wasn't a crush. It had stopped being a crush six months into knowing him. When she suppressed her feelings to keep him in her life, that was love. That "love" grew into "in love." Who knew it could happen in that order? The song that was playing on Justin's stereo when she opened her door still played in her head, a perfect song for tonight's scene, "Do I Have to Say the Words?"

"Weird. I'm definitely in a Bryan Adams phase."

9

Click, Click, Click

Not one "I Can't Quit Thinkin" thought had entered Lil's brain in the past two and a half days. Justin wanted to sleep with her. That thought and that thought alone was all she could try to process. No longer was Justin just a friend. Justin was a man. He was ready. No date four scenario was going to slow this down. She could never go back. She didn't want to go back, but what would going forward bring--or take?

She let her head fall back against the back of her chair in frustration at her lack of focus on work. She was working from home, still in her pajamas, though time was creeping into the afternoon hours. She thought of something and lifted her head upright, facing her home office computer screen.

"Isn't there a song?" she said to herself, opening the web beside the blank blog document on the screen.

Her fingers clicked in a search command. The screen showed the results. She was right. There was the song that perfectly described this moment of total distraction, "I Think About You."

"What the heck?!" she stared at the waiting videos at the artist's name, Bryan Adams.

She leaned back in her chair with a thud, considering the odds of this possibility, but shook her head, surrendering to the weird reality of it, then her thoughts took over again, and she covered her eyes with her hands.

"What's wrong with me?" she complained out loud, pondering why she had told Justin "no."

Why had she let what might have been the perfect moment pass her by? She let her hands fall to her lap.

"I said, 'no'?! I have fantasized about this moment for twenty-four months---no---twenty-four months with Justin, but a decade with a mystery man who turned out to be Justin! And I said, 'Not yet'?! I'm a freak!"

She *had* fantasized about it. She had given this mystery man qualities. She had designed clothes. She had determined the weather and how she would wear her hair. She was the wardrobe, casting, and set director rolled into one, and she was always the leading lady. She had spent as many hours creating the details as she had on imagining the act itself. She just hadn't cast the leading man, until now. She had covered five of the journalistic six in her imagination: what, when, where, how, and why. Only now, she was certain about the who.

Men were no different with their fantasies. They liked to think they were. She realized this similarity when she watched her grown brother setting up an Xbox 360 basketball game with his grown friends when he was home on a military leave. Forty minutes after they sat down to the game, she heard her mother say, "Y'all haven't even started the game yet? My supper's getting cold!" They had spent over half an hour designing their players. Lil understood that. If you're going to fantasize, do it right, she thought. Shame though, that men didn't spend that kind of time thinking about their love lives.

Lil would replay her first time in her mind over and again for days, weeks even. She would start with their first meeting, their first kiss, their first misunderstanding and reconciliation, all the way to their first time. She never dwelt on the details of the wedding. She'd been in enough of those to know weddings are the first bludgeoning of the romance. All the fuss about the wedding killed any hope of having a passionate first time. She cringed thinking every guest there knew the bride and groom were somewhere later that evening, "doing it," and assuming it wasn't their first time no matter how white the dress had been.

The wedding madness started with a huge diamond debt, then the multitude of decisions, the bickering with the mother over every little detail, the bridesmaids' faces at their dress choices, the disagreements with the alterations lady, the endless guest list meetings, the misprinted invitations, all things the bride would complain about with the fiancé which only led to battles with him. The bouquets that arrived looking more like the bride's mother's vision than the bride's, arriving after the photos were taken due to rain that froze traffic and forced the picture-taking inside a lobby. The groomsmen and new in-laws who embarrassed the bride's parents, the months of thank you notes, the bills, the bumping into someone you inadvertently overlooked during the guest list meetings no matter how many comparisons to other brides' lists you'd done.

In her mind, Lil would pick a setting for the necessary nuptials, then quickly jump over them to the honeymoon, and there she would dwell for days. Then she would create an entirely different situation and start all over.

The setting for her first time changed frequently. After a while, they all felt cliché. But before she could even get to the first time, the I-love-yous had to be spoken. She had some stipulations about saying "I love you." He had to say it first. And even after he said it, she couldn't just blurt it back to him. Who would believe that? Saying it then would just seem like a courtesy, an obligation. She would say it when it was time to say it, her time to say it, perhaps in a beautiful setting or after some huge gesture on his part, whatever that might be. She'd know it at the time, and it would be momentous. Her imaginary lover would wait for her to say it. Justin would wait.

And then there was the legend, Dos Amantes, Un Latido del Corazón: Two Lovers, One Heartbeat. She'd added this detail within the past two years. She'd discovered the legend because of her dissertation, "South America: the Language and Legends of Love." She'd found the article in one of the many journals she'd discovered at the Sterne Library, this one dealing with lost love legends of lost cultures. The article stood out because the publisher chose to print it in its original format, typed on an old typewriter, though it was written in the post-computer age. The old fashioned letters of the alphabet, different widths depending on the amount of ink absorbed into the paper as the

159

metal hammers hit different spots along the ink ribbon, added to the allure of the legend, as though Hemmingway might have tapped it out in a jungle retreat, his typewriter, the only sound breaking the monotony of the mosquitoes' buzz. A writer using this technology uses only the necessary words to tell his story. Just the sight of the pages put Lil in a romantic frame of mind, before she'd read even one word. The legend was worth the effort it must have taken to put it on paper.

Unfortunately, Lil had discovered the article after she had submitted her paper to the dissertation panel. When she finished her master's, Lil didn't know how to act with all the extra time she'd found herself with, and she continued to be pulled to the Sterne Library for a while, almost sad that the paper and the degree were finished. She couldn't have used the article anyway. The journal was worn out and missing pages, including the credits page for this particular article. Her online search for the paper to find the bibliography information was fruitless. She knew the legend was just primal mumbo jumbo junk, but she loved the idea of it, two people having the same heart rhythm, the same path, a shared purpose in life. A part of her believed it or wanted to. "Dos corazones con un ritmo, un amor, un deseo, un solo Dios, un plan, un camino, una vida--un imán divino les une." Two hearts with one rhythm, one love, one desire, one God, one plan, one path, united by a divine magnet.

As if she needed to bog down her search for the man of her dreams any more than she already had with her game-playing and all her other stipulations, she'd gone through a brief phase of slyly trying to test the theory during goodnight kisses, one finger on his neck, the other on her own, her eyes closed in hopes of matching pulses. She would take it as a sign to give the man a fourth date no matter how poorly the first three had gone. It was almost impossible to do, and the three times she managed it, the rhythms sounded like dueling drums, and she felt like an idiot.

"So what was that weird goodnight kiss you gave Chet last night?" Sims asked accusingly at coffee after Lil's third date with Sims' student teacher.

He was one of Lil's heart rhythm guinea pigs.

"What was weird about it?" June asked, taking the straw from her water and sticking it into Sims' coffee for a sip.

"He said he could have sworn Lil was checking his pulse."

"What?! That's crazy. Why would I do that?" Lil asked innocently.

"How do you hold a man's wrist and slip him the tongue?" Mac asked, baffled at the new weirdness Lil had thrown at them.

"His throat," Sims corrected Mac.

"Spill it, sister," Hinton demanded, her eyes narrowing in on Lil's. "You're just trying to freak out the guys we're setting you up with, aren't you?"

Lil was glad Chet finished his teaching requirement that week. And she was also glad the waitress dropped a coffee cup right behind Hinton, splattering her Armani suit, breaking Hot's first coffee cup, and breaking up the Wednesday coffee gathering in the nick of time.

She didn't want to test the heartbeat theory with Justin. She didn't want to know if her heartbeat didn't match his. She would just imagine that they were the same. That would be enough.

Justin. He was so much better than any imaginary lover she had created. His hands were warm. His kiss was tender. His arms were strong. His words were right, and his affection was real and passionate. So what was the problem?

Should she tell him he would be her first? Would his knowing soften any passion he might have shown her? She craved passion. Should she let him discover it afterward to find out he would rather have known? There could be only one once. She stared at the blank document on the computer screen, her fingers longing to be clicking out some fabulous article for the blog to keep her mind busy. Her fingers typed **Justin**. Then she back-clicked to erase it. Click, click, click. **Tell Him**, her fingers typed. Then she erased that. Click, click, click. **Don't Tell Him**. Click, click, click.

Lil had been instrumental yesterday, thank goodness, for distraction's sake, in the hippo-themed baby shower Sims had given for June. Each of the girls had their roles and responsibilities. Sims, of course, procured a baby hippo from the Birmingham Zoo to be there. "Generous contribution" didn't begin to explain how much it cost her. Tanner thought his mother was the coolest mom in the world, but he already thought that. Now the shower was a memory.

Tell Him. Click, click, click.

Thank goodness for the play. At least the play would keep her mind busy.

Don't Tell Him. Click, click, click.

Justin was giving exams and wrapping up semester grades. He called her over the weekend, and sent regular texts, all sweet.

"You sleep in an Auburn T-shirt?" he had texted.

How had he noticed that breach of propriety in his rush of emotions the night he woke her to make sure she had gotten home from his house safely?

Tell Him. Click, click, click.

Don't Tell Him. Click, click, click.

She looked over at the Internet page at the music video that still lit up half of her screen, and she clicked on the song that was still waiting there. While the soothing raspiness of Bryan Adams' familiar voice flowed from her laptop speaker, she reached into her bag and pulled out a stack of notebook paper, a ruler, and a number two pencil.

10

A Tear in the Tarp

The "Don't" column trumped the "Do" column 18 to 1, so Lil was driving to Justin's house to tell him. Why start listening to her lists now? "Justin deserves to know," had been the only entry in the "Do" column.

She knew she had time to go by his house, have the talk, get home to shower, and head to the theatre to get into makeup and wardrobe. She didn't have time to make a Do/Don't list to decide if she should call him to let him know she was coming. She knew he was there getting ready for his last two evening exams. She decided to take her chances. If they missed each other, then that would be a sign that she shouldn't tell him.

She walked up on Justin's porch. She could hear him playing the guitar. She stood there for a moment listening and changed her mind, not wanting to disturb him. She turned to leave then turned back around and regained her determination. She tapped on his door. The music stopped, and Justin opened the door, freshly showered with his hair glistening. He wasn't dressed for class yet. He'd just thrown on some gym shorts.

"Lil?" he smiled. "Hey, babe," he said, kissing her and opening the door farther for her to come in, leaning the guitar against the wall. "Is everything okay?" he asked, not able to read her expression.

"Everything is fine," she said. "I had just enough time between your exams and my performance to say hi. 'Hi,' " she added awkwardly.

"Hi," he stepped toward her and kissed her again. "Let me take your coat."

"I can't even stay that long," she said fidgeting, already changing her mind again. "You know, I misjudged the drive time here, and I see you're about to iron your shirt, and well, from the looks of the sky, it's finally about to storm, and that's going to slow traffic, so I'll just see you later, maybe tomorrow?"

"Lil, sit," Justin said. "What's on your mind?"

She sat on the edge of the sofa, still in her jacket. He waited. She exhaled.

"You know, I did come to talk to you about something, but it just seems silly now," she laughed, "so I'm gonna go beat that traffic."

"Lil," he said, insisting she talk.

She quieted herself, and straightened her posture.

"Okay, . . . Justin, . . . we don't really know as much as we thought we did about each other--"

"And that's what we're doing now, Lil," he comforted her apparent worry. "I love everything I already knew, and I love everything I'm discovering about you. Lil, I already know enough," Justin said looking intently at her to see if she understood how deep his feelings were for her. "I already know. The rest, . . . well," he looked around for something. "Look," he grabbed his wallet off the table, put it in her hands, and opened it up to his driver license. "My middle name is Gabriel."

He grabbed a pair of reading glasses off the table and placed them in her hands.

"I put these on around 6 every night when my eyes can't take another minute of looking at a Spanish paper or at the computer screen without them. We have time to learn the details," he said, "because I'm not going anywhere, Lil."

We have time, she thought. Leave.

"Lil, is this about what I told you about Ava, and . . . ?"

"Yeah," she said, smiling. "I mean no! I was saying 'yes,' agreeing with you that yes, we have time to learn all the stuff about each other! Not 'yeah' about the Ava story. I love the Ava story! I want to hear more of your stories. And 'yeah,' we have time to learn the rest about each other, all of our stories up until now, and that's why I said 'yeah.' Now I'm just rambling. You know, I am gonna go because you're right: We've got time."

She got up quickly, and hurried out the door. She got to the front steps and started running to the car. Thunder rumbled, vibrating the ground beneath her feet. It appeared they were about to get the long-awaited rain. She got in the car, shut the door, and thrust the keys toward the ignition, but hit the steering rod and dropped them on the floor. She leaned down, grabbed them, and Justin was there. The door was open. He was guiding her out of the car, into the first few sprinkles of rain.

"Tell me!" he insisted. "What is it, Lil? Just tell me!"

She had typed those words all day, and he was yelling the answer to her.

"Tell me!"

Thunder crashed, and rain fell like it had been building up on a tarp in the sky, and the tarp, no longer able to hold, tore, the definition of "the bottom fell out." For December, it was an oddly warm rain.

"I love you, Lil!" he shouted over the noise of the storm. "I love you!"

He was standing in the pouring rain, shouting, "I love you!"

"What more do I need to hear?" she thought. "How can I not shout it back to him?!"

"I've loved you for a long time!" Justin continued. "I think you have some crazy notion that I've been with a hundred girls, that I'm some Casanova. Lil, I don't even need half the fingers on one hand to tell you about that, and it isn't what you think. Let me tell you."

"No! I don't want to know about someone you loved, and I don't know which would be worse—hearing about you with someone you loved or with someone you didn't!"

"Lil," he said, taking her face in his hands and staring intently into her eyes, "you are the only one I've ever loved. I'm not just your fourth date, Lil. I'm your five hundred and fourth date! I've been dating you for a year and a half. For the last year, only you. You just didn't notice."

She watched his beautiful face saying these beautiful words.

"Justin," she started and couldn't finish.

"Lil!" he pleaded.

"You found her, Justin!" she shouted over the rain.

"I don't understand!" Justin shouted back.

"That girl," she said, "the one from my article . . . the last virgin . . . you found her," Lil said.

Justin looked intently at her. The realization of what she said, what it meant appearing on his face. The sky had emptied most of its rain, and the force of the storm lightened to a steady shower.

"Lily, . . . " he said her name, letting himself understand the enormity of what she had said.

His eyes moved around her face, from her eyes, to her lips, to her hair that he now touched with both hands, to her cheeks, her nose, back to her eyes. He held his gaze there, and his mouth curved into a glimpse of a smile as so much occurred to him about that word.

He kissed her gently, then with increasing force. He picked her up off the ground and kissed her, and set her back on her feet and kissed her. He pressed his cheek against hers, holding her close, his breath and voice in her ear.

"I already loved you, Lil," he almost whispered, "but hearing you say that . . . everything it means . . . the time . . . the choices . . . you waited . . . I didn't know . . . I didn't know how much that could mean to me . . . until now. Te amo, Lily."

He took her face in his hands and kissed her.

This kiss . . . words cannot explain.

But a song can, the one that was playing on the CD that Justin was strumming along to in his den when she'd gotten there, Bryan Adams' "I'll Always Be Right There." Lil could still hear it playing in her mind, and she let the song play through this kiss, through this part of her story.

11

Fair Rosalind

Justin stayed in his classroom for the hour after the first exam. He decided to stay there and grade those test papers while he waited on the students who were coming to take the last exam. The sooner he wrapped up this semester, the sooner he could focus on Lil. He looked up as he saw someone enter the classroom. He glanced at the clock.

"Julieta," he said, "you're very early. Muy temprano."

"Yo se," she answered, nodding.

Julieta got there early on purpose, telling her father she needed to get to the classroom and do some last-minute studying. With one car, and her father heading to work, he dropped her off early. Spanish-speaking students took Justin's classes to get their foreign language requirements accomplished. They learned in his class that though they might know how to speak the language, that still he could teach them plenty. He corrected errors in their semantics that different dialects undid, and he taught them proper syntax for when they were writing in Spanish, which wasn't often.

Julieta had one reason for getting there early tonight. Justin. She'd been flirting with him all semester. He was aware of the girls who batted their eyes at him, but never had he let girlish flirtations and his profession cross paths. Julieta set her books down and took off her long coat. She was wearing more makeup than most nights. Her heels were higher, her pants tighter, and her shirt cut more deeply than usual. It was the last night of her semester, and the last Spanish she had to take. She was not going to let this last moment get away from her.

"Just take a seat and do some final studying," Justin said and looked back at his papers.

She walked over to his desk. She rested her hip against the side of it, staring at him. He looked up at her.

"Go, Julieta. This isn't an easy exam," Justin said sternly, not letting her seductive posture interfere with his work.

She walked around to his side of the desk and leaned her rear against it, facing Justin.

"We need to talk, Julieta," Justin said, setting his pen down and removing the pair of glasses he'd gotten out of a drawer at home when he realized Lil had accidentally taken his other pair and his wallet when she had run to her car earlier at his house.

He pushed his chair back slightly so he could look up at her, forgetting that only the chair in his office had wheels. With no wheels, this chair screeched on the floor, and moved back only an inch. Julieta moved quickly, straddling Justin's lap. His reaction was fast. He pushed on the floor with his feet again to

171

slide the chair back so he could push her forward and get her off of his lap. The cinder block wall stood close behind them with little space between it and the desk. With twice the weight in the chair now, it moved only another inch. The momentum of his effort dug the back legs into the vinyl tile and lifted the front two off the ground, pushing Julieta's chest into his neck, her head above his, her long black hair flowing around him. She smiled at the result, her arms around his neck, resting on his shoulders. Justin grounded his feet and stood, lifting himself and her onto the floor in the same motion.

"Stop it!" he shouted. "Stop it, Julieta!" he shouted again.

With his hands on her hips where they had to be to get both of them out of the chair simultaneously, he pushed her away from him, and let go quickly, wiping the forced indiscretion from his palms on the side of his pants.

Justin was about to lecture Julieta, when the sound of something lightly hitting the floor near the entrance caused both of them to turn. He looked at the floor. A pair of reading glasses had fallen from the sloping surface of the first desk next to the door. Something on the desk above them that had not fallen drew his eyes back up. His wallet. Lil had been there. She had seen them in the chair. She had made not even a hint of a noise. No sound will erupt when a heart stops beating. Lil quickly and silently had placed Justin's wallet and glasses on the desk. She had turned, and as quietly as she could, she trotted to the stairwell four stories high in the foreign languages building.

She had gone to Justin's office first. He wasn't there. Another professor checked a diagram taped to the wall in the hallway, and told her Justin was in room 427. Now she ran. She made it to the stairwell and ran quietly down the first flight, twisting and turning in the square concrete funnel of stairs, careful not to let her shoes clank against the metal edge protector that was screwed to each step. On the second floor, she knew she was out of hearing, and she ran the last flights, squeezing between arriving students, not caring how much noise she made. How could she have been such a fool, she thought? How could she not know Justin was playing a game? Why would he do that to her? She ran.

Justin ran, too. He ran to the stairwell. He could hear her last few steps on the last few stairs. He started down the stairs, pushing past students coming and going, each turn slowing him down, each ugly wall glaring with a different primary paint color, smeared and dirty, counting his turns. Now only his pounding feet echoed off the concrete steps and walls. Lil was done with the stairs.

"Lil!" his voice echoed in the concrete well. "Lil!" with every three steps. "Lil!"

He had no idea where she had parked, how far away, how far a run. He had to catch her before she got to her car. He leaned over the railing and looked down the last flight of stairs. He grabbed the railing with one hand, pushed off with his feet, and hurled himself over into the space past the last flight, bouncing up from a squat where he landed.

"Lil!" he ran after her.

He could see her in the night. She was running through the parking lot toward the baseball field, slowed by two passing cars. He ran parallel in the grass to gain ground until the line of

173

cars on his side moved. He was gaining easily. He had run this desperately once when he was 10. Running across the grass, he clipped his chest, right next to his shoulder, hard on a metal statue hidden in the darkness on the school lawn. He clutched his shoulder as he ran, quickly cutting across the lot. Lil hadn't struggled to run like this since she tried to run from Blaze Hardaway in eleventh grade.

"Lil!"

Justin's hand firmly grabbed her arm. He spun her around into an embrace without her permission. She had the jerks, and he held her cheek against his chest, and her body against his, refusing, with his strength, to let her go.

"It wasn't what you think, Lil! She jumped into my lap! I pushed her away immediately! I stopped it, Lil, as soon as it happened!" Justin said desperately. "As soon as she did it, I stopped it, Lil! I stopped it!"

He held Lil longer, then slowly released her, holding her upper arms tightly.

"Come back with me!" Justin cried, pulling Lil back through the parking lot toward the building. "She'll tell you herself! She's just a girl! She'll tell you!"

Lil was shaking her head no.

"I have to go!" she yelled. "I'm late getting into makeup and wardrobe! I have to go!"

Justin held on to Lil's arm and turned back to the building.

"Julieta!" he shouted, looking up to the fourth floor.

All of the classroom doors opened onto a concrete balcony that wrapped around the entire square of the outside of the

Humanities building. A three and a half foot high concrete wall served as the railing. He knew Julieta could hear him.

"Julieta!" he yelled again.

"I have to go!" Lil insisted, not wanting to stay here for this.

"No!" Justin argued with her. "Julieta!" he demanded again toward the building.

Julieta shyly looked over the concrete wall.

"Tell her, Julieta!" Justin yelled at her. "¡Dígale!" he demanded again.

Lil wasn't paying attention to Justin's shouts anymore. She was looking at Julieta on the balcony. She saw Julieta's long, silky black hair, her dark eyes and olive skin, her dark red lips, her made-up face, her plunging shirt. The architect had left a few inches at the base of the balcony wall open to allow rain water to escape, and in those few inches, Lil could see Julieta's spiked heels and the beginning clue of how tight her pants were.

"Juliet," she thought in her mind, writing the tragic ending to the tragic love story in her head. "And I'm Rosalind," she thought. "You're Justin's type. I'm not." Lil knew Julieta would always be Justin's type.

She jerked her arm hard, pulling it from Justin's hand and ran to her car.

Justin stood there and watched her drive off. He turned back to the building. He knew Julieta would still be there. She wouldn't get her credit without this exam. He walked furiously up the stairs.

"She'll be at the theatre," he thought about Lil. "I can give this last test, and be waiting on her after her performance."

175

He breathed to regain his composure. When he got to his classroom, Julieta was sitting in her desk pretending to cram for the exam. He picked up his wallet. He didn't say a word. He was too angry to risk what he might say. His glare said it all. He pulled the stack of exams from his messenger bag and slammed them on the front of the desk, and hurled his glasses into the satchel.

"You date Angélica?" Julieta asked.

"Yes," Justin answered, wondering how Julieta recognized Lil from the play.

"She's beautiful," Julieta said. "She should go to Broadway."

Justin knew he wouldn't be able to pass that compliment along to Lil, having come from Julieta.

"Next time they ask her, maybe she will go," Julieta added.

"What do you mean, next time they ask?" Justin asked her.

"The scouts came from New York and offered her the part there. She turned it down," Julieta said. "You go with her, and you don't know this?" Julieta commented.

"How do *you* know it?" Justin asked.

"My father, he works in maintenance at the Alabama Theatre. I know everything down there. I've seen the play three times from backstage. Have you seen it?"

"Not yet," Justin answered, still angry.

"Profesor," Julieta said, "then you are too late. Tonight is the last performance."

Justin couldn't believe it. He was about to miss Lil's last night in her first ever role of leading lady. How could she not have reminded him? He started slamming everything he'd brought to the classroom into his satchel. Another student walked in and sat down, then another.

"¿Profesor? What are you doing?" Julieta said. "We have our final exam!"

"You give it to them!" Justin instructed Julieta.

"Okay, but the gringos are gonna cheat," Julieta stated the obvious.

"Don't let them. You're in charge," Justin said, slamming the stack of papers on Julieta's desk.

"You pass these out," he said to her.

Then he pointed to one of the other two who had arrived. "You take them up," he instructed.

Then he pointed to the third student.

"You take them to my office and lock it."

"What do we tell everyone?" Julieta asked.

"Tell them I had a play to catch!" Justin said, running out.

12

Only One Once

Parking for a final performance near the Alabama Theatre was time consuming, and Justin was out of time. Tonight's performance was sold out and still had a line of people hoping for admittance. The Alabama Theatre never had been the venue for a production that contained any nudity, and rumor had it that at this closing performance there would be some. Women and teenaged girls, not regular play attendees, had come out in droves hoping the nude scene, if there were one, would showcase Gene Hope, a town celebrity. Even more of the crowd were there hoping Matt Fowler who played Rodney, the play's villain, would be the one in his birthday suit. The blog's critic came again, though he'd attended opening night. Craig Jenkins came to cover the possibility of skin for SameSunNewsMark.com's review, secretly hoping the skin would belong to Lil.

Downtown Birmingham was swimming in parking decks, but Justin didn't have time to snake around those decks tonight. They would slow him down just as the stairs had. He circled the blocks, trying to find street parking. He looked for Lil's car where she normally tried to park and spotted it there before he turned from 18th Street South onto 5th Avenue North. Lil didn't like walking the parking decks at night alone when her performances were over, so she parked in the flat lot across the street from the Hugo Black Courthouse. Most of the bow-tie-wearing attorneys were gone by the time she got downtown, leaving the lot empty until the theatre crowd arrived.

Justin turned the corner after spotting Lil's car. Even in his rush, he shook his head at the thought of her walking the two short blocks to her car by herself in the dark from 3rd Avenue. Someone was vacating a parallel place, and he waited, though not as patiently as he normally would have. He slipped sloppily into the slot, leaving one tire on top of the curb, and he started running. He ran around the corner and down two blocks on 19th Street South. When he reached the corner of 3rd Avenue North, he saw the vertical "Alabama" marquee flashing in lights. He flew up the star-studded Walk of Fame sidewalk, but he saw none of it. Dean Jones, Louise Fletcher, Jim Nabors, Truman Copote, Pat Buttram, Fannie Flagg, Mary Badham, John Badham, Wayne Rogers, Kate Jackson, and Harper Lee--- he dashed across all of their sidewalk stars.

When Justin got inside to the Will Call window, he discovered that neither Lil nor Nick had left a ticket in his name. He ran to the ticket sales windows to the right of Will Call.

"Sold out," the man said, walking away from his window.

He ran back to the white-haired woman closing her Will Call window to try again to persuade her that Lil always gave Nick a ticket to leave at the window for him, but it was Nick's night off.

"I'm the leading lady's boyfriend!" Justin insisted to the woman.

"Of course you are, and I'm shaggin Rodney," she said about the play's villain. "We should all double date, Sailor," she said sarcastically, "but you don't have any tickets here, Casanova!" she repeated, slamming her window.

The people in charge of selling tickets and tearing them in half couldn't help him. They didn't know the people on the stage, and had no reason to believe the people on the other sides of their windows.

"Harlem!" Justin remembered, knocking on the glass. "Get Harlem!" Justin said, remembering Nick had introduced them once.

Harlem came to the front, but he couldn't remember Justin.

"Then call Nick!" Justin shouted at Harlem.

"I don't have his number! I just work with him! Who do you think you are, shoutin' at me?" Harlem shouted back.

"I'm sorry, man. Please, Harlem, find someone who can call Nick," Justin pleaded.

A few minutes later, a big burly guy in a plaid, flannel shirt and twenty pounds of keys hanging from his belt loop walked toward Justin, holding his cell phone out for Justin to take.

"Nick!" Justin said into the phone. "It's Justin! Lil Swann's Justin! Man! I almost let this play get away from me!"

"I thought you were out of the country or something," Nick said.

Lil had told Nick that Justin went abroad frequently.

"I held a seat each night, and Lil asked me after every performance if you'd made it," Nick said.

Justin's heart panged at the words.

"Glad you went tonight, man. I don't know how you'd tell a girl you missed her performance after she passed on Broadway for ya!"

Lil never mentioned to a soul, not even to her parents, that she'd been given the Broadway opportunity. Phillip Guwen had called her production people and asked them if she'd made a decision. Guwen assumed Lil would have been shouting his offer from the rooftops. Everyone around the theatre had whispered and wondered about why Lil would have passed on the chance to understudy the lead in a production at the Winter Garden Theatre on Broadway. Nick guessed it was because of Justin and told a few people. He instructed Justin to hand the phone back to the man in plaid. Nick okay'd it with him, told him where the available seat was, and the man asked another man wearing an Alabama Theatre badge to escort Justin to his seat.

"It's all we've got," the man said, showing Justin the chair on the aisle, next to the last row on the right side of the main level.

"It's perfect," Justin whispered as the play was already in its second scene.

The theatre building was an ornate golden masterpiece splashed in red velvet seats, the detailed carvings on the box seating suited for royalty, its Wurlitzer pipe organ, the reason for the building's salvation from parking deck pimps who would have torn down the architectural gem. No detail was missing. Even the ceiling was a sight to behold. Most people got there early to find parking so they could get to their seats quickly to have time to drink in the grandeur of one of the finest treasures in all of Alabama. Justin had no time to gaze around. Lil was on stage, and she was captivating.

Scene after scene passed. The crowd's laughter was background noise to Justin's anxious thoughts. The play was building toward its climax. Justin decided during a scene Lil wasn't in that they would be fine. He'd get up during the final bows, and find his way backstage. He might have to wait for some last-performance cast celebration, but he wasn't dumb to the fact that Lil might not be in the mood for that party tonight. He was glad he found her car before he parked his. He would try to keep an eye on it if nothing else worked.

The curtain drew on the climactic scene. Lil was standing there, in a forest green, satin gown, alone in a dark, woodsy park setting, at night. The atmosphere was in stark contrast to all the comical acts that had come before this one, clearly a statement on the playwright's part. Angelica was nervous, as the sun had gone down half an hour earlier, and her courter, Manley, who, she was told, was about to propose, was late. Another woman less classily clad than his Angelica, less clad in general than Angelica, easily had distracted Manley. Lil stood watching for him in the darkness, waiting. She knew Manley would come for her. He had promised. The villain, played by Matt Fowler, stood watching her from the trees.

Justin gripped the arms of his seat. It was hard watching Lil even pretend to be in this kind of predicament. Rodney emerged from the darkness, startling Angelica.

"I'm sorry to surprise you," he spoke, "but to see any woman in this place, at this hour, is surprising to me as well, pleasingly so, my lady," Rodney added, bowing to Angelica. "Welcome to my neck of the woods."

Angelica knew the villain, of course, from earlier scenes. He had played brilliant games to woo Angelica into his bed and to divert Manley's attention away from Angelica. He personally had provided Manley's present diversion. The crowd knew Manley would come bursting on stage at any minute to rescue Angelica, though right now they knew Manley was also in a place he shouldn't be, a situation they'd laughed about minutes earlier.

"I'm not alone," Angelica lied. "Manley is just within those trees. One scream will bring him running back to me," she continued.

"Then scream," Rodney instructed her, grinning.

His games from the first acts were over. He had bored of them, and he was ready to take his prize now, even though he hadn't won it.

"I will not scream," Angelica answered, knowing no ears were close enough to hear her anyway.

"Ah, but you will," Rodney said, smiling crudely. "Think you're too much of a lady?" Rodney asked moving closer to Angelica as she inched backward. "I've played numerous, tired, old games over the past weeks," he said, "but you've played your games as well, games older and sadder than mine,"

Rodney continued toward her, "you clinging to your purity, showing just enough of what we'll get if we wait for it, me pretending to wait for it. But this is the nineteenth century. The sun is shining on a new day. The old rules have faded away. Let's write some new ones."

Justin clenched his teeth and closed his ears to the dialogue. He shut his eyes deliberating whether to watch at all. He opened them. A ripple ran up his cheek from the tension in his jaw. The scene was affecting him physically. He wanted it to be over.

Rodney bolted toward Angelica, grabbing her, forcing his mouth on hers, ripping the bodice of her dress down, revealing her cleavage, lifted in the bones of her corset. The crowd gasped.

"Manley!" Angelica screamed into the air, but Rodney slapped her to the ground and stood over her with his back to the crowd.

He unfastened his pants and let them fall, his derriere, the only nudity in the play, but jolting to the senses, so real that there were no cat calls from the crowd, not even from the women and girls who had come to see just that nude moment.

Something in Angelica surrendered. Something in her knew the games, the wait, the fight had been futile back before she had even started fighting it. Something told her Manley was never who she thought he was. To the people in the first few rows, Angelica's tears looked real. All the young girls who had discussed on the ride downtown what it would be like to be with Matt Fowler, felt the loss of what was about to be stolen from Angelica, and they blamed Manley as much as they blamed Rodney. The danger was too real to make light of it. The crowd forgot they were at a comedy. The curtain dropped.

Justin moved his head around to let go of the tension that had built during the scene. He moved his shoulders and stretched his fingers out from the fists he had formed without realizing it. The crowd had gasped as a whole. They forgot to applaud, and their mutters about what had just happened continued as they waited for the next act.

The fourth act was brief, and the curtain rose on the fifth act. Angelica didn't appear in the final act. She had sailed across the ocean, with whispers from the play's aristocrats that she was a trollop. They claimed Manley had dodged one of those newfangled bullets, and he agreed, slightly distracted with a crabby itch he'd recently contracted. The last scene brought back the laughter. It tidied up all the loose ends, and took its sweet time doing so, at least to Justin.

The last curtain fell, and Justin stood and went behind the last row to watch the bows and keep a lookout for Lil. The characters came out in order of importance from least to most. Gene as "Manley," took his bow, followed by the villain, "Rodney," Matt Fowler, who'd gone al fresco in his last scene, earning him the next to the last bow on this evening. Pockets of people scattered around the crowd had this second opportunity to let out their "woo-hoos" that the tension of the moment had silenced while the actor had stood there bare-bottomed. The shouting went on for quite a while. The older people in the audience began laughing, remembering how they'd been in their youth. Then Fowler backed away from the edge of the stage with his arm outstretched, gesturing the anticipated

185

appearance from behind him of Angelica, Lil. The crowd went crazy with applause as they looked for Lil, but she didn't appear from behind as the others had. The applause grew, and parts of the crowd that had sat back down, rose to its feet again, but still, no Lil. Gene dashed back behind the scenes to see what was keeping her. He returned with a microphone and a stage-actor's grin. He raised the mic to his mouth.

"It appears our Angelica truly has sailed for better opportunities!"

The crowd's applause became thunderous. Some people plugged their ears with their fingers, and others lipped that they could feel the floor vibrating from the applause. Craig Jenkins would write that Lil Swann brought a new tone, a sadness, to the character of Angelica that made the play a whole new experience. He would write that Angelica's absence at the end was a stroke of genius.

Justin was running. Even before Gene Hope had returned with the mic and his announcement, Justin was running. He knew she had left. He was pushing past employees, and those in the crowd, mostly seniors, who were trying to beat the rush. Every door was employed. Justin waited as patiently as he could behind the white-haired couple struggling to get through the door at the same time, not wanting to be separated for even that moment in case the other lost his footing, as thresholds can be tricky. The thinning white-haired husband clutched his tennis-ball-bottomed cane while his wife's hands clenched his arm, determined to squeeze through the opening together.

"But she just gave up in that park scene! I hated it from that point on!" the woman lamented.

"It was her against the world, dear. When she realized Manley was just like all the others, man in general, I imagine, thus his name," he surmised, "she knew her battle was futile," her husband explained as they inched through the door. "Turned out to be more literary than comical. About time, but probably too late," he said.

"I understood it," she argued, "but I still hated it!"

Justin placed his hand on the door above their heads and pushed the door wider for them, and let them get far enough outside that he could squeeze past them. When he got to the parking lot, Lil's car was gone.

13

The Final Bow

Lil hadn't come home. Justin sat on her porch stoop waiting for her. Her car wasn't in the garage. He had opened it with the combination and checked the entrance from the garage, but it was locked. She'd had a good leeway to get to her car and leave. She didn't know Justin had been at the theatre. Where had she gone? He would wait. He would wait for her.

Lil had gone home though. She left the theatre a full thirty minutes before the final bows were taken. She'd gone straight to her car in her green satin gown. She had walked down 3rd Avenue North toward 18th Street South, away from the flashing marquee, in the opposite direction of the square path Justin had run to the theatre. She slowly walked across the stars on her side of the sidewalk, Stanleigh Malotte, James Hatcher, Tallulah Bankhead, Polly Holliday, George Lindsey, Nell Carter, Jack Hess, Phillip Alford, saying her good-byes to each one, as this had been her last night as leading lady. She didn't know if she'd ever play that part again. She crossed the street and stood on the lonely corner of the prayerful, boarded, vaudevillian Lyric Theater whose sidewalk stars would read Mae West, Roy Rogers and Trigger, Gene Autry, Milton Berle, Buster Keaton, Will Rogers, Sophie Tucker, and the Marx Brothers, if anyone cared. The forgotten Lyric's broken windows mirrored neighboring parking decks like a corner harlot fearful of the dreaded pimp, a few windows enviously reflecting the flashing lights across the street as the Lyric seemed to look back nostalgically, along with Lil, at the bright lights that flashed around "Alabama." Lil smiled a melancholy smile, holding the tears in her eyes.

"It was amazing . . . I'll never forget . . . goodbye," she said blowing a kiss from her hand back toward the place and everyone inside it, taking her bow, turning, and running the rest of the way to her car.

She drove straight home and started packing. She used all of her luggage. It might have been too little or too much. She didn't know. She never had packed for four weeks before. She had found Phillip Guwen's card in her purse backstage during the second act. He still needed her in New York as the second understudy. He told her he would make the necessary calls right then and have her ticket waiting at the airport that same night for a morning flight. She'd told Dottie in wardrobe she was leaving, and Gene Hope's announcement was true about Angelica sailing for better opportunities.

If Justin hadn't told her it was too dangerous to hide a key outside in case she ever locked herself out, he could have let

189

himself in, and the clues were all around. She had looked at the list of New York Dos and Don'ts. She had torn it in half and thrown away the one and only Don't: "Justin isn't in New York." Now, that seemed the perfect reason to go there. If Lil's front door had been anything other than solid wood, Justin would have been able to see the ripped, green gown lying on the floor of her living room, in front of the fireplace where she'd stepped out of it and walked away.

14

Auggie's Futon

Everyone has experienced this night. The night in that weird, third bedroom in someone else's house, that has its own unique smell and its own special quiet and creaks. The bedroom that isn't really a bedroom, where no comfort is possible, no sleep can be found, but the struggle to find it is never ending.

Lil went to June's house after she packed. She didn't know if Justin would come to her house after his exams, but she didn't want to be there if he did. She called June since June had no kids, and a late-night guest would disrupt fewer people's lives. Plus June, almost two weeks from her due date, was already on maternity leave, so it would be easier for her to take Lil to the airport in the morning. She turned off her cell phone and put it in a suitcase. June opened the door wearing her pajamas, whispering to Lil.

"Auggie went to bed at 8. He's leaving at 4 a.m. to meet his buddies to go deer hunting."

She signaled Lil to follow her down the hall.

"I don't have a guest room anymore," June whispered. "It's the baby's room now."

"I'm so sorry to barge in like this, June," Lil whispered back.

"It's fine," June said, leading Lil through the small fixer-upper to the third bedroom, the room Lil could only describe as June and Auggie's all-purpose, slash, storage, slash, where the heck do we put this baby crap, slash, Auggie's old futon, room."

June and Auggie had renovated the kitchen beautifully, and were about to start the living room when June discovered she was expecting, so all renovation monies shifted to the baby's room, and all their crap shifted to this one.

"Sorry about the mess."

"It's okay," Lil whispered.

She was glad she had brushed her teeth and gotten ready for bed at home. She thought June would be up a little while, and they could talk, and she'd be able to unwind some before trying to sleep.

"Tell me about it in the morning?" June whispered.

Lil nodded.

She would put up a fight to keep Justin out of her mind. The goal was to sleep and to begin the process of forgetting him.

She tried not to make much noise. She brought sweatpants and a long-sleeved T-shirt to sleep in, and she quietly changed into them. She had her own small bathroom at the end of the hall across from her room, the pink tile bathroom, but every bedroom was on this hallway, so even in there she had to be quiet. She pee'd and washed her hands, deciding to flush in the morning. She had a gut feeling the plumbing in this bathroom would roar like a dragon. In these old houses, even the clicking of the light switches could wake a comatose patient, and she heard Auggie snort in his sleep when she turned off the light. She tiptoed back across the hall.

She crawled onto Auggie's futon and pulled the nylon, kiddie-camping comforter over her. And the night started. She fell hard asleep for the first twenty minutes. The exhaustion from the heartbreak over Justin, added to the final performance of the long-running play, June's baby shower, and the pressures of work, really had been too much all at once. She woke to discover she had been right about the plumbing.

June flushed the toilet in the bathroom, the pink tile bathroom, the same bathroom Lil was using. Lil woke to the explosion of flushing followed by a whole rendition of noises in the pipes that died into a falsetto about six minutes later, ending with something that sounded like a Mack truck skidding into stop. There would be no falling back to sleep, only a sweaty, hard-fought effort throughout the night to try. She felt the weight of sadness sitting like a cinder block on her heart, and a tear rolled down her cheek.

"No," she told herself, wiping it harshly with her sleeve.

She was cold. The foam-stuffed comforter wouldn't hug her. It just sort of floated on top of her. Lil rolled herself in it tightly to force it to give her some feeling of being covered, but it still gave her no warmth. The room was dark in spite of the rectangular crack of light blazing around the door, jutting into

Lil's room in sharp rays. June had installed a nightlight in the hallway around month seven when her nighttime treks to the bathroom increased. She'd have to suggest to June to replace the 1000-watt bulb for a 20-watt. She closed her eyes and tried to position her head so that her eyes weren't in the line of fire. She got close to sleep, but even in those moments, bright flashes of exhaustion lit up behind her closed lids as if she had stood next to a strobe light for too long. She shifted, balling up and stretching out, but without even momentary comfort. She sat up to find a clock to see how much sleep she had missed already. There wasn't a clock in the room. Then cold turned to hot. The sweat pants and the long-sleeved shirt were too much, but they were all she had in the one bag she had brought inside. The comforter now seemed to weigh a ton. She wiped away another tear.

"No!" she told herself again. "Just go to sleep!" she ordered herself.

She kicked off the comforter, and willed herself to sleep. She was close, drifting into a sweaty, anxious, on-Auggie's-futon kind of sleep. Then June flushed the toilet again.

Two hours later Lil was still struggling on the futon to find the spot, the position, the temperature where sleep would find her. At least it felt like two hours. She sat up again, looking for a clock. She knew it shouldn't matter what time it was when precious sleep hours were ticking away, but it was making it worse for her not to know. She needed to do the math. She just had to know how much was lost and how much potential sleep was left. She got up and quietly felt her way past waiting packs of diapers, clipping her little toe on the corner of the unopened high chair box. She hopped the rest of the way, clutching her injured toe, to the dusty treadmill and felt for her watch where she'd left it. She went closer to the crack in the door and held her watch in the light. Two thirteen a.m.

She pushed her long sleeves up as high as she could, which just made her upper arms hotter. She pulled each of her pants legs up to her thighs, and the elastic squeezed them tightly. She was convinced she had a fever though she didn't. She crawled back in the bed, stretched, breathed in, and the toilet flushed.

Time seemed to drag and fly at the same time. From the feverish darkness, Lil heard voices. June was talking in low tones to Auggie who was putting on his camouflage. The tinkering in the kitchen included clacking sounds that hurt Lil's head like she suspected noise would hurt if she'd been hung-over. Her head throbbed. She heard the voices at the front door, June closing it, and Auggie cranking up and backing away from the house. Finally, Lil felt her body and her mind giving up the fight. And she had the peace of knowing the time because June had told her Auggie would be leaving at 4.

"Just this next hour, please," she mumbled.

The temperature was just right, and the futon accepted her position for the first time. Lil slipped into the land of the sleeping.

June flushed the toilet.

15

Birmingham-Shuttlesworth International Airport

Lil sat in June's passenger seat with her swollen eyes closed, smeared mascara underneath them, her head leaning on the window, bumping against it as the tires hit bad spots on the interstate, trying to sleep through June's conversation on the way to the airport. Two rings around her thighs still stung from where her sweatpants had cut off her circulation in the night.

"You'd be surprised how many times I pee'd last night," June said.

"Eight," Lil reported with her eyes closed.

"Really? That's my new record."

"Glad I could be there for it," Lil mumbled.

"I had to use the bathroom across from your room because ours is messed up. You should hear the noise ours makes when we flush it," June continued.

"Good night! Did the neighbors start a petition?" Lil asked.

"Mac is already at the airport," June said, "and Hint is coming right up behind us," she added having spotted Hinton's Lexus SUV right behind them. "Looks like she picked up Sims."

June shifted to her side-view mirror as Hinton crossed back and forth over the centerline.

"Good gosh a'mighty!" June exclaimed. "She's gonna kill Sims putting on makeup while she drives," she said watching Hinton swerve around, Sims fussing, grabbing for the steering wheel, and blowing her whistle that was already around her neck.

They were all headed to the airport in the first minutes of rush-hour traffic. June stayed up after she kissed Auggie goodbye. She had coffee waiting when Lil stumbled out of bed and threw on jeans at 4:50 a.m., not that Lil had gotten any sleep after Auggie left. Her flight would be leaving at 7. Lil explained to June about her opportunity to understudy on Broadway. June was so excited for Lil. When Lil explained she would be gone for a month, June insisted they wake the others up and get them on a bon voyage conference call. June had them all on speaker, the others in their beds. Lil told them about Phillip Guwen's offer, B. Merry's ditching the play, and her own plans to write her column from New York for the month. They started their goodbyes.

Sims shouted into the speaker, "Break a Leg!"

Mac joked, "Get your mom a Louie Vuitton knockoff!"

Hinton added, "Get laid!"

Lil started to cry. It was the first time June had ever seen Lil cry.

"What's she doing?" Hinton asked.

"Blubbering!" June answered.

"About what?" Sims asked.

"I don't know," June replied.

"We're coming over," Mac said.

"We're fix'n to leave for the airport," June told them.

"Then spill it!" Hinton ordered.

"Justin wanted to sleep with me!" Lil squalled.

They were all meeting at the airport.

They sat around a small table between Charley's Steakery and Mrs. Field's Cookies by Concourse C. Lil had her left arm across her stomach with her right elbow resting on the back of her left hand, her thumbnail between her front teeth.

Hinton was bent down theatrically hitting her head on the table, trying to get through to Lil.

"I'm a freak," Lil said.

"We know, sweetie," Mac agreed, sweetly patting Lil's arm.

Except for Hinton, they all looked like Sims today, wearing workout pants and exercise jackets zipped up over their pajama tops. Hinton threw on a navy pencil skirt, a blouse, and navy stilettos, and she put on a full face of makeup on the drive there. If there were ever any place she wanted to look like a successful businesswoman, it was the airport at 7 a.m. Lil hadn't told them much, just that she and Justin had decided to try dating, that they'd had two, good, simple first dates, that on the third date, Justin wanted to sleep with her, that she had said no, and that she'd seen him with another woman. She didn't report the "I love you." That was personal, and at this point, moot. She

198

was glad she hadn't told him she loved him that afternoon in the pouring rain.

"You've seen him with a million women!" Sims said. "You've had *three* dates! So what if he saw somebody else?! Y'all aren't married which means he's still up for grabs, so grab him and sleep with him!"

"You know the saddest part of it all," Lil said, ignoring Sims' advice. "I was worried that I'd lose Justin as a friend if I slept with him. Turns out, not sleeping with him--I lose him anyway."

"At least you'd have the memory of sleeping with him," Sims insisted.

"That's the thing," Lil said. "I don't think I could survive the memory if I didn't still have Justin."

Mac's bottom lip poked out, sweetly and sincerely, hurting for Lil.

Hinton wrapped her arm around Lil's back and laid her head on Lil's shoulder. June stood behind Lil and laid her head on top of Lil's. Sims reached across the table with both of her hands and held onto Lil's.

"Now boarding Delta flight 5039 nonstop to New York's LaGuardia Airport."

Lil had only enough time to give them a key to her place in case of an emergency and make them swear they wouldn't tell Justin where she was.

16

Act III, Take Three

Lil slept hard on the plane. The entire flight was silent in her head. She didn't hear the cart bumping along the sides of the seats, or the pilot's voice making announcements on the speaker, or the excited crowd of Alabamians loudly talking about their plans for their Christmas in New York, not even the tray going down and up next to her. She heard none of it. Total, unconscious sleep took her.

"Miss," the flight attendant said touching Lil's shoulder. "Ma'am, we've deplaned," she said as Lil looked at her.

"What?"

It took Lil a few seconds to realize where she was. She was the only passenger on the plane. She stood dizzily, her ponytail all bed-headed, her mouth dry. She had cried off all her makeup back at June's house. She saw the pilot deplaning and other flight attendants rolling their suitcases out of the plane. The attendant checked the overhead bin and found Lil's carryon and handed it to her. Lil walked down the aisle to the exit, holding onto the seats as she passed them, still half asleep.

She walked into the airport and stood there trying to remember what she was supposed to do next. The drunken fog of exhaustion held on tightly. Oh yeah, she remembered. A driver was supposed to be in the baggage area with her name on a sign. He had given up minutes earlier when it appeared to him that she wasn't in the crowd of passengers who had collected their luggage already, and he was walking around looking for the attractive blonde Mr. Guwen had described to him. Lil walked toward what she hoped would soon be her baggage carousel. Her driver was walking toward her with her name on the sign up against his leg. They passed each other. She woke enough to find her way to baggage and discover her lonely suitcases on their merry-go-round ride alone. An airport employee was moving them for the next batch of luggage that had already arrived. She rolled the miss-matching suitcases to a bench and called Mr. Guwen.

"I'm so sorry. I didn't sleep even 30 minutes last night," she explained the predicament of missing his driver.

"That must have been some cast party. It's fine, Lil. Sit still. I'll call the driver to come back to you at baggage. I'm going to take very good care of you while you're in New York. I want you in that bed. From the foyer, the right corner bedroom. I won't be home until 11 or so anyway. Sweet dreams," he added.

He was nice, Lil thought. She hoped he had a real bed waiting for her, still sore from Auggie's futon. She just wanted to brush her teeth and go to sleep.

201

Lil had been to New York three times before with the girls, so it wasn't a sin to rest her eyes on the ride to Mr. Guwen's apartment. The driver turned into a gorgeous motor court and helped her out of the car.

"Oh, it's beautiful!" she exclaimed about every part of the building.

"All limestone," the driver pointed out to her, "just like the Empire State Building."

She wondered if any of the stone had come from an Alabama quarry. The thought of being in New York, wrapped in a tower of Alabama rock felt comforting.

The driver took Lil's luggage up for her. She entered the unit behind him. While he went to put her bags in her room, Lil walked through the foyer into the living room to have a look. Stunning was too weak a word. She dug through her purse to give the driver a few dollars as he returned from the bedroom where he had placed her bags.

"Miss," he said, "Mr. Guwen has paid for you. Please put your money away," he smiled.

She knew she had a month to take the tour, so she brushed her teeth and went straight to bed. She slept for hours.

She woke rested, got up and pulled back the curtain. Manhattan. Time Warner Center and the Columbus Circle Monument out of her bedroom window, Trump International Tower just up the street. One side of her mouth twitched to a momentary smile that disappeared as she remembered. She closed her eyes, decided to focus on everything new, and inhaled the fresh start.

She went into her bathroom and started the shower. She stepped back to the bedroom for the bathroom items she'd packed and went back into the bath. While she watched the drops falling from the showerhead, she felt her body accepting the new energy her sleep had provided. She was relieved to be here. She would enjoy her time alone, meeting new people and welcoming the healing that comes with time and distance. She would dive into all the adventure of what New York had to offer her.

She undressed and stepped into the shower. She adjusted the water that was too hot and let it wash over her. She bathed and shampooed. She reached past Mr. Guwen's oversized guest towel to the smaller one she had packed. She had thoroughly thought through her stay with Mr. Guwen and considered the awkwardness of his having to contend with her wet towels. Not knowing before she arrived if his place would have a laundry, she packed her own towels. She noticed a plush red robe on a mahogany hanger, along with slippers and an engraved card, welcoming the "Guest" to enjoy. She felt of its extravagant fabric, caressed her cheek with the sleeve, and ran her finger along the golden monogrammed threads of the cursive "G." She placed her clean foot on top of the slipper, resisting the urge to let her foot sink inside its softness, and saw that the size would "fit all." She reached for her own robe and walked out of the bath barefooted.

She dressed and poked her head in the other rooms, the white galley kitchen, the gracious dining room, both facing the city views. She walked through the living room quickly to steal a peek at Mr. Guwen's master room before he got home. It had lush, green park views, the same as the living room. She made her way back to the living room and took it all in, the parquet floors, the Juliet balcony, the white, leather furniture, but mostly, the uncommon New York sight of green. No matter where she stood in the room, Lil had a clear view straight into the Central Park trees as if she were out among them, late at night, alone. She would start Act III over again, right here. Where else could be better than New York City?

Lil noticed a full-color booklet about the building's history on the small Duncan Phyfe table to her right. She browsed through it. Robert A. M. Stern Architects worked with the Zeckendorf developers who had bought the land for the building from a shipping family, the Goulandris, for $401 million. She pondered why the extra $1 million, like $.99 added to $400. There had to be a story there. She had a fleeting thought of wondering if Justin's family in Greece knew the Goulandris. Then she reminded herself that she was supposed to be forgetting. Lil kept reading. Phillip Guwen's unit was in the lower section of the structure called "the house" facing Central Park. The limestone came from a quarry in Indiana. Oh, well, she thought, replacing the booklet. She turned and stretched out theatrically on the tufted, white chaise lounge. She jumped when she saw a man out of the side of her eye.

"I'm sorry to surprise you," he said, smiling.

Phillip Guwen had come home.

"My leading lady," he said, slightly bowing his head theatrically. "Welcome to my neck of the woods," he smiled.

17

Break the Chain

Justin gave up his watch at Lil's townhouse around 2 a.m. Lil wasn't answering his calls. He went home and sat on his sofa. He woke stretched out on it the next morning, late. He called her. No answer. It was Tuesday. He would sit in on his department meeting, and then he'd call her again. After work he went back to her house, but again no answer at the door. He called again, her cell and her office. No Lil. He went back to her house later, late enough that she should have been there, but she wasn't.

Wednesday. He thought he'd drop by Hot's to try to find her at coffee. She wasn't there. None of the crowd was. He didn't want to concern her parents in this personal matter as a first resort, only a last one. He went to his office and started searching her friends' names, searching for numbers where he could reach them. It was late, so he decided he'd call them the next day.

He called Sims at 6:45 a.m. to catch her before her first gym class.

"Hi, Justin," she almost seemed to expect his call. "No, she's not staying with me. No, I don't know where she is. I'll let her know you're looking for her."

"Justin!" Mac was overacting. "What a surprise! . . . Lil? No, I haven't seen her. She's just busy, I'm sure. I'll let her know 'you really needed to see her.' "

"Well, Justin, you'd know where she is sooner than I would these days," Hinton said, resisting the urge to call him "Sailor." "I'll let her know you're looking."

"Hmmm," he thought. "They all said they'd let her know."

"June," Justin said into the phone, "will you please meet me for coffee? Please."

Justin wasn't buying the stone wall. He suspected Lil was staying with one of them. He met June at Jack's in Homewood at 8 a.m. and started telling her about him and Lil.

"No matter how I asked her to dinner or a movie," Justin said, "she never realized I was asking her out on a date. She was a student the first six months, so I couldn't date her. Then we'd been friends long enough that it just seemed to be friends having dinner. I talked to her father about my feelings on Thanksgiving Day. I have his permission to pursue her affections. I went to Hot's that day to talk to you all about her, but I got stuck in traffic and got there too late, and she was there already. I've had feelings for Lil for a long time, June, and I needed to hold her in my arms and kiss her. When your date thinks she's at dinner with a friend, it's a little weird to start kissing her. I should have been more direct with her, but I didn't want to lose her friendship. I started the conversation in front of her fireplace that night. We've been kissing ever since."

Justin told June of his time together with Lil over the past weeks. When he finished explaining what happened with Julieta and the play, June had to wipe tears from her eyes at the romance of it all.

"It's my hormones," she said as Justin left the table and came back with a few napkins for her. "It's just that Lil has waited and dreamed so long about these kinds of things, with all of us telling her they'd never happen," she wiped her tears. "She's always writing the play of her life in her head. She always planned to drop the curtain on Act II in Tuscaloosa, and start Act III with Mr. Forever. She's our romantic. I'm rambling, but I have to ask," June said, wondering if Lil had kept anything else a secret. "Justin, did y'all, well, you know, did ja?" she blurted out.

"No," Justin said. "Not that I wasn't holding myself back every night, but I knew, with Lil, it was worth the wait. I love her, June."

Those words made June cry even harder into her napkin.

"I have to fix things, June. Her birthday is coming up, and I'm planning this trip--" Justin started, but June jerked down her napkin at the word birthday.

She was suddenly concerned.

"Justin, you have to go to her!" she said, snatching her phone from her purse.

"I'm trying to find her! That's why I'm here! Is she staying with you?" he asked.

She hit a number on her speed dial, and looked up at him, "No!"

The phone was dialing the wrong number, and June started over, again looking up at Justin.

"She's in New York!" she shouted, getting frustrated with her phone that was now ringing on speaker. "She's an understudy in that play."

"Hey, hot mama!" Mac's voice answered.

"Break the chain! Break the chain!" June shouted at Mac.

"What's going on?!" Mac asked eagerly, as though she were expecting some sort of report from June.

"No time! Break the chain!" June shouted as she slid a napkin toward herself and snapped her fingers at Justin to hand her a pen. He did.

"She said he'd be smooth and suave," Mac said. "Was he suave?"

"Of course he was!" June said, "Now break the damn chain already, Mac!"

"Fifteen!" Mac shouted. "Call me back!"

June wrote "15" on the napkin, hung up from Mac, and dialed Hinton.

"June, what's going on?" Justin watched the scene.

"Talk to me, gorgeous," Hinton answered.

"Break the chain!" June shouted.

"Convincing, was he?" Hinton asked, remembering Lil said he would be.

"Positively!" June shouted.

"Apartment 3LM!" Hinton squealed. "Call me back!"

June had conference called the others on her way to Jack's to let them know she was meeting with Justin near her house. They were waiting on a report of the meeting.

"June?" Justin asked as June kept dialing, this time to Sims, but she got Sims' voicemail, so she tried her again.

"It's the chain!" June explained to Justin, waiting for Sims to pick up. "Apparently a weaker one than Lil had hoped for," June said dialing. "Lil gave each one of us a part of her address in New York, so no single one of us, no one link would be weak and give in and give it to you. But she didn't tell us everything you just told me!"

"CPW," Sims answered without saying hello.

Mac had already called her. Sims was glad to give the information. She hadn't agreed in the first place to keep Justin in the dark.

"And I've got the name," June said, pulling a scratch piece of paper from her purse and adding a name to the address on the napkin."

June tossed her phone back in her purse, opened the napkin, and put all the information together.

"Phillip Guwen, 15 CPW, Number 3LM" she read it as she wrote it, and slid it over to Justin, adding "wherever that is."

"Central Park West," he told her. "This is where she's staying?" he asked. "Who's Phillip Guwen?"

"One of the play's producers," June answered. "He's letting her stay with him."

Justin didn't like the sound of that.

"Justin, Lil may have been all talk, but she said at coffee that last time you joined us, that she was going to lose her virginity before her 26th birthday. Lil has given up on Mr. Right. She's decided to start Act III again with 'Mr. Whoever's Right Here in My Bed.' You have to find her!"

Justin knew Lil well enough to know she had just been talking at Hot's that day, but he also knew her heart was broken at the moment. He didn't know this Phillip Guwen, but he knew men, and Lil was beautiful and sweet and smart and funny. And vulnerable and weak and crushed, if she felt anything like he did. And she was staying in this man's house. Justin reached over and kissed June on the cheek.

"I'll walk you to your car," he said, standing up.

"I don't walk, Justin; I waddle," June said. "And you don't have time to wait on that! Just go!" she shouted.

He did.

June balled into her napkin, and started the conference call to the weak links of the broken chain on her way to the toilet.

18

Manley

"Who could that be?" Lil wondered. She was alone in this New York apartment late at night, and someone was knocking on the door. Phillip wasn't in yet. She wasn't tall enough to see through the peephole. Should she open a New York door?

"Who is it?" she called.

There was a second of pause on the other side where Justin stood, as he let his head fall back, his knees buckle slightly, and his hand touch his chest in relief at the sound of Lil's voice. He had gotten there fast. If anyone could work a plane schedule, it was Justin, but it was Christmas time, so getting there at all was difficult. Getting up to the apartment had not been easy either, but Justin's parents had many benefactors, some they'd gone to medical school with, now doctors in New York, whose desires to serve in missions were outweighed by time constraints and understandable fears of third-world dangers and diseases. Not everyone hears the call to mission work, but others gladly offered financial support in admiration of those who did. Justin's name was always included on the notes that had accompanied their checks to his parents.

"It's Justin," his voice met her ears.

Lil hesitated a couple of seconds wondering how?

She unlocked and opened the door.

Everything rushed at her, her feelings for Justin and the scene with Julieta.

"Never open a door in New York City when you can't see who's on the other side of it," Justin said.

He had lived in Midtown West at one time, better known as Hell's Kitchen. He knew this city.

"How?" Lil simply asked him.

"Well, at first, you might think your chain is weak, but in fact, your chain is strong," he said.

"They told you?" Lil said.

"They might be the Wednesday firing squad, but they know a love story when they hear it," Justin said. "Lil, let me talk to you."

Lil stepped back from the door and let Justin enter. He didn't notice his elaborate surroundings.

"You by yourself?" he asked as she closed the door.

Lil nodded. "Phillip works late. Mr. Guwen," she changed it.

Justin wished she had said "Mr. Guwen" first.

"I'm just his guest here, so . . .," Lil thought about it, " . . . but I guess he wouldn't mind."

Justin didn't care if Guwen minded. He was coming in, and he was getting Lil out.

"Lil, I love you," he said with no time to waste. "I wouldn't hurt you for any reason ever. You've had time to think about what you saw, and there's nothing else I can tell you about it. All I can ask is for you to believe me."

The door opened, and Phillip Guwen walked in with a bottle of champagne.

"Did I interrupt anything, Lil?" he asked, sizing up Justin.

Phillip was a handsome man, tall, starting to gray at the temples prematurely. At 6'1" and broad shouldered, he made an impressive entrance, practiced during his years in theatre.

"Justin, this is Phillip Guwen, a producer for the play and my gracious host here. Phillip," Lil said, "this is . . . my friend, Justin Rock. Justin flew up to see me unexpectedly. He just got here a few seconds before you did," she explained, not wanting Guwen to think she had brought a man up to his apartment.

"Justin, good to meet you. Any friend of Lil's," and they shook hands. "Please, let me pour you a drink. I was about to order up some food for me and Lil, but you're wel--" he was saying when Justin interrupted.

"That won't be necessary. I'm taking Lil out, if she'll do me the honor," Justin looked at Lil.

He wasn't here for Guwen's champagne and hor d'oeuvres. He was here for Lil.

"Oh," Lil said. "I'm not dressed, but," she looked from Justin to Phillip and back to Justin.

She didn't know what Justin might say if she declined, and she didn't want a scene in Mr. Guwen's apartment. She wanted to talk to Justin, at least to try to salvage their friendship, but she didn't want to appear rude to Phillip who had opened his home to her.

Phillip had called on his ride home to tell Lil he was looking forward to a relaxing night at home, toasting his next production, and he was just glad to know he would get to share the night with her. He had sent her flowers two days before with a note thanking her for dropping everything and flying out the way she had, telling her the building's private chef would be preparing a special late-night dinner for the two of them. He told her he should have reminded her to pack at least one evening gown. She would be representing their production at different events, and he would have his girl at Sak's pick out a gown especially for her, as well as a bathing suit in case she wanted to swim laps in the pool.

The store had delivered two packages a few hours earlier. Lil had spread the gown out on the chaise for Phillip to approve of the store's selection when he got home. She had left the swimsuit in the box. It was quite skimpy, and she had no intentions of wearing it. Phillip had been such a gracious, attentive host. He had taken her to dinner the second night and lunch today. He had insisted she join him, saying he hated eating alone, and if she didn't accompany him that he would be sitting at a table for one.

"You look beautiful," Justin assured her. "Mr. Guwen wouldn't want to keep us apart after my long flight here," he added. "Just grab a coat. It's cold."

Lil walked to her room to brush her teeth and get her jacket.

"Justin, please, come join me in the den while you wait on Lil," Guwen said jovially and loud enough for Lil to hear as she walked to her room.

Justin took the few steps into the den. A vase crammed with at least three-dozen coral roses sat on the buffet, the card still attached. A butter yellow gown, the tags still hanging on it, was displayed on a chaise lounge. Guwen was working fast, and if Justin was correct, whether Lil knew it or not, in Guwen's mind, the last nights with Lil had been preliminary work.

"Talk down in Alabama has it," Guwen said pouring himself some Scotch, his jovial tone gone, and his voice lower, "that Lil's flight here was something of a red-eye. It seems her eyes were really red, some misunderstanding with a cheating beau," he said.

"Yes, the one misunderstanding in a million that really was innocent," Justin said, shaking his head no to the glass Guwen was offering him.

Guwen laughed.

"Of course it was, Justin. It stops being fun when the trap slams shut on our foot, doesn't it? Then it's all gnaw, gnaw, gnaw, work, work, work. And you flew up here to win her trust back," Guwen continued. "There's a funny thing about trust, Justin. Doubt. Doubt always has a way of creeping back in. Lil," Guwen said smiling again, seeing Lil come into the room. They all walked to the door.

"Don't keep my girl out too late. I need her in the bed," Guwen said looking at Justin, "rested," he added, smiling at Lil,

215

then looking back at Justin. "Justin, let me call my driver to pull my car around for you. I hate to think of a good ole Alabama boy trying to find his way around this big jungle of ours," Guwen grinned. "I think I'd feel better having Lil in *my* car."

"Not necessary," Justin said escorting Lil out, not playing Guwen's game. "We aren't going far. The whole island is only thirteen miles long. Alabama has driveways longer than that."

Justin followed Lil then looked back in at Guwen who stood in the doorway.

"Don't wait up," Justin said low enough that only Guwen could hear him.

19

An Apple in the Big Apple

Justin whistled for a cab.

"89 Mercer Street," he said to the driver.

That would be the only conversation in the taxi. Justin resisted the urge to take Lil's hand. He had lost that privilege for now. At Bar 89, Lil answered Justin's first question with "Booth." Lil sat on the booth side, and Justin sat in a chair across from her. He pulled his cell phone from his pocket and laid it on the table.

"You got an iPhone?" Lil said, looking at the new phone.

"Yes, I bought it today."

She didn't know why the realization that he'd broken their phone pact stung, after all that had transpired already, but it did. And the thought of Justin standing in the Verizon store before catching his plane made his spontaneous New York attempt at reconciliation seem far less romantic, Lil thought. It wouldn't work in a play.

"Actually," Justin said, "I bought two of them."

"What?" Lil said.

"Yes, do you know the maintenance supervisor at the Alabama Theatre?"

"No," Lil said.

"Mr. Alvarez?"

"Oh, yes, I think I know who you're talking about," Lil remembered.

"I dropped the other one off for him," Justin explained.

"Why would you do that?" she asked.

"Well, I need to be able to FaceTime. I was expecting the call several minutes ago," he said as the waiter came over for their order. "I don't normally order for you," Justin said to Lil, "but you might want to try the burger. It's one of three reasons I brought you to Soho," he explained.

Lil nodded to the waiter who said he'd place the order and bring them two waters. Justin's phone started vibrating, and he answered it.

"¿Señor Alvarez, cómo está?" Justin said into the phone. "Un momento, let me put you on FaceTime."

Justin got up and sat next to Lil in her booth so she could see Mr. Alvarez.

"Buenas noches, Justín. Estoy bien. ¿Cómo está?" Mr. Alvarez said.

"Bien, bien," Justin replied. "Señor Alvarez, I have Miss Swann here with me."

"¿Pueden verme?" Mr. Alvarez asked.

"Yes, we can see you, Señor," Justin answered.

Lil was so confused.

"Miss Angélica, you are so talented in the play," Mr. Alvarez said to Lil.

"Thank you, Señor Alvarez," Lil said sincerely. "We couldn't have these productions if it weren't for you and your staff. Thank you so much for your hard work."

Lil thought she heard a girl start crying in the background, and she looked at Justin, confused.

"Miss Angélica," the man continued. "Lo siento, so sorry for my daughter's behavior," he said.

"What?" Lil said quietly to Justin so that Mr. Alvarez couldn't hear her, not knowing what Mr. Alvarez meant.

Justin pointed to the phone, letting Lil know to keep listening.

"Julieta, she is a good girl, but she has gotten with bad friends, and what she did to sit with Señor Justín in his chair with him was wrong. She will say the Rosary many times, Miss Angélica."

Lil was surprised. She put her hands over her mouth. Mr. Alvarez disappeared from the screen, and the view wobbled around, then it stilled, and Julieta appeared on the screen.

"I'm so sorry, Miss Swann," Julieta was crying. "Profesor didn't like when I sat on his lap," she said.

Without all her makeup, and making these apologies in front of her father, Julieta looked 15-years-old.

"Profesor pushed me away and told me to stop. I am so sorry this hurt you," Julieta cried.

"Julieta," Lil said sweetly with tears welled in her eyes, her face showing her acceptance and surprise, "thank you so much for saying you are sorry. It is a hard thing to do. I'm sure your

219

father was upset with you when he heard these things because he loves you, and he doesn't want you to be this way with any man, but I am certain tonight he can tell you he is proud."

Justin found Lil's hand. He wasn't expecting Lil to say anything to Julieta and her father, but what she had said was perfect.

"You are so beautiful, Julieta," Lil continued, "just as you are tonight without all that makeup. Do not be in any hurry to find a man. Get that college degree. The right man, he and you will find each other when the time is right. Watch for him. Julieta, wait for him."

"Thank you," Julieta said. "You are sweet," Julieta said, giving the phone back to her father.

Justin turned the screen to himself, and Lil put her hands back over her mouth again.

"Señor, otra vez, lo siento por lo de mi hija," Mr. Alvarez said.

"Gracias. Thank you, Señor Alvarez," Justin said. "Adios."

Lil threw herself into Justin's arms right there in the booth. He got the good kissin. She would keep the Verizon store scene in her script. And she would add a song.

"Lil?" a Southern accent ended the moment.

In Lil's mind, the voice made the sound of the turntable needle scratching across the record before she could even put music with the scene.

"Lil, is that you?"

"Oh, hey, Miss Waltha!" Lil said knowing her mother would be calling any minute after Miss Waltha let her know about her unexpected encounter with her daughter slobbering all over some long-haired hippie in a restaurant in New York City at going on midnight.

"Your mama told us to watch for you, that you had gotten a big Broadway role, and I told her the odds of us seeing you in a city of 8 million people was slim to none, but it's a small world, idnit? We just stepped in here to use the potties, but you should see 'em. You couldn't pay me to pee in here. I'm gonna have to call your mama and tell her I'm lookin at you right now!" she said, digging in her purse for her phone.

"I'll tell her!" Lil insisted. "You just enjoy your trip," Lil said, mentally editing this moment out of her scene. "It was so good to see you."

Justin was right about the burgers. Lil wasn't even hungry until the waiter brought hers to her. They talked only briefly about what had happened with Julieta, and they would never talk about it again.

"My type?" Justin asked, repeating Lil's words.

"Exotic," Lil answered.

"Exotic?" Justin laughed. "Lil, if you knew where I grew up, you'd know you are the exotic one. I'm sitting in a booth in New York City! If you were paying close attention to the scenes in our story, you'd know you're the one, Lil."

How did he know they had scenes in a story?

"Tell me about this Broadway play," Justin said.

"It's shutting down in two weeks instead of four. They're keeping it open for the Christmas and New Year's crowd, and then they're closing it. I'm done in six more days, unless I sign papers with Mr. Guwen, but there's no point in that," Lil explained. "Everything behind the scenes is falling apart. Ticket sells are dismal without Merry. Phillip is trying to save face with the other two producers since he's the one who signed her. They've made more money than they even hoped to make, but he needed to get contracts signed on his next production before this show closed early, and he managed to do that today. He wanted to celebrate tonight."

"That means you'll still be here over Christmas," Justin said.

"My first one ever not at home," Lil said, "and with Peter away, it'll be hard for my parents."

"You don't owe this crowd here anything," Justin said.

"I made a verbal commitment through the next few days, so I owe them that," Lil explained. Justin nodded.

"Still, a week more of Broadway," Justin smiled, pretending he was happy for her.

"Eh," Lil said, as though she were disappointed in the whole experience. "It isn't what I thought, not that I thought I was going on stage or anything," she added. "I'm third in line for that, but it's just as well. I wouldn't go on even if both of the others broke all four of their legs."

"Why not?" Justin asked.

"Well, in this production, Rodney drops trou every night, but not until he rips Angelica completely naked from her throat to her waist, then rips her gown from the bottom up. And the curtain doesn't close until she's been thoroughly rapped upon," Lil finished, looking up at Justin.

"I'm a girl from Alabama in Manhattan, with a shot in a million at a Broadway play, who would refuse the role, because apparently, no matter how the opportunity is presented, I won't 'do it,' " she put in finger quotes. "It's the never-ending story of my life."

Justin started laughing, hard laughing, the vibrating, totally-into-the-complete-humor-of-it-all laughing. His arm down the back of the booth, he laid his head on Lil's shoulder with his face in her neck, and kept laughing. She started laughing with him.

"I love you," he said.

"So what are the other two reasons you brought me here?" Lil asked, remembering Justin had said he had three reasons.

"The bathrooms," he replied.

He took her to the bathrooms. She looked through the glass doors at the toilets.

"Huh," was all she could muster.

"Like peeing out in the open, isn't it?" he smiled.

Lil remembered her promise to herself to experience everything New York has to offer, and she went inside to see what would happen. She came out smiling.

"You're two for two," she told him. "Third reason?"

The third reason would require a quick walk up the street.

20

The 'ho' in "Soho"

"So when will they get here?" Lil asked about the two girls in whose tiny student studio Lil and Justin stood.

The girls were students at NYU Law School, with housing up the street from Bar 89. Justin's parents had been good friends with their parents, and Justin had known the girls most of their lives. They'd arranged for a friend to let Justin and Lil in the building.

"No idea," Justin answered, flipping on the lights.

It took him some serious persuasion on the walk from the restaurant to convince Lil to stay here for the night and get her things in the morning from Guwen's apartment. She argued all the way up to the studio that doing so would be the "height of rudeness," and, after Mr. Guwen's "more than gracious invitation and hospitality, socially unforgivable." She couldn't act on her other impulse of "at least having the common courtesy of calling him," but that alternative was "socially unthinkable" as it was well after midnight.

"If my mother knew I was returning that man's kindness with this inappropriate display of disregard, she'd disown me," Lil argued, looking around the apartment.

"And if your father knew you were staying with the man, he'd beat your mother to it," Justin said.

"I feel so bad," Lil continued, concerned. "I can just picture Phillip waiting up for me."

"Yeah, I can picture him waiting up for you, too," Justin said under his breath, his concern different from Lil's.

"All my things are there, and," Lil was saying, when Justin lifted a Louis Vuitton bag up to show her.

"Hinton's bag with some things she packed for you," Justin explained. "She met me at an off-ramp on my way to the airport. You left them a key to your place, and she agreed to pack an overnight bag for me for this situation."

"*Hinton*? Did you have to pick *Hinton* to pack the bag?" Lil asked wondering what leopard skin atrocity was waiting beyond that zipper.

If there were such a thing as underwear made out of cotton candy, Lil knew it was waiting for her in Hinton's bag. She wondered if Hinton had gone to her townhouse at all and packed any of her things or if she had found some still operating Frederick's of Hollywood in Crestwood on the way to the airport.

Justin and Lil eventually made themselves as comfortable as Lil could be, imposing on strangers, their legs stretched down the length of the sofa in opposite directions, each one's back against the opposite arm rest, facing each other. Lil would not hear of Justin being anywhere inappropriately near her when the two residents of the apartment showed up. She had embarrassed her mother, long distance, enough for one night.

"So where are you staying?" she asked him.

"I have a buddy who has a sofa in his office," Justin said, looking at her, drinking in that she was with him.

"I have to pay these girls," Lil said. "Six nights with a stranger in your home is weird."

"They're family friends. It's all good," Justin said. "They leave for break in a couple of days."

They looked at each other and smiled, both of them comfortable in the relief of being together.

"Lil, I want to take you somewhere," Justin started. "I want to show you a place that will help you understand me better."

"Where?" Lil asked.

"A village, a small tribal village in Ecuador," he said. "I spent time there when I was a boy. My parents started a medical clinic nearby. I was going a few weeks ago, but I postponed the trip. I have to finish a job I started there. For other reasons, it's the perfect place to take you. It isn't exactly beautiful," Justin admitted, "and, Lil, it's dangerous, so I want you to think about it while you're here. I would be with you all the time, and I would take my best care of you, but there's always danger to consider on this type of trip. I'll understand if you don't want to go. Do you have a passport?" he asked.

"Yes, from when I did my Spanish study in Cancun. Would I have to have any shots?" she asked.

"Yes," he answered.

"Will there be electricity?"

He shook his head no.

"Just think about it," he said.

"What's the name of the place, and I'll research it," Lil said.

Justin just laughed.

"You're so cute. Good luck with that search," he said. "Oh, I almost forgot. I got you something," he said, reaching over the back of the sofa and taking a beautifully wrapped gift from the sofa table.

Lil accepted the small, rectangular box and slowly opened it. She looked at the contents of the box, then down the length of the couch, into his eyes.

"Justin, how sweet," she said.

This was it, the huge gesture she knew she would recognize when she saw it, sitting on this second-hand sofa, in this dinky flat, wearing jeans and a T-shirt. Not at all how she'd imagined it, but simply perfect. This was the night she would say it.

"In case Hinton forgot to pack one," Justin said about the Oral B Soft 40 toothbrush Lil was holding.

"Justin," Lil said, changing her tone, "there's something I have to tell you."

"Okay. Should I brace myself for it?" he asked seriously.

She nodded.

Justin sat up straight and prepared himself for what she would say.

"I'm ready," he said.

"Justin," Lil said, "I love you."

He smiled at her antagonistically.

"You know I'm coming over there, right?" he said.

She smiled, and he was there, lying on top of the blanket she had spread over her legs, kissing her passionately. He stopped kissing her long enough to look into her eyes and say, "It's about time."

"I know," she agreed. "I had this stupid rule that you had to say it first," she admitted.

"Too bad you broke your own rule," he said then kissed her again.

She pushed his shoulders away from her and said, "No I didn't. You said it first. You said it that day in the rain."

"True, after you had already said it on the phone," he smiled, moving back in for a kiss, which she stopped.

"What are you talking about?"

"That day I met you at the ER for your father's faux heart attack."

Lil thought about it.

"Ahhh, no, that doesn't count. I was pretending you were my mother. I said, 'I love you' to calm my fictional mother's nerves since, allegedly, my imaginary father was having a fake heart attack."

"If you say so," Justin smiled.

"I *do* say so!" Lil said.

"My story will always be that you said it first," Justin teased her. "For the next hundred years, that's how I'll tell it."

"But that's not--"

"But that's what I'm telling our kids," he smiled, still teasing her, "right after I tell them you fainted when I kissed you at the end of our first date."

"Our kids?" Lil asked.

228

That time, she didn't stop him from kissing her.

"Whoa! Get a room!" the two girls joked as they walked in.

"Huh," Lil said quietly in Justin's ear, "I'm pretty sure I just heard my Mama drop dead."

Lil stepped into the hall to tell Justin goodnight.

"I'll pick you up at the airport when you get back," Justin said, caressing Lil's hand.

He was going to help her move her things over in the morning and was flying out right after. He had come to New York to find her, to prove to her he was innocent, and to get her out of Phillip Guwen's house. Lil looked down and watched his fingers softly touch hers. He reached in his pocket and pulled out a suede pouch. He stuck his thumb and index finger in the pouch and pulled out a chain with a beautiful cross on it.

"Merry Christmas, Lil," he said.

Lil looked at the cross. She had never seen one like it. Two entwined circles rested on the horizontal line of the cross.

"It's beautiful, Justin," she said reaching up to kiss him. "I have a gift for you on my dresser at home," she said as he clasped the chain around her neck. "If I had known, well, everything that has happened was going to happen, I would have gotten Hint to pack it. Of course, if I had known *everything* that was going to happen, I probably wouldn't even be here and . . ."

He kissed Lil softly in the middle of her rambling.

Justin gave her the iPhone and told her he'd be picking the other one up from Mr. Alvarez.

"I really need to see you while we're apart," he explained about FaceTime again.

He hadn't broken the phone pact after all. He opened the door for her to go inside, and waited to hear her lock it.

Janine was pulling out the sleeper from inside the sofa.

"Oh, you don't have to do that!" Lil rushed to help her.

She had to let these girls know that she really hadn't been raised by wolves. How embarrassing! She'd been in the hall smooching while this girl was struggling to fix her a place to sleep. She was sure they now thought Justin had hooked up with white trash.

"That's okay," Janine said. "This is where I'll sleep. Chloe and I alternate weeks taking the bed and the sofa," she explained. "There's a futon in that walk-in closet behind those doors," she said pointing to a pair of closet doors. "Sorry about the mess in there," Janine added about the closet.

"It's perfect," Lil smiled.

She waited on her turn in the tiny bath to brush her teeth and wash her face. The time had come to unzip the bag. Right on top was Justin's Christmas gift. Hinton had seen it on Lil's dresser, the watch with three different time zones on the face for when Justin was on his world travels. She'd give it to him in the morning before he left. Her clothes were right underneath.

"Huh. Turns out Hinton went shopping *and* to my place," Lil thought, holding up a crotchless, red lace body suit and a green T-shirt that read "L the V."

Lil slept in her clothes.

21

Googling Earth

L il couldn't help but search Google Earth during her free time the next day in New York. She was really nervous about this trip, scared, a better word. She zoomed in all over Ecuador. So much of it was rocky, volcanic terrain, softened by jungle canopies. The Mariscal Sucre Airport looked like a strip of asphalt, a short one at that, sandwiched in the middle of the financial district of Quito. It looked like an airstrip a small town like Eufaula or Opelika, Alabama, might have, and this was the country's capital. Thank goodness the larger new airport had opened. The view of the longitude, latitude Justin had given her of the village's location showed only the tops of jungle trees. The camera views were fascinating though, and exiting Google Earth was difficult for Lil.

The conference call to the girls about Justin's coming to New York, followed by their discussion of this trip didn't calm her worries. None of her friends was excited about the location, even though they hoped a trip together would seal the deal with Lil and Justin. Even Hinton's jokes about "jungle lovin" and Mac's discussion about Justin in a Tarzan cloth didn't lighten Lil's worry. Their only news from home was that June had no signs of labor yet with just a little more than a week to go, according to the due date.

Lil stretched out on the sofa in the Soho apartment and tried to focus on her latest blog, "Don't Let the Lyric Theatre Crumble," about helping Birmingham Landmarks, Inc.'s "Light up the Lyric" campaign to renovate the historic Lyric Theatre. Instead, her fingers clicked their way to a map of South America. She looked at earthquake-prone Chili and swallowed hard. Next, her eyes calculated how close she'd be to the remnants of the Hugo Chavez regime and the current turmoil, and she didn't like it. She'd be even closer to Colombia. All she knew about Colombia was what Claudia, a student from Bogota, had told her college geography class, all having to do with the drug cartels there. Lil figured those guys were always on prop planes to the jungles of Ecuador checking on their crops. She was hoping the village would be close to the coast or to Peru, not that she knew anything about Peru, until Justin explained the often dangerous border issues Ecuador has with Peru and apologized that this wouldn't be a beach trip either. They would be a few degrees past central Ecuador, one step out of the Andes, slightly east, into the Oriente, part of the Amazon rainforest. Lil decided the best option for calming her worries was to quit researching, but she couldn't.

She looked up Ecuadorian tribes, and the pictures backed up her imagination. The photos were reminders of the *National Geographic* magazines that rested on her grandfather's ottoman when she was a child. She was surprised at how moderate the temperatures literally at the equator were going to be, at least compared to the summer ones that Alabama experienced. She was used to humidity. She'd need shorts and jeans. The days would be perfect twelve-hour days, 6 to 6. She hoped to see some monkeys. Justin assured her she would. He told her monkeys were almost as commonplace as squirrels are in Alabama. She reread Justin's email explaining her flight arrangements.

Lil would be traveling alone since Justin would be going a week before her. Her plane would leave the Birmingham-Shuttlesworth International Airport for Atlanta's Hartsfield-Jackson Airport, from there, direct to Quito, Ecuador. The new, larger Quito International Airport on the Tababela plateau was open for business, and that would be her first landing in Ecuador. From there, a much smaller plane would leave from a private hanger with only thirteen other passengers, making a second stop, then a final descent to a short landing strip behind a chain-link fence topped with barbed wire, in the middle of Nowhere, as the place unofficially was called, next to a 30' X 20' cinder block building that she would pass through and out the front door. Justin promised he would be there waiting. His instructions included her not striking up any conversations with passengers starting on the Atlanta leg of her flight, and not because Justin was a jealous person; he wasn't. She would discover the other passengers were using his advice, too, though they'd never met him, as their eyes assumed the worst about those around them.

Justin was right about researching the village. Lil tried some other ideas. She decided to type in his parents' names thinking maybe some article about them with photos in the village might exist. She found two articles, but no photos. His parents had established numerous medical clinics in places in South America. They also had started Christian churches. They had done a phenomenal job raising funds in the states. Justin had told her they were both deceased, but he never had told her how. She just assumed illness, especially considering their vocations.

The second article was written about their deaths. Suicides five years ago. Their bodies were found with one other missionary in what had been determined to be a group suicide. Justin was mentioned as their one surviving child, a student at Duke University School of Medicine at the time. She knew he had a double major in science and language, but she never knew he had been in medical school. Would he ever want to talk about this tragedy? Certainly he needed to talk about it, especially with her.

"Hey, girl," Janine said, coming in from her last class before she and Chloe left for Christmas break. "Let's go get those shots."

Justin had booked an appointment for Lil at a clinic in Manhattan to get the vaccinations she would need for the trip so they'd have time to take effect. Janine said she'd go with her.

Lil wondered if these two friends knew about Justin's parents. She wouldn't ask.

Lil woke before the sun rose on Christmas morning to the sound of the iPhone vibrating. Justin sent her a text. She enlarged the photo and laughed at the three faces looking at her: Justin, her dad, and Auggie, all wearing camo, clearly in the woods, deer hunting.

"Don't worry. I'll have your dad home in time to share lunchtime with your mother!" Justin's text read.

Lil texted June.

"Tell Auggie thanks for taking Justin and my dad hunting!"

"Thank Auggie?" June answered. "He didn't sleep a wink last night! He was too excited that Justin was finally going to teach him how to hunt with a spear. Auggie thought bow and spear season would never get here!"

Lil was confused. She remembered the bow on Justin's wall that she had always thought was art.

A few hours later, her phone vibrated again, and she smiled at the second photo of the day: Justin, her mom, and her dad posing in their aprons and hairnets as they helped serve Christmas lunch to the crowd at the Johnny Mack Mission. She'd never seen such big smiles on her parents' faces. They FaceTimed her at dinner. She had takeout. They were at the table around her mom's usual dishes. Justin joined hands with her parents and led them in prayer. Lil had never heard Justin pray.

" 'For unto us a child is born, unto us a son is given: and the government shall be upon his shoulder: and his name shall be called Wonderful, Counsellor, The mighty God, The everlasting Father, The Prince of Peace.'[15] Thirty-three years later, that same child, now a man, died, nailed to a cross, taking onto himself the world's sins. 'Then said Jesus, Father, forgive them; for they know not what they do.'[16] On the third day, an angel of the Lord declared, ' . . he is risen, as he said . . ..'[17] And the arisen Lord told His disciples, 'All power is given unto me in heaven and in earth. Go ye therefore, and teach all nations, baptizing them in the name of the Father, and of the Son, and of the Holy Ghost: Teaching them to observe all things whatsoever I have commanded you: and, lo, I am with you always, [even] unto the end of the world.'[18] Today, dear Father God, we remember, and we thank You for this Child, our Savior, Your only begotten Son, Jesus. Amen."

Two days later, Justin picked Lil up at the airport. Their embrace was all she had hoped it would be. He took her straight to a clinic in downtown Birmingham. He hadn't told her she needed to have blood drawn for the trip. He had gone for his workup while she was in New York. He introduced her to the staff because, of course, he had worked with them before. The nurse came in the room to give Justin his paperwork while Lil squeezed the stress ball.

"Clean bill of health, Justin," the nurse said, reaching the paper out to him as he leaned against the counter with his arms crossed.

"Just hand it to Lil," Justin instructed the nurse without uncrossing his arms.

Lil looked at Justin as she took the paper, and he raised his eyebrows to her. Lil looked at the paper. She realized he'd had most of these tests for her benefit. Justin had been tested for everything under the sun, and he wanted Lil to know.

Lil's mouth fell open, embarrassed at what everyone there must be thinking about her, about her and Justin. She sat up a little and pushed the paper onto the chair seat under her bottom to hide it from anyone else who might walk in.

"You're so cute," Justin said, shaking his head.

Afterward, they went by June's for Lil's car, and Lil followed Justin to his house to visit before she left for Montgomery again on business for the next couple of days. She had some getting ahead to do for work since there would be no Wi-Fi in her jungle retreat.

Montgomery would be something of a jungle itself as the heated session was coming to a close, and outsiders had converged on the town--elected officials, media, lobbyists, fourth graders' buses packed with little learners, citizens fighting for their causes, shoppers and museum-goers from smaller towns. A jungle analogy started in the capital in the mid-1900s with a legend that capuchin monkeys had once escaped from Montgomery's forgotten Oak Park Zoo. Lil knew the story was true. She had a videotaped interview with the teenaged mastermind, a man now in his 80s, his renegade youth visible in his twinkling blue eyes as he told her the story of how he and three of his culprit-compadres had sneaked into that zoo as young boys, stretched a ladder across the moat that kept the capuchins and woolly monkeys on what was called Monkey Island, and watched the creatures cross that ladder and run wild around the zoo. He said the story was exaggerated about the animals overtaking the town, claiming many went right back across the ladder to the island where they knew their food, water, and safety had always been. But he wouldn't go public with his story, at least not until his friends had passed on, not convinced the statute of limitations had expired. Lil assured him she'd keep his secret until that time. She had a couple of meetings under the canopy of Montgomery's famed, green-roofed buildings and other work there to wrap up before she left for Ecuador.

Justin was flying out in a few days, and she would depart by herself a week later. He told Lil he had work in the village he needed to finish, and he wanted to make sure everything was ready for her.

Justin was washing a small load of clothes, and they would be all he would pack. He had instructed Lil to do the same. She was following all of his instructions to the letter. She was scared about where they were going. His parents' deaths frightened her, and they happened only a few hours' drive away from where they would be staying.

"Oh, here, take this!" she said holding out his health report from the clinic.

He smiled at her.

"You needed to know," he simply said about his good checkup, leaving the form in her hand. "I had no doubt, and I didn't want you to either. Let me tell you something about the teachings of the Apoya Tribe," Justin said, leaving his packing to sit by her.

"The tribal priests teach that a woman's body accepts and recognizes the first man she ever lays with. He becomes a part of her, part of her actual physical makeup. If any other man

238

were to enter there, her body would recognize that he did not belong there. Her body, every cell, would begin to fight this forbidden presence, which could lead to illness and worse for the woman. The Apoyas teach that when a woman joins physically with a man, that his god becomes her god. In their jungles, it matters who his god is. A 12-year-old boy hearing these things doesn't forget them. I cannot dwell on what ifs, and I cannot set back the clock. I only can tell you that I was safe. The only woman I won't use protection with is my bride," he explained.

"Is this tribe in the village we're going to?" she asked, uncomfortably changing the subject.

"Yes," Justin said.

"You were right," she admitted. "The internet wasn't much help."

He pulled a couple of duffle bags from a closet, stuck an old pair of running shoes in one, and tossed the bags to a corner of the room to pack later.

"I searched your parents, thinking maybe there was an article about them with photographs of the village."

Justin stopped and looked up at her. He knew what she would have found with that search. Their eyes studied each other.

"You can talk to me about it," Lil said.

"Nothing to talk about," he said, walking into the kitchen.

Lil followed him.

"Justin, you probably ought to talk about it."

"The suicides?" he asked.

She nodded.

"They weren't suicides, Lil," Justin said.

"But the newspapers . . . how sure can you be?" she asked.

"This sure," he said, pulling his shirt off so she could look at his scar.

He walked to her.

"A clinic was attacked when I was 10 years old. We were asleep. I woke to my father lifting me out of bed and out a window. 'Run to the trees and keep running!' he told me," Justin continued. "He went to help get others out. I ran to the trees and kept running, just like he told me. Then I turned around. I couldn't leave them. I ran back, even harder than I'd run away. I was 10. I wasn't leaving without my parents. A spear pierced my shoulder. I saw the attackers. They took the bodies and arranged them. There were no suicides, even though the papers reported there had been. Papers don't cover these tribes unless an American or other foreigner is involved in an incident. These tribes decide their laws, they tend to their dead, and they provide their own justice," Justin said and continued. "That's all I remember from that night. I passed out. My father found me. They survived that attack. They had run, too. They took me, eventually, to the place we are going, if you still want to join me. Maybe you shouldn't, Lil. I haven't slept well since I asked you to go. Maybe I'm being selfish. That was over twenty years ago. The attack my parents were killed in happened fifteen years later, a long way from this village. But I've changed my mind about the whole idea of you . . . I'm sorry I . . ."

Lil pressed her lips into his and quieted him, calmed him, comforted him, and excited him.

240

Justin was leaving on New Year's Day. All Lil wanted to do for New Year's Eve was stop by to see her parents, make a brief appearance at Mac's big bash, then spend the rest of the night at home in front of her fireplace in Justin's arms.

"I can arrange that," Justin suavely smiled at her request.

Lil picked Justin up the next morning and took him to the airport.

The entire time at Hot's the next afternoon was spent discussing Lil's trip. Lil was more a silent target of the conversation than a participant. She suffered through a half hour of terms like "hammock humping" and "shrub shaggin." Lil was relieved when the senior ladies showed up and sat beside them, striking up a conversation between the two tables, but her relief was temporary. She discovered they were cruder than her crowd when Lorraine tossed out the term "man-spear." Lil mentally blocked out the entire discussion of tree vines, which took on a whole Circ de Soleil theme. Redheaded Gladys had several methods for getting grass stains out of actual knee skin, but she suggested her hydrogen peroxide recipe as it could serve a dual purpose, jungles posing unsterile situations and all. Hallie was disappointed that she didn't know about Lil's trip sooner or she would have brought the Jane costume she wore just this past Halloween. Thurston Howell III's name came up in ways it should never come up, jump-starting Dixie's argument that big men need lovin' too, at which point, the Skipper made a cameo.[19]

Mac swapped plastic surgeon cards with Lorraine. Hinton got some tips from Mabel on making blond believable once the grays start coming in, as well as suggestions on how to work a Dr. Scholl's foot pad unnoticeably into an open-toed, slingback stiletto. Sims shared some stretching techniques with Dixie who suggested a specific jogging bra to keep Sims' "puppies" right up there where they were at the moment. She made a quick trip to the ladies room with Sims to prove it. June, Lorraine, and Mabel teased Lil with their rendition of the Steve Miller Band's "Jungle Love." Turned out, the older women knew all the lyrics. Mac left with a bag that contained a borrowed bustier. Lorraine secretly arranged to borrow it from Mac before Lil got back from Ecuador. Lil left not even aware she was humming "Jungle Love." The others went home and made love to their husbands. Every single one of them.

22

The Heart of Ecuador

Justin was waiting at the entrance to the airstrip's cinder block building where Lil would be exiting. She had deplaned behind the rectangular structure that contained some benches and a guy behind a bulletproof window exchanging what, she didn't know as she passed through. Ecuador was on the U.S. dollar system, so it wasn't a currency swap. She was relieved to see Justin there, exactly where he said he would be.

Justin was different, tan, not exactly relaxed, but comfortable and happy to see her heading toward him. His hair was down, his face, scruffy. He looked fresh, strong, and healthy. She sped up, working her way around a couple of stragglers. Two armed men stood at the door, blocking the entrance to Justin and the others awaiting passengers and those dropping off the next ones. When Lil finally reached him, she jumped up into his arms, letting her bag drop beside his feet. He nodded to a man behind her who had been on the flight with her, who nodded back and returned to the plane. Justin put her down quickly, then leaned down and picked up her bag.

"You don't know where you are," Justin smiled at her naïveté. "Never put a bag down while you're here. Now, a proper kiss," he said, wrapping his arms back around her with her bag in his hand.

"Justin!" she whispered.

He realized what her tone implied.

"Oh," he laughed, "no, there really is a pistol in my pocket."

"What?" Lil said.

"Yeah," he chuckled, "you *don't* know where you are," he said again, turning her to go to the vehicle and quickly leading her by the hand.

Justin had instructed her to bring only one bag, a carryon with the fewest clothing items for the short four-day stay, just the essentials, and she had brought only that, a duffle with necessary clothes, a toothbrush and paste, blush, lip gloss, moisturizer, hand sanitizer, mosquito cream, sunscreen, a brush, and a first-aid kit in case Justin hadn't thought of it. He had given her the bad news that nothing electrical would work anyway, so no hairdryer would be worth the trouble. Even her phone would be useless, so she didn't pack it. She had a moment of regret about that one on the plane, remembering she could have snapped a few photos before the battery died. Justin assured her he would have everything she needed when she got there.

The sounds--her plane taking back off, rickety vehicles coming and going and honking and braking--met her in the middle of Nowhere. She didn't know what to expect, but she wasn't expecting already to be seeing dirt roads and chickens.

"Calle de Gallina," he told her the name of the dirt road.

"Chicken Street," she translated.

He held her bag in one hand, her hand in the other as he looked for someone in particular. He was keenly aware of everyone moving around them as if he'd been trained to be suspicious. It was that intense focus he always gave her, but now it was focused all around her. He pulled his bottom lip in and whistled. A vehicle pulled up in front of them, the beaten up kind used on African safaris with a wooden panel running down each side, only on this one, the panels were missing, windows were cracked, there was a hole where the radio used to be, and the air conditioner hadn't worked in years. They'd have a better vehicle soon. Justin's calls in New York to get up to the third floor of 15 CPW had been fruitful in that effort, too. He opened the back door, tossed her bag to the back, and picked up a few items to clear her way into the vehicle.

"Lily, el es San Puente," Justin introduced Lil to the driver. "San Puente will take us to the village. It's a long drive. Get comfortable."

"Mucho gusto," Lil said to San Puente, who nodded. "Saint Bridge," she said to Justin, translating the driver's name.

"He is exactly that for us," Justin said, motioning for Lil to get in the truck.

She noticed all the items Justin had moved, a bow, arrows in a leather cylinder, and a rifle. Another rifle leaned from the front passenger floorboard against San Puente's leg. A pistol rested on the seat beside San Puente. Justin got in beside Lil, shut the door, and San Puente jerked into drive. Justin smiled at her, stretching his left arm behind her along the back of the seat. He turned his head and started looking out of the windows, one at a time, scanning whatever might lie beyond the truck.

As they drove away from the other vehicles and all the other noises except for the rumbling of their own car, Justin relaxed, but only a little. The truck bounced hard, frequently, so there would be no getting comfortable. Lil found herself holding onto the torn leather of the seats to keep from going airborne a couple of times. Justin looked relaxed, natural, in tune with the moment, as if he were at home in these circumstances. She wondered how far from Nowhere into nowhere a dirt road could last.

She looked out of the window to her left at the landscape, not wanting to break the silence until Justin did. Then she felt his lips kiss her neck. She turned to face him with a smile. He winked a suave wink at her, and she realized, he doesn't know. He doesn't know he's suave. That realization never occurred to her before. He isn't even trying, she thought. He moistened his lips and kissed her slowly on the mouth. San Puente had no rearview mirror, so the kiss was just theirs. Then Justin turned his head to look back out of the windows. She could see there would be no other distractions, but she was comforted in knowing he knew this place, that she was with him, and he was there to keep her safe.

How she fell asleep, she would never know. Sleeping in a bumper car at an amusement park would be easier. The flight had completely exhausted her. She was lying across the seat, and the truck was stopped. She sat up to see she was the only one in the truck, and it was rocking a bit and tilted.

"Justin?" she said, looking out of the window to her right where he had been sitting.

"Here," he said from the opposite side.

She turned to his voice.

"We're fine," he said. "Flat tire. We'll go through at least one more before we get there. Do you need to get out?"

"How does a girl, well, 'make water,' in the wilds of Ecuador?" she asked, knowing the inevitable answer.

He opened the door. He had the pistol stuffed in the front of his jeans, the bow over his shoulder, the quiver strap across his chest, and the rifle in his hand. A new addition, a leather holster, was strapped around his thigh containing a knife. San Puente was on the other side of the car with his rifle aimed in the opposite direction from the one Justin was watching, his pistol sticking out of the back of his pants. The car jack was being lowered.

"Who's changing the tire?" Lil asked.

"Santito Pablo," Justin said, walking Lil away from the truck. "We picked him up a few minutes before the flat. San Puente dropped him off close to his mother's village to check on her on our way to get you. She sent him to us when he was small. She wants him in our Christian village. Here, behind this tree," Justin said, leading her to the thickest trunked tree in sight.

"I'll be just on the other side," he said. "Quickly."

"This explains Bar 89, doesn't it?" Lil said.

247

A minute later she stood beside him.

"I can mark that off my 'bucket list,' " she commented.

"Maybe I'll get you a bucket for your list," he said with a grin. "Where we're headed, I have a feeling you'll soon be marking off things you never knew would be on any list."

She thought about her list. Maybe he would be marking something off for her himself, she thought, but back home, not here.

They walked back to the car. That was the most conversation they had had all day. Santito Pablo was putting the jack back in the rear of the truck as they returned.

"Listo, San Puente," Santito Pablo said, climbing into the front seat. Ready.

Lil noticed Pablo was wearing the old running shoes she had seen Justin pack. Justin and San Puente each faced away from the vehicle on opposite sides, aiming their weapons into the distance as they looked for anything as far away as the horizon, backing their way to the vehicle. Three door slams later, the truck lurched forward.

"Buen trabajo, Santito," Justin said. "Muy rápido. Ha estado practicando."

Lil understood without asking, the importance of quickly changing a tire in this environment. She was glad Justin bragged on Santito Pablo's rapid work. Thirteen-year-old Pablo smiled at the compliment. He took a pistol from the glove compartment, held it on his lap, and assumed his role of manning the front passenger window.

"I hope y'all are gripping those guns in case of wild animals," Lil said, sort of questioningly.

"I hope we are, too," Justin answered.

He wasn't joking. He looked at her to see her reaction. She nodded at him that she understood, but showed no fear or concern, not that she didn't have any. He had enough on his mind at the moment not to have to add her anxiety to his current job. She was glad to be with him. He had told her the place was dangerous, though her father would have liked Justin a lot less had he known where she was.

Her parents had only a few questions when she told them "Ecuador." Justin had visited with them about the trip while Lil was still in New York. He assured her father he would be armed the entire time and that he and Lil would have separate beds, close enough, however, for him to know Lil was safe.

"Isn't that where the Galápagos Islands are?" her mother had asked her.

"Exactly," Lil had smiled and added a nod, hoping the nod would imply that she and Justin would be on those islands.

"Beautiful beaches, I hear," her father had added.

"That's what I hear," Lil had added.

She didn't know what Justin had left them thinking, but she left them thinking those things.

Justin was right. One more tire would blow, then all the men in the car seemed to relax. Even this boy, Pablo, at almost 13, had earned the title, "man." Every muscle in his body was defined from constant use, sneaking through jungle villages alone, gripping a pistol, so different from boys his age back home. They eventually passed some invisible line of danger. Their postures softened, and the weapons relaxed in their grips.

"Oh, look!" Lil squealed excitedly, pointing out Justin's window, thrilled to have spotted her first monkey.

"How cute!" she squealed again, leaning across Justin's lap to get a better look.

Justin casually turned his head to see the monkey running at full speed. He was familiar with the flight patterns of fleeing monkeys, and he reached up and shut the sunroof.

"It's just like the ones at the zoo!" Lil exclaimed with a huge grin.

"This one has it a little tougher than the ones at the zoo, Babe," Justin said, manually rolling up his window. "Gato," Justin said, touching San Puente's shoulder, as he reached the width of the truck and rolled up Lil's window as well, while Pablo and San Puente rolled up theirs.

"No, it's a monkey. 'Mono,' " Lil said monkey in Spanish, correcting Justin who had said cat.

She was still smiling, watching it run.

"Lil, why don't you look out your window and see if you see any over there," Justin suggested.

"Why would I do that when I can just watch this--," Lil was saying when a jaguar came out of nowhere and snapped the monkey up in its jaws.

Her mouth dropped open, and her eyes widened. She looked at Justin, stunned, and he smiled at her.

"I tried to warn you, Babe," he smiled. "Welcome to Ecuador."

23

Papá Noel

"¡San Justín! ¡San Justín! ¡Regresaste!" the voices of small children shouted outside of the vehicle, so happy that Justin had returned as he promised. Lil lifted her head from Justin's shoulder and opened her eyes. Justin turned to his open window and waved and smiled at the kids who were running alongside the vehicle. Lil looked around. The trees, each one different, were breathtaking. The canopy of trees had been increasing exponentially since their last tire change. The mathematics of the rapid increase in their numbers, changed the line of them into a curve as they entered the jungle. The trees would be the things she would talk about the most to the girls when she described the place to them later.

"It's so green," she said, even during the trip to Justin who was smiling at her repetition of the word. "I mean, *green*," she would say again, using her hands to show the burst of color.

She heard herself saying "green" more loudly each time as she tried to translate the intensity of the color she was seeing. Every now and then a burst of other colors would appear from the thick green cover as a toucan or parrot stuck its beak through to size up the sojourners.

They had arrived at a village with what looked like mud houses covered in growing grass, a number of tents scattered around, some straw huts, and a few women over outdoor grills. They drove past a few of these structures and stopped. Justin jumped out and scooped up the first child to run up to him. He tossed the little boy high into the air.

"¡Más, San Justín!" the boy giggled, wanting another toss.

"Uno más," Justin said, and gave him a second toss, and the next child tugged on his pants leg.

"Yo voy después!" the boy squealed.

"No, no, no," a man's booming bass voice scolded as he approached the scene. "¡Justín esta cansado! ¡Mas tarde! ¡Mas tarde!" he said, tenderly shooing the children who had no intention of leaving Justin's side yet whether Justin was tired or not.

Lil got out of the car and forgot her stiffness. She enjoyed the sight of Justin's tiny, barefooted fans. It was a beautiful sight. She turned to see who commanded the bass voice and was moved at the appearance of a black man, wearing the most colorful robes, clearly religious coverings.

"¡Justín!" he said, embracing Justin tightly.

"!Papá! !Venga!"

Justin took the man over to Lil.

"Ella es Lily," Justin said. "Lily, this is Papá Noel."

The man took both of Lil's hands in his. He looked at her face with endearment.

"Ah, I always knew Justín would find the most beautiful of women. An exotic beauty indeed, Justín," he said.

Lil looked at Justin accusingly.

Justin shrugged at her, smiling.

"I didn't say a word! Not a word," Justin claimed his innocence.

"So this is Santa Claus?" Lil asked, remembering Padre Rivera's words from Justin's church at home.

"Yes, a long story from years ago," Justin said.

"Papá," Lil said, "mucho gusto."

"Let me take you to your Poco Dolor," Papá said.

Lil looked questioningly at Justin at the word dolor, poco dolor, little ache or pain. Justin winked that he'd tell her later. He retrieved Lil's bag from the truck where San Puente waited to pull away, and handed it to Papá. Lil and Papá started making their way to the Poco Dolor. Santito Pablo tossed the rifle over to Justin and pointed to where he had laid his bow and arrows for him and got back in the truck with San Puente. Justin walked over and patted Santito's arm that rested on the car window ledge.

"Santito Pablo! Gracias! Y San Puente, muchísimo gracias otra vez!" Justin said. "Vivimos para ver un otro día."

"Esta vez, mi amigo!" San Puente shouted as he pulled away.

Justin's father had said those words often to his drivers years ago after such a journey. San Puente had been the last one of his drivers.

253

"Thank you so much! We live to see another day!"

San Puente would always answer, "This time, my friend."

Lil's dwelling was in what appeared to have been at one time a plaza or center of the village. A woman had taken Lil's bag from Papá Noel, leaving Papá outside of the dwelling to wait for Justin. Papá had explained to Lil that for him to enter the Poco Dolor with her would be inappropriate, even to carry her bag.

The 140-square-foot, rectangular mud house was constructed against a small hill, a simple two-bedroom structure with a three-quarter twin bed in each of its two rooms. A wall containing a wide, doorless opening on one end, separated the rooms from each other. The beds were the only beds in the village. They sat high off the floor, with gorgeous hand-carved posts and feather-stuffed mattresses and pillows. The front door wasn't centered. It was pushed to the right, opening into one bedroom, not the other. The Poco Dolor was fourteen feet across and ten feet deep. This dwelling was the only structure in the village that had wooden floors, quite a luxury. It had a porch of sorts, an extravagant detail Lil had noticed. Though the house was extremely primitive, Lil recognized that the villagers had put her up in the finest they had to offer.

The grass that grew all over the structure was covered in buds of some flower just waiting to open. The porch was merely a small four-foot deep, eight-foot long dirt space in front of the entrance side of the house, with a makeshift tin roof stuck into the mud on the house side. Stone columns supported the sheet of tin on its outer edges. The two columns grew out of a forty-inch high stone wall and reached up to the corners of the tin roofing, creating a space between the front of the house and the stone wall, giving the feeling of a front porch. A hook screw was attached to a stone on the inner sides of both columns. A thick wire stretched between the hooks, and a couple of empty clothesline clips hung there waiting for some laundry to put them to good use. The surrounding trees looked unreal to Lil, as if Hollywood had stepped in and enlarged the leaves to an unbelievable size, big enough to make Lil's mother's prized Elephant Ear shrub look like a bush of four-leaf clovers. Everything was either green or dirt-colored, except for the stark white, unopened buds all over the dwelling's exterior, making the mud house the clear focal point of the plaza.

The woman escorted Lil into the mud house.

"Me llamo Margarita," the woman introduced herself.

"Daisy," Lil smiled at her name. "Mucho gusto, Margarita," Lil said. "Me llamo Lily, como la flor."

"¿Cual cuarto quiere usted, Señorita Lily?" Which bed do you prefer?

Lil didn't know if the woman would be in the other bed like some tribal chaperone or helper, but she was drawn to the second bed for no particular reason. Perhaps that room felt more private since the front door opened into the other room. She noticed both spaces contained what appeared to be a shorter than normal closet door, but out of courtesy, she decided to look in them later, after Margarita left.

"Gracias," Lil said to Margarita who had placed Lil's bag on the second bed and had come over to where Lil stood.

255

The woman placed her bare foot next to Lil's as if she were comparing the two in size. Pablo seemed to be the only one here who wore shoes. She walked behind Lil and placed her hands on the outsides of Lil's shoulders, then stood with her shoulder touching Lil's and looked down the length of Lil's height to the floor. She compared her arm length and waist level to Lil's as though she were literally sizing Lil up.

"¿Puedo preguntar ¿cuántos años tiene?" Margarita asked.

Lil thought about the strange question, "How old are you?" and realized for all intents and purposes, she was already twenty-six, just days away from her birthday. She might as well get used to saying it.

"Tengo veintiseis años," Lil answered.

Twenty-six. It didn't sound as bad as she thought it would.

"Gracias. Bienvenida, Señorita Lily," the woman welcomed Lil to the village, nodding her goodbye, then left.

Lil took the opportunity to look in her short closet. It contained only a wooden chair. She walked to the closet in the other space, and again a wooden chair. The dwelling offered barely enough room for the bed in each room, so it made perfect sense to tuck the chair out of the way until it was needed.

"Utilitarians," she said.

She looked up as Justin approached, running his fingers through his hair, pushing it back from his face. He stopped in the entrance, gripping the top of the door opening in one hand, the side frame with the other, leaning against it. They smiled at each other.

"Quaint, huh," he said about the space, walking in, noticing her bag was on the second bed. She nodded.

"Who sleeps there?" she asked about the first bed.

"I do," he said. "Is that okay?"

She exhaled.

"Better than okay! 'Thank goodness okay!' " she answered, relieved.

"Do you need to rest?" he asked walking over to her, pushing a strand of her hair away from her face. She shook her head no.

"What's the first thing you want to do?" Justin asked her.

"Brush my teeth," she smiled.

"Okay," he smiled back.

"Tell me about this place, Justin, why you brought me here."

"I will. I'll show you around, but first let me explain the water."

"Okay."

"Don't drink it, under any circumstance."

"That bad?" she asked.

"Worse. Don't let the shower water go in your mouth," he continued. "Don't eat any vegetable unless you check with me first. Only fish the men bring in at breakfast and again at supper. The villagers eat only fruit picked from the trees, not off the ground or picked by anyone else. You don't know if someone else got it from the ground. You're not at home. You don't wash the fruit because the water will contaminate it. We cook everything. The word for water in most of these tribes is 'P,' " Justin explained.

"Ahhh," Lil said, remembering Justin's story about drinking only P when he a boy. "Okay, I think I'll eat only what you're eating, when you're eating it," she said, noticing how thirsty she was all of a sudden upon discovering the lack of clean water.

"Where is this shower?" she asked.

"There are two. The women will show you the one you would use if you shower while we're here."

"*If?*" she said.

"We go as many days as we can without taking one," Justin explained. "The water may be nasty, but it's precious. The only thing they treasure here more, are their trees, but that's another story. San Puente brings food and tubs of treated water from the clinic for the showers and the cooking pots. I brought trunks with me on my flight from Quito. They are filled with bottled water. Use that water even to brush your teeth," he said, knowing she was a tooth-brushing maniac.

"Why is the water so bad?"

"Different reasons. The latest, this world's love of crude."

"Oil?"

"Yes. This earth, she will give us everything we need, but it's our duty to take care of her, to take what she gives with care and humble respect. Some of the drilling in places here was like a violation. Some men behave differently under the cover of the jungle. Those who did here, left the mess for these small tribes to suffer. Many don't know what has happened here, but they need to know. A 'there-but-by-the-grace-of-God' attitude, won't help any of us. In a very real way, this is everyone's yard. These rainforests are most likely the heart of the whole, the health of us all, and one day it will be too late. I won't take you any farther east into the forest than this. We'll stay near the mountains, near moving water, and the clinic."

"Where are the trunks?" she asked, already thirsty. "And where is your bag?"

"Outside. I wanted you to pick your bed first," he said. "I stayed in a hut until you got here."

He went out and returned with one trunk, then another, next his bags, and a compact, hard case with a handle. The trunks were heavy for any individual man, but he managed. He removed a few water containers, more like canteens than bottles, then slid the trunk against the wall under his bed. He brought the second trunk containing more water and water filters and set it on the floor in the opening between the rooms.

"This one has wheels if you'll just roll it under your bed for me," he said. "It isn't as heavy as the other one. It contains more water and filters from the Waves for Water people. I'll show you how to use the filter. San Puente, Santito Pablo, and I distribute them around the different villages," he said, standing up, raising his arm to wipe his face on the shoulder and sleeve of his T-shirt.

"Clean water and sewage systems, the fine line between civilized and third world," he said. "A civil engineer and skilled plumbers—the difference between life and death." he added. "You'll appreciate clean water more when you get home, and you'll wonder what we did to deserve it. We take every sip for granted," he said, walking back to the porch to grab his duffle bags.

"It rolls easy enough," Lil said, securing the trunk under the bed the same as Justin had done with the other trunk, "but how in the world did you lift these?" she asked. "You should have gotten another man to help you."

"No other man is allowed in this dwelling but me," he explained from the other room. "They're heavy, but I've lifted them many times."

"Is that what I think it is?" Lil asked pointing to the small case.

"A typewriter," Justin nodded. "It's all that works in these jungles. My parents used it to write for medical journals. I used it, too. I brought supplies to replace the ribbon and give it a tune-up. The s is dropping." He sounded nostalgic and tired.

"Do you need to rest, Justin?" she asked, remembering she had napped off and on, but he had not relaxed for a moment of their drive.

"I do, but not until bedtime, and that will be soon, so let's get you to a sink to brush those pearly whites and start the tour," he said.

"Okay, I'll get my toothbrush," she said going back to her bedroom.

She unzipped her bag and retrieved her toothbrush and toothpaste. She heard a metal container making contact with the wooden floor behind her. She turned around to see Justin walking away from the shared opening where he'd placed a blue metal bucket and one of the water canteens.

"What's that?" she shouted from her room.

"The sink," he said from his room. "And the toilet," he added. "Told you I would get you a bucket."

260

A roll of toilet paper came flying into her room from his, landing on the foot of her bed. She could hear him laughing.

24

The Grand Tour

Lil brushed her teeth before Justin showed her around the village. She spit into the bucket and swished with the bottled water. If there had been a window, she would have dumped the spit and water out of it, but there was no window. She decided she'd dump it when Justin wasn't around. It wasn't a very lady-like bucket. She dabbed her mouth with her sleeve, and walked through the opening to join Justin.

He was getting a T-shirt from his bag. She watched him. He was fit, beautifully toned, a fitness that a man would have if his work required physical labor, but Justin was a teacher, at least at the moment. Her eyes moved over to his scar.

"Is this where that happened?" she asked.

He looked up to see what she meant, and saw that her line of vision was directed at his scar.

"No," he said pulling out a shirt, and putting it on. "But this village is where I came afterwards," he continued as he zipped his bag and placed it under his bed by the trunk. "Papá's wife, Esperanza, took care of me whenever my parents left for the clinics," he added, checking his pistol and tightening the holster on his leg.

"I'll have to thank her," Lil said.

"You'll have to wait until you're in Heaven then," he said reaching his hand out for her to take. "So, will you please wait a very, very long time to thank her?" he smiled, walking over and kissing her.

"Why is his name Papá Noel?" Lil asked.

"When he first came to this village, he told the people about the birth of Jesus and how people celebrate Christmas around the world. Weeks later, when he got to the laying of the palm branches and the death and resurrection of Christ, an older boy went over to him. He said to Papá, 'You have brought us this knowledge of this man Jesus, God's Son, Who would save us, so you must be this Papá Noel we have heard about,' " Justin continued.

"How beautiful," Lil exclaimed.

"That boy was San Puente," Justin said, taking Lil's hand and kissing it. "I'm so glad you're here, Lil," he said. "Now, let's take the grand tour."

They walked out under the tin roof.

"Where do we start?" she asked.

"It's really more of a stroll than a tour. Not much to see."

"What are those smooth places on the ground on each side of this house?" she asked.

"Two other houses just like this one used to stand in those places. They went unused for so long and untended as well, that they eventually crumbled and were removed. Papá insisted this one be saved, and my parents helped him start the process. The people helped, and here it stands, not used as often as in years past, but maintained at least."

"Why wouldn't they use it?" Lil asked. "And what a shame about the other two. This one has a certain beauty. What are these flower buds growing all over it?" she asked.

"Lirio de Cereza," Justin smiled, knowing the meaning wouldn't be lost on Lil.

"Cherry Lilies? You're totally making that up," Lil accused him.

"I thought you might say that, but no, that's their real name," Justin chuckled. "They don't open every year. In the off years, the buds appear, and the people get hopeful, then the buds just die. My father used to have a photo of the three mud houses covered in the flowers. It was beautiful."

"Maybe this time," Lil said looking at the buds.

They held hands and strolled through the place where they had entered with San Puente earlier. Justin spoke to people who were at their leisure with no sunlight left, torches lit low to the ground, away from the vegetation overhead. He called them by name, even the children who still jumped into his arms. At a couple of tents, they sat for a moment and ate a bite of cooked fish and bread. Justin nodded to Lil if it was okay to accept what was offered at each place.

"Taste this," he said, handing her a clay cup of black coffee, "but only a sip or two. Any more than that and you won't sleep for days," he kidded. "It's strong for the men who stand watch tonight."

It was without a doubt the best coffee she'd ever had.

"What is the other language I hear some of the older people speaking?" Lil asked.

"Lenguaba," Justin said. "It's disappearing. Most of what you'll hear is Spanish, no English in this village except for Papá. The village's elder still speaks Sabiojo, which historians claim is extinct," Justin said. "Other villages nearby speak Lenguaba. One other tribe speaks Aldeabla."

"And you understand all of these?" Lil asked.

"Enough of each one," Justin said.

"So many languages," Lil said.

"You just got back from the real jungle," Justin said. "Hundreds of languages walking around New York City. This is just a handful."

Teenaged boys prepared to douse the torches, and the crowd of people gathered for Papá Noel to pray for their safety through the night. He thanked God that Justin was back among them, and that Lily was here beside Justin. He touched the heads of the children as they skipped by him into their mothers' arms as an extra blessing, saying with each little noggin, "Y este niño, Padre, y éste, por favor, y esta hija, también, y este hijo, Dios . . .." And this child, Father, and this one, please, and this daughter, too, and this son, God . . ..

"More tomorrow," Justin said to Lil.

They strolled back to the Poco Dolor.

"We'll go in that direction tomorrow," Justin said, pointing in the opposite direction from their dwelling than they had walked today. "I have something to show you there."

An older boy sat in front of their porch, leaning back against the stone wall, with a worn guitar at his side in the dirt. He stood when he saw them approaching and nodded to Justin.

"Gracias, Juanito," Justin said to him. "Y agárralo," Justin said, reaching into his back pocket and tossing something shiny to Juanito.

Juanito caught it, looked at it, and smiled.

"¡Muchísimo gracias, San Justín!" Juanito exclaimed about the guitar capo, grabbing the instrument from the ground, untying the string that was tied tightly around the third fret of the guitar's neck, and attaching the capo in its place.

"Esto le ayudará a tocar esa nueva canción," Justin said. This will help you play that new song. "Hasta mañana," Justin said, sending Juanito on his way.

The boy appeared to Lil to have been guarding the place while they were gone.

"Just another ritual extended to special visitors," Justin said about Juanito's presence.

Justin stepped in front of her and entered the dwelling first, which was completely out of character for him. He turned immediately toward her room, and from the opening there, inspected the area. He could see totally under the bed, clear to the wall that no one was present and turned to her standing behind him.

"Okay, you ate two bites of fish, so go brush your teeth," he teased. "When you're done, I'll brush and dump the bucket."

"No!" Lil shrieked.

"What do you mean, 'no'?" he asked. "I *do* have to brush, too, you know."

"I mean, no, not in the same bucket! I don't want you looking at my spit!" Lil said embarrassed, walking briskly to her room and looking in the bucket.

"Looking at your spit?" he asked, smiling from the opening. "You really don't have a clue of how I grew up, do you? On any given day, your spit might have been the prettiest thing I had to look at," Justin smiled through the opening to her room.

"Okay, here, come get it and use it first," she said, grimacing at all the spit he was about see.

"Hand it here," he said from where he stood, laughing at her.

"Are you that tired?"

"I can't come into your room, Lil," he explained.

"Why not?" she asked.

"Unless you are in danger or are inviting me into your bed, I am not to cross this threshold," Justin said. "It's their way. But if you're inviting me into you bed, . . . " he smiled.

"Well, if I had chosen the other bed, how would you have managed getting from the front door to this room without crossing my room?" she asked.

"But you didn't choose that bed."

"But if I had?" she repeated.

"In this village, there are no what ifs, only what is. It makes for fewer depression pills," Justin explained. "And you chose that one," he said pointing to her bed.

"Are you saying I chose correctly?"

"I didn't say that," he smiled, "but you did."

"I did say it, or I did choose correctly?" she asked, meeting him in the doorway.

"Both," he said taking the bucket from her and walking to his room with it.

"What else do I need to know about this village?" she asked, getting her pajamas out of her bag, but before he could answer, she realized what else they were going to have to share that bucket for, and she dashed to the opening and exclaimed, "We're going to need a second bucket!"

Justin laughed harder than he'd laughed in weeks.

25

What Is, Not What Ifs

They both slept soundly. Lil was surprised at that fact when she woke. After the ride there, she thought she might dream a few different scenarios about whatever Justin and San Puente had been watching for out the car windows. The mud walls kept the room's temperature at just the right level. Not a single dream disturbed her rest. She wafted into unconsciousness as she surrendered to a peaceful, completely-away-from-the-world sleep. No sun peeked past the mud to wake her, but eventually the beginning of a ray of light entered through the open door, casting a glare off a silver, metal bucket that sat in the shared threshold.

"He's wonderful," she thought at the simple sight of her own bucket.

The smell of fish grilling rode in on the sun's ray.

"Justin?" she said quietly so she wouldn't wake him if he were still sleeping, but wondering if he were there.

She got up and moved into the light just enough to stick her arm into it to see her watch. It was 5:59 a.m. She peeked around the wall, but Justin wasn't there. She calculated the hours that had passed from the shower she took before her flight.

"You can do it, girl," she told herself.

She took a bottle of water, thought about using the bucket to wash her face before she brushed her teeth, then thought of all the times and ways that thing had been used, and reconsidered. She turned yesterday's shirt inside out, poured some water on it, and freshened her face with it. She wore so little makeup anyway, that after her journey and first day, none was left to wash off. The water felt good, and the moisturizer felt even better.

She brushed her teeth, combed her hair, and braided a loose fishtail ponytail that curved toward one side, gliding over her left shoulder. She'd gotten more sun than she'd anticipated the day before through the vehicle's sunroof, so the blush was pointless. She dotted sunscreen on her face, and mixed it with a bit of mosquito repellent for her arms and legs. She dabbed a bit of pink gloss on her lips, slipped into a pair of khaki shorts and a billowing ivory blouse. Years of mentally scripting her wardrobe paid off. She was hoping for that fresh, earthy, how-do-you-look-so-effortlessly-beautiful-in-the-jungle look, like she'd seen in safari movies. She had forgotten a mirror, so she only could hope she was presentable. She slipped on her shoes, tidied her bed, grabbed the water bottle with half its contents remaining, glanced down at the bucket knowing she'd better get ready for its other use, picked it up, and walked to the door.

Justin sat on the stone wall watching the sunrise. He had slipped on his jeans and reclined against the stone column, his left leg hanging down the outside of the wall, the other, bent, with his foot on the wall, his right arm stretched across his bent knee, holding a half-empty water canteen. He was deep in thought, remembering times in this village, years earlier, thinking about his parents, Papá Noel's wife, his childhood playmates. This morning, he remembered in particular, a girl and a time fifteen years past.

Her name was Calla. She was different from the other girls in the village. The details of her life had been planned for her from the beginning, sooner even, and that fact was the sadness of her days. She never knew her mother. She was her mother's first and only child, but her mother died of an infection before Calla was old enough to call her madre. No Apoya man was to raise a daughter without a wife. Tradition held that sons could stay with their fathers, but daughters passed to another family if one would have them. In Calla's case, they all wanted her, not that she came with riches, but she came from a chief's line, royalty in these jungles. But Calla's father would not part with her. He bucked tribal tradition and kept the daughter because he had loved her mother dearly. And he loved Calla with all his heart. He intended to raise her to survive these jungles, just as he would have reared a boy. And in Calla's case, he needed to protect her. He knew that if her purity were breached, it would cost her her life. He was determined to guard it until she wed.

Calla's grandfather, the last of the chiefs, was too old and feeble to persuade his son-in-law otherwise. Tribal chiefs were being replaced with religious profits, priests of sorts, men who captivated different tribes with their claims of knowledge of different gods. Calla's mother had no brothers. Her mother was the only one of the chief's daughters who was wed to an Apoya man and the only hope that the royal family's bloodline would continue another generation. If the chief died without passing on his blessing to a grandson, the line would end with him. Since Calla's mother didn't live to have a son, Calla's grandfather would be the final chief, and the priests would replace Calla's family as royalty. Her grandfather took comfort in knowing Papá Noel would lead his tribe.

No women helped raise Calla. They merely pointed out how wrong her father was doing everything, especially concerning the daughter of tribal royalty, and even more especially because Calla was promised before she existed to be wed to the first born son of the neighboring Lado priest. The Apoyas and the Lados were allies, a necessary relationship because of rising tensions with the Tomenava tribe. Calla's marriage was meant to tie the two tribes by blood when her first child was born, so it was imperative that she be untouched when given to the Lado priest's first son. The Apoya women feared that Calla's masculine upbringing would make her unacceptable to the priest. But Calla's father raised her his way, to take care of herself, teaching her everything he would have taught a son.

The only other stipulation the neighboring Lado priest had was that Calla was not to be taught the beliefs that the new Apoya priest, Papá Noel, spouted. The Lado priest would indoctrinate her into his religion when she joined his tribe, and he didn't want to have to undo Papá Noel's teachings. His request was easy to abide, as the girls in Calla's tribe were not allowed to attend Papá's lessons. Though Papá struggled to convince the Apoyas that their daughters, too, should be educated, the Apoya men ignored his pleadings and made sure their wives and daughters were occupied otherwise. Esperanza made certain to be busy with the girls, perhaps singing songs while she worked with them and their mothers over the food and the laundry, songs that happened to teach things Papá was teaching the boys. But Calla's father didn't allow her even this time with the other girls. She had her instructions, both from her grandfather and the Lado priest. With Calla, when told she couldn't do something, she quietly and respectfully accepted the instruction . . . as a challenge.

Calla was a few months older than Justin. In these villages, the young children played together and helped in the village doing whatever chores they could, while their parents and older siblings worked. When they were around 9 years old, the boys would go off with their fathers to learn to hunt and tend the land. The girls stayed with their mothers to cook, to tend to the youngest, and to nurse the elderly, all the girls but Calla. Calla was always by her father's side. She could shoot an arrow as well as any boy her age, drag a boar three times her weight, skin it, gut it, and cook it. The other girls looked down on her, something they never would have done had her mother lived and gone on to birth a son. The boys saw her as unnatural, as competition, though they would never admit it. She was Justin's match with an arrow, a spear, and a knife, but unlike the other boys, Justin liked that this girl challenged them.

As the other children reached their teens, Calla found herself with fewer peers, and soon, only Justin would speak to her, but the opportunity to do so was rare and at best, brief. The two had only moments without her father's watchful eyes on them, like the minutes it would take to gut a kill before moving on to the next one. During these hurried encounters, Calla would ask, in blunt phrases, what Papá Noel had taught them on the previous evening. She would listen to Justin's answer, pretending she didn't care. Justin was glad she asked. He would tell her as much as he could before her father sternly called her back to his side.

No romance was burgeoning between them. No, theirs was an unspoken relationship of understanding, a mutual respect. Each one knew the life laid out before the other. Justin understood why she never smiled, though he wondered what she would look like if she did.

At 18, Calla was considered well past her prime, an old maid. The years had ticked away as the neighboring Lado priest fathered only daughters, no son for Calla to marry. Calla's fading grandfather and the Lado priest reached a new agreement; Calla would now marry the old priest instead, a man in his late sixties. The chapters of her life had been written before her birth--a story she had no voice in--and the plot now took a grimmer path than she even imagined.

It was a rainy night, the kind Justin slept best in, with the sound of the water striking the vegetation that served as a roof in the hut he used now, a few yards from the dwelling he had shared with his parents in his childhood. His parents were away for days, sometimes weeks at a time working in the clinics. He usually worked with them, but during the harvest,

274

Justin would stay in the village to help the men with their crops.

He heard the steps coming. He rose to his elbows, put the poison dart between his lips and waited. She pulled the curtain to her right, stepped inside, and their eyes met. Justin lowered his hand and waited for her to speak. Her hair was dripping water, and her garments stuck to her Apoya skin as she looked down at him.

"Ayúdame," Calla said to Justin. Help me.

Justin nodded. He knew her nuptials to the old priest were the next evening.

"We'll need water for a few days' journey," he said, agreeing to help her flee before she even asked.

"No," she answered. "I will keep my family's vow to marry. It always has been my fate. Their priest is old. It will not be forever."

"Then help you how?"

She studied his eyes and breathed hard. Then she answered.

"Thou shalt have no other gods before me," she quoted the Biblical commandment.[20] "As a little girl, my village taught me that the first man I lie with, when I lie with him, his god becomes my god and my children's god. That man's god is not the God of Abraham."

"Calla, you know who your God is. You know when this man takes you . . . you know that is not how God works. That is only superstition."

"I know here who my God is," Calla said touching her heart. "But here," she reached to her temple, "here, is where Diablo will torture me with worry for the souls of my children during my nights for years to come. I will die at my own hands before

275

I birth a child whose soul will belong to a block of wood that will fuel the fire in the pit. Help me, Justín. Ayúdame, por favor."

Justin looked into her sad face. He knew her faith was based on stolen minutes of learning, mixed with a lifetime of tribal lore, and he understood what she was asking.

"Calla, he will kill you when he discovers."

"The elder, she has shown me a way to trick him."

"But if it doesn't work, he surely will kill you."

"I am ready. In death, I have salvation."

They studied each other's eyes.

Indecision does not exist in these jungles. Here, where death can come with the soundless pouncing of four speckled legs, with the blowing of a single dart, with one invisible bacterial cell, decisions come quickly. In these jungles, adulthood comes far sooner than in other places, places considered by those living in them, more advanced, more civil.

The rain increased in intensity. Justin reached for a supply box from the many his parents stacked in his hut. He opened it, and tore from a ream, one small square package containing protection, and looked back at Calla. She pushed her clothing off her shoulders, let it drop to the ground, and walked to Justin.

As she left his hut, she turned back to meet Justin's eyes, and ever so slightly, she smiled. She was beautiful when she smiled. One day, Justin would tell Lil about Calla, Santito Pablo's mother. Pablo was the only son Calla's old Lado husband fathered. Calla had sneaked Pablo to the Apoya village when he was one, claiming to her husband that while she was washing their garments, that a croc had snatched their precious child and dragged him to the bottom of the water.

The Lados revered the crocodile. They and other tribes believed when the crocs died, all other animals would follow. Thus, the old priest found solace in that while the croc stole his only son, life would continue for all other living creatures, including man. The priest celebrated, choking through his tears, his son's having provided sustenance to the reptile.

Calla grieved for months. Her grief was real. She hated lying to her husband and causing him such despair, and she missed Pablo to the depths of her soul, but she knew Papá and Esperanza would love Pablito as their own. Papá and Esperanza took Pablo and moved, for a while, to a more distant village, until Pablo was older, where Calla's deception would go undiscovered. They had no choice. The priest would have killed Calla if he had discovered what she had done. They returned with the boy when Calla's grandfather, the Apoya chief, died.

Calla knew Pablo would be raised a Christian. Then, with the Lado priest's markings on the tops of his feet, hidden by the shoes Justin always provided, Pablo could return to her tribe when his father died. As the only son, Pablo would lead her village, and it would become a Christian tribe. She used the years in between to organize groups of young girls, convincing her husband to allow them to go to the clinic to learn vital nursing skills for their tribe. She learned, too, and used their breaks to gather the girls to listen to the missionaries and to teach them the art of shooting arrows. She was a silent leader to these girls. Her father and her life had equipped her for that role.

She prayed daily that at the end, that her husband would forgive her, that he would recognize Pablo as his son and give him the priest's blessing before he closed his eyes for the final time. She worked hard in her tribe and served the priest diligently in daily retribution for her secret sin. She cared tenderly for her husband over the years and waited for the priest to die.

A bird flapped loudly out of the buds of the Cherry Lilies behind Justin, and he glanced quickly in that direction, startled out of his memory. He reached over to the vines and plucked a tiny, unopened, white bud from the mass of green leaves. He leaned back against the column and rolled the stem of the bud back and forth between his thumb and index finger. The flower brought back another memory, one from here in this plaza, a sweet one he would never forget. One he would soon share with Lil.

Justin felt Lil's presence behind him, though she had made no sound. He turned to see her standing in the door of the Poco Dolor. She had set down the bucket, and she stood still to let him finish whatever memory he was reliving. She was enjoying the view, both of him and the sunrise in front of him. He smiled at her like her presence there completed both the scene and the memory.

He stood up, walked to her, took her in his arms and kissed her as if he were about to make love to her. Her hands moved across his shirtless torso, starting with his chest and abdomen, and softly gliding to his sides and back, and up across his broad shoulders.

He led her to the wall, sat back up on it, and helped her up, securing her between his legs, reclining her back against his chest to share the sunrise with him.

"Your hair is wet," she realized. "You took a shower!" she turned to accuse him.

"Trust me. You should be glad I did. I took the run today."

"What is the run?"

"The men run the perimeter of their tribal land before the sun rises. They are checking their land, their livestock, their crops, marking their territory each day for the neighboring tribes to see. When I am here, I fill in for one man each day so he can stay with his family. That's why I run back home."

"What were you thinking about just now?" she asked him.

"A day when I was 12," he said. "By that tree there," he pointed. "I was there by that tree the first time I ever saw the Cherry Lilies in bloom. Just one of those moments when details come flooding back," he said.

She closed her eyes and rested in his arms.

"Did you sleep well?" Justin asked.

"Surprisingly well. Not one dream, just Bryan Adams playing in my mind, and total rest."

"It wasn't Bryan Adams," Justin chuckled.

"It's *my* mind," Lil reminded him.

"It was Juanito," Justin assured her, still laughing. "He's teaching himself guitar when I'm not here to help him. He sat here while I was on the run in the dark hours of the morning. He was playing his guitar. He plays by ear. I brought him a CD player a couple of years ago that I bought at a yard sale. It had a burned CD left in it—all Bryan Adams songs. I bought

279

the same songs and made another CD for myself so I could try to keep up with him. Haven't you noticed that's what's always playing in my car? I've listened to more Bryan Adams in the last year than Bryan Adams has. I bring Juanito a box of batteries for the player every time I come. He won't accept a new CD until he's mastered this one. He's working on his last, new piece. He's out-playing me for sure. Pretty good, isn't he?"

"*Really* good," Lil said, a smile forming on her lips as she realized the sweet reason why Bryan Adams had been on her mind so often.

She breathed in the fresh air and listened to the sounds of grazing stock and the chatter of birds, deciding to make some memories of her own. This view was not how she had imagined Justin's trips abroad. Not a concrete building in sight, no monuments built by men for men, no retail stores, no towers with lights, no girls in stilettos. These places were Justin's places. This village and others like it were Justin's abroad. He truly was the man she wanted. He was the one she had waited for, and he had been worth that wait.

"When we get home," she thought.

She looked down the length of Justin's leg to his bare foot resting on the stone wall.

"I noticed you brought shoes to Pablo. I would have bought him a new pair and gathered up some pairs for a few more children if you had told me they are all barefooted," Lil said.

Justin shook his head.

"Adorning your feet can cost you your life here," Justin said. "Toes clutching to tree bark speed up the climb when a predator is in pursuit. Toes gripping dirt at the edge of a water bank can be the difference between life and death. A bare foot can detect solid ground or sinking sand more quickly," he explained. "Pablo wears them for other reasons. An old broken-in pair eliminates blisters and draws less attention. So I break the shoes in for him."

Justin leaned forward, lifting Lil up with him, at the sound of a woman's voice coming toward them. She was a small, toothless old woman, wearing a colorful kimono-fashioned robe, her face creased with more lines than Lil imagined possible on one face. Her back was curved from age, and she chanted as she came. Justin guided Lil from the wall with his firm hands and stood behind her out of respect for the approaching elder of the village. As she drew closer, Lil saw that she was holding something on her hands. She continued chanting her way toward them. Lil watched and listened as she got closer. The chant wasn't in English, and very little of it was in Spanish, so Lil had no idea what the meaning of the song was. The woman reached their dwelling and stopped walking until she finished her chant. Lil picked up on the words "Poco Dolor," and remembered that's what Papá Noel called the mud house the day before. She'd have to remember to ask Justin why the Apoyas called the mud house the "small pain."

Lil could see that the woman was carrying fresh bed linens, folded neatly in a square. Finished with her song, the woman walked to where they stood. She studied Lil's face, but since Justin had not spoken to her, Lil did not either. Lil was approaching this experience with a "do as Justin says and as Justin does" approach so as not to offend the Apoya people.

Out of courtesy though, Lil instinctively began to reach for the linens and thank the woman for bringing them, but Justin stilled her arms. When Lil turned her head and looked up at Justin, he merely shook his head. The old woman left them where they stood and walked into the room and began to change the beds.

"Well, I have to say," Lil whispered to Justin, "the last thing I was expecting here was turn-down service."

It took the woman a few minutes to change both beds and chant a blessing over both of them.

"Sabiojo," Justin answered Lil's facial request to remind her of the language she was hearing. "Her generation will be the last that knows it," he added. "My mother spoke pieces of it with her beautifully. She tried to teach them all the importance of keeping it alive, but that's more than a one-woman job."

They stopped and listened to the blessing, and Lil listened for any Spanish to try to make out some of what the woman was saying.

"Catching any of that?" Justin asked Lil. "She does add some Spanish at times."

"Not really," Lil said, continuing to listen and decipher any part of the chant.

"Well, I got that part," Lil said, excitedly, "but she's just talking about her chore of changing the beds, now. 'La primera sábana,' " Lil repeated the part she'd understood in Spanish. "But those are the second linens," Lil corrected the woman to Justin.

"Well, those are the first ones she has changed," he suggested.

"Strange service in such a primitive place," Lil said. "I love the way these people ask God to bless everything, right down to the pillow you rest your head on at night."

As the old woman left, they could see Papá Noel hurrying toward them.

"¡Justín! ¡Justín!"

Something was wrong.

"Papá, what is it?" Justin asked.

"It is time, Justín," Papá said. "We must prepare."

"It cannot be time!" Justin argued, as if saying it loudly would will it. "It is too soon!" Justin insisted. "What is it?!" he seemed to be calculating. "Seven, eight weeks?" he looked at Papá who nodded. "She cannot be here now!" Justin said indicating Lil with his eyes. "It's too dangerous!"

"Perhaps this is God's way of stopping it all, mi hijo," Papá said.

Justin looked at Lil who had no idea of what this was about.

"She has to go!" Justin said, meaning Lil. "Send Juanito for San Puente! Santito Pablo becomes a watch today! She has to leave! Today!" he insisted.

"Justin, I just got here!" Lil jumped in.

"I know, my son," Papá said placing his hand on Justin's shoulder. "San Puente will be coming soon from the clinic. No more fires today. The women will stay in their tents."

The two men embraced, and Papá turned to the direction from which he had come and hurried away.

"What is it, Justin?!" Lil said.

283

With no apparent harm in sight, she had no clue to what was happening. Justin's face was firm and intent, defiant even. She had never seen him like this. She was scared.

He went quickly into the dwelling with her following closely. He pulled a black T-shirt from his bag and forced it over his head. He pulled his hair into a ponytail. He angrily grabbed his bow and slid it over his head and around his chest.

"Put your hair up as tight and as close to your head as you can," he said. "Did you pack any jeans?"

She nodded.

"Put them on. You have to cover your legs," he instructed her.

He reached in his bag and pulled out a hat and tossed it to the end of his bed next to where she stood.

"Then put this on. Change into a plain T-shirt," he finished.

"No!" he changed his mind as she turned to go do what he said.

He reached in his bag and grabbed another of his shirts, and tossed it to her.

"One of mine."

She caught it and turned to go change. She could hear the noises from her side of the dwelling--Justin intently preparing for something. Whatever "something" was, it involved his checking his weapons. When she finished changing, she walked back over to where he stood waiting for her. His bow was across his chest, his quiver strapped across it, too. His knife was on his thigh, and the rifle waited against the wall. He looked up to inspect her. His shirt swallowed her, and the hat covering her hair made her look like a man. So much for her effortless safari beauty hopes. He walked to her and kissed her. He pushed some stray, blond strands better hidden up in the hat.

"Your beautiful face gives it all away," he said, seriously.

He held her tightly, leaning down to press his face into her neck, kissing it before he released his embrace.

"I love you, Lil," he said with that intense look.

"I love you, too," she said.

"This isn't going to be the trip I thought it would be," he said. "I never should have brought you here. My reasons . . .," he left that thought. "Here, we deal with what is, not what ifs. You have to do everything I say, how I say it, when I say it."

He wasn't asking her.

"Yes," she said, meaning it.

She had no problem following Justin's lead. His mother, his father, his whole life had equipped him for the role.

"Starting with this," he said reaching to the floor and picking up the bucket.

She looked up at him embarrassed.

"Now," he said with no ounce of teasing. "And quickly. It may be the only chance you get today."

She squeezed her eyes closed tightly and crinkled her nose while receiving the bucket. She retrieved her roll of toilet paper and hand sanitizer and turned and followed him outside. He showed her where to go, and he raised his rifle into the wilderness while she was out of his sight. She wondered who was out there. Who was on the other side of that scope? She had wondered that the entire car trip here. But something about being here, from the moment she laid eyes on Justin when the plane landed, told her he would tell her what she needed to know when she needed to know it. She knew he would tell her soon who was out there because apparently whoever it was, was coming. She had sneaked a bottle of water along when she grabbed the toilet tissue, to clean the bucket. To her, that was a precious use of a precious bottle, and Justin would just have to understand. She was surprised how easily she managed everything, and she was quickly back to where Justin stood.

"That wasn't so bad, now, was it?" He reached for the bucket, but she instinctively pulled it back.

"No!" she protested.

"Then put it back in your room, and we'll talk," he said, not able to resist a smile.

When she returned to where he stood, Justin was holding his pistol, with the grip facing her. The gun was different from the ones she had used back home, so the next part of the conversation involved Justin telling her how to use it and how to reload it. Then he raised her shirt and slid the point of it down the front of her jeans the way he had been wearing it. He turned her around and retrieved two ammunition magazines from his back pockets, placing one in each of her pockets.

"If you hesitate, it could cost both of us our lives," he explained, not caring if her hesitation would cost him his life, just hoping that saying so to her, would convince her to squeeze the trigger if the moment called for it.

He had no doubt that she loved him, and he was not above using that love to make her save herself. She nodded.

"The neighboring tribes are peaceful, but one is becoming less so, the Tomenava tribe," he started to explain. "The

Apoyas have not had any serious trouble from them, but there is a situation between the tribes now that could change that.

"A young woman here in the Apoya tribe is expecting a child. She is married. The Apoya couple has two daughters together. A Tomenava man claims the child she is carrying now is his. Her husband is quiet. He is not sure. Until the husband speaks for the woman and this child, claiming them both as his, not he, his brothers, nor his cousins will fight for the wife or the child. He doesn't want the child if it isn't his, but he is quiet in case it is. It all started when this pregnant woman's sister ran off to the Tomenava tribe and slept with the Tomenava high priest, Singozo."

"Why did she do that?" Lil asked.

"Her husband took a second wife. Apoya men have not taken multiple wives in three generations, and his doing so shamed her. She said she would rather be one of dozens of wives than one of two. When she left, her husband refused to go get her. He denounced her and their three daughters along with her.

"When the woman who is now in labor discovered what her sister had done, she took her nieces in, but even her husband doesn't want the girls. She defied him by bringing them into their tent, which was a bold and dangerous choice for her. She later slipped off in the night to bring her sister back to this village. This laboring woman went to get her sister away from the idol worshipper. Singozo raped her, and left her on the border. She was found on the morning run the next day," Justin explained.

287

"Singozo has persuaded the Tomenava men to worship the idol Virilo. He has taught them that all women belong to all men, for their pleasure and for their service. They pass the women around in that village. Singozo gets them first. He has sworn to take this child. If it is a son, he will raise him as an idol priest; if it is a daughter, . . . I can't speak the words," Justin said shaking his head. "He refuses to let the mother keep the baby and says he will kill the child before it is raised in this tribe. Her husband can denounce her as his wife. If he does, he denounces their two daughters as well.

"Her husband's silence is making the tribe weak. He is one of 13 brothers. They must respect his wishes in the matter and remain silent as well, until he decides. The Apoya men believe that to sleep with a woman who has been violated by a Tomenava man is akin to sleeping with someone who has been with Satan. These Apoya men believe this violation of this woman leaves her defiled in a way they can't reconcile, though the violation was forced upon her. Thirteen men in this part of the country is a small army. Without this father, his brothers and cousins, I don't know how long we could defend the mother, the baby, her daughters and the nieces from her sister she now cares for, from the Tomenava. That many silent men leave this village entirely vulnerable. If these men don't stand up for this unborn child, if this husband does not claim it as his own, Singozo will come for the woman and child, her daughters, and the nieces that she now mothers, and that will be just the beginning. They will be forced to worship his idols, and they will be passed around to the men of his village . . . many times over," Justin continued.

"Today, all the women must stay out of sight when the Tomenava men come, and they will come. Even the touch of a Tomenava man's hand is considered defiling to them. Singozo will come when he hears of her labor, and he will not come alone. By now he knows, and he's been making his way here. He's out there now, waiting."

"What do we do?" Lil asked.

"For now, I watch, and you pray. Take your pillow and place it on the floor under your knees and stay on them until you can't stay on them anymore. Pray for God's will to be done, for the safety of us all. And, Lil, pray that this child is a boy."

She understood now the seven or eight weeks from Justin's words with Papá. The baby is coming prematurely. Papá must think if the baby is too premature to survive, that God's plan could be to save the lives of the men who would have fought for it and the lives of the women and girls who would be lost without a fight. Perhaps that is what Papá is praying, Lil thought, that the Lord just takes the baby during the birth. With the husband and his brothers refusing to fight, fewer Apoya men and Justin would be left to fight, Justin who can't even speak the words of what that tribe would do to a baby girl who might be born. That must be why he is praying for a boy, Lil thought, but she also thought that the hope for a son might be wrong. Maybe this Singozo wouldn't want his own daughter passed around to the men of his tribe. Maybe he would leave a little girl here, in this tribe, better than her suffering what she would suffer in his village. Surely this Singozo would have enough heart not to want this horror for his own daughter. But

289

Justin said pray for a boy, so she would. Justin had an understanding of this place, these customs, these people, as if he were truly one of them.

"I'll be outside, watching. Stay inside," he said. "There will be no more fires today. I'll bring you yesterday's bread."

"Don't worry," Lil said. "I've never felt like praying more desperately in my life than I do right now."

Justin went outside, and Lil put her pillow on the floor and prepared to kneel beside her bed to pray.

26

Can See, but Still Am Blind

The hours were nerve-wracking. The heat was heavy. The wondering, unbearable. A young boy brought Justin a basket of bread. No fires, no children playing, nothing but a bird cawing and eventually another one answering, then a cow snorting a fly from her nose. The women and girls were staying out of sight. The Tomenava priest would be coming. The few women who were allowed to assist in the delivery had been in the labor hut of the expectant mother hours before the sun rose. Every two minutes Lil had heard the shrieking of the woman from what sounded like a long way away, screams that made their way to the dwelling as if carried on the wind, but there was no wind, just a dead heat. Now, no break existed between her shrieks. San Puente would not have spare tires until the next day. Without them, he could make only short journeys. Lil would have to stay.

The day-old bread was hard, but Lil's stomach was empty, so it tasted like a delicacy. She sucked each broken piece to soften it so she could chew it, swallowing and washing it down with hot, bottled water. She wondered if the water was ruined now, mixed with the heat. She put her eye to the opening of the flask to see if the liner was plastic, but she couldn't tell. She broke another piece of bread and sucked on it.

The bread was just the right amount of salty. It reminded her of Saltine crackers on Communion Sundays when she was a girl, when ushers passed trays of broken Saltines to serve as Jesus' body and grape juice to symbolize His blood. She would sit through the rest of the service savoring the remnants of the cracker, lifting a crumb from a molar or two with her tongue, sucking it to make it last. She would dash straight to the cookie cabinet when she got home, tear open a box of Saltines and eat one every time she passed the box throughout the day, taking a bite and sucking it, making one cracker last five minutes.

"I forget how good these crackers are, Mama, until Communion Sunday," she would say to her mother. "Can we start buying grape juice? That's the best stuff in the world," she'd add, remembering the single last drop in the communion cup that she'd try to suck out, more like inhale out of the cup at church so as not to make a slurping sound.

She'd wait for the simultaneous clicking of the congregation's cups as they placed them, now empty, in the slots attached to the backs of the pews in front of them. She hoped the mass clicking of cups would mask any sucking sound she might accidentally make trying to savor that last drop that she refused to allow to elude her in the bottom of her own cup.

The bread she sucked now brought back all those memories. It also reminded her of how thirsty she was, and she swished another sip from the canteen, thankful Justin had brought the water to this village.

Lil tried to keep her thoughts positive. She caught herself wondering what Justin was thinking by bringing her here. It wasn't even a beautiful place, not really. She knew other parts of Ecuador were probably breathtaking, but not this plot of it. Then she'd jerk her thoughts back and defend him.

He told me it was dangerous, and he could have had no idea this woman would go into labor early. He thought that event was two months away. But he knew the kind of danger this place held, and he knew she didn't understand that kind of danger, not really.

Then she'd jerk back to the positive. But the next minute would pull her back.

Not even a beach, not a meadow, nothing even worth photographing, not here. How does a girl from Alabama end up in a place like this, she asked herself. She could hear her mother's voice on the drive home from church on the Sundays their congregation had prayed for members who were going off on their first foreign missions.

"There are plenty of hungry people that need feeding and souls that need saving right here at home where it's safe."

Then she'd remind herself that Justin intended none of this. She hadn't even seen much of the place, hardly any of it, and now she was a prisoner to this mud dwelling. If she had to run, she wouldn't even know where to run. Then she thought of Justin, and how he must be feeling about having brought her here. Seeing him right now might calm her, but he told her to stay inside.

Justin had been watching for hours. He stood, he walked, he squatted, but his focus was sharp, scanning the horizon for anything that moved. He saw Papá Noel coming off in the distance.

"Justín!"

Papá hurried over to Justin. Lil got up from were she now rested, stretched on her back across her bed, and hurried to the door to hear. Her knees, through the pillow and her jeans, were bruised from her hours of prayer.

"Parto de nalgas," Papá said. "It is breech."

No one from inside the labor hut had told Papá Noel this news. He had been outside, praying and listening for anything he could hear from within the hut about the goings on inside. He saw the doula's blood-covered, white robe when she walked past the curtain that hung from the entrance to the hut. The cracks on each side of the curtain were small, but red on white is not hard to miss. The mind knows what red on white means every time it sees it. Red on the white dental napkin clipped around a reclining neck means not enough flossing. Red on a white football jersey means a bloody nose, a missing tooth. Red on a white cotton ball means the dreaded finger prick is over. This much red on a white doula gown in this village means a man will be digging at least one hole. Papá had heard with his own ears their words for breech. These types of deliveries in this village rarely ended well. Not for the baby or the mother. In the hut in these hours was woman's work, only woman's work, no matter how it ended. It was the only work the men left totally to their women.

The men often criticized how the supper tasted or the way the wife handled the children, but the men wanted no part of the curse of delivery that God placed upon this lowly gender. It was their punishment, and they were to suffer it alone.

The women reigned over these hours like four-star generals. No video cameras recorded the happenings, no balloons wafted to the ceiling, no chocolate cigars exchanged hands. No smiles, no "ooing," no "cooing," not even when the result was good. A child here made life more difficult, someone else to feed and keep well. The women loved their babies and their older children with the deepest of affection, and there would be smiles on other days over a new life, but on this day, the reality of epiduraless pain, another life and soul to save in this wilderness, was a burden. More often than not, in this land without antibiotics or even clean water, it was still easier to save the life than it was the soul. Few people ever came to try to help change that.

A doula would take staunch, unsmiling pride in handing a child to the father on most of these days. She would present the naked baby to the man just outside of the hut and stand there while he looked the creature over like a bargain hunter at a flea market trying to determine if he had been handed junk or treasure. He looked first for the sex. A boy would elicit a nod. A boy could offer far more help in surviving these jungles than a girl. A girl would take as much work to rear, and he'd be handing her away too soon after the effort to some other man.

He would inspect the child carefully as if he were deciding to keep it or not, as the price would be high.

The doula would stand there watching him with her hard attitude, both of them, emotionless. The father would count fingers and toes, feel the rims of the baby's ears, run his dirty fingers along the upper and lower gum lines, push his hands into its hair as if a defect might be hiding there. He'd lift it up over his head and look under at its backside. The doula would wait as if to ask, "Is this one good enough? Is this one finally the one to make up for that fruit? We handed you that fruit, but you ate it. Does *this* child fix it, or do we have to keep doing this until we get it right? Do we have to keep suffering the pain because you crawled on top of us again? Which son will satisfy you so we can be done?" The father would eventually nod, hand the baby back to the doula to return it to the exhausted mother inside the hut. He'd leave and go back to sleep, not really caring that another child had entered the earth until it was old enough to be of some use to him. For the first few years, it was the mother's.

"There is much blood," Papá continued.

"She tested negative?" Justin asked.

"For everything," Papá said. "Her husband, too."

"That's two out of three," Justin said.

Justin stepped into the dwelling. He reached under his bed and retrieved one of the bags lying on the floor. He unzipped it and checked the contents. It was filled with medical supplies. Lil could see blue scrub material, medicines, and packaged needles. She thought about the tiny first aid kit she'd packed.

He zipped it up. He dumped all his clothes and toiletries from the other bag on the bed, slid the trunk out and started throwing water bottles into the empty bag.

"He's warmed the water up for us on a day we have no fires," Justin said meaning God.

With no electricity, not much of anything, in a place like this, Lil realized, it's easier to give God the credit for everything. Justin has known this all along, Lil thought.

He slid the trunk back.

"Justin, your shampoo lid came open. It's all over the bed," Lil noticed, picking up the bottle and snapping the lid tight.

"Let's go," he said to Lil. "The elder can change the bed later. I'm not leaving you alone."

He touched her stomach to make sure she still had the pistol where he'd placed it. He was still carrying his rifle and was covered in his other weapons. She was relieved she was going with them. As they walked away from their dwelling, Lil saw Juanito, with his guitar and a spear, take his place on the ground in front of their porch where she'd first seen him the night before. They all hurried through the village.

"What can Justin do?" she asked Papá, as they walked briskly behind Justin. "He's not a doctor," she added.

"Lily, in our villages, we need good medical care. Justín has been practicing medicine since he was a 10-year-old boy, probably longer. He learned with his hands at the sides of his mother and his father who were fine physicians, their voices always in his ears, in these jungles and others. His skill is not his problem. The sex of this baby and its mother are."

"What do you mean?" she asked.

297

"He cannot touch this mother. It is not allowed. He cannot even look upon her naked body. It would be considered as much of a violation as the one that may have created this child. And if this baby is a girl, he cannot touch her either. Not even to save her life. Not until she is clothed for the first time at a ritual the elder will perform on the third day from her birth. If she lives."

"This is why Justin was praying for the child to be a male!" she realized. Now she understood. "Please, Lord, let it be a boy!" she whispered, horrified.

She had prayed that prayer when Justin asked her to, but only once, not like the dozens of times in the hours she had been on her knees begging God to keep Justin alive and her, too, so she could be with him, and San Puente so he could get them home and, then, of course, the child and the mother and Papá Noel and the others. She should have realized, for Justin to request any specific need from God Almighty, there had been a reason behind it.

"Please, Lord, a little boy," she asked again.

Twenty men stood outside of the hut, brothers and cousins to the husband. They were waiting to see if their relative would claim the child as his. They were armed with spears and poisoned darts, ready for Singozo. When they reached the hut, Papá Noel sent the young girl at the entrance in for the doula. The girl was one of the three nieces of the woman in labor, a daughter of this laboring woman's sister who had left to be with Singozo. This woman, now fighting to get this baby out from inside of her, was now responsible for five young daughters.

Lil looked at the youth and realized this day could end with five motherless girls.

A middle-aged woman came to the door, the doula. She was wearing a long white gown and a white headpiece tied tightly around her head. She wore surgical gloves and pulled her surgical mask down under her chin to face Papá. Visiting doctors in mission clinics taught doulas as much as they could, when the women would come to them. Smears of blood streaked her dress, and Lil was instantly glad she had eaten only bread. The screams coming from inside the hut were making her queasy. Papá said something in a language to the woman that Lil did not understand, but Justin did. Without a word, the doula went back inside.

Papá looked at Justin, who nodded. Lil could hear a man's voice inside arguing with the woman. The painful shrieks of the woman in labor never subsided. Her labor screams turned into shouts of words Lil couldn't make out. The other voices calmed, but continued to talk. The laboring woman's screaming came with no relief. Lil wanted to go home.

Justin sat the two bags on the ground. He and Papá Noel seemed so calm, but Lil wanted to charge in and do something, anything to help stop the screaming, anything to help this woman.

The same old woman who had changed their bed linens earlier walked out of the hut. She looked at the two men and nodded. Justin knelt down in front of her, and she began to chant. As if her words were instructing him, he bowed his head and closed his eyes. She continued chanting. She inhaled deeply, focusing on the air she was taking in, then she blew on

299

her index finger until all of her breath was expelled. She touched one of Justin's closed eyes with her finger and hummed a solitary note for the same amount of time that it had taken to exhale the air she had inhaled. She did the same with her other index finger, touching his other eye. She reached into her pocket and retrieved a strip of white linen. She took the linen, holding one end in each hand and passed it across Justin's closed eyes, back and forth, again and again, pressing her thumbs in to keep contact with each eye as the linen crossed the bridge of his nose. She continued to chant, and he held out his hands. She pulled a larger piece of linen from her other pocket and ran it in every direction around his hands, making sure to go between each of his fingers. All this, this slow, tedious ritual, while the woman in the hut was screaming in pain.

Justin was patient with their rituals. He knew what to expect as if he'd done this or seen this before. The old woman circled around him, stopping in front of him. She instructed him to open his eyes, then gave him further instructions and went back into the tent. Justin stood and retrieved the bags without Papá's help. He would be going in alone.

He took one step toward the hut, but stopped abruptly as the husband of the woman in labor stepped from inside and blocked his way. Justin was not surprised to see the man at the delivery. The husband had claimed he would be the first to see the head of this child forcing its way from this "whore's womb," as he put it on his loudest drunken evenings that had been many since they'd found her lying on the border that morning seven months earlier. He told her she should have begged the Tomenava priest to kill her when he was finished with her so that he could more quickly take another wife.

He was waiting the crowning of this baby's head for a reason. The Tomenava men claimed their sons who would be priests entered this world with shiny, hairless heads, ready for the burning of the priest's marking that they placed on the children's scalps when they were one. It was true that their tribe's children were mostly hairless at birth, while the children of the Apoyas entered the world with thick, matted curls, but not always, so they would never know for sure which man fathered this child. This man had told his wife, when the shiny scalp emerged between her wicked legs, that he would rip the child out himself and kill him before Singozo had a chance to take him and raise him under his wooden idol. He swore his knife would be even swifter to cut the throat of a daughter to save her from what the Tomenava satan would do to her. No one knew when the alcohol left him how much of anything he said had been true, but there he was, the first Apoya father ever, standing in the door of a labor hut. Perhaps this baby had heard this husband's threatening words, and turned itself around in its mother's womb to keep its head from crowning first.

"Bring her," he ordered speaking Spanish, pointing at Lil, "your woman, so she will know where your eyes are and judge for herself."

"Sí," Justin answered.

The man went back inside, and Justin stepped over to Lil.

"What is this? What is going on?" she asked.

"The elder has performed a ceremony," Papá said, "where, though Justin has eyes and can see, he is blind to the nakedness

301

of this woman who is giving birth. If he accidentally touches her, although he touches, he cannot feel."

While Papá Noel was explaining the ritual to Lil, Justin was retrieving items from the medical bag.

"Accidentally touches her?" Lil asked. "Justin still can't help her?"

"No, not without the husband's permission," Papá said. "He won't give it, but at least Justin can go inside now. He'll be of some help there."

"The husband is going to let them die, isn't he?" Lil said. "He wants them to die, doesn't he?"

"Put these on her," Justin said, handing Papá a scrub gown, a mask and gloves.

He removed the bow and arrows and put his own scrub shirt on top of his T-shirt. He pulled the mask down around his neck. Whatever he was allowed to do beyond that curtain would be done with a bow and a pouch of arrows strapped around his chest. He replaced them, and handed Papá his rifle. Last, he pulled on his surgical gloves.

"Reach behind the gown," Justin instructed Lil, "and slide the pistol to a position where you can rest your hand on it comfortably."

Lil did.

"Keep your hand on it," he instructed.

"I'm not shooting the husband!" Lil said, confused.

Justin smiled for the first time in hours.

"Let's go in," Justin said walking in ahead of her, his smile already gone.

27

The Labor Hut

J ustin walked past the curtain, and held it to the side for Lil to enter. He nodded his head once to the women and tried to take in as much as he could to factor the situation as quickly as he could. Lil had told herself not to look at anything that would make her faint, but she couldn't help but look at the face of the laboring mother. Seventeen. She couldn't have been older than seventeen. She was just a girl, and this was her third labor.

"Please, Lord, help her, and please, let Justin help her," Lil prayed.

This hut wasn't the regular labor hut. This girl and this child she labored to unleash would never be allowed in the labor hut where other women, undefiled women, would give birth. The Apoya's doula would not dirty her hands on this woman and her child. If she had, she would not have been allowed to touch the other women in the village during the labors to come. A doula from another tribe was here. This doula's daughter had died in childbirth months earlier. Her pregnancy, too, had been the result of a rape. This doula saw her own daughter's death as a gift; she would have died soon anyway, a long, drawn-out death, from the disease the rapist had given her. The doula cared for the grandchild the best she could, but she died, too, from the same disease. This doula's defiance, her presence in the hut now, marked her courage, but she was not happy there were men among them. It was still her labor hut.

Justin knew something in this doula's heart was good because she had come for this woman and this child. His eyes met the doula's, and in her language he said thank you, using words that told her of the blessing she would receive from the One who knew the hardships this would cause her. There it was--Lil saw it--that focus as his eyes spoke to this woman, then as he scanned the room to catch up on the last fourteen hours of what had happened here. This place or one like it was where it started, she realized, in these situations, in these jungles, that intense focus. Had he not grown up the way he had, he never would have looked at her the way he did. Thank goodness he liked what he saw when he looked at her, she thought, because he was looking past the surface to what lay within.

Lil watched Justin's eyes. Watching him take in the sights was all she could do. Watching him kept her own eyes away from anything she would not be able to handle. She tried to read from his face anything that would give her hope for this girl and this child.

The girl's screams were waning, not because the pain was, but because her blood pressure was disappearing. She had lost too much of the precious red fluid. The doula had blood to give the girl because when Justin arrived in Ecuador, he had made sure there would be blood to give. He always gave blood his first day at the hospital in Quito, along with a few nurses who were always willing to help him. Justin was a universal donor. With a fresh bandage on his arm and his pockets stuffed with hundred dollar bills, he would spend the next couple of days collecting other supplies that benefactors arranged to send him from other countries, countries that had fewer regulations than the United States had when it came to transporting drugs and other liquids. He would return for the blood and start the remainder of his journey, not knowing how many of his supplies, if any, would appear at his final landing, but that was out of his control.

Ice was his next biggest obstacle, keeping that blood cold. Two solid blocks of ice with a space carved out between them were frozen to fit snuggly into a cooler. The blocks were placed together with the bags of blood nestled in the hollowed center. The second Justin lifted the cooler to begin the final leg of his trek, that ice would begin to melt. The cooler would never leave his hand. He guarded it as though he were guarding the life of a king's child.

On the last flight, Justin would sit in the small prop plane among the other flyers who frequented these jungles of Ecuador, all by now, including him, openly wearing weapons, most letting them rest in their hands on top of the single brief cases they transported. Eventually, the plane would land in a field with four-foot high grass, and every man would exit quickly and run to a darkly tinted, awaiting SUV. Justin, his pockets now empty, would disembark, and quickly unload his own supplies from the small cargo hold. While still in their seats, the pilot and copilot aimed guns into the distance and ordered Justin to move faster, threatening to take off with his supplies still in the plane and with his head hanging from the propeller, and Justin knew they were serious. Within minutes of landing, they would taxi away while Justin ducked. San Puente would pull up, jump out, and quickly help him load the boxes into the truck, first plugging the cooler into the truck's cigarette lighter, the one piece of equipment in that banged up truck they were certain to keep in working order. As fast as the plane had come and gone, Justin and San Puente, too, would slam their doors and speed away. Sitting in those fields for long wasn't wise.

They would deliver the cooler to the nearest clinic forty minutes from the village, leaving some of the new supplies there as well. The clinic had the facility to store the blood until its generators overheated. They ran the generators only when they were fortunate enough to have blood. Papá Noel had sent San Puente to the clinic to retrieve the blood in the dark morning hours, just in case. He brought this doula as well.

Justin spoke to the doula in Spanish. Lil was relieved. She hated not knowing what was happening.

"How long ago did you start the transfusion?" he asked the doula.

"Hace quince minutos," she answered.

He smiled and nodded at her answer, though he knew fifteen minutes ago was at least two hours too late. Nothing he could do about that now. His goal was to hang on to the invitation into this hut as long as he could, and the only way to do that was to keep this doula on his side. He had learned early that tribal leaders must save face if he were to continue to be welcome in their villages, their clinics, and their labor huts.

Others were in the hut as well. The toothless elder sat in a chair, to witness. She would not be shunned for being here as the doula surely would be. The elder was allowed to be anywhere she felt she needed to be. Witnessing events, whether happy or tragic, with her own eyes, was the only way an elder gained wisdom. The three daughters of the laboring woman's sister were there, as was one of her own children, her 5-year-old daughter, to help with the birth. The laboring woman's husband, sweating whiskey, sat as far back into the shadows as a small hut would allow. No one else, no experienced women would come. Husbands had forbidden the others who wanted to help from coming to this hut.

"What is this medicine here?" Justin asked indicating the intravenous catheter taking medicine through the back of the girl's hand.

The doula gruffly told him what it was, and though the drug was doing no harm, it was providing no help in this situation. Two questions so quickly angered the doula.

"Again, you have taken such good care," Justin said. Her face didn't show it, but that comment softened her, and she took pride that the others had heard it. "Do you have any antibiotic in your supplies?" he asked, mentioning a specific one.

307

"No," she answered.

"I'm sure you had been hoping you had," he said, whether she was aware she needed this drug or not.

It was not lost on Lil that Justin was helping this mother through a doula who lacked experience, while helping the doula save face, all without the authority to touch the patient.

"Of course!" the doula said, defiantly, though she had never even heard of the drug Justin mentioned.

"If I have some," he said, knowing he did, "I will gladly offer it. I should have enough for you to change that medicine and enter the antibiotic into that same IV catheter you have established already in the mother's vein, as well as into the baby's vein when it comes," he instructed, with the sound of assumption that she already knew these things, whether she did or not. "It is the best I have to fight any infection because of the premature birth," he said, not mentioning the unavoidably unsterile surroundings. "What's mine is yours," he added.

He went to his bag, covered the table with a sterile cloth, retrieved the medicine, and placed it on the table for the doula. He laid a smaller catheter, IV tubing, needle, and syringe, for the baby next to it, and a clean needle and syringe for the mother. His hands desperately wanted to prepare the medicine and get it into that girl's body. If he had the authority, the drug already would have been changed, and that baby already would be in this world.

"I'm honored I got here in time to assist with what's about to happen now," he said, "watching life come into this world. I'm ready," he said. " I know you are, so I will step out of your way," he said, not telling her what to do, but letting her know to begin something now.

Another minute could be too late.

"Forgive me if I say the steps out loud as you go. It's a habit I've had since I stood at my mother's side," he said, making sure to say his mother's side instead of his father's side, though both had been skilled in this situation. "Speaking it aloud helps me remember her guiding words to me," Justin said, certain this woman had met his mother in the past and respected her work among their villages.

His mother had introduced these tribes to the word "doula," and made sure many of these women had more nursing skills than the term implied. Justin's guiding instructions to her began.

The doula administered the antibiotic to the mother, and Justin let a small blowing exhale release from his lungs through barely parted lips, unnoticed by the others, except for Lil. He was relieved the medicine could start its work. Lil saw his relief, and she admired his calm approach. She had seen all the blood now, all the signs of impending death that she thought would make her faint, but they were background sights and sounds to her. Her gaze and her ears were focused on Justin. He changed his language to Sabiojo, and said something to the elder, who glanced over at Lil. Then he continued, turning back to the doula, now speaking in Lenguaba. Lil could hear the guttural changes in the different languages and knew he was changing between the few he had told her about. She knew when Justin changed languages, that he had very specific reasons for doing so.

Justin had reasons for everything he did. He needed the younger generations here who spoke only Spanish, not to understand the next conversation between him and the doula because even the doula would have to pretend he wasn't instructing her on her own profession. He knew she had exhausted her experience, and she knew it too. She had to move her pride over, and he was going to help her do that. If she didn't get that baby out now, it would be a matter of who would see God first, the child or its mother.

He started talking, and she followed his instructions. Lil watched; she watched Justin. There was no need to listen to the words; she understood none of them. She watched his face and listened to his voice, how he taught, encouraged, and helped. His parents must have been this way with him. Lil thought of them and of Justin at their sides as a boy. When the doula's frustration rose high with angry tones at the horrible task at her hands, screaming at Justin at the top of her lungs, he remained calm for her and the mother. However, the mother was now unconscious, but that was a temporary blessing, and he needed to get to her next.

Lil loved him, with every guiding word, even more, with every nod of encouragement, more, with the sight of his fingers squeezing his own thighs to keep himself from shoving this woman out of his way and grabbing that baby himself, she loved him more. She was lost in this emotion, but brought back to the room by the sound of one short cry that lasted only a second. The baby's. She couldn't see the baby. The husband had stepped in the way, holding a fishing knife. She hadn't even realized it, but he had found a spot between them to watch for the baby's head. Her hand felt for the pistol.

All she could see was the husband's back. Was the child a boy or a girl? Did it have a shiny, bald head, or was it covered in matted curls? She couldn't see! She saw the man's head move its stare up to his wife's face. She had regained consciousness. Then the man turned and walked out of the hut. The twenty men outside followed him away from the labor hut.

The child lay in the doula's hands. A boy. A tiny boy. He wasn't bald, but he had no massive amount of hair either. The man had left not knowing, but he had left, and that was all that the woman who struggled for life on the table needed to know. He would not fight for this child that could be his. His uncles would not fight for him. But in this moment, Justin would.

Justin took the precious life from the doula, and went to work clearing the air passages for the child. He instructed the girls to bring him the warm bottled water and start a fire to warm blankets. He reached for the medicine and established an IV catheter for the baby. He closed his eyes and listened through the stethoscope that he gently held on the baby's chest, a tiny chest that wasn't much bigger than the silver circle Justin held on it. He kept his eyes closed, listening to this tiny heart slowly beating in the jungles of Ecuador, near the center of the earth.

Lil could see the confidence of his knowing what to do, but she also knew there was only so much he could do in this setting. This baby's chances were slim. Justin spoke calmly to the doula while he worked on the child, giving her instructions of what to be doing for the mother. Lil gave the mother small sips of water, knowing how good it must feel and taste. The small crowd in the hut moved like a MASH unit after a long battle.

"Justín!" Papá Noel shouted to Justin from outside the hut.

Lil was to the left of the door, between the mother and the place where Justin and the baby's two cousins stood tending to the baby. The doula was to the right of the bed, still helping the woman, with the woman's daughter assisting her. Farther to the right sat the elder, in a chair like the ones in the Poco Dolor closets, watching the events unfold. They all jerked their heads toward Papá Noel's shout. The curtain was ripped from its nails, and Singozo entered carrying a machete.

Singozo was massive, and his shiny, bald head was tattooed with the Tomenava high priest markings. Four men armed with spears pushed up close behind him, just outside the entrance.

The doula threw a blanket over the mother and started a verbal defense of her labor hut, screaming something at Singozo who stood at the entrance. She screamed it for a long time. He allowed her this loud monologue while he looked around the small hut as if he couldn't hear a word she shouted.

Lil's legs trembled. She took in as much of what was happening as she could and turned her face to Justin. Justin already had his bow in his hand and an arrow in its string. He had known what Papá's shouts meant, and in the seconds that had passed between his shouts and the ripping of the blanket at the entrance, Justin prepared to defend whomever one solitary arrow could defend. Lil slowly moved her hand to her pistol. Her way might be quicker than his. She wanted to wake up. This was unreal.

"What am I doing in Ecuador?! This isn't my life!" she thought.

Her whole body trembled, and something was happening to her skin, something cold and clammy that she knew a dog could smell. Real fear. It will be quick, she told herself. Whatever it is, it will be quick. Quicker than this labor. She feared that her twitching muscles would involuntarily pull her trigger. She could see past the four men to Papá Noel. His rifle was aimed at them, but she wondered if he would really pull the trigger on five lost souls. Her hand gripped the pistol. She didn't wonder if she'd pull the trigger. She knew she would. She would squeeze it as many times as it would fire to save Justin.

"I'll take the boy now," Singozo said in Spanish.

"He needs medical care," Justin said. "He won't live an hour without it."

"I don't care," Singozo said.

Singozo looked at the girl on the table. He doubted she would survive the hour. Pity, too, he thought; she was pretty, but useless to him now. He glanced at the daughters around the room, taking in their frames and features. Then he saw Lil. A strand of her blond hair had fallen from her hat. He smiled.

"I heard of your woman. I haven't seen hair that color in years," he said and stepped toward Lil.

That's when Lil heard it--the sound she'd only heard in movies--the slicing an arrow makes cutting the air. It stabbed the ground just in front of Singozo's walking toes. He jerked his head toward Justin.

"Where I come from, Singozo," Justin said in English, pulling the string back on his second arrow, "we treat our women better than you do. You could say we'd die for them."

He knew Singozo spoke English.

"That one," Justin said about Lil, "I'll die for. Or you will. Either way."

Singozo laughed as if to die for a woman was the dumbest thing he'd ever heard.

Justin stepped once away from the baby and toward Lil, and, merely, said, "Lil," and she knew he wanted her behind him. She stepped closer to Justin, just close enough to reach for one of the young girls and pull the girl behind her. The girl dragged her sister who was holding the baby behind Lil as well, but Lil didn't step completely behind Justin. She needed a clear shot at Singozo.

"Then I will take just the boy," Singozo said, "today," he added, glancing at the girls who peeked out from behind Lil.

Not once since he entered the hut had Singozo referred to the baby as his son. Twice he'd referred to the child as "the boy." Justin knew these tribes. He knew all too well that the men always referred to their boys as "my son," "mi hijo," as if "mi hijo" were an actual name, always. Singozo was not convinced this boy was his child, and Justin knew it. Singozo's tribe would never accept the boy as a priest, and Justin knew that reality would soon bring shame to Singozo.

"He oído las historias sobre la madre que regalaría su hijo en vez de cortarlo por el medio," Singozo said. Then he smiled. "Cortaré éste el medio primero y duermo bien esta noche." I've heard your tales of the mother who would give her child away

314

instead of cutting it in half. I will cut this one in half first and sleep well tonight.

He stepped toward the child, but Justin retrieved his knife and blocked Singozo's way. Without hesitation, Lil stepped foward and pulled out her gun. Singozo smiled at her foolish courage, but he wasn't the only one in the hut who was smiling. The elder watched Lil. When she saw Lil raise the pistol and point it at Singozo, a smile creased across the wrinkles in her face, showing her completely toothless gums. Lil put her other hand on the weapon, and steadied her first hand, ready to fire, Her hands weren't shaking anymore. She knew what she might have to do. And she was equipped for it. Her father had made sure of that.

The elder stood up from her chair. She mumbled something to Justin and started one of her chants. She literally shoved past Singozo, not afraid that any touch of his skin would defile her, and at her age, not even caring if it did. She was not afraid of his big knife. She shoved her way past the other four as well, as if their spears were mere sticks, and this crowd of fools was playing childish games. She no longer concerned herself with the birth, near deaths, nor threats of the labor hut. She pushed her way out to get on with her next chores. They all let her pass like one would let any crazy old loon pass.

"Do your men speak English?" Justin said quickly in English to get Singozo's attention away from Lil and her gun.

He didn't want her to have to live with memories of anything worse than she'd already seen that day. He just wanted her to live.

315

Singozo shook his head no. Justin needed for Lil to understand everything he was going to say and for Singozo's men not to understand.

"Lil, don't lower your gun yet, but don't fire it either, not yet," Justin instructed. "Singozo has four men with him here, but there are many more men out in the trees waiting for any sound to pull them in. Singozo," Justin said to the man, "I don't believe you want this child," Justin continued. "You do not want to spend your life with a boy that your tribe will never accept as a high priest, a boy who, when he's grown, will more than likely look like another man. What Tomenava priest would want that life? I think you are looking for a reason to start a war. I have an offer that should be acceptable to you. I take the child when I leave. I find a place to take him, a place far from here. Don't start this war for a child who probably won't even survive the night, Singozo. Leave this child with me."

"And how will I know you have taken him?" Singozo said.

"You'll have to trust me," Justin said.

"No, no," Singozo laughed. "That would require faith. I have to see with my own eyes."

He looked back at Lil.

"Your woman will hold him without a blanket through the roof in your truck as you drive past our land so we witness it."

"The child will not survive," Justin said.

Singozo smiled. "I don't care," he said.

Justin nodded agreement.

316

"Okay, Lil," Justin said. "He will tell you in his language, Aldeabla, for his men to hear, to lower your gun, and you will lower it."

Both Lil and Singozo knew Justin was allowing Singozo to keep his pride in tact in front of his men. Not to do so could have harsh, future repercussions. Singozo nodded to Justin, then shouted some harsh words at Lil. She lowered her gun upon his words. Then he pushed past his men, out of the hut, and they turned and followed him.

"Singozo!" Justin shouted, now speaking Spanish from the opening of the hut. "The church is finished. The front door faces your village. We will all meet our Maker soon. It's best to meet Him here first. Papá Noel would like to introduce you to the Maker's Son. Put down your weapons soon and come."

It was not lost on Lil that Justin had said those words in Spanish. He knew Singozo would not come, but his invitation, in Spanish, was for the other four with him.

The men left, Singozo laughing at Justin's invitation to church.

Justin explained to the mother the agreement he had come to with Singozo. Justin's promise to find a Christian home for her boy gave her great joy, joy for her son.

"¡Gracias, San Justín!" she exclaimed to Justin. Then she looked to Lil. "¡Gracias, Señorita! ¡Muchas gracias!"

Justin took the young girl's hands, and Lil listened with tears running down her cheeks as the two bowed their heads and closed their eyes, and began to pray.

" . . . Venga Tu reino. Hágase Tu voluntad así en la tierra como en el cielo . . . "

Lil quietly joined them in English, "Thy kingdom come . . .."

28

La Primera Sábana

Justin did all he could with the medicines he had to help the baby and assist the doula in helping the mother. San Puente came and transported the mother, her baby, her older daughter, and the doula to the clinic. He would return as soon as he could to take Justin, Lil, and the baby on their journey to the nearest town with better facilities. San Puente had much work to do to arrange for the papers and transportation, but he had done so many times before. He was a saint among the missionaries and villages.

Justin and Lil walked back toward their dwelling.

"How are you liking my vacation so far?" he asked, smiling.

Lil smiled. She wasn't exactly ready to joke about it.

"East side of Birmingham," she managed to say, "not such a dangerous place, is it?"

Justin laughed.

"Lil, you've never looked more beautiful in all the time I've known you than you do right now," Justin said, "but I bet you'd like to shower."

"Yes!" Lil exclaimed. "And I want to brush my teeth!"

Juanito was planted in front of the stone wall of their mud house, and the elder was coming toward them. She had come out of their dwelling with the sheets that the shampoo had sullied, bundled in her arms. She was chanting her blessings as she walked.

"When we were in the labor hut, I told her we needed new linens," Justin explained.

"During all of that?" Lil asked.

"I knew it was the one thing that had impressed you since we arrived, the turn-down service," he smiled.

The old woman walked past them, chanting, and for the first time she smiled at Lil.

"I understood that part of what she just said," Lil said straining to understand some more of the woman's chant, as the elder swapped among the several tongues she spoke.

"El poco dolor," Lil said, "the small pain," she translated, though she knew Justin understood every word the old woman said in every language she said it in.

She knew the woman was referring to the mud house where she and Justin were staying.

"And there it is again!" Lil said, still listening to the woman who was passing them.

" 'La primera sábana,' clear as a bell in Spanish," Lil quoted the woman, "and that was the *third* bed change!" she protested.

Justin just smiled and pulled Lil closer to him as they walked.

They scrubbed their hands. The fires had been burning since Singozo left with his men, everything in the village postponed much later than usual because of the day's happenings. The midnight hour had passed. Justin said they should eat before the men doused the cooking fires, then shower. No fish that night, but the grilled plantains were delicious.

"I'll walk you to the Poco Dolor so you can brush your teeth and get your toiletries," Justin said, "and the women will come take you to the shower."

When Lil walked out of the mud house holding her bath items and change of clothes, a group of women dressed in white were waiting outside for her. Justin was sitting on the wall.

"They'll take you to your shower. Mine is this way," he pointed in a different direction.

Lil walked to him and whispered.

"I get to bathe myself, right?"

He nodded and guided her over to the women, saying something Lil didn't understand. She hoped he was telling them that all she needed were directions. One woman took Lil's things for her, and they took Lil by her hands, smiled at her, and guided her away from Justin. Justin grabbed his soaps and razor and jogged in the opposite direction.

Lil never expected to have warm water. The women filled the primitive plumbing with buckets of water heated over a fire. Justin would tell her later about the showers. Juanito's family built them. Juanito's family members were fontaneros, plomeros. Plumbers. The shower system was based on the same premise that fountains are, recirculating water. In this case, the pump at the system's heart was powered by human energy, these women's, two of them Juanito's sisters, fontaneras.

The water was the most soothing water Lil had ever felt. The women worked together so smoothly that Lil never had a moment without a warm stream falling over her. She showered quickly, shampooed, conditioned, and ran a razor up her legs. She remembered to keep the water out of her mouth, and maneuvered to keep it out of her ears the best she could.

She shyly peeked around the curtain to reach for her towel. Two of the women stood there holding a different one out for her, a beautifully bleached, soft, white towel. She ran into it, not because she was cold, but because of the awkwardness of these strangers seeing her naked. Even backstage in wardrobe, she'd never been totally nude. A third woman insisted that Lil sit on a wooden stool while she combed and tended to her hair for her. The other two rubbed her legs and arms with some lotion that smelled most closely like cocoa butter than anything else Lil could compare it to, but whatever it was, Lil hoped they'd send some home with her when she left. The last two women approached her with a gown. It was a simple but gorgeous, white gown, softer even than the towel had been.

"I have some clothes. Mi ropa está allí," she motioned to what she had brought with her from the mud house.

They shook their heads no. Lil slipped her arms into the awaiting gown's sleeves that reached to her elbows, and the women wrapped the gown around her. The gown closed across

Lil's front, the first side concealing her, the second overlapping the first, the outer layer curving under one breast, where on her side, ribbons there met up with other ribbons on the other edge of the gown. Twenty-six ribbons paired together, closely lined the edges running down Lil's side. One woman held the gown together while another tied bows with each pair of ribbons, working her way down to the last pair that came just below Lil's hip at the top of her thigh. The gown hugged her curves magnificently. The sheer number of ribbons added tremendously to the beauty of the gown.

The gown was open from the last bow to the ground, but the overlapping of the fabric concealed Lil just enough, allowing her leg to peek ever so slightly when she walked. The gown reached past her feet, and a few extra inches gathered romantically on the ground. She forgot how awkward she felt a few minutes before, and admired the beauty of the gown, not made from any fancy laces, just a simple, soft fabric.

"Perfecto, Margarita," one of the women said to Margarita, implying that Margarita had made the gown.

Margarita knelt down and held open a soft white, handmade slipper, fashioned like a ballet slipper, and helped Lil place each foot inside each slipper. The fit, again, was perfect. Lil and Margarita smiled at each other, as Lil remembered that Margarita had made rudimentary measurements of her the day she arrived.

The women escorted Lil toward her dwelling along the earthen paths lit by torches. Lil held up the length of the gown as she walked to keep it clean from the dirt. Halfway there, she saw Justin waiting for her. He had on fresh jeans with his knife strapped to his leg and his rifle in his hand. He was wearing a beautiful white shirt she'd never seen him wear before. Papá Noel stood next to him. When he saw Lil approaching with the other women, Papá touched Justin on the back and walked away. The women stopped walking. Margarita kissed Lil on the cheek and stayed back with the others to let Lil join Justin alone. He took her hand and led her into the Poco Dolor.

"You are the most beautiful woman my eyes have ever seen," he said, caressing Lil's hair when they got inside.

He lifted her chin and kissed her, just one, long kiss, though she wanted more.

Justin went to the side of his bed, stood the gun in the corner, and tightened the knife holster.

"Are you sleeping with your knife?" Lil asked.

"All the men are guarding the rest of the night in case Singozo has a change of heart. He's certainly not a man of honor. I'm not taking chances. I have to get you home safely, Lil."

She went and sat on her bed while he said these things, wondering if she was supposed to sleep in this gown or change into her things now. It was soft enough. She thought she would keep it on. She didn't want to take it off just yet.

"I'm going to watch outside for the next hour, Lil," Justin said from her doorway. "The other men guarded and slept in shifts during the day. I'll be right out front. The torches will burn all night. Try to rest," he told her.

He pulled the pistol from where it was stuck in his jeans.

"Keep this beside you," he said.

She went to take it from him. He was one step into her room when she met him and took the gun. She wondered if he realized he had passed the threshold. For him to enter her room, Lil knew he thought she was still in danger. Perhaps he just didn't notice where he was standing.

Singozo had seen Lil, and Justin knew what that meant. He knew a blond-haired, blue-eyed woman was uncommon among these tribes. Singozo would consider Lil quite a find. Justin also knew a woman who looked as different as Lil would be impossible for Singozo to keep for long. He would have to dispose of her quickly, but he would have to kill Justin first, to get to Lil.

Lil tried to sleep, but as tired as she should be, she replayed the day. She should have felt more at ease knowing Justin was outside watching, but she desired to have him inside, nearer to her. She placed her pillow on the floor and spent an hour in prayer, thanking God for their safety and asking for continued blessings on the mother, her son, and all her daughters. She remembered Justin's invitation to Singozo and his men to come to church, and she prayed that they would.

An hour into Justin's watch, Lil got up. She just needed to glance out the door. She saw Justin across the plaza talking to some of the men. She could see the top of Juanito's head as he squatted, guarding the Poco Dolor on the other side of the stone wall. Even the twenty men outside the labor hut earlier were way in the distance, standing watch for their wives and daughters. She noticed a shifting of the guard. Justin was getting ready to come inside. Now she would rest. Just a little longer before the sun would rise.

She walked back to her room. She forgot to lift the hem of the gown, and she stepped on top of it, tripping herself. Struggling to keep her balance, she knocked over the bucket, which clattered across the floor, rolling underneath the bed, and she fell in all the clamor. Justin heard the noise and ran to the mud house. He jumped over Juanito who ducked, cleared the stone wall, and ran inside.

"Lil!"

"I'm fine," Lil answered, "just clumsy."

Justin had already leaned down and scooped her into his arms.

"Justin," she said, her face close to his, "you're on my side of the dwelling."

"It's okay," he answered. "I thought you were in danger," he said, gently putting her down. "Juanito!" Justin shouted over his shoulder. "Gracias, amigo. Eso es todo por esta noche," he said, thanking Juanito and sending him on his way.

Juanito picked up his spear and his resting guitar and jogged to the far side of the plaza and into the trees to join his father and brothers who were keeping watch. He sat beside them as they stood with their spears and looked at his father who nodded at Juanito.

"Toque su guitarra hasta que salga el sol, mi hijo," his father granted him permission to play his guitar until the sun rose, which would be soon.

Juanito smiled his thanks. He placed his guitar in his lap, clamped the capo across the strings of the third fret, and played without error the song he had been working on, Bryan Adams' "Here I Am."

A drizzle began to tap the trees, the large leaves of which provided shelter for the men underneath them, standing watch. The light from the torches danced around each raindrop, surviving the soft rain to illuminate the space in the Poco Dolor through the open door. The notes from Juanito's steel strings rode in on the warm breeze.

Justin looked at every feature on Lil's face. He ran his hands into her hair and slowly moved his face close to hers. He kissed her softly on each side of her lips, letting his mouth touch the outer edges of hers. He let his nose graze her cheeks, breathing her. He pulled back just slightly, moved his hands to her neck, looked into her blue eyes, and kissed her passionately. His hands felt their way down her form until they reached her waist, and his lips moved to where his hands had been on her neck. He continued to feel his way down her body, reaching behind her to the small of her back, and he pulled her close, pressing her against him, moving his lips back to hers, and he kissed her intensely.

"Te amo, Lily," Justin whispered, his lips still touching hers as he spoke.

He kissed her passionately between his words.

"Te quiero, Lily . . . Te necesito, Lily."

I love you, Lily. I want you, Lily. I need you, Lily. And he kissed her again.

"Marry me, Lil," Justin whispered.

"Yes, yes, Justin," Lil whispered back as a tear fell from the outer corner of each of her eyes.

She answered with a passionate kiss, moving her hands into Justin's hair. She was ready. He lifted her into his arms again,

327

and took her to his side of the Poco Dolor. He closed the door, and laid her gently on his bed. The soft light of the torches coming in around the door's edges gave them just enough light. He removed his shirt and unfastened the holster around his thigh. He unbuttoned his jeans and dropped them to the floor, and lay beside her.

The kissing lasted an eternity. He started with her mouth, her cheeks, her ears and neck, down to her collarbone, and back to her mouth. His felt the roundness of her breasts, and caressed them, around and down to her waist and stomach, sliding up again to her breasts. His hands looked more masculine than usual as they untied the twenty-six ribbons that concealed her. He pushed the fabric from his way, opening the gown in both directions, and gazed upon her.

"Dulce perfección," he whispered, and his kisses moved over her to where the gown had once stopped him.

He lifted Lil's back from the mattress, moved the gown out from underneath her, reached up and draped it around the post of the bed. His lips returned to her mouth, her neck, her breasts, her stomach. No woman's body had ever been given such attention and affection before.

She could feel the length of his body against her side, every part of him warm, moving and kissing her, caressing her. Then he was on top of her. His mouth found hers, and his body moved in waves. She felt him. He was ready. He loved her. He had waited for her, and she was ready.

"Justin!" she gasped, out of breath.

He lifted his eyes to hers, but she didn't say anything else. She just breathed heavily, looking into his eyes.

"Un poco dolor," he said softly.

She understood.

He moved to where he had waited to be. Lil closed her eyes, and pushed her head back into the pillow, moving with him as he moved with the waves of his body. He slid his hands between her and the mattress, sliding them down, past the small of her back, lifting her there ever so slightly, and he moved, and she moved with him, her hands running from his broad shoulders to the lowest part of his back. It was Justin. Justin! Their breathing increased, Justin's becoming heavier and heavier. His motion became increasingly stronger. She felt his mouth again on her breasts, and his movements increased. A panting took Lil. A rapid, unexpected panting, quicker and quicker. The sound of it excited Justin's motions even more, and he could control the moment no longer. One masculine groan left him, then a smaller one and a smaller one. He let his face fall against Lil's neck for a few seconds, breathing in the completeness of it all. He lifted his face to hers and kissed her lips as if for the first time. He returned his face to her neck and let the weight of his body relax on top of hers, his breathing starting to slow.

Lil wrapped her arms around him, moving her hands up into his hair. She stroked it between her fingers wondering how his heavy body felt so light at the moment, noticing that every part of their bodies fit together, and adoring the thin layer of sweat that held them glued there for what she wished could be forever. She wished he would stay right where he was throughout the night. He raised his head from her fingers that still caressed his hair and began to lift himself from her, thinking he was too heavy. She moved her hands to his lower back to stop him.

"Not yet," she said.

She could feel his pulse in every part of him. Even the bed pulsed beneath them. She slowly reached her hand up to her throat, and felt for her own pulse. She closed her eyes, and a smile relaxed across her face.

"Dos corazones, un ritmo," she whispered. Two hearts, one rhythm.

Justin looked at her.

"Un imán divino les une," he finished the thought. A Divine magnet unites them.

"Yes! But how?

"I wrote about that legend for a journal," he replied.

She lifted herself up against him. The panting took her again, just as unexpected as the first time, quick, breathing pants, that made Justin want her again, and their bodies started their motions, and Justin groaned again. He sank on top of her. He wrapped his arms underneath and around her and rolled to his back, taking her with him, looking up at her face. She found her new position on top of him, their legs stretched the length of the bed.

"Really?" Justin said, smiling, and Lil started laughing, nodding her head and laying her forehead against his chest.

"This bodes well for me," he said, smiling, raising Lil's face in his hands to look at her.

"Pretty well for me, too," she said breathlessly, smiling back at him.

"Even that is part of the Maker's creation," he said.

Lil had never thought of it like that before. She shifted to his side, opposite the side she started on, and stretched her arm across him, settled her cheek into his chest, closed her eyes, and listened to his heart beating. She felt Justin lift his head from the pillow. His hand left her arm that it had held and stretched across the sheet to where she had been lying and gently rubbed it.

"Lil," Justin said.

Lil lifted her head, and her eyes moved to where his hand caressed the sheet. A stain was there of the most beautiful red she'd ever seen.

"La Primera Sábana," Justin told her. "The First Sheet," he translated.

A tear rolled down Lil's cheek.

"La Primera Sábana! That's what the elder has been saying!" Lil realized. "This is what she meant," Lil began to understand it all. "The First Sheet," she repeated Justin's words as another tear rolled down her cheek.

Justin kissed her. He turned on his side and faced her. He stroked her hair, preparing to share part of his life with her.

"This village is where my parents brought me for my chest to heal," he started. "They sent me to Greece when I was well. By then I had turned 11, and at 12, I came back. I woke one morning early. I could hear children outside, earlier than usual. My parents were still asleep. They'd had a long night at the clinic. I got up without waking them. I came here to the plaza where I had followed the voices. Mothers sat among their children. Their sons were running shirtless around them. Their daughters, all wearing white, were sitting around them and in

331

their laps. The younger ones were toddling around their mothers. Men sat among the trees, with drums waiting in their laps. Papá Noel stood out in the center wearing a white robe, facing the mud houses, the three that were here then," Justin said. "A man came out of this one, and a woman wearing a white gown, followed him. He had a bundle of white fabric in his arms. He climbed up on the stone wall. He put one corner of the material in a clip on the wire stretched between the columns. He stepped down the wall and clipped the opposite corner of the fabric. Then he let go, and the rest of the sheet fell open, and my eyes were fixed on a red stain on that sheet. At 12, I instinctively knew what that sheet meant. The crowd cheered. The women stood with their daughters, taking their hands and dancing in playful circles. The men lightly patted their drums. The man smiled back at the woman, then looked at Papá Noel and nodded. Papá smiled a grand smile, lifted his arms, and began to chant the Blessing of the First Sheet," Justin said. "La Bendición de La Primera Sábana."

"This is why you brought me here," Lil said, knowing, the tears falling from her eyes.

She never had cried as much in her entire life as she had over her time with Justin. But no one would have been able to contain the tears today.

"This hut is called El Poco Dolor, the little pain," Justin continued. "My mother came up behind me where I watched, and she explained. She told me when the blood touched the sheet, the man was married to the woman. She explained that the man had taken the woman as his wife, and the sheet, for him, was for the other men to know she was his and only his.

332

For the woman, the sheet was for her husband, so he would know she had saved herself for him, she had waited, and no one could ever say otherwise."

Lil listened.

"That closet," he motioned to the door with the chair beyond it, "the elder woman would sit behind the door and watch through the cracks to make sure the girl used no trickery."

"Justin, please tell me," Lil started.

Justin laughed, "No, Lil, I wouldn't want a woman watching either."

He told her all the parts of the ritual of The First Sheet. Juanito, who had guarded the mud house, was there to make sure no other man entered the Poco Dolor except for Justin. Had Lil chosen the first bed beyond the entrance, Justin would not have been allowed to sleep in the Poco Dolor with her. Had he taken Lil in her bed in the other room, he would have been doomed to a life of being henpecked, but because he took her in his bed, he would be the head of their home.

"Lil," he looked into her eyes, "may I present your First Sheet?" Justin asked.

Lil nodded, wiping her tears. He reached up and gave Lil her gown. He put on his jeans. While Justin took the sheet from the bed, Lil slipped into the gown, tying the ribbons, understanding now, why Margarita needed to know how old she was, how long she had waited, so she would know how many ribbons to sew on the beautiful, white gown.

Justin took Lil's hand and led her behind him out the door and to the porch. The sun was about to rise. The first face she saw across the plaza was Papá Noel's. He was wearing a white robe. He smiled at Lil who was already gazing upon the small gathering of people, the women with their daughters who were all dressed in white, the boys running at their play, and the men with their drums among the trees. Justin was already on the wall when she looked to him, the first corner already clipped. He walked down the wall and clipped the opposite corner, and let the sheet fall. The crowd smiled at the sight of The First Sheet. The women and their children stood and playfully started dancing. Justin nodded to Papá Noel, and Papá began La Bendición de La Primera Sábana, the Blessing of the First Sheet, as the men began to tap their drums.

"Señora!" a young girl shouted to Lil as she ran past Lil and Justin to the house.

Lil turned to her at the word "Señora," "Mrs." The girl was picking flowers from the side of the house, Cherry Lilies. They had started to bloom, not all of them, but the first few. The tiny petals were white, and from the center, a burst of red pistil flamed up within a guarding circumference of red stamen. Lil turned to Justin who wrapped his arms around her. The little girl took Lil's hand and led her out into the plaza. The women wanted her to dance among their daughters for a while.

Justin turned to see the elder walking from behind him, over to Papá Noel. She smiled and nodded to Papá. Justin looked back from where she had come. As the elder walked out of the plaza, she turned and winked at Justin as he walked over to Papá.

"Papá Noel, please tell me the elder was not in there," Justin said.

"Justín, it is our way, my son. Your Lily waited for you, mi hijo. She deserves for you to know completely that she was saved for you. This can be your one secret from your wife, Lily. Keep it in your heart, and treasure Lily when you think on it. This was her treasure, her sacrifice to give to you," Papá told Justin.

"Sacrifice," Justin repeated, considering Papá Noel's word.

"Of course. Es verdad, mi hijo. Everything God created serves a purpose. Every part of the woman's body was created as it is for a reason. This part of her that she has given you, this sacrifice of her purity, Justín, was signified with blood. God often uses blood to make sacrifices evident. In this village, Lily will always be considered pure. As long as you are the only man she is ever with, she will always be Justín's Virgin."

Lil returned to where Justin stood. Papá smiled at Lil, and stepped back to let Justin share this time with her.

"While we are here, Lil," Justin said, "we are man and wife." Then he leaned in to Lil's ear and whispered. "Don't worry, Lil, I won't hold you to it," he said, then he leaned back and looked into her eyes, "unless you let me," he added, dropping to both of his knees. "You said 'yes,' earlier. Will you let me hold you to it?" he smiled.

Tears rushed again to Lil's eyes. Justin reached for both of her hands.

"Will you be my wife, Lily?" Justin asked.

Lil nodded through her tears, unable to speak, and the drums got louder, and the small, watching crowd celebrated again.

"Will you marry me today?" Justin asked, standing.

"Of course, but how will this be legal at home? Alabama requires blood tests," Lil answered, "and there's paperwork--"

"Papá Noel is authorized," Justin said. "I have the papers ready, and your blood test at the clinic was for this moment. In my heart," Justin nodded toward the sheet, "we are already married."

Too good to be true, Lil thought.

"Yes!" Lil exclaimed. "Yes, Justin!"

Justin took her in his arms, lifted her feet from the ground, and kissed her while he lowered her again. He led Lil across the square in the direction he had promised to show her on their second day of touring the village. The crowd followed, still celebrating, still tapping their drums. They crossed through the trees, into thick plush grass, and through an opening. Lil could see a church. It was a small replica of Justin's church at home. Just beyond it was a beautiful body of water with a gorgeous waterfall behind it. Lil looked at Justin. The beauty of what she was seeing showed on her face.

"We built this church when my parents were alive," Justin said. "My church at home raised the money. I've been working on one major change in the structure over the last year," Justin continued. "We removed the back wall and replaced it, replicating the front. Now both sides make an entrance so that the Tomenava people will feel welcome to come," Justin said.

They stood in front of "Justín's church" as the people called it, no matter how strongly Justin asked them to stop calling it that. Papá Noel performed a marriage ceremony for Justin and Lil. Justin placed a simple platinum band on Lil's finger. He had kept it in his pocket the entire time she had been there. Lil would get him one when they got home, and they'd have a simple ceremony at Justin's church in Birmingham with little Ava at Lil's side, so Lil's family and their friends could come. No array of flowers or reception, just a simple ribbon around a grouping of Calla lilies in Lil's hands, vows spoken among loved ones, and a really good taco behind The Gas Boy at Tafoya's afterward.

Lil saw that life could be even better than fantasy. Justin had proven them all wrong, even her. She wished Hinton, Mac, Sims, and June could see all that was happening and share the moment with them. She wished her parents and Peter and Ava could hear the laughter and the drums, the singing and the celebrating. She wished the girls could see the dancing, and the gown, and Justin's beautiful face. Never had she seen Justin more gorgeously handsome than he was in these hours. If even just in a photograph, she wished she could show them. She knew the girls would be so happy for her and with her. It all had been worth the wait.

The girls were right about one thing though. She'd have to get her first list and add one more entry in the "Do" column. And it would start with the letter "O."

29

Act V: *Dénouement*

Justin and Lil didn't live happily ever after. That would be a fantasy. They lived joyfully and passionately ever after, but they had heartbreaking times as well.

Justin continued to travel to the places where he'd grown up helping his parents. Lil went with him whenever she could. Justin brought back a jar of Cherry Lilies for Lil whenever he saw them in bloom. He had only one slump in employment, but that brief moment coincided with one of the highlights of Lil's writing career. Lil did fairly well with a small book called *The Virgin's Undercover Guide to Dating.* The book was brilliantly marketed by local bookstores. Women and girls would buy the book from the stores' female employees who would ring up the purchases at a "secret" cash register in the stock section in the back of the stores. Mothers and fathers, grandmothers and aunts had a good time with their daughters, granddaughters, and nieces, ringing the stores' back doorbells and escorting the girls in for the stealthy purchase. Sorority sisters bought the book for their new, little sisters. Sunday School teachers brought their older teen classes in on their way to movie and bowling outings.

Lil gradually made renovations to their East Birmingham bungalow. She gave birth to two daughters, Ava Rose and Lula Margarita, followed by two miscarriages, both boys. Those two losses magnified the blessing that had become part of their lives. Six months after their wedding, Justin took his first trip back to the village to help start rebuilding the two other Pocos Dolores. He returned to the Birmingham airport with two precious packages. One was a box of photographs Santito Pablo had taken from among the trees on the morning Justin hung Lil's First Sheet, using a camera Justin had given him and taught him how to use. Justin had the photos made into a book that he gave to Lil on their first anniversary.

The other package was even more precious: the baby boy born in the labor hut. He now had the thickest head of curls Lil had ever seen on a baby. Lil eagerly met them at the airport. They sat in the seats where Justin deplaned, and Lil kissed Justin Noel on the forehead. They called him Joel.

"Did you hear any news of his mother?" she asked Justin about the baby's birth mother.

"Lil, my parents taught me as a boy, not to ask about patients they had treated. In those jungles, the news is so often not good. I was instructed to provide care to the people to the best of my ability, then to let life move forward."

Lil nodded her understanding.

But Justin *had* asked about the mother. She had survived only two days after the birth. The doula took the woman's daughters and nieces and loved them as her own. It was the second and last secret Justin ever kept from Lil, but he didn't want Lil's heart to hurt every time she looked at their little boy.

Justin had been wise to stand guard and have the other men do the same the night he took Lil to his bed. Singozo was coming for her. The sister of the mother in the labor hut, the woman who had run off from her husband to be with Singozo, she heard Singozo planning with the other men to return to the Apoya village. She knew Singozo wouldn't stop with the exotic American woman. She knew he was going back for her daughters and nieces, too. He had said so. She sliced his throat just minutes before he was to leave for the Apoya village where Lil and Justin were. Then she fled.

Joel gave his parents a bit of trouble in high school. Justin said nothing worse than he'd given his aunt and uncle in Greece. After graduation, Joel played a pivotal role in helping Justin with his work in different villages on future travels, building churches and assisting in the medical clinics. Joel returned to school at UAB and became a surgeon, and he eventually moved to South America. Ava graduated from law school in global affairs. Lula became a pediatric nurse and married Padre Rivera's grandson.

But heartache is part of every life. Some of the greatest joys happen alongside the greatest tragedies. Little Zach did receive a heart. Tanner's. Sims' Tanner was killed in a car accident. His grandmother was driving. She died of a heart attack a week later. Sims had a breakdown. Lil, Hint, Mac, and June alternated days going to Sims' house. They would let themselves in with their keys, put dinner in her refrigerator or in the oven, and walk through her sun-filled house to the bedroom that stayed dark for three months. They crawled in bed next to Sims and held her. They never once said, "Time will heal," "Tanner wouldn't want you to be this way," or "Maybe if you got out in the sunshine." They simply embraced her where she lay and said, "I love you, Sims," until Sam got home.

Tanner had met Zach. He had watched the Barons practice with Zach and Justin during spring training, as Justin had promised they would. Lil and Sims were with them. They gently wheeled Zach across the street from the clinic to the field. Sitting in the sunshine, Zach told Tanner about the device that was working hard in his chest. Tanner understood Zach's plight.

"I wish I could give you my heart," Tanner had said to Zach. "Mine would let you run as fast as that guy!" he pointed to the player sliding into home.

It wasn't just a made up line in a script. Justin, Lil, and Sims heard it with their own ears. They heard how sincerely Tanner had said it. Replaying Tanner's words in her mind is what got Sims through her grief.

"Here feel it," Tanner had said to Zach.

Zach laid a flat palm against Tanner's chest, but couldn't feel anything, so they decided to compare pulses.

"Cool! They're the same!" Tanner had noticed.

"Yeah!" Zach agreed.

Justin and Lil turned to each other and smiled. Drawn together as if by a Divine magnet.

The night it happened, all the girls and their husbands rushed to the hospital. While Sam walked up the hall to tell all the grandparents, Hinton and June clung to each other in the hospital chapel where Lil held onto Sims and rocked her back and forth in the pew. Mac sat next to them, her tear-streaked face bowed in prayer.

Justin left Lil there, and drove quickly down 18th Street South. He steered with his left hand while his right hand gripped the precious cooler that was buckled in his passenger seat. As he turned onto 16th Street South, he peered up and out of the front windshield, into the night sky just in time to see the helicopter land on the roof of the Right Hand Surgical Mission. Justin's college friends and benefactors, Cooper and Lee Ann, had flown to the Birmingham-Shuttlesworth International Airport as soon as Justin called them, and the copter was waiting there to get them to the Mission. Kilgro, Deano, and Lauren would be there any minute. They were already in town for a medical convention. Their specialties were organ transplant and anesthesiology. They and many others would do whatever they could now to help Zach.

In the years to come, Sims and Sam would have two more little boys, both given the middle name Tanner. They weren't the only ones named for that precious soul. The next hippopotamus born at the Birmingham Zoo was also given the name Tanner.

Hinton and Mac each had another baby, both girls, and June had three daughters. During Mac's second pregnancy, the doctor ordered her to bed during the last trimester. Hinton asked Big Daddy if she could help on the lot while Mac was on bed-rest; Hinton was bored with her workless days. She outsold every dealer there and got close to Mac's record, but she couldn't reach it no matter how hard she tried. As Mac lay in bed one night, sleeping, Jack working in bed beside her, Mac heard Hinton's voice in what she thought was a dream. She smiled at the humor of it as she woke to see all 54-flat-screen inches of Hinton saying, "And only Big Daddy can put you in this one at this price."

Mac raised herself up onto her elbows. She let her eyes adjust to make sure she was really seeing what she appeared to be seeing---Hinton doing one of her commercials.

"Come see us, down at Big Daddy's Imports," Hinton continued.

"Don't you say it!" Mac threatened TV Hinton. "Don't you do it!"

" . . . and let me take ya for a ride," Hinton said, crinkling her nose at the camera, and the camera loved her.

"Oh, no she didn't!" Mac shrieked, springing up from the mattress.

Jack had to hold Mac down. Mac didn't have to worry though, for two reasons. One she figured out herself while Jack was telling her to calm down, gently pushing her shoulders back to the pillow, as Mac angled to see the TV around his head. She noticed the camera angle was suspiciously set from

Hinton's empire waist and up to her face, and her boobs looked, well, the way boobs look when you're pregnant. Mac was right.

The second reason occurred the very next day. Hinton had a customer that would change everything for her. The most beautiful woman Hinton had ever seen, a 38-year-old black woman, drove onto the car lot in a shiny, red Lamborghini. Hinton walked out to get to her first.

"You might rather grab that gentleman over there looking at that Bentley," the woman said, getting out of her car. "I'm not buying, just selling."

But Jet was already shaking the other man's hand.

Hinton looked through the car windows at the woman's pristine car to discover a tiny baby girl, asleep in a rear-facing car seat.

"Let's take it for a spin," Hinton said.

They talked while Hinton drove. The woman's name was Gracie Waters. She was an attorney, a successful one. She was lightening her material load, she explained to Hinton, selling everything she owned. She was going to quit her job and find one that would pay the bills, but allow her time to leave a good mark on this world. A recent mission trip to Uganda with her church had changed her life, starting with little Poppy in the back seat. Gracie had adopted the baby girl in Africa. Poppy's birth mother had sneaked her daughter to the people on Gracie's church mission with all the paperwork they would need to take the baby out of the country, saving her daughter from genital mutilation. Hinton never had heard of such an inhumane horror. Gracie said she could no longer sleep at night.

344

"I just have to do this," Gracie said, as Hinton pulled into a parking deck and shut off the car. "What are we doing here?" Gracie asked Hinton.

"I want to introduce you to my husband," Hinton explained.

Two weeks later, Gracie laid the keys to a gas-efficient, company-owned Ford Escape on her new desk and sat in her new chair in her new office in Denton's firm, where she would handle only pro bono cases, with a carte blanche vacation calendar, no questions asked.

Gracie's first assignment was to set up a nonprofit organization for Hinton. Within five years, Hinton was the most successful chair of charitable causes in the state. The first item Hinton placed on her desk was Amy Vanderbilt's etiquette book, the one she'd received at her Swann Academy graduation in seventh grade. The corners were dented and frayed from all the times it had crashed to the floor from being balanced on her head. The pages were dog-eared from when she'd depended on it heavily during all her wedding preparations. She didn't want a new etiquette book. This old one put a smile on her face just as it was. Anyway, there were no new rules.

Justin was a huge adviser to Hinton, and he was an occasional recipient of Hinton's fundraising. The first donation Hinton received came from an anonymous contributor, a worn envelope with $1700 in twenty-dollar bills that Justin delivered to her. She could just make out an erased "L. V." on the outside of the envelope, which reminded her of a green T-shirt. Justin never told her that the money had come from Mrs. Swann, Hinton's new Director of Dining. Mrs. Swann had given it to Justin to give to Hinton, and she asked him to keep her secret.

"I read somewhere that it's best in these situations to keep your left hand from knowing what your right hand is doing," Mrs. Swann smiled.

"Yes," Justin returned the smile, "I've read that myself," he said, embracing his mother-in-law.

Mrs. Swann also named Hinton's nonprofit.

"It might sound a little corny," she said about the name she had come to the first board meeting with, totally excited about, "but we can think about it," she said, clearing her throat, preparing to say it. " 'Good Manna's,' " she said, and waited. "Just a suggestion," she added, uncomfortably, trying to read the expressions on the others' faces as they sat there silently. "You know, we don't even have to put that one on the flip chart," she added, feeling embarrassed now that she'd said it out loud.

"No, we don't," Hinton said. "We just need to put it on the letterhead and our business cards."

"Really?" Mrs. Swann said, truly surprised.

"It's perfect."

"Then I have one other suggestion?" Mrs. Swann said timidly, among this group of young businesswomen.

"Let's hear it."

"Well, I've never understood why charities spend a fortune to make less than one. I say we at least start by hosting iced water teas, serve only iced water, you know, like the sororities do the first day of rush. Maybe have some trays with tiny cakelike bread, like manna. The donors can come in and out quickly, make their donations, and get back to their hectic lives. People who would like to give but don't like the hoopla surrounding events might come. Is that stupid? Does that sound corny?"

And that's what they did. June tapped her glass against Hinton's at their first successful iced water tea and toasted the new nonprofit.

"Here's to drinking pee."

Hinton handed her small volunteer staff different sized envelopes at Christmas, bonuses for which she had used her own money. Mrs. Swann's was a nonrefundable gift card to the Louis Vuitton store in Atlanta. The note said, "Nothing we've done this year would have been possible without you. Buy that purse! Merry Christmas. Love, Hinton."

The second contribution given to Hinton's nonprofit came from Mac. Mac left her new baby girl at home with a sitter to visit Hinton in the maternity ward and welcome Hint's new baby girl into the world. Mac handed Hinton a check matching Hinton's car sales profit from the time Mac had been on bed-rest.

"You done good, girl," Mac said. "Really good."

June's first daughter was the first girl born to any of them. The Hot Aunts arrived, one at a time, to June's hospital room, Lil getting there first. Sims dropped Tanner off with grandparents and got there next, running into the bathroom to wash her hands. June, with tears welled up in her eyes, holding her bundle, looked up at Lil, and whispered, "I want her to wait."

Lil kissed June's forehead and smiled.

"June, I'm so thankful I waited and didn't miss out on Justin and Ecuador," Lil said brushing June's hair back with her fingers, "and I'm so thankful Sims didn't miss out on Tanner," Lil continued as Sims walked to the bed, assured June her hands were clean, and caressed the baby girl's soft hand.

The hour-old child grasped Sims' pinky. Lil continued.

"We'll all be here with you to love her, to help guide her when you ask, to pray for her, and to speak for her when her voice alone isn't enough," Lil added, reaching her arm around Sims. "Then we'll wait to see all the paths she chooses. Maybe she'll forge a few new ones."

Hinton and Mac walked in with white porcelain cups filled with steaming hot coffee that they'd helped themselves to in the nurses' break room, setting them on a nearby table.

"Make room for two more Hot Aunts!" Hinton announced.

They all crowded around their new addition as Mrs. Swann came in with Amy Vanderbilt's book, a journal for "Baby's First Visitors" to sign, a pad to record gifts and flowers, and a box of thank you notes, the envelopes already stamped.

Years later, Lil's mother had a stroke. Justin was wonderful with her and with Lil's brother Peter who returned from the Middle East, having lost his left foot in an explosion during a military mission. Lil's father died two years after his wife's stroke. Lil handled the funeral arrangements. The headstone read, "Daddy . . . there was just something about him."

San Puente called one morning at 3 a.m. to let Justin know Papá Noel had been killed, along with two missionaries, in an attack on a medical clinic five hours away from the village. The papers reported it as a group suicide. Justin, Lil, and San Puente knew it wasn't.

The two of them lived long lives. Justin died at 92. He had taken to bed for two weeks. He called Lil into the room one afternoon.

"What, darling?" Lil asked.

"I just really needed to see you, Lil" Justin said, closing his eyes.

"Then you have to open your eyes," Lil said, smiling.

"I will," Justin answered, "but first, I want to picture you in that black dress with the lace sleeves."

Tears rolled down Lil's smiling face. She knew. Justin always kept his promises. She sat on the edge of the bed, and leaned over and kissed his sweet, warm lips.

"I'll be there waiting for you, Lil."

That was the last promise Justin made to Lil.

Lil grieved Justin's passing for the next two months, holding her children and her six grandchildren in her arms as often as she could. She died from what only could be described as a broken heart.

"I'm so sorry to leave you so soon after you've lost your father," Lil said to her children who held her hands around her bed.

"I really need to see him," Lil explained, caressing an ache in her chest.

They couldn't believe how fast her health had deteriorated. Just a few months earlier, she had been so vibrant in her role of Daisy in "Driving Miss Daisy," at the beautifully renovated Lyric Theatre. Lil had been overwhelmed to see the stars lining the sidewalk in front of the Lyric, listing the names of the stars from its former glory and all the additional stars who had performed since its renovation. She paused each night and smiled at the name engraved on one star in particular: Bryan Adams'. Years earlier, his performance was the theatre's grand reopening act.

"What is it, Mama?" Lula asked, listening with her stethoscope to the heart her mother was constantly caressing. "The doctor says she doesn't detect anything definitive in your tests."

"Un poco dolor," Lil explained. "They aren't all bad ones," she said, confusing her daughters at times.

She talked about reunions to come with Mac and Sims, her parents, Tanner, Papá Noel, meeting Justin's parents, and thanking Esperanza. She talked about them with confidence. She knew she'd see each one of them.

"He said he would be waiting for me," she reminded them frequently about their father's promise to her. "He will be waiting for me. He said he would," she would say, smiling, repeating herself over and over.

Ava and Lula buried their mother in a beautiful white, antique gown. They were there, as were Joel and June and Hinton, all beside her when she died. Lil had been sleeping. A smile lit up her resting face, and she said, "You never break a

350

promise." Just that simple. And they all knew Justin had met her.

Joel took the next earliest flight to Ecuador, holding a memorial service for both of his parents for the Apoya people at Justín's church. He spread twenty-six jars of dried Cherry Lilies around the mud houses. The next blooming of the Cherry Lilies was so huge that other tribes traveled to see them. A few stayed for services in Justín's church while they were there. Almost all of them met their Maker while they listened to barefooted San Pablo preach.

Joel saw a young girl admiring the blooms growing on the Pocos Dolores. Her father walked over to his daughter and put his arm around her shoulders.

"Hay una leyenda sobre estas flores rojas, mi hija. Es una historia hermosa del amor. 'La leyenda del Lirio de Justín.' Vamos. Te contaré la historia de amor mientras caminamos a nuestro pueblo." "There is a legend about these flowers, my daughter," he explained. "It is a beautiful story of love. 'The Legend of Justin's Lily.' Come. I'll tell you about it on our walk home to our village."

Joel smiled. What a beautiful way for a daughter to hear about the birds and the bees. He thought about his mother's dissertation, and now she was starring in a love legend of her own. What a beautiful circle. What a beautiful mark on this world.

Justin and Lil had few material things to leave their children. They'd never been collectors of things. Lil left them one special box. It contained a manuscript, typed on an old

351

typewriter, bound with a simple string. Underneath it was a leather photo album, a book Justin had given Lil on their first anniversary. A handwritten note rested on top.

Act III was the highlight of my life. It started when a divine magnet drew your father's hand to mine, as we reached for the same book in the library, The Heart of Ecuador. I've written our story for you. I think it's worth your time. It takes a little patience, but they say that's a virtue. Play some music while you read it. Life is so much fuller with music. And remember, true treasures are worth the wait. May your lives be filled with pocos dolores and joy. We'll be watching for you, but don't rush. We'll be there forever.

Love, Mama.

Underneath was the title page.

The First Sheet. La Primera Sábana.

Final Curtain

30

Act IV: *The falling action, with one or two unresolved issues*

ut this is all too much, too quickly. Let's take Lil's
advice and wait. What a sin to skip over all the
good stuff, and there was such good stuff. Lil had
waited for passion, and Justin had so much to give her, so let's
go back a bunch of scenes, and let her have it. All the way back
to the quaint celebration in front of the Poco Dolor where her
First Sheet blew in the breeze and little girls in white celebrated
around her.

San Puente arrived soon after their union, he and the doula,
bringing the tiny boy to them. He pulled up in front of the Poco
Dolor where Lil and Justin were saying their good-byes to the
Apoyas and Papá Noel. He honked the horn in the brand new
Land Rover, donated by Justin's benefactors from home. As
they made their way to the truck, Lil and Justin gave the
children final embraces. San Puente rolled down the electric
window.

"San Justín, aire frio como hielo!" San Puente said. Ice cold air.

"San Justín!" Juanito was running up to where they stood, carrying his CD player.

Justin and Lil turned and waited for him.

"He aprendido todas las canciónes. He acabado," Juanito said, smiling, retrieving the CD from the player and holding it out for Justin to take.

He had learned every song on the disk.

"Quedatelo, mi amigo," Justin said, telling Juanito to keep the CD.

Justin reached into his bag and retrieved a new disk and held it out for Juanito to take.

"Toma este ahora. El artista se llama Bruno Mars." Take this one. The artist is named Bruno Mars.

Juanito placed the new disk in the player and pressed the play button. The rhythm of Bruno and B.o.B singing "Nothin on You," drifted from the speakers, and the Apoya men joined in with their drums.

"Dame el otro, Juanito," San Puente said, reaching for the Adams' CD through the vehicle's window.

Juanito gave it to him.

Santito Pablo positioned himself in the passenger seat with a pistol in his lap. Lil stood in the sunroof, holding the naked baby boy as protectively as she could. Justin sat in the center of the back seat, holding Lil's hips to steady her over the rough terrain.

354

A few minutes into the ride, San Puente stuck the Adams CD into the truck's CD player and turned it up. The truck vibrated as Bryan Adams belted out "The Best of Me" across Ecuador. Lil smiled, hearing the song.

"Full circle," she said, kissing the top of the baby's head.

Twenty minutes later, Lil told Justin she was worried about the baby.

"I think you need to hold him, Justin," she said, concerned. "You're so much warmer than I am."

Justin stood and took the baby. The three of them finished the trip standing together. San Puente had arranged for a medical team to meet them at the first clinic past the Tomenava land. The baby survived the trip, but they didn't know for how long. They kissed the child and watched as the nurses took him away. They both embraced Santito Pablo, then San Puente.

"Vivimos para ver un otro día, mi amigo," Justin said to San Puente as his father had said.

"Esta vez, mi amigo," San Puente shouted as he pulled away.

The music continued to play in Lil's mind as she and Justin stood outside of Hot's Café, looking in at Hinton, June, Mac, and Sims, who were talking to the older women at the next table. They couldn't wait until Wednesday. They bumped their coffee date up to the day after Lil and Justin returned from their trip. Justin kissed Lil, and she went in alone to tell her friends their news. He could see they had what must be an early, green, birthday cake waiting on the table with twenty-six candles. Tanner was sitting in half of Sims' chair with her, his finger already in the icing. Justin watched through the glass as the girls asked the one question Lil knew they'd ask first, their fingers forming Ls and Vs. He watched Lil's smiling lips answer, "Yes!" He watched them all squeal and clap and jump up and hug her. Then he watched Lil's lips say, "And no." He laughed to see their expressions fall as they sank back into their seats, and Hinton literally knocked her head against the table. He left to let Lil explain it all.

He got in their old BMW, shut the door, exhaled, and closed his eyes.

"Thank You, dear Father God," he said.

Then he reached in his pocket, pulled out his iPhone, and texted Lil.

"Have fun, but hurry home. I really need to see you."

Lil replied.

"Come back! June's water just broke!"

Glossary

Aldeabla—**aldea**: world village; **habla**: speak (like world)

Apoya—apoyar, to lean for support (as on God)

Calla—**callar**—to shut up; **acallar**—to silence

Fontanero--plumber

El Poco Dolor—the little pain

La Primera Sábana--The First Sheet

Lado—beside, nearby

Lenguaba—**lengua**: language; **guava**: fruit of guava tree, i.e., apple guava; language of the garden

Lirio de Cereza—Cherry Lily

P or Pi (pee)—word for water for many Ecuadorian tribes

Papá Noel—Santa Claus

Plomera—plumber

Puerto de guantes—glove compartment

Sabiojo—sabio/ojo: wise eye

San Puente—Saint Bridge

Singozo—sin gozo: without joy

Tomenava—tomen Ava: they take Ava

Thank you . . .

Thank you for reading Lil's story. Thank you for waiting for the gobsmacking. Sometimes that's how life works. I hope it was worth the wait.

Thank you to my family. Encouragement whenever I needed it. I love you.

Thank you to those who helped with editing and to others who shared with me their thoughts: Joan, Sunny, Darlene, Gail, Nancy, Ann Marie, and Libby. Muchísimo gracias to my Spanish mentors: Ronnie, Justin, and Ana. Also to Martha George and Karen Russell. To my eyes in Manhattan—Buzz, and to my medical terms expert—Jill, thank you. Thank you, Chris, at Rocky Heights Print and Binding. Thank you, Les, for the capo. Thanks to a squire I know. Thank you, Bryan Adams, for music that speaks to the heart and makes the knees go weak, no matter what year is printed on the calendar. And much gratitude, Bettie Bland, for your contagious love of literature and writing.

Thank You, dear Father God.

Endnotes

[1] Conrad, Joseph. *Heart of Darkness and Selected Short Fiction.* Consulting Ed. Dir. George Stade. New York: Barnes & Noble Books, 2003. 115. Print.

[2] The Holy Bible, King James Version. *Ecclesiastes 1:9.* New York: Cambridge Edition: 1769; King James Bible Online, 2014. Web 8 March 2014. <http://www.kingjamesbibleonline.org/ Ecclesiastes-1-9/>.

[3] The Holy Bible, King James Version. *Luke 6.31.* New York: Cambridge Edition: 1769; King James Bible Online, 2014. Web 8 March 2014. <http://www.kingjamesbibleonline.org/Luke-6-31/>.

[4] Williams, Tennessee. *The Theatre of Tennessee Williams.* Vol. I. New York: New Directions Publ., 1971. 481. Print.

[5] Austen, Jane. *Pride and Prejudice.* New York: New American Library, 1980. Print.

[6] *Law.justia.com. Perdue v. Green; Motlow v. Green.* 1101337; 1101506. Alabama Supreme Court. October Term 2012-2013. PDF. 62-74, 66. Web. 8 May 2014. http://law.justia.com/cases/alabama/supreme-court/2013/1101337.html.

SaveAlabamaPACT.com. Files: "PACTopinion.pdf Version 1." *Perdue v. Green; Motlow v. Green.* 1101337; 1101506. Alabama Supreme Court. October Term 2012-2013. 62-74, 66. Web. 2 May 2014.

http://www.facebook.com/groups/savealpact/10151610
458678200/.

Perdue v. Green, Motlow v. Green, 127 So.3d 343,
407-411, 408 (Alabama Supreme Court, 2013).

[7] *Law.justia.com. Perdue v. Green; Motlow v. Green.*
1101337; 1101506. Alabama Supreme Court. October
Term 2012-2013. PDF. 8-10. Web. 8 May 2014.
http://law.justia.com/cases/alabama/supreme-
court/2013/1101337.html.

SaveAlabamaPACT.com. Files: "PACTopinion.pdf
version 1." *Perdue v. Green; Motlow v. Green.*
1101337; 1101506. Alabama Supreme Court. October
Term 2012-2013. 8-10. Web. 2 May 2014.
http://www.facebook.com/groups/savealpact/10151610
458678200/.

*Perdue v. Green, Motlow v. Green,*127 So.3d 343,
356-360, 386-387 (Alabama Supreme Court, 2013).

[8] *Law.justia.com. Perdue v. Green; Motlow v. Green.*
1101337; 1101506. Alabama Supreme Court. October
Term 2012-2013. PDF. 10-11. Web. 8 May 2014.
http://law.justia.com/cases/alabama/supreme-
court/2013/1101337.html.

SaveAlabamaPACT.com. Files: "PACTopinion.pdf
version 1." *Perdue v. Green; Motlow v. Green.*
1101337; 1101506. Alabama Supreme Court. October
Term 2012-2013. 10-11. Web. 2 May 2014.

http://www.facebook.com/groups/savealpact/10151610
458678200/.

Perdue v. Green, Motlow v. Green. 127 So. 3d 343,
387 (Alabama Supreme Court, 2013).

[9] Myerson, Allen R. "O Governor, Won't You Buy Me
a Mercedes Plant?" *The New York Times: Business
Day.* N.p., 01 Sept. 1996. Web. 27 Dec. 2013.
http://www.nytimes.com/1996/09/01/business/o-
governor-won't-you-buy-me-a-mercedes-
plant.html?pagewanted=all&src=pm.

[10] Amy, Jeff. "Alabama state and local aid to
ThyssenKrupp tops $1 billion after vote." *Mobile
Press-Register.* N.p., 28 Apr. 2011. Web. 8 May 2014.
http://blog.al.com/live/2011/04/alabama_state_and_loca
l_aid_to.html.

[11] Privett, Greg. "13 Investigates: Business Tax
Incentives." Alabamas13.com. 6 Dec. 2013. Web. 14
May 2014.
http://www.alabamas13.com/story/24154899/13-
investigates-business-tax-incentives.

[12] *Law.justia.com. Perdue v. Green; Motlow v. Green.*
1101337; 1101506. Alabama Supreme Court. October
Term 2012-2013. PDF. 61, 67. Web. 8 May 2014.
http://law.justia.com/cases/alabama/supreme-
court/2013/1101337.html.

SaveAlabamaPACT.com. Files: "PACTopinion.pdf
version 1." *Perdue v. Green; Motlow v. Green.*

1101337; 1101506. Alabama Supreme Court. October Term 2012-2013. 61, 67. Web. 2 May 2014. http://www.facebook.com/groups/savealpact/10151610 458678200/.

Perdue v. Green, Motlow v. Green,127 So.3d 343, 406, 409 "Conclusion," and "Chief Justice Moore, (concurring in part and dissenting in part)." (Alabama Supreme Court, 2013).

[13] Fulgham v The State. 46 Ala. 143. (Supreme Court of Alabama, June Term 1871). Thomas/West: 2008. Web. 10 May 2014. http://faculty.law.miami.edu/zfenton/documents/Fulgha mvState.pdf.

[14] The Holy Bible, King James Version. *Matt*hew 6:10. New York: Cambridge Edition: 1769; King James Bible Online, 2014. Web 8 March 2014. http://www.kingjamesbibleonline.org/ Matthew-6-10/.

[15] The Holy Bible, King James Version. *Isaiah 9:6*. New York: Cambridge Edition: 1769; King James Bible Online, 2014. Web 8 March 2014. http://www.kingjamesbibleonline.org/ Isaiah-9-6/.

[16] The Holy Bible, King James Version. *Luke 23:34*. New York: Cambridge Edition: 1769; King James Bible Online, 2014. Web 8 March 2014. http://www.kingjamesbibleonline.org/ Luke-23-34/.

[17] The Holy Bible, King James Version. *Matthew 28:6.* New York: Cambridge Edition: 1769; King James Bible Online, 2014. Web 8 March 2014. http://www.kingjamesbibleonline.org/ Matthew-28-6/.

[18] The Holy Bible, King James Version. *Matthew 28:18-20.* New York: Cambridge Edition: 1769; King James Bible Online, 2014. Web. 8 March 2014. http://www.kingjamesbibleonline.org/ Matthew-28-18_28-20/.

[19] *Gilligan's Island.* Actor Jim Backus as Thurston Howell, III; Actor Alan Hale, Jr. as The Skipper. Sherwood Schwartz, creator. United Artists Television. CBS: September 26, 1964 to April 17, 1967.

[20] The Holy Bible, King James Version. *Exodus 20:3.* New York: Cambridge Edition: 1769; King James Bible Online, 2014. Web 8 March 2014. http://www.kingjamesbibleonline.org/ Exodus-20-3/.

To find out who your Alabama legislators are and to contact them:
http://www.legislature.state.al.us/
House of Representatives: 334-242-7600
Senate: 334-242-7800

To contact Alabama's Governor by email, just search the web for the current governor's name. The switchboard number is 334-242-7100; fax is 334-353-0004.

Made in the USA
Charleston, SC
09 December 2014